J.L. Underwood

The Women of the Confederacy

Outlook

J.L. Underwood

The Women of the Confederacy

1. Auflage | ISBN: 978-3-73262-122-4

Erscheinungsort: Frankfurt am Main, Deutschland

Erscheinungsjahr: 2018

Outlook Verlag GmbH, Frankfurt.

THE WOMEN OF THE CONFEDERACY

In which is presented the heroism of the women of the Confederacy with accounts of their trials during the War and the period of Reconstruction, with their ultimate triumph over adversity. Their motives and their achievements as told by writers and orators now preserved in permanent form.

BY

REV. J. L. UNDERWOOD

Master of Arts, Mercer University, Captain and Chaplain in the Confederate Army

NEW YORK AND WASHINGTON
THE NEALE PUBLISHING COMPANY
1906

By
J. L. UNDERWOOD

Yours Truly,
J. L. Underwood –

DEDICATION

To the memory of Mrs. Elizabeth Thomas Curry, whose remains rest under the live oaks at Bainbridge, Ga., who cheerfully gave every available member of her family to the Confederate Cause, and with her own hands made their gray jackets, and who gave to the author her Christian patriot daughter, who has been the companion, the joy and the crown of his long and happy life, this volume is most affectionately dedicated.

PREFACE

It is remarkable that after a lapse of forty years the people of this country, from the President down, are manifesting a more lively interest than ever in the history of the women of the Confederacy. Bodily affliction only has prevented the author from rendering at an earlier date the service to their memory and the cause of the South which he feels that he has done in preparing this volume. His friends, Dr. J. Wm. Jones, and the lamented Dr. J. L. M. Curry, of Richmond, Va., made the suggestion of this work several years ago. They both rendered material assistance in the preparation of the lecture which appears in this volume as the author's tribute in the Symposium, and to Doctor Jones the author is greatly indebted for the practical brotherly assistance he has continued to render.

Thanks are due to the Virginia State Librarian, Mr. C. D. Kennedy, and his assistants, for kind attentions. The author is under obligations to the lady members of the Confederate Memorial Literary Society of Richmond, especially to Mrs. Lizzie Carey Daniels, Corresponding Secretary, and Mrs. Katherine C. Stiles, Vice-Regent of the Georgia Department of the Confederate Museum. In many ways great and valuable service was kindly rendered by Miss Isabel Maury, the intelligent House Regent of the Museum. To his old Commander, Gen. S. D. Lee, now General Commander of Confederate Veterans, he is under obligation for his practical help; also to Gen. Marcus J. Wright. In making selections from the works of others, great pains have been taken to give proper credit for all matter quoted. The author's home has been for more than thirty years his delightful Pearland Cottage, in the suburbs of Camilla, Ga. On account of his afflictions he has moved his family to Blakeley, Ga., while he himself may remain some time for medical treatment here in Richmond. The book is sent forth from an invalid's room with a fervent prayer that it may do good in all sections of our beloved country. Much of the work has been done under severe pain and great weakness, and special indulgence is asked for any defects.

J. L. Underwood.

Kellam's Hospital,
Richmond, Va.

INTRODUCTION BY REV. DR. J. B. HAWTHORNE

Richmond, Va., *January 30th, 1906.*

Only within the last two years have I had the opportunity to cultivate an intimate personal acquaintance with Rev. J. L. Underwood, but as the greater part of our lives have been spent in the States of Georgia and Alabama, I have been quite familiar with his career through a period which embraces a half century. Wherever he is known he is highly esteemed for his intellectual gifts and culture, his fluency and eloquence in speech, his genial manner, his high moral and Christian ideals, and his unflinching fealty to what he believes to be his country's welfare. No man who followed the Confederate flag had a clearer understanding or a more profound appreciation of what he was fighting for. No man watched and studied more carefully the progress of the contest. No man interpreted more accurately the spirit, purposes, and conduct of the contending armies. When the struggle closed no man foresaw with more distinctness what was in the womb of the future for the defeated South. His cultivated intellect, his high moral and Christian character, his personal observations and experiences, his residence and travels in Europe, his extensive acquaintance and correspondence with public men, North and South, and his present devotion to the interests of our united country, render him pre-eminently qualified for the task of delineating some features of the greatest war of modern times.

I have been permitted to read the manuscript of Mr. Underwood's book, entitled, "The Women of the Confederacy." I do not hesitate to pronounce it a valuable and enduring contribution to our country's history. There is not a page in it that is dull or commonplace. No man who starts to read it will lay it aside until he has reached the conclusion of it. The author's definitions of the relations of each sovereign State to the Federal Union and of her rights under the Federal Constitution are exact. His argument in support of the Constitutional right of secession amounts to a demonstration. His interpretation of the long series of political events which drove the South into secession is clear, just and convincing. His tributes to the patriotism and valor of the Southern women are brilliant and thrilling without the semblance of extravagance. His description of the vandalism of Sherman's army in its march through Georgia and South Carolina cannot fail to kindle a flame of indignation in the heart of any civilized man who reads it. His anecdotes, both humorous and pathetic, are well chosen.

The section of this book which relates most directly to "The Women of the Confederacy," including Mr. Underwood's tribute in the Symposium to their memory, is by far the most thrilling and meritorious part of it. Into this the author has put his best material, his deepest emotions, his finest sentiments, and his most eloquent words. To the conduct of Southern women in that unprecedented ordeal, history furnishes no parallel. Through many generations to come it will be the favorite theme of the poets and orators.

I need no prophetic gift to see that this book will be immensely popular and extensively circulated. Its aged and afflicted author has done a work in writing it which deserves the gratitude and applause of his fellow countrymen.

J. B. HAWTHORNE.

INTRODUCTION BY REV. DR. J. WM. JONES

J. WM. JONES,
Secretary and Superintendent,
Confederate Memorial Association,
109 N. 29th Street.

RICHMOND, VA.,
January 23, 1906.

I have carefully examined the manuscript of Mr. J. L. Underwood on "The Women of the Confederacy" and I take great pleasure in saying that in my judgment it is a book of very great interest and value, and if properly published and pushed I have no doubt that it would have a very wide sale.

Mr. Underwood has given a great deal of time to the collecting of material for his book, and has had great advantages in doing so in having had free access to the libraries of Richmond, and his book abounds in touching and thrilling incidents, which present as no other book that has been published does the true story of our Confederate women, their sufferings and privations; their heroism and efficiency in promoting the Confederate cause. I do not hesitate to say that it is worthy of publication, and of wide circulation.

J. WM. JONES.

AUTHOR'S INTRODUCTION

One of the last things the great Henry W. Grady said, was: "If I die, I die serving the South, the land I love so well. My father died fighting for it. I am proud to die speaking for it." The author of this volume fought for the South and is now so afflicted that he can no longer hope to speak for the South, but he will be happy to die writing for it. Not half has yet been told of the best part of the South, her women.

The Apostle John, on finishing his gospel story of Christ, said: "And there are many other things which Jesus did, the which if they could be written every one, I suppose that even the world itself could not contain the books that should be written." While at work preparing this volume, Mr. C. D. Kennedy, the courteous State librarian of Virginia, said to the writer it would "take a whole library to tell all about the Confederate women." As in the life of Christ, only a small part can be told; and only a small part is necessary.

It is remarkable that the life of Christ was the most tragic, thrilling, and beneficent life the world ever saw. And yet it is all told in four booklets of simple incidents. Those four little books have been worth more to the world than all other books combined. Neither is there any system in the gospel record. There was no system in Christ's life. It could not be told in a consecutive biography nor in a scientific treatise. Science and system all fail when it comes to telling of a life of such love and labor and sorrow.

It is not sacrilegious to say the same thing when we come to tell of the heroic lives, the courage, the trials, the work of the Confederate women. We can only give incidents, and these incidents tell all the rest.

Fortunately the author, while a patient in a Richmond hospital, has been strong enough to search the libraries of the city and gather material scattered among the Confederate records already made. With them and his own original sketches, it is hoped that a contribution of some value has been made to a good cause. The story of the Southern women is worth studying; and the author tells in his eulogy his estimate of their great virtues. Then he shows that his estimate is not from partiality or ignorance by giving a symposium of tributes from others, some from the North and some from Europe.

It may surprise some that so much attention is given to holding up the righteousness of the cause in which these women labored and suffered. Why not? The great cause ennobled them, and they adorned the Confederate cause. The truth must be told from both directions. This is the ground idea of this humble volume.

It is hoped that it will fill a good place in our Southern literature, suggesting further investigation on the same line. It has been a work of love, a comfort to him in the days of very fearful bodily affliction. He is conscious of the feebleness of his work and much indulgence is asked for.

The author deems his subject a consecrated theme. And he rejoices that he could labor at his task amid the consecrated memories of dear old Richmond, where he has had the assistance and the smiles of encouragement from the noble women who continue to keep guard over Hollywood and Oakwood Cemeteries, the Soldiers' Home, and the Home for Confederate Women, and keep vestal watch in the Confederate Museum.

Not a line is written in sectional prejudice or tainted by a touch of hate. The author was a Confederate soldier. He hates sham, injustice, falsehood, and hypocrisy everywhere, but he loves his fellow men, and still bears the old soldier's respect and warm hand for the true soldiers who fought on the other side. The barbarities of bummers and brutal commanders must be repudiated by us all that the honor of true soldiers like McClellan, Rosecrans, Thomas, and Buell, on the one side, and Lee, Jackson and Johnston on the other, may stand forth in its true light.

When our broad-brained and big-hearted President Roosevelt has just stepped down from the White House to tell on Capitol Hill at Richmond and at the feet of the monuments of Lee and Jackson, his great admiration for the Confederate soldiers and the Confederate women, it is time for us all to take a fresh look at their heroic lives.

J. L. Underwood.

Kellam's Hospital,
Richmond, Va., April 1st, 1906.

CHAPTER I
SYMPOSIUM OF TRIBUTES TO CONFEDERATE WOMEN

MRS. VARINA JEFFERSON DAVIS

From her invalid chair in New York the revered and beloved wife of the great chieftain of the Confederacy writes a personal letter to the author of this volume, from which he takes the liberty of publishing the following extract. There is something peculiarly touching in this testimonial which will be prized and kept as a precious heirloom throughout our Southern land:

HOTEL GERARD,
123 West Forty-fourth Street, New York.
October 25, 1905.

MY DEAR MR. UNDERWOOD:

* * * I do not know in all history a finer subject than the heroism of our Southern women, God bless them. I have never forgotten our dear Mrs. Robt. E. Lee, sitting in her arm chair, where she was chained by the most agonizing form of rheumatism, cutting with her dear aching hands soldiers' gloves from waste pieces of their Confederate uniforms furnished to her from the government shops. These she persuaded her girl visitors to sew into gloves for the soldiers. Certainly these scraps were of immense use to all those who could get them, for I do not know how many children's jackets which kept the soldiers' children warm, I had pieced out of these scraps by a poor woman who sat in the basement of the mansion and made them for them.

The ladies picked their old silk pieces into fragments, and spun them into gloves, stockings, and scarfs for the soldiers' necks, etc.; cut up their house linen and scraped it into lint; tore up their sheets and rolled them into bandages; and toasted sweet potato slices brown, and made substitutes for coffee. They put two tablespoonfuls of sorghum molasses into the water boiled for coffee instead of sugar, and used none other for their little children and families. They covered their old shoes with old kid gloves or with pieces of silk and their little feet looked charming and natty in them. In the country they made their own candles, and one lady sent me three cakes of sweet soap and a small jar of soft soap made from the skin, bones and refuse bits of hams boiled for her family. Another sent the most exquisite unbleached flax thread, of the smoothest and finest quality, spun by herself. I have never been able to get such thread again. I am still quite feeble, so I must close with the hope that your health will steadily improve and the assurance that I am,

Yours sincerely,
V. JEFFERSON DAVIS.

TRIBUTE OF PRESIDENT JEFFERSON DAVIS

[From Dr. Craven's Prison Life of Jefferson Davis.]

If asked for his sublimest ideal of what women should be in time of war, he said he would point to the dear women of his people as he had seen them during the recent struggle. "The Spartan mother sent her boy, bidding him return with honor, either carrying his shield or on it. The women of the South sent forth their sons, directing them to return with victory; to return with wounds disabling them from further service, or never to return at all. All they had was flung into the contest—beauty, grace, passion, ornaments. The exquisite frivolities so dear to the sex were cast aside; their songs, if they had any heart to sing, were patriotic; their trinkets were flung into the crucible; the carpets from their floors were portioned out as blankets to the suffering soldiers of their cause; women bred to every refinement of luxury wore homespuns made by their own hands. When materials for army balloons were wanted the richest silk dresses were sent in and there was only competition to secure their acceptance. As nurses for the sick, as encouragers and providers for the combatants, as angels of charity and mercy, adopting as their own all children made orphans in defence of their homes, as patient and beautiful household deities, accepting every sacrifice with unconcern, and lightening the burdens of war by every art, blandishment, and labor proper to their sphere, the dear women of his people deserved to take rank with the highest heroines of the grandest days of the greatest centuries."

TRIBUTE OF A WOUNDED SOLDIER

A beautiful Southern girl, on her daily mission of love and mercy in one of our hospitals, asked a badly wounded soldier boy what she could do for him. He replied: "I am greatly obliged to you, but it is too late for you to do anything for me. I am so badly wounded that I can't live long."

"Will you not let me pray for you?" said the sweet girl. "I hope that I am one of the Lord's daughters, and I would like to ask Him to help you."

Looking intently into her beautiful face he replied: "Yes, do pray at once, and ask the Lord to let me be his son-in-law."

TRIBUTE OF A FEDERAL PRIVATE SOLDIER

There is no more popular living hero of the Federal army of the war between the States than Corporal Tanner, who is Commander of the Grand Army of the Republic. He left both legs on a Southern battlefield and is a universal favorite of the Confederate Veterans. The following is an extract from his speech at the Wheeler Memorial in Atlanta, Ga., in March, 1906:

"The Union forces would have achieved success, in my opinion, eighteen months sooner than they did if it had not been for the women of the South. Why do I say this? Because it is of world-wide knowledge that men never carried cause forward to the dread arbitrament of the battlefield, who were so intensely supported by the prayers and by the efforts of the gentler sex, as were you men of the South. Every mother's son of you knew that if you didn't keep exact step to the music of Dixie and the Bonny Blue Flag, if you did not tread the very front line of battle when the contest was on, knew in short that if you returned home in aught but soldierly honor, that the very fires of hell would not scorch and consume your unshriven souls as you would be scorched and consumed by the scorn and contempt of your womanhood."

JOSEPH E. JOHNSTON'S TRIBUTE

As to the charge of want of loyalty or zeal in the war, I assert, from as much opportunity for observation as any individual had, that no people ever displayed so much, under such circumstances, and with so little flagging, for so long a time continuously. This was proved by the long service of the troops without pay and under exposure to such hardships, from the cause above mentioned, as modern troops have rarely endured; by the voluntary contributions of food and clothing sent to the army from every district that furnished a regiment; by the general and continued submission of the people to the tyranny of the impressment system as practiced—such a tyranny as, I believe, no other high-spirited people ever endured—and by the sympathy and aid given in every house to all professing to belong to the army, or to be on the way to join it. And this spirit continued not only after all hope of success had died but after the final confession of defeat by their military commanders.

But, even if the men of the South had not been zealous in the cause, the patriotism of their mothers and wives and sisters would have inspired them with zeal or shamed them into its imitation. The women of the South exhibited that feeling wherever it could be exercised: in the army, by distributing clothing with their own hands; at the railroad stations and their own homes, by feeding the marching soldiers; and, above all, in the hospitals, where they rivaled the Sisters of Charity. I am happy in the belief that their devoted patriotism and gentle charity are to be richly rewarded.

STONEWALL JACKSON'S FEMALE SOLDIERS

In the southern part of Virginia the women had become almost shoeless and sent a petition to General Jackson to grant the detail of a shoemaker to make shoes for them. Here is his reply, in a letter of November 14, 1862: "Be assured that I feel a deep and abiding interest in our female soldiers. They are patriots in the truest sense of the word, and I more and more admire them."

GEN. J. B. GORDON'S TRIBUTE

Back of the armies, on the farms, in the towns and cities, the fingers of Southern women were busy knitting socks and sewing seams of coarse trousers and gray jackets for the soldiers at the front.

From Mrs. Lee and her daughters to the humblest country matrons and maidens, their busy needles were stitching, stitching, stitching, day and night. The anxious commander, General Lee, thanked them for their efforts to bring greater comfort to the cold feet and shivering limbs of his half-clad men. He wrote letters expressing appreciation of the bags of socks and shirts as they came in. He said he could almost hear, in the stillness of the night, the needles click as they flew through the meshes. Every click was a prayer, every stitch a tear. His tributes were tender and constant to these glorious women for their labor and sacrifice for Southern independence.

GENERAL FORREST'S TRIBUTE

There is a story told of General Forrest which shows his opinion of the pluck and devotion of the Southern women. He was drawing up his men in line of battle one day, and it was evident that a sharp encounter was about to take place. Some ladies ran from a house which happened to stand just in front of his line, and asked him anxiously, "What shall we do, General, what shall we do?" Strong in his faith that they only wished to help in some way, he replied, "I really don't see that you can do much, except to stand on stumps, wave your bonnets and shout, 'Hurrah, boys.'"

TRIBUTE OF GEN. M. C. BUTLER

Who of those trying days does not recall the shifts which the Southern people had to adopt to provide for the sick and wounded: the utilization of barks and herbs for the concoction of drugs, the preparation of appliances for hospitals and field infirmaries? What surgeons in any age or in any war excelled the Confederate surgeons in skill, ingenuity or courage?

Who does not recall the sleepless and patient vigilance, the heroic fortitude and untiring tenderness of the fair Southern women in providing articles of comfort and usefulness for their kindred in the field, preparing with their dainty hands from their scanty supplies, food and clothing for the Confederate soldiers; establishing homes and hospitals for the sick and disabled, and ministering to their wants with a gentle kindness that alleviated so much suffering and pain? Do the annals of any country or of any period furnish higher proofs of self-sacrificing courage, self-abnegation, and more steadfast devotion than was exercised by the Southern women during the whole progress of our desperate struggle? If so, I have failed to discover it.

The suffering of the men from privations and hunger, from the wounds of battle and the sickness of camp, were mild inconveniences when compared with the anguish of soul suffered by the women at home, and yet they bore it all with surpassing heroism. No pen can ever do justice to their imperishable renown. The shot and shell of invading armies could not intimidate, nor could the rude presence of a sometimes ruthless enemy deter their dauntless souls. To my mind there has been nothing in history or past experiences comparable to their fortitude, courage, and devotion. Instances may be cited where the women of a country battling for its rights and liberties have sustained themselves under the hardest fate and made great sacrifices for the cause they loved and the men they honored and respected, but I challenge comparison in any period of the world's history with the sufferings, anxieties, fidelities, and firmness of the fair, delicate women of the South during the struggle for Southern independence and since its disastrous determination. Disappointed in the failure of a cause for which they had suffered so much, baffled in the fondest hopes of an earnest patriotism, impoverished by the iron hand of relentless war, desolated in their hearts by the cruel fate of unsuccessful battle, and bereft of the tenderest ties that bound them to earth, mourning over the most dismal prospect that ever converted the happiest, fairest land to waste and desolation, consumed by anxiety and the darkest forebodings for the future, they have never lowered the exalted crest of true Southern womanhood, nor pandered to a sentiment that would compromise with dishonor. They have found time, amid the want and anxiety of desolated homes, to keep fresh and green the graves of their dead soldiers, when thrift and comfort might have followed cringing and convenient oblivion of the past. They had the courage to build monuments to their dead, and work with that beautiful faith and silent energy which makes kinship to angels, and lights up with the fire from heaven the restless power of woman's boundless capabilities. When men have flagged and faltered, dallied with dishonor and fallen, the women of the South have rebuilt the altars of patriotism and relumed the fires of devotion to country in the hearts of halting manhood. They have borne the burden of their own griefs and vitalized the spirit and firmness of the men.

All honor, all hail, to woman's matchless achievements, and thanks, a thousand thanks, for the grand triumph and priceless example of her devoted heroism. Appropriately may she have exclaimed:

"Here I and Sorrow sit.

This is my throne; let kings come bow to it."

TRIBUTE OF GEN. MARCUS J. WRIGHT

I know that it were needless to say that the character and conduct of the women of the South during our late war stand out equally with those of any age or country, and deserve to go down in history as affording an example of fortitude, bravery, affection and patriotism that it is impossible to surpass: and I am further proud to say that the women of the Northern States exhibited in that war a devotion and patriotism to their country and its cause deserving of all praise.

TRIBUTE OF DR. J. L. M. CURRY

[Civil History of the Confederate States, pages 171-174.]

We hear and read much of delicately pampered "females" in ancient Rome and modern Paris and Newport, but in the time of which I speak in this Southland of ours, womanhood was richly and heavily endowed with duties and occupations and highest social functions, as wife and mother and neighbor, and these responsibilities and duties underlay our society in its structure and permanence as solid foundations. Instead of superficial adornments and supine inaction, the intellectual sympathies and interests of these women were large, and they undertook, with wise and just guidance, the management of household and farms and servants, leaving the men free for war and civil government. These noble and resolute women were the mothers of the Gracchi, of the men who built up the greatness of the Union and accomplished the unexampled achievements of the Confederacy. Knowing no position more exalted and paramount than that of wife and mother, with the responsibilities which attach to miniature empire, the training of children and guidance of slaves, each one was as Caesar would have had his companion, above reproach and above suspicion; and whose purity was so prized that a violation of personal dignity was resented and punished, by all worthy to be sons and husbands and fathers of such women, with the death of the violator. "Strength and dignity were her clothing; she opened her mouth with wisdom, and the law of kindness was on her tongue. She looked well to the ways of her household, and she ate not the bread of idleness. Her children rose up and called her blessed; her husband also."

When inequality was threatened and States were to be degraded to counties, and the South became one great battlefield, and every citizen was aiding in the terrible conflict, the mothers, wives, sisters, daughters, with extraordinary unanimity and fervor, rallied to the support of their imperilled land. While the older women from intelligent conviction were ready to sustain the South, political events and the necessity of confronting privations, trials, and sorrows developed girlhood into the maturity and self-reliance of womanhood. Anxious women with willing hands and loving hearts rushed eagerly to every place which sickness or destitution or the ravages of war invade, enduring sacrifices, displaying unsurpassed fortitude and heroism. Churches were converted into hospitals or places for making, collecting, and shipping clothing and needed supplies. Innumerable private homes adjacent to battlefields were filled with the sick and wounded. It was not uncommon to see grandmother and youthful maiden engaged in making socks, hats, and other needed articles. Untrained, these women entered the fields of labor with the spirit of Christ, rose into queenly dignity, and enrolled themselves among the immortals.

ADDRESS OF COL. W. R. AYLETT BEFORE PICKETT CAMP

[In Southern Historical Papers, Volume 22, page 60.]

I claim for Camp Pickett the paternity of the first of the public expressions, in the form of a Confederate woman's monument. On the 16th day of January, 1890, in an address made by me, upon the presentation of General Pickett's portrait to this camp by Mrs. Jennings, as my remarks, published in the Richmond *Dispatch* of the 17th of January, 1890, will show, I urged that steps be taken to erect a monument to the women of the Southern Confederacy, and you applauded the suggestion. But this idea, and the execution of it, is something in which none of us should claim exclusive glory and ownership. The monument should be carried not alone upon the shoulders of the infantry, artillery, cavalry, engineers and sailors of the Confederacy, but should be urged forward by the hearts and hands of the whole South. And wherever a Northern man has a Southern wife (and a good many Northern men of taste have them) let them help, too, for God never gave him a nobler or richer blessing. The place for such a monument, it seems to me, should be by the side of the Confederate soldier on Libby Hill. It is not well for a man to be alone, nor woman either. To place her elsewhere would make a perpetual stag of him, and a perpetual wall-flower of her. Companions in glory and suffering, let them go down the corridors of time side by side, the representatives of a race of heroes.

GEN. BRADLEY T. JOHNSON'S SPEECH AT THE DEDICATION OF SOUTH'S MUSEUM

What Our Women Stood

[In Southern Historical Papers, Volume 23, pages 368-370.]

Evil dies, good lives; and the time will come when all the world will realize that the failure of the Confederacy was a great misfortune to humanity, and will be the source of unnumbered woes to liberty. Washington might have failed; Kosciusko and Robert E. Lee did fail; but I believe history will award a higher place to them, unsuccessful, than to Suwarrow and to Grant, victorious. This great and noble cause, the principles of which I have attempted to formulate for you, was defended with a genius and a chivalry of men and women never equalled by any race. My heart melts now at the memory of those days.

Just realize it: There is not a hearth and home in Virginia that has not heard the sound of hostile cannon; there is not a family which has not buried kin slain in battle. Of all the examples of that heroic time; of all figures that will live in the music of the poet or the pictures of the painter, the one that stands in the foreground, the one that will be glorified with the halo of the heroine, is the woman—mother, sister, lover—who gave her life and heart to the cause. And the woman and girl, remote from cities and towns, back in the woods, away from railways or telegraph.

Thomas Nelson Page has given us a picture of her in his story of "Darby." I thank him for "Darby Stanly." I knew the boy and loved him well, for I have seen him and his cousins on the march, in camp, and on the battlefield, lying in ranks, stark, with his face to the foe and his musket grasped in his cold hands. I can recall what talk there was at a "meetin'" about the "Black Republicans" coming down here to interfere with us, and how we "warn't goin' to 'low it," and how the boys would square their shoulders to see if the girls were looking at 'em, and how the girls would preen their new muslins and calicoes, and see if the boys were "noticen'," and how by Tuesday news came that Captain Thornton was forming his company at the court-house, and how the mother packed up his little "duds" in her boy's school satchel and tied it on his back, and kissed him and bade him good-bye, and watched him, as well as she could see, as he went down the walk to the front gate, and as he turned into the "big road," and as he got to the corner, turned round and took off his hat and swung it around his head, and then disappeared out of her life forever. For, after Cold Harbor, his body could never be found nor his grave identified, though a dozen saw him die. And then, for days and for weeks and for months, alone, the mother lived this lonely life, waiting for news. The war had taken her only son, and she was a widow; but from that day to this, no human being has ever heard a word of repining from her lips. Those who suffer most complain least.

Or, I recall that story of Bishop-General Polk, about the woman in the mountains of Tennessee, with six sons. Five of them were in the army, and when it was announced to her that her eldest born had been killed in battle, the mother simply said: "The Lord's will be done. Eddie (her baby) will be fourteen next spring, and he can take Billy's place."

The hero of this great epoch is the son I have described, as his mother and sister will be the heroines. For years, day and night, winter and summer, without pay, with no hope of promotion nor of winning a name or making a mark, the Confederate boy-soldier trod the straight and thorny path of duty. Half-clothed, whole-starved, he tramps, night after night, his solitary post on picket. No one can see him. Five minutes' walk down the road will put him beyond recall, and twenty minutes further and he will be in the Yankee lines, where pay, food, clothes, quiet, and safety all await him. Think of the tens of thousands of boys subjected to this temptation, and how few yielded! Think of how many dreamed of such relief from danger and hardship! But, while I glorify the chivalry, the fortitude, and the fidelity of the private soldier, I do not intend to minimize the valor, the endurance, or the gallantry of those who led him.

GOVERNOR C. T. O'FERRALL'S TRIBUTE

[In Southern Historical Papers, Volume 23, pages 361-362.]

I think I can say boldly that the bloody strife of 1861 to 1865 developed in the men of the South traits of character as ennobling and as exalting as ever adorned men since the day-dawn of creation. I think I can proclaim confidently that, for courage and daring chivalry and bravery, the world has never seen the superiors of the Southern soldiers. I think I can assert defiantly that the annals of time present no leaves more brilliant than those upon which are recorded the deeds and achievements of the followers of the Southern Cross. I think I can proclaim triumphantly that, from the South's beloved President, and the peerless commander of her armies in the field, down to the private in her ranks, there was a display of patriotism perhaps unequalled (certainly never surpassed) since this passion was implanted in the human breast.

But as grand as the South was in her sons, she was grander in her daughters; as sublime as she was in her men, she was sublimer in her women.

History is replete with bright and beautiful examples of woman's devotion to home and birthland; of her fortitude, trials, and sufferings in her country's cause, and the women of the Confederacy added many luminous pages to what had already been most graphically written.

Yes, these Spartan wives and mothers, with husbands or sons, or both, at the front, directed the farming operations, supporting their families and supplying the armies; they sewed, knitted, weaved, and spun; then in the hospitals they were ministering angels, turning the heated pillow, smoothing the wrinkled cot, cooling the parched lips, stroking the burning brow, staunching the flowing blood, binding up the gaping wounds, trimming the midnight taper, and sitting in the stillness, only broken by the groans of the sick and wounded, pointing the departing spirit the way to God; closing the sightless eyes and then following the bier to Hollywood or some humble spot, and then dropping the purest tear.

They saw the flames licking the clouds, as their homes, with their clinging memories, were reduced to ashes; they heard of the carnage of battle, followed by the mother's deep moan, the wife's low sob—for, alas! she could not weep—the orphan's wail, and the sister's lament. But amid flame, carnage, death, and lamentations, though their land was reddening with blood, and their beloved ones were falling like leaves in autumn, they stood, like heroines, firm, steadfast, and constant.

Oh! women of the Confederacy, your fame is deathless; you need not monument nor sculptured stone to perpetuate it. Young maidens, gather at the feet of some Confederate matron in some reminiscent hour, and listen to her story of those days, now more than thirty years past, and hear how God gave her courage, fortitude, and strength to bear her privations, and bereavements, and live.

TRIBUTE OF JUDGE J. H. REAGAN, OF TEXAS, POSTMASTER-GENERAL OF CONFEDERATE STATES

I never felt my inability to do justice to any subject so keenly as I do when attempting to do justice to the character, services, and devotion of the women of the Confederacy. They gave to the armies their husbands, fathers, sons, and brothers, with aching hearts, and bade them good-bye with sobs and tears. But they believed their sacrifice was due to their country and her cause. They assumed the care of their homes and of the children and aged. Many of them who had been reared in ease and luxury had to engage in all the drudgery of the farm and shop. Many of them worked in the fields to raise means of feeding their families. Spinning-wheels and looms were multiplied where none had been seen before, to enable them to clothe their families and furnish clothing for the loved ones in the army, to whom, with messages of love and encouragement, they were, whenever they could, sending something to wear or eat. And like angels of mercy they visited and attended the hospitals, with lint and bandages for the wounded, and medicine for the sick, and such nourishment as they could for both, and their holy prayers at all times went to the throne of God for the safety of those dear to them and for the success of the Confederate cause. There was a courage and a moral heroism in their lives superior to that which animated our brave men, for the men were stimulated by the presence of their associates, the hope of applause, and by the excitements of battle. While the noble women, in the seclusion and quietude of their homes, were inspired by a moral courage which could only come from God and the love of country.

GENERAL FREEMANTLE (OF THE BRITISH ARMY)

[In "Three Months in Southern Lines."]

It has often been remarked to me that when this war is over the independence of the country will be due in a great measure to the women: for they declare that had the women been desponding they never could have gone through with it. But, on the contrary, the women have invariably set an example to the men of patience, devotion, and determination. Naturally proud and with an innate contempt for the Yankees, Southern women have been rendered furious and desperate by the proceedings of Butler, Milroy, and other such Federal officers. They are all prepared to undergo any hardship and misfortunes rather than submit to the rule of such people; and they use every argument which women can employ to infuse the same spirit into their male relatives.

SHERMAN'S "TOUGH SET"

After Sherman took possession of Savannah he soon issued orders, driving out of the city the wives of Confederate officers and soldiers. While these women were packing their trunks, he sent soldiers to watch them.

The ladies sent a remonstrance to the general, and here is his reply:

"You women are the toughest set I ever knew. The men would have given up long ago but for you. I believe you would keep this war up for thirty years."

TRIBUTE OF GENERAL BUELL

The following are some of the words quoted from General Buell, one of the most high-toned and gallant of the Federal generals, and who saved the Federal army from complete defeat at the battle of Shiloh. This appeared in the *Century Magazine*, and afterward in the third volume of "Battles and Leaders in the Civil War." After speaking of the confidence of the Southern soldier in his commander, General Buell then speaks of another influence which nerved the heart of the Confederate soldier to valorous deeds:

"Nor must we give slight importance to the influence of Southern women who, in agony of heart, girded the sword upon their loved ones and bade them go. It was expected that these various influences would give a confidence to leadership that would tend to bold adventure and leave its mark upon the contest.

"Yes; the Confederate soldier has gone down in all histories as the most peerless, most gallant and matchless hero the world ever produced."

TRIBUTE OF JUDGE ALTON B. PARKER, OF NEW YORK

Nothing in all recorded history of mankind has been more pathetic, more heroic, more deserving of admiration and sympathy than the attitude of the Southern people since 1865. As fate would have it, their defeat in war was the smallest of their woes, because it would neither threaten nor bring dishonor. But the new *post-bellum* contest with military power, with theft and robbery, with poverty and enforced domination of a race lately in slavery, forced as it was without time for recovery, and that, too, in their own homes, required a courage a little less than superhuman.

HEROIC MEN AND WOMEN

[President Roosevelt, in his speech at Richmond, October 18, 1905.]

Great though the meed of praise is which is due the South for the soldierly valor of her sons displayed during the four years of war, I think that even greater praise is due her for what her people have accomplished during the forty years of peace which followed. For forty years the South has made not merely a courageous, but at times a desperate struggle, as she has striven for moral and material well-being. Her success has been extraordinary, and all citizens of our common country should feel joy and pride in it; for any great deed done, or any fine qualities shown, by one group of Americans, of necessity reflects credit upon all Americans. Only a heroic people could have battled successfully against the conditions with which the people of the South found themselves face to face at the end of the civil war. There had been utter destruction and disaster, and wholly new business and social problems had to be faced with the scantiest means. The economic and political fabric had to be readjusted in the midst of dire want, of grinding poverty. The future of the broken, war-swept South seemed beyond hope, and if her sons and daughters had been of weaker fiber there would have been in very truth no hope. But the men and the sons of the men who had faced with unfaltering front every alternation of good and evil fortune from Manassas to Appomattox, and the women, their wives and mothers, whose courage and endurance had reached an even higher heroic level—these men and these women set themselves undauntedly to the great task before them. For twenty years the struggle was hard and at times doubtful. Then the splendid qualities of your manhood and womanhood told, as they were bound to tell, and the wealth of your extraordinary natural resources began to be shown. Now the teeming riches of mine and field and factory attest the prosperity of those who are all the stronger because of the trials and struggles through which this prosperity has come. You stand loyally to your traditions and memories; you also stand loyal for our great common country of to-day and for our common flag, which symbolizes all that is brightest and most hopeful for the future of mankind; you face the new age in the spirit of the age. Alike in your material and in your spiritual and intellectual development you stand abreast of the foremost in the world's progress.

THE WOMEN OF THE SOUTH

[Joel Chandler Harris, in Southern Historical Papers.]

Southern women have been heretofore referred to only as the standards of fiction. There are three pieces of fiction that have had a long and popular run in what may be described in a large way as the North American mind. One is that the stage representations of negro characters are true to life; another is that the poor white trash of the South are utterly worthless and thriftless; and the other is that the white woman of the South lived in a state of idleness during the days of slavery, swinging and languishing in hammocks while bevies of pickaninnies cooled the tropical air with long-handled fans made of peacock tails.

Preposterous as they are, age has made these fictions respectable, especially in the North. They strut about in good company, and sometimes a sober historian goes so far as to employ them for the purpose of bolstering up his sectional theories, or, what is still worse, his prejudices.

I do not know that these fictions are important, or that they are even interesting. If there was an explosion every time truth was outrun by his notorious competitor, the man who sleeps late of a morning would wake up with a snort and imagine that the universe was the victim of a fierce and prolonged bombardment.

Wives of Planters

The busiest women the world has ever seen were the wives and daughters of the Southern planters during the days of slavery. They were busy from morning until night, and sometimes far into the night. They were practically at the head of the commissary and sanitary departments of the plantation. It was a part of their duty to see that the negroes were properly fed, clothed, and shod. They did not, it is true, go into the market and purchase the supplies; that was a matter that could be attended to by even a dull-witted man; but after the supplies were bought it was the woman's intelligent management that caused them to be properly distributed.

I have never yet heard of a Southern woman who surrendered the keys of her smoke-house and store-room to an overseer. The distribution of the supplies, however, was a comparatively small item. Take, for example, the clothing provided for, say, one hundred negroes, male and female, large and small. The cloth was bought in bolts, though occasionally a considerable portion was woven on the plantation on the old-fashioned hand-looms. Whether bought or woven, the cloth had to be cut out and made into garments. Who was to superintend and see to all this if not a woman? Who was at the head of the domestic establishment? There were seamstresses to make up the clothes, but all the details and preparations had to be looked after by the mistress, and it oftentimes fell to her lot to go down on her knees on the floor and cut out the garments for hours at a time.

Sanitary Experts

And then there was the health of the negroes—a very important item where a twenty-year-old field hand was worth $1,500 in gold. Who was to look after the sick when, as frequently happened, the physician was miles away? Who, indeed, if not the mistress? It was natural, therefore—and not only natural, but absolutely necessary—that a part of the store-room should be an apothecary's shop on a small scale, and that the Southern woman should know what to prescribe in all the simpler forms of disease. It is to be borne in mind that when the negroes came in from their work the plantation became a domestic establishment, and its demands were such that it was necessary for a woman to be at the head of it. On the energy, the industry and the apt management of the mistress the success of the plantation depended to a great extent. It was not often these qualities were lacking, either, for they were absolutely essential to the success, the comfort, and the moral discipline of the establishment.

Queen of the Kitchen

Then there was the kitchen. No Southern woman could afford to turn that important department over to a negro cook. Such a thing was not to be thought of. The mistress of the plantation was also the mistress of the kitchen. In order to teach their negroes the art of cooking, the Southern women had to know how to cook themselves, and they were compelled to gain their knowledge by practical experience, for the kitchen is one of the places where theories cannot be entertained. There are negro women still living who got their training in the plantation kitchen, under the eyes of their mistresses, and their cooking is a spur to the appetite and a remedy for indigestion. It is no wonder that a Georgia woman, when she heard the negroes were really free, gave a sigh of relief and exclaimed: "Thank heaven! I shall have to work for them no more!"

These Southern women were the outgrowth of the plantation system, the result of six or seven generations of development. On that system they placed the impress of their humanity and refinement; and the outcome of it is to be seen in the condition of the negro race to-day. In the sphere of their homes and in their social relations they exercised a power and influence that has no parallel in history. As they were themselves, so they trained their daughters to be.

In This Generation

As the vine was, so must the fruit be. I have tried to describe the mistress of the plantation for the reason that her characteristics and tendencies have been transmitted to the Southern women of this generation and to the young girls who are growing into womanhood. It is inevitable, however, that certain of these characteristics should be modified or amplified according as the circumstances of an environment altogether new may demand.

I know of no more beautiful or romantic civilization than that which blossomed under the plantation system, and yet, in the natural order of things, it would have inevitably run to caste distinctions. It had social ideals that were impracticable, and it had literary ideals that were foolish; nevertheless, after everything had been said, caste distinctions under the plantation system would have been less distasteful than those which are now in process of organization in some parts of this country.

Whatever the development of Southern civilization might have been under the old system it has come under the domination of the new. That the new has been strengthened and sweetened thereby I think will not be denied by impartial observers who have no pet theories to nurse. Women of to-day still possess the characteristics that made their mothers and their grandmothers beautiful and gracious; still possess the refinement that built up a rare civilization amid unpromising surroundings; still possess the energy and patience and gentleness that wrought order and discipline on the plantations.

An Inheritance of Graciousness

Take, for example, the home life of the plantation. It was larger, ampler, and more perfect than that which exists in the republic to-day, not because it was more leisurely and freer from care, but because the aims and purposes of the various members of the family were more concentrated. The hospitality that was a feature of it was more unrestrained and simpler, because it bore no relation whatever to the demands and suggestions of what is now known in Sunday newspapers as "Society."

The home life of the old plantation has had a marked influence on the Southern women of to-day in their struggles with adverse circumstances.

They lack, for one thing, the assurance of those who have inherited the knack of making their way among strangers. The poetic young Bostonian who has been writing recently of "The Mannerless Sex" and "The Ruthless Sex" could never have made the Southern woman a text for his articles, and I trust that for generations yet to come they will retain the gentleness and the graciousness that belong to them by right of inheritance.

A Beneficent Influence

Comparatively speaking, it has been but a few years since the Southern woman has been compelled by circumstances to seek a wider and more profitable field for her talent, her energy, and her industry than the home and fireside afford, and the experience of these few years has demonstrated the fact that she is amply able to take care of herself. In shaping and developing what is called the new literary movement in the South, she has shown herself to be a far more versatile worker than the men, more artistic and more conscientious. She has made herself in art, in science, and in schools; she has taken a place in the ranks of the journalists; she has a place on the stage and the platform; she is to be found in many of the trades that are next door to the arts, in the professions and in business; she is stenographing, typewriting, clerking, dairying, gardening. She is to be found, in short, wherever there is room for her, and her field is always widening.

I think she will exercise a mellowing and restraining influence on the ripping and snorting age just ahead of us—the rattling and groaning age of electricity. What part she may play in the woman's rights movement of the future it is difficult to say. Just now she has no aptitude in that direction. She has been taught to believe that the influences that are the result of a happy home-life are more powerful and more important elements of politics than the casting of a ballot; and in this belief she seems to be with an overwhelming majority of American women—the mothers and daughters who are the hope and pride of the Republic.

Yet she is an earnest and untiring temperance worker. Conservative in all other directions, she is inclined to be somewhat radical in her crusade against rum. She is inclined to fret and grieve a little over the fact that public opinion failed to keep pace with her desires. The wheels of legislation do not move fast enough for her, and she is inclined to wonder at it. In the innocence of her heart she has never suspected that there is a demijohn in the legislative committee-room.

There is no question and no movement of real importance in which she is not interested. Her devotion and self-sacrifice in the past have consecrated her to the future, and her sufferings and privations have taught her the blessings of charity in its largest and best interpretation.

EULOGY ON CONFEDERATE WOMEN, BY J. L. UNDERWOOD, DELIVERED IN 1896

[The author offers as his tribute to the memory of the Confederate Women the following lecture just as it came from his brain and heart in 1896. It was delivered mainly for the benefit of the Confederate Monument in Cuthbert, Ga. A very serious lip cancer soon interrupted all lecture work and finally landed him in Kellam's Hospital in Richmond, Va.]

Ever since 1861 the women of the South have been laying flowers on the graves of Confederate soldiers and building monuments to their memory. The humblest of surviving veterans begs the privilege of offering a wreath of evergreen and immortelles to the memory of the Confederate women. To the genuine woman, no bouquet is acceptable, not even the kiss of affection is welcome, unless hallowed by respect. Horatio Seymour, the great governorof New York, said that the South, prior to 1861, produced "the best men and the best women the world ever saw." In the early part of the spring of 1861, your speaker heard M. Laboulaye, one of the foremost men of France in literature and public life, in a public lecture at the Sorbourne in Paris, utter the following memorable words: "I am told that in America a lady can travel alone from Baltimore to New Orleans and will all the way be protected and assisted. A country where woman is respected as she is in the Southern States of the American Republic,—a country where women so richly deserve that respect,—others may say what they please about slavery in that sunny land, but that's the country for me." This profound admiration, expressed by the good and great of the world, while it fills the heart, must surely temper the words of a Southern writer.

That man is not qualified to admire one woman who sees no good in other women. Blind partiality is stupid idolatry. The just historian of Southern women will say nothing in disparagement of the warm-hearted fraus of Germany, the tasteful, tidy, sparkling women of France, our rosy cousins of old England, and especially those bustling, bright little creatures up North, who make things so lively everywhere. When Titian and Correggio put woman on canvas she is their Italian woman; Murillo paints her as the lustrous, dark-eyed beauty of his own Spain. Meissonier's women are French women, and when Rubens paints an angel or unfallen Eve, she is the fat chubby girl of Holland. But Raphael, in his celebrated Madonna, the greatest of all paintings, forgets all nationality, and his picture is just that of a woman. Oh for something of this cosmopolitan spirit in our sacred task. Nor must history degenerate into panegyric. Weeds are near the flower-garden, and there are thorns among the roses. Even among the brave Confederate soldiers there were some shirkers and cowards. We had our "hospital rats" and "butter-milk-rangers." In the battle there were some who suddenly got very thirsty and ran away to get water. As one of these was rushing from a hot fire to the rear one day, his colonel shouted to him, "What are you running for? I wouldn't be a baby." "I wish I was a baby, and a gal baby at that"—was the reply. Another one in Gordon's command, in another battle, was making tracks to the rear as fast as he could. General J. B. Gordon shouted, "Stop there, Jim; what makes you run?" "Because I can't fly," was his reply, as he leaped the fence. So our Confederate women were not all paragons nor angels; not if you let their poor husbands tell it. An old soldier in Atlanta has sued for a divorce from his wife on the plea that during a long life she has allowed him only four years of peace, and that was when he was away in the war.

About the time of the surrender in 1865, a Federal brigade, on its march to take possession of a Georgia city, halted near a farm. As usual the soldiers went in to get supplies of milk, chickens, etc., offering to pay for everything. The old gentleman of the farm when he heard of their approach had taken to the woods. His wife stood her ground, and, seizing her first opportunity to let the Yankees "know what she thought of them," let out upon their devoted heads a torrent of woman's fury. Her tongue fought the war over again. They became enraged and literally "cleaned up" the farm, taking mules, wagons, corn, chickens,—everything in sight. When they had gone the old farmer came in and when he saw "wide o'er the plain the wreck of ruin laid" he became desperate. Finally, on the advice of his neighbors, he went to the headquarters of the general in the city and laid before him his pitiful complaint. That officer told him he could not help him. "If you people give my soldiers a civil treatment, I shall see that they respect your property and pay for everything they get; but when they are abused and insulted as they were at your house, I can't restrain them, nor shall I try." "But, see here, General, it is my mules and other property that they have taken, and I have not abused your soldiers; it was my wife." "But, sir, you ought to make your wife hold her tongue." "Well, now, General, I have been trying that forty years, and if you and your whole army can't make her hold her tongue, how in the world can you expect me to do it?" The general saw the situation and kindly ordered everything which had been taken to be given back to the old farmer.

It has been said that the South has been busy making history and others busy writing it. Our own people must write it, and our children must study it. For more than twenty-five years the life of the South was the drama of the nineteenth century; and no drama is complete without woman's part in it. The war between the Southern and Northern States was one of the bloodiest in history. The Southern States claimed the right of secession from the Union—a right which during the first seventy years of the Nation's life was never questioned. The Northern States claimed the right to coerce our States back into what they called the Union—a right never before thought of.

The die of war was cast, the Rubicon of coercion was crossed, the gauntlet of blood was thrown down, when the Northern States sent ships and soldiers to hold Fort Sumter on South Carolina's soil. Again and again had the Southern States asked the Northern States for the fish of peace; they were given the serpent of Seward's "irrepressible conflict." They asked for the bread of simple right; they were given the stone of invasion. The reinforcement of Fort Sumter was a declaration of war on the South.

Then, and not till then, did Beauregard's cannon thunder forth the protest for the rights of States, and the tocsin rang out from the Potomac to the Rio Grande. The ultimatum was cowardly submission to sectional dictation. There is something better than peace; that is liberty. There is something dearer than a people's life; that is a people's manhood. The South wanted no war; had prepared for no war; and had but few arms, no navy, few factories and railroads. With a small population, she was cut off by an effective blockade from the rest of the world. The Northern States had the national army, navy, treasury and flag, and all Europe from which to draw soldiers and supplies.

The South, after mustering every able-bodied man, could enroll, in all, but 600,000 soldiers, while she fought 2,600,000. Never was there a war continued for four years at such fearful odds. And yet Richmond, the Confederate capital, almost in sight of Washington, was only captured when Sherman and Sheridan, the modern Atillas, had flanked it with walls of fire, and pillaged the country in its rear. Never has there been a war in which the weaker so long and so effectually held the stronger at bay or so often defeated them on the field of battle; never a war in which the valor of the finally vanquished was so respected by foes and so universally applauded by the world. The mention of no battle, from Manassas to Appomattox, from Shiloh to Franklin, brings a blush to the Confederate soldier. The world congratulates the Federal soldier on his pension and the Confederate soldier on his valor. The surrender of Lee's 7,800 to Grant's 130,000 and the roll of 357,679 Federal soldiers living to-day in the Grand Army of the Republic measure the odds against us. The reduction of the Federal forces to 1,500,000 during the war and the present pension roll of 800,000 tell our work. Our poor South was never vanquished. Her sad fate was simply to be worn out, starved out, burned out, to die out.

Generously, but truthfully, did Professor Worseley, of England, in his poem on Robert E. Lee, say of the ill-fated Confederacy,

“Thy Troy is fallen, thy dear land
  Is marred beneath the spoiler’s heel;
I cannot trust my trembling hand
  To write the things I feel.

“Ah, realm of tombs! but let her bear
  This blazon to the end of times;
No nation rose so white and fair
  Or fell so pure of crimes.”

After the surrender a poor Southern soldier was wending his way down the lane over the “red old hills of Georgia.” His old gray jacket that his wife had woven and his mother made, was all tattered and torn; the old greasy haversack and cedar canteen hung by his side. From under his bullet-pierced hat there beamed eyes that had seen many a battlefield. Said one of his neighbors: “Hello, John; the Yankees whipped you, did they?” “No, we just wore ourselves out whipping them.” “Well, what are you going to do now, John?” “Why, I’m going home, kiss Mary, and make a crop and get ready to whip ’em again.”

That “Mary” is our theme to-day. Others have told of Confederate soldiers on the battlefield. God help me to tell of the soldier’s “other-self” behind the battlefield. The brave Southern army was defending home. The arm of the hero is nerved by his heart, and the heart of John was Mary, and Mary was the soul of the South. In peace woman was the queen of that Arcadia which God’s blessings made our sunny land, and never has there been a war in which her enthusiasm was so intense and her heroic cooperation so conspicuous. Her effectual and practical work in the departments of the commissary, the quartermaster and the surgeon, and her magic influence at home and on the spirit of the army, were something wonderful. The Federal General Atkins, of Sherman’s army, said to a Carolina lady: “You women keep up this war. We are fighting you. What right have you to expect anything from us?”

And yet in all she was woman,—nothing but woman. “And the Lord said it is not good for man to be alone; I will make a help-meet for him.” In Paradise she was the rib of man’s side; in Paradise lost she bears woman’s heavy share of his labors and his fate. The history of the South of 1861 will go down to the centuries with its immortal lesson that woman’s power is greatest, her work most beneficent and her career most splendid when she moves in the orbit assigned her by Heaven as the help-meet of man. It is the glory of Southern life and society that with us woman is no “flaring Jezebel” but our own modest Vashti.

Thank God the Confederate woman was no Lady Macbeth, plotting treason for the advancement of her husband; but the loyal daughter Cordelia, clinging to her old father Lear in his wrongs; no fanatical Catherine de Medici, thirsting for Huguenot blood, but the sweet Florence Nightingale, hovering over the battlefield with,

"The balm that drops on wounds of woe,

From woman's pitying eye,"

and making the dying bed of the patriot feel "soft as downy pillows are." She was no Herodias, calling for the head of an enemy, but the humble Mary, breaking the alabaster box to anoint the martyr of her cause; weeping at His cross and watching at His grave. She was no fierce Clytimnestra, but the loving Antigone leading the blind old Oedipus, or digging the grave of her brother Polynices; no Amazon Camilla, "*Agmen agens equitum et florentes aere catervas*," but the Roman Cornelia, proud of her jewel Gracchi sons, and laying them upon the altar of her country; no Helen, heartless in her beauty, but the gentle Creusa, following her husband to be crushed in the ruins of her ill-fated Troy; no cruel Juno, seeking revenge for wounded pride, but a pure Vesta, keeping alive the fires of American patriotism; no Charlotte Corday, plunging a dagger into the heart of the tyrant Marat, but the calm Madame Roland, under the guillotine of the Jacobins, raised to sever her proud but all womanly head, and crying to her countrymen, "Oh, Liberty, what crimes are committed in thy name!" Who begrudges a moment for the record of her patriotic services and unremitting toil? Who does not see in her a glorious lesson?

Thank God! the clash of arms has long ago ceased. The temple of Janus is closed. But the war of pens, the contest of history, is upon us. For years Southern women had been written down as soulless ciphers or weakling wives, dragged by reckless husbands into an unholy cause. Text books of so- called history, teeming with such falsehoods, have been thrust even into Southern schools. It is high time to protest. Before God we tell them our mothers were not dupes, but women; they and our men were not rebels, but patriots, obedient to every law, loyal to every compact, State and National, of their country; true, gloriously true, to every lesson taught by Washington and Jefferson, and moved by every impulse that has made this country great.

But there must be no gall in the inkstand of history. No man can justly record the truth of the Confederate war who has not risen above the passions and prejudices incident to such terrible convulsions. No man with malice to the North can write justly of the South. No man can appreciate our great Jefferson

Davis, who can see nothing good in President Lincoln. No man can describe the glory of Lee and Jackson, who shuts his eyes to the soldiership of McClellan, the patriotism of Hancock, the generosity of Grant, and the knighthood of McPherson and Custer.

But don't let us go too far in this direction. We might fall into the other extreme of hypocritical "gush." Let us be careful; yea, honest. About the best we could do in war times is well shown in the preaching of a good old Alabama country Baptist preacher in the darker days of the war. He was a thorough Southerner and "brim full of secesh," as we used to say, and at the same time a devout Christian. He was of the old-fashioned type and talked a little through his nose. His text was the great day when the good people will be gathered to Heaven from the four corners of the world. Warming up to his theme he said: "And oh, my brethren,—ah; in the day of redemption the redeemed of the Lord will come flocking from the four corners of the earth,— ah! They will come from the East on the wings of the morning,—ah! I hear them shouting Hallelujah, as they strike their harps of gold—ah! And they'll come from the West shouting Hosanna in the highest,—ah! and you'll see them coming in crowds from the South,—ah; with palms of victory in their hands, ah! And they'll come from the,—well, I reckon may be a few of them will come from the North." Oh that's about the way men, women and children down South felt for twenty years. But, we've moved up on that. Christians grow in grace, you know. The war is over. There are no enemies now. We now believe a great many will come from the North. Our old preacher would not now have a misgiving about all four of the corners.

A few weeks after the surrender of Vicksburg, a large number of sick paroled Confederate soldiers were sent home on a Federal steamer by way of New Orleans and Mobile. The speaker was among them. He had been promoted to the chaplaincy of the Thirtieth Alabama Regiment and soon found himself strong enough at least to bury the dead as our poor fellows dropped away every day. The Federal guard on the boat was under command of Lieutenant Winslow, of Massachusetts, and a nobler and bigger hearted soldier never wore a sword. Between New Orleans and Mobile it was necessary to bury our dead in the Gulf. Having no coffins the Federal lieutenant and the Confederate chaplain would lay the body, wrapped in the old blanket or quilt, on a plank and then bind it with ropes and, fastening heavy irons to the feet, we would gently lower it and let it sink down, down in the briny deep, the cleanest grave man ever saw. The Northern lieutenant not only took off his cap and bowed in reverence when the Confederate chaplain prayed, but with his own hands assisted in all the details of every burial. So let the North and the South together bury the dead animosities of the past, take the corpse of bitter falsehood, the prolific mother of prejudice and hatred, bind it with the cords of patriotism and sink it into the ocean of oblivion. But publish the truth. The truth lives and ought to live. Truth never does harm; but, with God and man, it is the peace angel of reconciliation. Let the testimony be the truth, the whole truth, and nothing but the truth and our people will abide by it and every patriot will welcome the verdict.

Who were the women of 1861? My old Tennessee father used to teach me that there is a great deal more in the stock of people than there is in horses. Blood will tell. These women were the direct descendants of those bold, hardy Englishmen, who, under John Smith, Lord Delaware, Lord Baltimore and General Oglethorpe made settlements on the Southern shores and those who, from time to time, were added to their colonies. They were broad men, bringing broad ideas. They came, not because they were driven out of England, but because they wanted to come to America; who thought it no sin to bring the best things of old England, and give them a new and better growth in the new world; who first gave the new world trial by jury and the election of governors by popular vote. English cavaliers who knew how to be gentlemen, even in the forest. This was the leading blood. From time to time it was made stronger by a considerable addition of Scotch and Scotch-Irish and an occasional healthful cross with the very best people of the North, more soulful and impulsive by some of the blood of Ireland, and more vivacious by the French Huguenot in the Carolinas and the Creole in Louisiana. There thus grew up a new English race—English, but not too English; English but American-English blood, of which old England is proud to-day. With little or no immigration for many years from other people, this blood under ourbalmy sun produced a race of its own—a Southern people, as Klopstock says of the sweet strong language of Germany, "Gesondert, ungemischt und nur sich selber gleich." Distinct, unmixed and only like itself.

This was the blood that made America great, the blood from which the South gave her Washington and so many men like Henry, Jefferson, Madison and Monroe; that out of seventy-two first years of this Republic furnished the President for fifty-two years; the Chief Justice all the time, and the leaders of Senates and of Cabinets; the blood of Calhoun and Clay and Lowndes and Pinkney and Benton and Crawford; Cobb and Berrien, Hall and Jenkins, Toombs and Stevens; the blood that produced our Washington, Sumter and Marion to achieve our independence of Great Britain; Scott and Jackson to fight the war of 1812, Clark and Jackson to conquer from the Indians all the splendid country between the mountains and the Mississippi, and Taylor and Scott to win vast territories from Mexico.

This was the blood that so often showed how naturally and gracefully a Southern woman could step from a country home to adorn the White House at

Washington; the blood that made the South famous for its women, stars at the capital and at Saratoga; favorites in London and Paris; and queenly ladies in their homes, whether that home was a log cabin in the forest or a mansion by the sea. It was common for Northern and European people to praise the taste of Southern women, especially in matters of dress. They did have remarkable taste in dressing, for they had a form to dress and a face to adorn that dress. Neither war nor poverty could mar their grace of form nor beauty of face.

It is said of the great Bishop Bascomb, of the Southern Methodist Church, that, in the early years of his ministry, he was so handsome and graceful in person, and so neat in his dress, that a great many of his brethren were prejudiced against him as being what they called "too much of a dandy." For a long time the young orator was sent on mountain circuits to bring him down to the level of plain old-fashioned Methodism. It was proposed to one of his mountain members who was very bitter about the preacher's fine clothes that he give Bascomb a suit of homespun. The offer was gladly accepted, and on the day for Bascomb's appearance in the plain clothes the old brother was early on the church grounds to glory in having made the city preacher look like other folks. Imagine his chagrin when Bascomb walked up, looking in homespun as he looked in broadcloth, an Apollo in form and a Brummel in style. "Well I do declare!" said the old man. "Go it, brother Bascomb; I give it up; It ain't your clothes that's so pretty, it's jist you." So our Southern women were just as charming in the shuck hats and home-made cotton dresses of 1864, as in the silks and satins of 1860.

But by their fruits ye shall know them. Walk with me on the streets of Richmond and Charleston. Go with me to any of our country churches throughout these Southern States and I will show you, among the many poor daughters of these women, that same classic face that tells of the blood in their veins. Go with me back to the Confederate army and you will see in such generals as the Lees, Albert Sidney Johnston, Breckinridge, Toombs, the Colquitts, Gordon, Evans, Gracie, Jeb. Stuart, Price, Hampton, Tracy, Ramseur, Ashby and thousands of private soldiers that face and form that tell of the knightly blood in the veins of the mothers that bore them.

South Georgia is to be congratulated that in the Confederate monument recently unveiled at Cuthbert, the artist has at least given what is sadly lacking in other Confederate monuments to private soldiers, the genuine face of the Southern soldier, that face which is a just compliment to the Confederate mother. The artists who cast some other monuments in the South had seen too little of Southern people, and had put on some of our monuments the pug nose and bullet head of other people.

Our mothers and grandmothers lived mostly in the country, and drank in a splendid vigor from the ozone of field, and forest, and mountain. They were trained mostly at home by private teachers or in common schools run on common sense principles, and in "the old-time religion," without "isms," fanaticism, or cant. They were taught the philosophy of life by fathers who thought and manners by mothers who were the soul of inborn refinement. They thought for themselves, and indulged no craze for things new, and they aped no foreigners. In conversation they didn't end every sentence with the interrogation point, but followed nature and let their voices fall at periods. They never said "thanks," but in the good old English of Addison and Goldsmith, said "I thank you." They never spoke of a sweetheart as "my fellow," and would have scorned such a word as "mash." They never walked "arm clutch," nor allowed Sunday newspapers to make five-cent museums of their pictures. Their entertainments were famous for elegance and pleasure, but they had no euchre-clubs. Indeed, we doubt if many of them ever heard of a woman's club of any kind. They were fond of "society," but would have had a profound contempt for that so-called "society" of our day, in which the man is a prince who can lead the german, spend money for bouquets and part his hair in the middle. They didn't wear bloomers, nor did many of them ever dress decolette. They were clothed and in their right mind. They never mounted platforms to speak nor pulpits to preach, and yet their influence and inspiration gave Southern pulpits and platforms a world-wide fame. Their highest ambition was to be president of home. They were Southern women everywhere, at home and abroad, in church and on the streets, in parlor and kitchen, when they rode, when they walked. Gentle, but brave; modest, but independent. Seeking no recognition, the true Southern woman found it already won by her worth; courting no attention, at every turn it met her, to do willing homage to her native grace and genuine womanhood.

Now, to appreciate the enthusiasm of such women in the Confederate war, you must remember that great principles were at stake in that struggle, and that woman grasps great principles as clearly as man, and with a zeal known only to herself. See with what prompt intuition and sober enthusiasm woman received the Christian religion. Martha, of Bethany, uttered the great keynote of the Christian creed long before an apostle penned a line. The primitive evangelist Timothy, the favorite of the great Apostle Paul, was trained by his grandmother Lois and his mother Eunice; and the pulpit orator Apollos studied at the feet of Priscilla. The great lamented Dr. Thornwell, of South Carolina, who was justly called the "John C. Calhoun of the Presbyterian Church" of the United States, loved to tell it that he learned his theology from his poor old country Baptist mother. In politics, as in religion, our mothers may not have read much, and they talked less, but they heard much and thought the more. Before the war the reproach was often hurled at Southern men that they talked politics. God's true people talked religion from Abel to the invention of the art of printing. They had a religion to talk. Our fathers did talk politics, for, thank God, they had politics worth talking—not the picayune politics of the demagogue office-seeker of our day; not the almighty dollar politics of the bloated bond-holder and the trusts, the one-idea craze of the silver mine-owner, nor the tariff greed of the manufacturer; not the imported European communism that would crush one class to build up another, not the wild anarchy that would pull down everything above it and blast everything around it.

The South was intensely American, and her people loved American politics and talked American politics. She entered into the Revolutionary war with all her soul. Southern statesmanship lifted that struggle from a mere rebellion to a war of nations by manly secession from Great Britain in North Carolina's declaration of independence at Mecklenburg. The Philadelphia declaration was drawn up by the South's Jefferson and proposed by Virginia. This was the great secession of 1776. To the Revolutionary war the South sent one hundred out of every two hundred and nine men of military age, while the North sent one hundred out of every two hundred and twenty-seven. (We quote from the official report of General Knox, Secretary of War.) Virginia sent 56,721 men. South Carolina sent 31,000 men, while New York, with more than double her military population, sent 29,830. New Hampshire, with double the population of South Carolina, sent only 18,000. The little Southern States sent more men in proportion to population than even Massachusetts and Connecticut, who did their part so well in that war.

It was Southern politics that proposed the great union of the sovereign States in 1787. To that union the three States of Virginia, North Carolina, and Georgia have added out of their own bosoms ten more great States. These Southern States were the mothers of States, and most naturally did they talk of States and State's rights.

Southern politics, prevailing in the national councils against the bitter protests of New England, carried through the war of 1812; added Florida to the Union, and, by the purchase of Louisiana, all the Trans-Mississippi valley from the Gulf to Canada. It was Southern politics against the furious opposition of New England that annexed Texas, and, by the war with Mexico, brought in the vast territory far away to the Pacific. The South sent 45,000 volunteers to the Mexican war; the whole North, with three times the population, sent 23,000. Thus the South was the mother of territories, and was it not natural that she should talk of territories and of her rights in the territories?

In political platforms, in legislative enactments, and notably in the election of Mr. Lincoln in 1860, the more populous North declared that the Southern

States should be shut out from all share in the territories bought with common treasure and blood. Our women, a child, a negro, could see the iniquity of the claim.

The action of the North in regard to national territory was an edict, too, that the negroes, through no fault of their own, should be shut up in one little corner of the country.

Then when the South sought the only alternative left her, that of peaceable secession, her right to go was justified by the terms of the Constitution; by the distinct understanding among the sovereign States when they entered the Union, more directly insisted and put on record by the three States of Virginia, New York, and Rhode Island than any other State; by the secession convention of New England in the war of 1812; by the Northern secession convention in Ohio in 1859 and the reiterated declarations of Henry Ward Beecher, and by Wendell Phillips, and Horace Greeley, William Lloyd Garrison and the other great leaders of Northern thought in 1860.

As to coercing the States back into the Union, President Buchanan well said at the time there was "not a shadow of authority" for it, and Governor Seymour, of New York, truthfully said "coercion is revolution."

Again, remember that wrongs pierce deeper into the heart of woman than into the more callous soul of man. For years vast multitudes of the people of the North had kept up a furious war against the South in books and newspapers; in pulpits and religious conventions; in political platforms and State assemblies. Oh, it makes the blood run cold to think of the relentless malignity of the fanaticism of those days. No parlors nor churches too sacred for bitter onslaught on Southern people; no epithets too vile; no slanders too black; no curses too deadly to be hurled at Southern men and women. But war,—yes, blood-red war was really, and almost formally declared by the Northern endorsement of Henry Ward Beecher's "Sharpe's rifles" crusade against Southern settlers in Kansas; and the war of 1861 was actually begun by John Brown's murderous raid at Harper's Ferry in Virginia in 1859. The North made him a hero martyr. John Brown's rifle shot in Virginia only alarmed the angel of peace. The Northern applause of John Brown drove her away from our unhappy land. By his apotheosis the Northern people made his rifle shot at Harper's Ferry the skirmish firing of the impending war, to be answered by our manly cannon at Charleston in 1861. Puritan intolerance scourged Roger Williams out of Massachusetts for nonconformity in religion; and Puritanism scourged the South out of the Union in 1861 for nonconformity in politics. The Southern woman's heart felt to the very core and resented as only woman can resent, the sting of that merciless lash.

This is an age of monuments, and your speaker has undertaken to erect one in book form to the memory of Confederate women. When this thought comes to be put in marble or brass, as it will some day soon, let that monument rest on the broad granite foundation of truth. Then as the artist begins to put in bas relief the symbols of the virtues of the Southern women of 1861, and the souvenirs of her heroic life, let the first scene be that of a scroll, the Constitution of the United States, held in the unsullied hands of the great Jefferson Davis, as he marches out from the United States court, under whose warrants he had been held for treason, again a free man. Let that picture tell of the undying loyalty of our mother and her people to the organic law of the land: that Southern men wrote it and their sons have ever honored and loved it: Tell it in Gath, publish it in the streets of Aekelon, that those who crushed us were the men who despised, hawked at and cursed the Constitution.

The South at Montgomery swore fresh allegiance to the Constitution handed down by our American fathers, and carried with her through all the wilderness march the sacred old Ark of the Covenant. And when our Confederate head, the peerless Jefferson Davis, our chosen standard bearer of State sovereignty and home rule, was brought to trial, bearing in himself the alleged sins of us all, charged with being a rebel, that document showed him to be a stainless patriot; and though the mob of millions was shouting, "Crucify him, crucify him!" the highest courts of the Federal Government declared by his quiet and silent, but significant release, as Pilate did of Jesus, "We find no fault in this man." The Constitution of the United States is a standing declaration of the sinlessness of the Confederate cause.

Let the artist next put on the monument a picture of an old negro woman, the old Southern "mammy," with the child of her mistress in her arms. Near by let old Uncle Jacob be leading the little white boy, while down in the cornfield near by are seen Jacob's sons and daughters at work singing the cheerful songs which the poor negro now has heart to sing no more. In the distance picture the faithful Bob or Mingo coming from the battlefield, bearing the dead body of his young master.

Let that picture tell to all generations the story of slavery. We had slavery, but, thank God, it was Southern slavery,—Christian slavery. Truth will explain the paradox, if there was any paradox. It had its evils, and nobody blushes because we had it, nor whines because it is gone. But as for any sin of the South in it, let the first stone of condemnation be thrown by that people who had no fathers cruel to their children, no husbands harsh to their wives, and no rich man unjust to the poor laborer.

The South never enslaved a single negro, never brought one to America. Georgia was the first of the settlements to forbid slavery, and Georgia and Virginia were the foremost States in cutting off the slave trade. The colony of

Virginia petitioned twenty times against the continuance of the slave trade. The negroes were enslaved by their own savage chiefs in Africa. England and the Northern people brought them to America and sold them for gold. The Dutch brought twenty to Virginia, but were forbidden to bring any more. When found less profitable in the colder climate of the North, the negroes were sold South to become valuable tillers of the soil, and, after the invention of the cotton gin, to make the country rich. The Northern people at a good profit sold their slaves down South, put the money at interest, suddenly got pious, and waged a fierce war on the people who bought them. That's history.

In 1861, on the first Sunday after the news of the fall of Fort Sumter reached England, the author, in company with a friend from Pennsylvania, who was an anti-slavery man, attended services in Mr. Spurgeon's chapel in London. The great city was wrapped in the deepest gloom. The war storm in America was expected to ruin manufactures and trade throughout Great Britain. Mr. Spurgeon and his people seemed bowed down with sorrow. On returning to our hotel my Northern friend remarked that he knew I didn't approve of Spurgeon's prayer about slavery. I said to him, "R——, just there you are mistaken. Some of my people in Alabama some time ago burned Spurgeon's books because of some of his abolition views, but when I go home and tell them how this great Christian prayed to-day they will respect his honesty and sincerity. We blame nobody for being anti-slavery, but we do abominate fanatical abolitionism. Spurgeon is no fanatic. Listen to this Englishman: 'O God, our people are in the ashes of woe. A dreadful war beyond the ocean has cut off our commerce and closed our factories, and thousands of our poor must sadly suffer. The people of the American States are bone of our bone and flesh of our flesh. O Lord, pity them, and pity us. O God, they and we have sinned in enslaving our fellow men. England put slavery on her colonies against the protest of those Southern people, and England must suffer Thy judgments for her part. Forgive the North, forgive the South, and forgive England. O pity especially the people of that section where the war will bear so heavily and pity the poor everywhere.'

"Now, R——, that's a Christian prayer that we respect; and while Spurgeon goes back one hundred and fifty and even two hundred years and tells the truth about slavery, and for his English people, even to-day, shoulders their responsibility in this matter, how are thousands (thank God, but not all) of your Northern preachers in your churches at the North praying to-day? 'We thank Thee, Lord, that this war has come. Somebody will get hurt, but we people up this way will come out all right because we are so innocent and so righteous. O Lord, we thank Thee that we are holy and not as other men are, especially these wicked Southern people. We thank Thee for short memories; that we have forgotten that we brought the negroes from Africa, kept them as long as it paid us, and then sold them to these Southerners; that we have forgotten that when Virginia and Maryland wanted to put an end to the slave trade, we out-voted them and kept the slave trade open until 1808. Lord, we could have seceded from these savage Southern States long ago and got rid of any connection with slavery, for we believed in secession until just now. But, Lord, if we let the South go, as Mr. Lincoln says, where will we get our revenues? We thank Thee too that we have forgotten that those Southerners can't get rid of the negroes without kicking them into the Gulf of Mexico. Lord, we thank Thee that we can see nothing but our own righteousness. We have tried to reform those wicked Southerners and make them good like ourselves, but we couldn't. Now, Lord, we have brought on a war and we turn it over to Thee. We'll hire Dutchmen and Irishmen to help Thee do our fighting, and we'll stand off and enjoy the fun. Now, as Thou art about to pour out the vials of Thy mighty wrath upon the abominable Southern people, do, Lord, just give 'em—fits.' Now, R——, there's the difference between honest anti-slavery in England and the hypocrisy of the crusade in America."

The truth is that in Southern homes, the negro prospered and multiplied as no other laboring class has ever done. The South shared with him its bread, its medicines, its homes and its churches. M. de La Tours, the eminent French hygienist, truthfully said that "The slaves of the South were the best fed and the best cared for laborers that the world ever saw." No chain-gang, no penitentiary, for the negro, no lynchings, and no crimes to be lynched for, when the negro was under the influence of our mothers and grandmothers. God forgive the fanatic who in later days put folly in his head and the devil in his heart. Our mothers trusted him and he trusted them. All through the war, while nearly all the white men were away in the army, the negro slave was the protector and the support of Southern families. Our mothers would have died for the negroes, and negroes would have died for them. In Wilson's raid near Columbus, Ga., his soldiers were about to destroy a patch of cane belonging to a widow. The brave woman took her gun and declared she would shoot the first man that touched her property. In their rage they raised their rifles to shoot her down. Just then her old cook rushed in between them, saying, "If you are going to kill 'old miss,' you'll have to kill me, too."

When Sherman was plundering South Carolina, some of his soldiers heard that a young lady had a very fine gold watch concealed in her bosom. They demanded it, and on her refusal they were about to seize her, when Delia, her faithful servant, defied them. "Fore God, buckra, if one of younner put your nasty hand on dis chile of my ole missus you got to knock Delia down fust."

The monument to the Southern woman will be a monument to our faithful old Dinahs and Delias too. The old ex-slaves will gather at its base and as the tears stream down their dusky cheeks they will say, as they say now, "Dat's de best friend the poor nigger ever had," and enlightened negroes, like Booker Washington, will tell the true story that out of slavery the North got money, the South got ruin, and the negro got civilization, Christianity, and contentment.

Let the next picture be an ear of corn, a spinning-wheel, and a hand-loom. Ceres was the goddess of the Sunny South, and the staff of our armies was the corn of our own fields. The South, however prosperous, was not made up of rich people. Not one man in ten owned a slave; not one slave holder in ten was wealthy. The small farms, many of them under the care of the soldier's wife and the faithful old negro foreman, and many more tilled by the soldier's boys under the eye of their mother, yielded a very large share of the Confederate supplies. While Minerva taught our men war she taught our women household work, and quickly did she make Southern beauties Arachnes at the loom and Penelopes with the knitting needles. They knew how to adorn the parlor and play the piano, but, when necessity came, like Lemuel's mother, they "sought wool and flax and wrought diligently with their hands," or even, like Rebecca, they could go out into the field and draw water for the cattle; or, like Ruth, hold the plow steady in the furrows, or glean grain at harvest time. False histories have pictured our mothers as doll babies. Let that monument tell of the wonderful pluck, energy, and strength, while it tells of the patriotism of the smartest and sweetest and bravest and strongest doll babies the world ever saw.

The artist must do his best when he puts on that monument a little white hand —the well-shaped, classic hand of the Southern woman. In that hand must be held the little white handkerchief. What a part that handkerchief played in the war! Old soldiers, as you rode off down the lane, again and again you turned to take the farewell look at home, sweet home, and there was that little white handkerchief waving at the gate; or when your company left the railroad station there, all around, were the good women of the neighborhood, and as you looked far back down the track these little white flags bade you woman's "good bye and God bless you." You never forgot it. Whether we marched past country homes or through the streets of cities, woman's heart-cheer greeted us in the handkerchief from the window. Perhaps it was held in the rheumatic hand of Mrs. General Lee as she looked out from her knitting in her Richmond home, or, later on we could see behind it the sad, mourning sleeve of Stonewall Jackson's widow. I tell you, my countrymen, the bonny blue flag or the Southern Cross was the banner of the soldier on the battlefield, but the little white handkerchief was our sacred banner behind the battlefield. The one, in the hands of the color sergeants, guided our movements in the army; but the other, in woman's hand, inspired our movements everywhere.

Put here a knapsack, the rough, old, oil-cloth knapsack of the Confederate soldier. Poor fellow! he had but few clothes in it, but it contained something dearer to him than clothes—letters from home. He kept them all, the most of them written on the blank side of old wall paper and inclosed in brown envelopes, which perhaps had been turned so as to be twice used. When our poor boys were killed, their letters were gathered by the chaplains, litter bearers and burial details, to be sent to their homes. I am not going to tell what sort of letters were found in many knapsacks on our battlefields, but it is a fact, borne out by the testimony of these men, that never was there found a letter from a Confederate soldier's wife to her husband whose words would make the most modest blush, or in which she exerted any of her woman's power or used any of woman's arts to decoy him from the army. Here is a specimen of a letter from home in a Confederate knapsack:

MITCHELL COUNTY, GA., *July 20, 1863.*

Mr. Jno. Iverson,
Company B, Fourth Regiment, Army of Virginia.

DEAR JOHN:

This leaves us all getting along very well. Nobody sick, and we finished laying by the corn. The cattle are fat and the hogs doing finely. We sell some butter and eggs every week. We have plenty to eat, and know that it's only you that's having a hard time. But we are all so proud that you are fighting for your country. Will be so glad when you can get a furlough, but we know that you must, and will stick to your post of duty. Willie and Jennie send kisses to their brave papa. We never forget to pray for you. If you get killed, darling, God will take care of us and we'll all meet in heaven.

Your,
MARY.

That's the way they wrote. Let that knapsack tell forever of the fortitude, the purity, the loyalty and refinement of the Southern woman.

Let the next picture be the humble hospital couch.

"Up and down through the wards where the fever
Stalks, noisome, and gaunt, and impure;
You must go with your steadfast endeavor
To comfort, to counsel, to cure.
I grant you the task is superhuman,
But strength will be given to you
To do for those loved ones what woman
Alone in her pity can do."

Our women gave their carpets to make blankets, their dresses to be made into shirts for the soldiers, and their linen to furnish lint for their wounds, and then, clad in homespun, they gave themselves. Nearly every town and village in the South had its Soldiers' Aid Society and its hospital. Thousands and thousands of the poor fellows were taken to private houses, even away out in the country, and tenderly cared for. There was scarcely a woman near a battlefield or a railroad who did not nurse a soldier. Nearly every woman in Richmond served regularly on hospital committees. One of these, a Mrs. Roland, was blind, and her sweet guitar and sweeter song cheered many a poor hero. One of the songs of these days was "Let me kiss him for his Mother." Here's a story to show how woman's petting, which always spoils a boy and sometimes a husband, occasionally found a hard case in a Confederate soldier. Among the sick in Richmond was a brave young fellow, who was a great favorite and the only son of a widowed mother, who was far away beyond the Mississippi. One morning the report got out that he was dying in the hospital, and one of the prettiest and sweetest young ladies in the city was so touched by the sad story that she determined to go and kiss him for his mother. She hastened to the ward where the poor youth was lying high up on one of the upper tiers of bunks and quickly told her mission to the nurses. "I don't know him, but oh, its so sad, and I have come to 'kiss him for his mother' away out in Texas." Now he wasn't dying at all, but was much better, and as he peeped at the sweet face, the rascal, raising his head over the edge of the bunk, said, "Never mind the old lady, miss, just go it on your own hook." Now that's just the thanks these ununiformed sisters of mercy sometimes got for their pains.

Put on this monument a pair of crutches. You never see the bright star of womanhood until it shines in the darkness of man's misfortune. It is the furnace of man's suffering that brings out the pure gold of her love. Here's a specimen. On a cold winter day, when Lee's army was marching through one of the lower sections of Virginia, some of the veterans were completely barefooted, and the Sixth Georgia Regiment was passing. A plain country woman was standing in the group by the road side. "Lord, a mercy," said she, "there's a poor soldier ain't go no shoes," and off came hers in a jiffy and she ordered her negro woman standing by to give hers up, too. The good woman wore number threes, and the soldier who got them was Jake Quarles, of Company B, Dade County, Georgia, who wore number twelves.

Soon after the war I once expressed my sympathy to a young lady friend who was about to marry a young one-armed soldier. "I want no sympathy. I think it a great privilege and honor to be the wife of a man who lost his arm fighting for my country," was her prompt reply. That's your Southern girl.

When John Redding, of Randolph County, Ga., was brought home wounded from Chickamauga, it was found necessary to amputate his leg. On the day fixed for the dangerous operation, his many friends were gathered at his father's country home. Among them was Miss Carrie McNeil, to whom he was engaged. After he had passed safely through the ordeal she, of course, was allowed to be the first to go in to see him. They were left alone for a while. The next to go in was an aunt of Miss Carrie's, and as she shook hands with poor John and was about to pass on, he said, "Ain't you going to kiss me, too?" Ah, what a tale that question told. The gallant soldier had offered to release his betrothed from her engagement, but she said, "No, no, John, I can't give you up, and I love you better than ever," and a kiss had sealed their holy love.

When Tom Phipps, of Randolph County, Ga., came home on crutches he offered to release Miss Maggie Pharham from her engagement. "No, Tom," she said. "We can make a living." There are hundreds of these noble, God-given Carrie McNeils and Maggie Pharhams all over our war-wrecked South.

Let the next emblem be the oak riven by the lightning, and the tender ivy entwining itself around it. Let it tell of the sufferings of the refugee father and the wreck of the old man in the track of such vandals as Sherman, Hunter, Sheridan, Milroy and Kilpatrick. Let it tell of the horrors of the years of so-called peace that followed the war. Northern soldiers killed our young men in war; politicians killed our old men in peace. Sherman burned houses from Atlanta to Bentonville. Thad Stevens in Congress blighted every acre of ground from Baltimore to San Antonio. The war of shot and shell lasted four years; the war of blind, revengeful reconstruction legislation lasted twenty years. War marshalled our enemies on the battlefield; reconstruction made enemies of the men who had held our plow handles and stood around our tables. War put the South under the rule of soldiers; reconstruction put us under the heel of the rapacious carpet-bagger and negro plunderers. War crushed some of our people. Vindictive legislation crushed all our people. War made the South an Aceldama; reconstruction made it a Gehenna. Grant held back the red right hands of Stanton and Holt from the throats of Lee and his paroled soldiers: alas, Lincoln was dead, and his patriotic arm was not there to hold back Thad Stevens and his revolutionary congress from our prostrate citizens.

Amid these horrors our young men could hope, but to our old men was nothing left but despair. Robbed of their property after peace was declared, without a dollar of compensation, their lands made valueless or confiscated; they themselves disfranchised and their slaves made their political masters, too old to change and recuperate, too old to hope even, but too manly to whine, they stood as desolate and uncomplaining as that old oak.

Do you see that tender vine binding up the shattered tree and hiding its wounds? That is Southern woman clinging closer and more tenderly to father and husband when the storms beat upon him, comforting as only such Christian women can comfort; smiling only as such heroines can smile; with "toil-beat nerves, and care-worn eye," helping only as such women can help. In the schoolroom and behind the counter, over the sewing machine and the cooking stove, in garden and field, everywhere showing the gems of Southern character washed up from its depths by the ocean of Southern woe.

Let the last symbol on the monument be the clasped right hands of the Union. These Southern women of 1861 were the daughters of the great American Union. Their fathers under the leadership of Jefferson, Madison and Washington, had proposed the Union, devised the Union, loved the Union, and, under Clay and Calhoun and Benton, had preserved the Union. As an inducement for union between the original States, without which the Northern States would not come into it, Virginia, the great mother of the Union, gave up all her splendid territory north of the Ohio, embracing what is now Ohio, Illinois, Indiana, Wisconsin, and Michigan, and agreed that they should be made States without slavery. She afterwards gave Kentucky. North Carolina gave Tennessee, and Georgia gave Alabama and Mississippi. Southern influence and Southern statesmanship made the Union strong at home and respected abroad by the war of 1812, which was gallantly fought by the South and bitterly opposed by New England—opposed to the very verge of secession from the Union in the Hartford convention. The Southern States had shown their devotion to the Union by yielding to the compromises on the tariff, the bounty, and the territorial questions. The South demanded no tariff tribute, no bounties and no internal improvements as the price of her devotion to the Union. She loved the Union for the Union's sake. All that she demanded was that in the territory, while it was territory, belonging to the government, her sons, with their families, white and black, should have an equal share.

John C. Calhoun was not a disunionist. The nullification ordinance of South Carolina, "the Hotspur of the Union," was not secession. It was the protest of a sovereign State against unconstitutional Federal taxation levied through the tariff on the consumer, not for government revenue, but for the benefit of the manufacturer. The nation heard the manly voice of the little State, and Calhoun and Clay stood side by side in the great compromise that followed. Calhoun and his people loved the Union, but they wanted a union that was a union. True religion is that which is laid down in the Bible, not theory nor sentiment. True political union is the union formed by the Sovereign States and expressed in the Constitution. Constitutional union was the only true union. Everything else was a mere sentiment or a sham. History will yet hold that the secession of the Southern States in 1861 was itself a union movement. The Northern States had destroyed the old union. By their numerous nullification acts in State assemblies they had repudiated the legislative branch of the government; by their defiance of the Supreme Court they had virtually abolished the judiciary, the second branch; and in 1860, by the sectional platform of the dominant party and the election of a sectional president, they had denationalized the executive branch of the government. Where was the union? Gone, utterly gone. South Carolina only cut herself off from the union-breakers and attached herself to such States as clung to the Constitution and Union of the fathers. Secession in 1861 meant the preservation of the union of 1787. Coercion in 1861 was rebellion against the Federal compact and death of the old Union. The Star-Spangled Banner became the labarum of invasion, and the Southern Cross the standard of all the Union that was left.

The Union that our fathers and mothers loved lay buried for twenty-five years. From March, 1861, to March, 1885, any true Southern man in the national capital found himself a stranger in a strange land, and was looked upon as a political Pariah by those in power,—an intruder even in the house of his fathers. Every government office all over the land in the hands of the Northern States. What a travesty of union! The North a dictator, the South a satrapy. The Northern man, lord; the Southern man, a vassal.

But, thank God, the resurrection came; the door-stone of the tomb was rolled away by the national election of Cleveland in 1884. "The Southern States are in the Union, and they shall have their equal rights," was the slogan of the triumphant party. Then go to the capital and you find the first national administration since Buchanan—Bayard, the champion of the South, in the first place in the Cabinet, and by his side the Confederate leaders, Lamar and

Garland. About the first act of the administration was to appoint General Lawton, the quartermaster-general of the Confederate army, to one of the most conspicuous embassies in Europe, Curry to Spain and other Confederates wherever there was a place for them. The sons of our Southern mothers were no longer under the ban. Peace, real peace, had come. The Union, real union, was herself again.

Again in 1892 the electoral votes of the Northern States alone were sufficient to make Grover Cleveland, the great pacificator, twice the choice of the solid South, again President of the United States. Once more there is a national Cabinet, the South having half of it, with a Confederate colonel in command of the navy, another minister to France, another to Mexico, another to Guatemala—Southern men at Madrid and Constantinople; and when this country needs a man to represent her in the crisis in Cuba to a Virginia Lee is given the conspicuous honor.

The last unjust election law is repealed; the last taint taken from the fair name of Confederate officers. The North has extended the right hand of union. The South has grasped it; and withered be the arm that would tear those hands asunder.

Image of the Southern Woman Surmounting the Monument

High above these hands, artist, place the crowning statue of the Southern woman. Let it be the queenly form of the proudest of the proud mothers of Southern chivalry. Let her sweet, calm image face the north,—no frown on her brow,—no scorn on her lip. Let her happy, hopeful smile tell the world that Southern womanhood felt most sadly the Union broken, and hails most joyfully the Union restored.

My countrymen, we have a country! In the name of God, our mothers, asthey look down from heaven, beseech you to preserve it.

The art of sculpture was finished in ancient Greece, and the statue of Venus de Medici will never be surpassed. In it the artist has put in marble the perfect form, face, majesty and grace of woman. The ancients in their sensual materialism adored beauty in form and feature and many moderns worship at the same shrine. The German poet Heine, when an invalid in Paris, had himself carried every day in a roller chair to the Tuilleries, to gaze upon the marble beauty of Venus de Milo. If in our age, the artist ever attempts to sculpture the true woman, the woman with soul, the Christian Psyche, with heart as perfect as her face, with character more charming than her form, the modern Praxitiles will take for his model the Southern woman, from among your mothers and grandmothers. They are your models in character now. To you much is given; of you will much be required. Study your mothers and may Heaven help you to learn the God-given lesson.

Young men, the model man, Jesus Christ, the divine Saviour of our world, asked for no carved stone, no statue to his memory. He wanted no marble cathedral. He demanded living monuments,—men and women to set forth in holy lives the lessons of his example. From childhood He honored his mother, nor did He forget her on the cross.

With something of his exalted spirit your mothers, who have gone before you, demand of you not a chiseled monument, but they do beseech you to honor them in manly life. Hold sacred the very blood they gave you. Lay hold of their lofty principles; drink in their noble spirit. Set forth their glorious patriotism, and you will be a crown to them, a blessing to your country, and an honor to your God.

CHAPTER II
THEIR WORK

INTRODUCTION TO WOMAN'S WORK

[By J. L. Underwood.]

Throughout the South the women went to work from the first drum-beat. A great deal of it was done privately, the left hand itself hardly knowing what the modest, humble right hand was doing. In nearly every neighborhood soldiers' aid societies, or relief associations, were organized and did systematic and efficient work throughout the four years. Supplies of every kind were constantly gathered and forwarded where most needed. The old men and women did an immense amount of work.

In all the railroad towns, hospitals and wayside houses were established for the benefit of the travelling soldier. These were maintained and managed almost exclusively by the women. They prepared as best they could such articles as pickles and preserves and other delicacies for the use of the hospitals. They sent testaments and other good books and good preachers to the army, and being nearly all women of practical piety, they helped greatly to infuse that spirit of patriotism which gave such strength to the Confederate army. The world has never known an army in which there were so many earnest, practical Christians like Jackson, Cobb, Lee, Polk, Price, and Gordon among the commanding officers, where there were so many ministers of the gospel of good standing who were fighting soldiers, and so many men in ranks who were God-fearing men. The world has never known an army where so many officers and soldiers came from homes where there were pious wives, mothers, and sisters. The inspiration of the knightly hearts of the Confederacy was home and the inspiration of a pious home was godly woman. The world will never know how effective were the prayers and letters of the women at home in those great religious revivals with which the Confederate army was so often and so richly blessed. Thousands of men who entered the army wicked men went home or to their graves genuine Christians. The war ended; but the good woman's work never ends. Our Confederate women began immediately to look after the soldiers' orphans and the soldiers' graves. In all directions the Confederate monuments have been erected mainly by their efforts. Soldiers' homes have been established and in some few of the States homes provided for the Confederate widows. It is safe to say that women collected two-thirds of the money raised for all these objects. It is their dead they are honoring. And they will continue to break the alabaster box. Let them alone.

THE SOUTHERN WOMAN'S SONG

[Confederate Scrap Book.]

Stitch, stitch, stitch.
Little needle, swiftly fly,
Brightly glitter as you go;
Every time that you pass by
Warms my heart with pity's glow.
Dreams of comfort that will cheer,
Dreams of courage you will bring,
Through winter's cold, the volunteer.
Smile on me like flowers in spring.
Stitch, stitch, stitch.
Swiftly, little needle, fly,
Through this flannel, soft and warm;
Though with cold the soldiers sigh,
This will sure keep out the storm.
Set the buttons close and tight,
Out to shut the winter's damp;
There'll be none to fix them right
In the soldier's tented camp.
Stitch, stitch, stitch.
Ah! needle, do not linger;
Close the thread, make fine the knot;
There'll be no dainty finger
To arrange a seam forgot.
Though small and tiny you may be,
Do all that you are able.

A mouse a lion once set free,
  As says the pretty fable.
      Stitch, stitch, stitch.
Swiftly, little needle, glide.
  Thine's a pleasant labor;
To clothe the soldier be thy pride,
  While he wields the sabre.
Ours are tireless hearts and hands;
  To Southern wives and mothers,
All who join our warlike bands
  Are our friends and brothers.
      Stitch, stitch, stitch.
Little needle, swiftly fly;
  From morning until eve,
As the moments pass thee by,
  These substantial comforts weave.
Busy thoughts are at our hearts—
  Thoughts of hopeful cheer,
As we toil, till day departs,
  For the noble volunteer.
      Quick, quick, quick.
Swiftly, little needle, go;
  For our homes' most pleasant fires
Let a loving greeting flow
  To our brothers and our sires;
We have tears for those who fall,
  Smiles for those who laugh at fears;
Hope and sympathy for all—
  Every noble volunteer.

THE LADIES OF RICHMOND

The editor of the Lynchburg *Republican*, writing to his paper in June, 1862, says:

The ladies of Richmond, as of Lynchburg, and indeed of the whole country, are making for themselves a fame which will live in all future history, and brilliantly illuminate the brightest pages of the Republic's history.

Discarding all false ceremony and giving full vent to those feelings and sentiments of devotion which make her the noblest part of God's creation and the fondest object of man's existence, the ladies of this city from all ranks have gone into the hospitals and are hourly engaged in ministering to the wants and relieving the sufferings of their countrymen.

Mothers and sisters could not be more unremitting in their attention to their own blood than these women are to those whom they have never seen before, and may never see again. They feed them, nurse them, and by their presence and sympathy cheer and encourage them. "Man's inhumanity to man makes countless millions mourn," but woman's sympathy would heal every wound and make glad every heart.

THE HOSPITAL AFTER SEVEN PINES

[Richmond During the War, pages 135-136.]

On this evening, as a kind woman bent over the stalwart figure of a noble Georgian, and washed from his hair and beard the stiffened mud of the Chickahominy, where he fell from a wound through the upper portion of the right lung, and then gently bathed the bleeding gash left by the Minie ball, as he groaned and feebly opened his eyes, he grasped her hand, and in broken whispers, faint from suffering, gasping for breath, "I could-bear-all-this-for-myself-alone-but my-wife and my-six little-ones," (and then the large tears rolled down his weather-beaten cheeks,) and overcome he could only add, "Oh, God! oh, God!-how will-they endure it?" She bent her head and wept in sympathy. The tall man's frame was shaking with agony. She placed to his fevered lips a cooling draught, and whispered: "Think of yourself just now; God may raise you up to them, and if not, He will provide for and comfort them." He feebly grasped her hand once more, and a look of gratitude stole over his manly face, and he whispered, "God bless you! God bless you! God bless you! kind stranger!"

BURIAL OF LATANE

["The next squadron moved to the front under the lamented Captain Latane, making a most brilliant and successful charge with drawn sabres upon the enemy's picked ground, and after a hotly-contested, hand-to-hand conflict put him to flight, but not until the gallant captain had sealed his devotion to his native soil with his blood."—Official Report of the Pamunkey Expedition, Gen. J. E. B. Stuart, C. S. A., 1862.]

[From a private letter.]

Lieutenant Latane carried his brother's dead body to Mrs. Brockenbrough's plantation an hour or two after his death. On this sad and lonely errand he met a party of Yankees, who followed him to Mrs. B.'s gate, and stopping there, told him that as soon as he had placed his brother's body in friendly hands he must surrender himself prisoner. * * * Mrs. B. sent for an Episcopal clergyman to perform the funeral ceremonies, but the enemy would not permit him to pass. Then, with a few other ladies, a fair-haired little girl, her apron filled with white flowers, and a few faithful slaves, who stood reverently near, a pious Virginia matron read the solemn and beautiful burial service over the cold, still form of one of the noblest gentlemen and most intrepid officers in the Confederate army. She watched the sods heaped upon the coffin-lid, then sinking on her knees, in sight and hearing of the foe, she committed his soul's welfare and the stricken hearts he had left behind him to the mercy of the "All-Father."

"And when Virginia, leaning on her spear,

Victrix et vidua, the conflict done,

Shall raise her mailed hand to wipe the tear

That starts as she recalls each martyred son,

No prouder memory her breast shall sway,

Than thine, our early lost, lamented Latane!"

MAKING CLOTHES FOR THE SOLDIERS

[In Our Women in the War, pages 453-454.]

Money was almost as unavailable as material with us for a time. "Uncle Sam's" treasury was not accessible to "rebels." Our government was young, and Confederate bonds and money yet in their infancy. We could do nothing more than wait developments, and try to meet emergencies as they trooped up before us. In the meantime, children grew apace. Our village stores were emptied and deserted. Our armies in the field became grand realities. All resources were cut off. Our government could poorly provide food and clothing and ammunition for its armies. Then it was our mothers' wit was tested and did in no sort disappoint our expectations. Spinning-wheels, looms and dye-pots were soon brought into requisition. Wool of home production was especially converted, by loving hands, into warm flannels and heavy garments, with soft scarfs and snugly-fitted leggings, to shield our dear boys from Virginia's wintry blasts and fast-falling snows. Later on, when the wants and privations of the army grew more pressing, societies were formed to provide supplies for the general demand. Southern homes withheld nothing that could add to the soldiers' comfort. Every available fragment of material was converted into some kind of garment. After the stores of blankets in each home had been given, carpets were utilized in their stead and portioned out to the suffering soldiers. Wool mattresses were ripped open, recarded, and woven into coverings and clothing. Bits of new woolen fabrics, left from former garments, were ravelled, carded, mixed with cotton and spun and knitted into socks. Old and worn garments were carried through the same process. Even rabbits' fur was mixed with cotton and silk, and appeared again in the form of neat and comfortable gloves. Begging committees went forth (and be it truthfully said, the writer never knew of a single one being turned away empty) to gather up the offerings from mansion and hamlet, which were soon cut up, packed, and forwarded with all possible speed to the soldiers.

And who can tell what pleasure we took in filling boxes with substantials and such dainties as we could secure for the hospitals. Old men and little boys were occupied in winding thread and holding brooches, and even knitting on the socks when the mystery of "turning the heel" had been passed. The little spinning-wheel, turned by a treadle, became a fascination to the girls, and with its busy hum was mingled oft times the merry strain of patriotic songs.

"Our wagon's plenty big enough, the running
gear is good,

'Tis stiffened with cotton round the sides and
made of Southern wood;

Carolina is the driver, with Georgia by her side;

Virginia'll hold the flag up and we'll take a ride."

THE INGENUITY OF SOUTHERN WOMEN

[Our Women in the War, pages 454-455.]

During all that time, when every woman vied with the other in working for the soldiers, there were needs at home too urgent to be disregarded. These, too, had to be met, and how was not long the question. For those very women who had been reared in ease and affluence soon learned practically that "necessity is the mother of invention," and the story of their ingenuity, if all told, might surprise their Northern sisters, who always regarded them as inefficient, pleasure-loving members of society. Whatever may have been the fault of their institutions and rearing, the war certainly brought out the true woman, and no woman of any age or nation ever entered, heart and soul, more enthusiastically into their country's contest than those who now mourn the "Lost Cause." While our armies were victorious in the field hope lured us on. We bore our share of privations cheerfully and gladly.

We replaced our worn dresses with homespuns, planning and devising checks and plaids, and intermingling colors with the skill of professional "designers." The samples we interchanged were homespuns of our last weaving, not A. T. Stuart's or John Wanamaker's sample envelopes, with their elaborate display of rich and costly fabrics. Our mothers' silk stockings, of ante-bellum date, were ravelled with patience and transformed into the prettiest of neat-fitting gloves. The writer remembers never to have been more pleased than she was by the possession of a trim pair of boots made of the tanned skins of some half-dozen squirrels. They were so much softer and finer than the ordinary heavy calf-skin affairs to be bought at the village "shoe shop," that no Northern maiden was ever more pleased with her ten-dollar boots. Our hats, made of palmetto and rye straw, were becoming and pretty without lace, tips, or flowers. Our jackets were made of the fathers' old-fashioned cloaks, in vogue some forty years agone—those of that style represented in the pictures of Mr. Calhoun—doing splendid service by supplying all the girls in the family at once. We even made palmetto jewelry of exquisite designs, intermingled with our hair, that we might keep even with the boys who wore "palmetto cockades." The flowers we wore were nature's own beautiful, fragrant blossoms, sometimes, when in a patriotic mood, nestled, with symbolic cotton balls. For our calico dresses, if ever so fortunate as to find one, we sometimes paid a hundred dollars, and for the spool of cotton that made it from ten to twenty dollars. The buttons we used were oftentimes cut from a gourd into sizes required and covered with cloth, they having the advantage of pasteboard because they were rounded. On children's clothes persimmon seed in their natural state, with two holes drilled through them, were found both neat and durable. In short, we fastened all our garments after true Confederate style, without the aid of Madame Demorest's guide book or Worth's Parisian models, and suffered from none of Miss Flora McFlimsey's harassing dilemmas.

MRS. LEE AND THE SOCKS

R. E. Lee, in his recollections of his father, General Lee, says:

"His letters to my mother tell how much his men were in need. My mother was an invalid from rheumatism, and confined to a roller chair. To help the cause with her own hands, as far as she could, she was constantly occupied in knitting socks for the soldiers, and induced all around her to do the same. She sent them directly to my father and he always acknowledged them."

It was well known in the army what great pleasure it gave the General to distribute these socks.

FITTING OUT A SOLDIER

[Mrs. Roger A. Pryor's Reminiscences of Peace and War, pages 131-133.]

When I returned to my father's home in Petersburg I found my friends possessed with an intense spirit of patriotism. The First, Second and Third Virginia were already mustered into service; my husband was colonel of the Third Virginia Infantry. The men were to be equipped for service immediately. All of "the boys" were going—the three Manys, Will Johnson, Berry Stainback, Ned Graham; all the young, dancing set, the young lawyers and doctors—everybody, in short, except bank presidents, druggists, a doctor or two (over age), and young boys under sixteen. To be idle was torture. We women resolved ourselves into a sewing society, resting not on Sundays. Sewing-machines were put into the churches, which became depots for flannel, muslin, strong linen, and even uniform cloth. When the hour for meeting arrived, the sewing class would be summoned by the ringing of the church bell. My dear Agnes was visiting in Petersburg, and was my faithful ally in all my work. We instituted a monster sewing class, which we hugely enjoyed, to meet daily at my home on Market street. My colonel was to be fitted out as never was colonel before. He was ordered to Norfolk with his regiment to protect the seaboard. I was proud of his colonelship, and much exercised because he had no shoulder-straps. I undertook to embroider them myself. We had not then decided upon the star for our colonels' insignia, and I supposed he would wear the eagle like all the colonels I had ever known. We embroidered bullion fringe, cut it in lengths, and made eagles, probably of some extinct species, for the like were unknown in Audubon's time, and have not since been discovered. However, they were accepted, admired, and, what is worse, worn.

The Confederate soldier was furnished at the beginning of the war with a gun, pistol, canteen, tin cup, haversack, and knapsack—no inconsiderable weight to be borne in a march. The knapsack contained a fatigue jacket, one or two blankets, an oil-cloth, several suits of underclothing, several pairs of white gloves, collars, neckties, and handkerchiefs. Each mess purchased a mess-chest containing dishes, bowls, plates, knives, forks, spoons, cruets, spice-boxes, glasses, etc. Each mess also owned a frying-pan, oven, coffee-pot, and camp-kettle. The uniforms were of the finest cadet cloth and gold lace. This outfit—although not comparable to that of the Federal soldier, many of whom had "Saratoga" trunks in the baggage train—was considered sumptuous by the Confederate volunteer. As if these were not enough, we taxed our ingenuity to add sundry comforts, weighing little, by which we might give a touch of refinement to the soldier's knapsack.

There was absolutely nothing which a man might possibly use that we did not make for them. We embroidered cases for razors, for soap and sponge, and cute morocco affairs for needles, thread, and courtplaster, with a little pocket lined with a bank note. "How perfectly ridiculous," do you say? Nothing is ridiculous that helps anxious women to bear their lot—cheats them with the hope that they are doing good.

THE THIMBLE BRIGADE

[From Dickison and His Men, pages 161-162.]

With prayerful hearts, the devoted women of Marion formed themselves into societies for united efforts in behalf of our gallant defenders.

At Orange Lake, we formed a Soldiers' Relief Association, playfully called the "Thimble Brigade;" and, with earnest faith in the blessing of God upon our work, we began our mission of love. With grateful hearts we labored to provide comforts for the brave soldiers, who around their campfires were keeping watch for us. The following notice will be read by our sisterhood with mingled emotions of pleasure and sadness:

"In this number of the Ocala *Home Journal* will be found the proceedings of a meeting of the ladies of the neighborhood of Orange Lake, held for the purpose of organizing a 'Soldiers' Friend' Association. They have not only succeeded in perfecting their organization, but have already accomplished a great deal for the benefit of the soldiers. They have made thirty pairs of pants for the soldiers at Fernandina, the ladies furnishing the material from their own private stores, besides knitting socks and making other garments. The manner in which they have commenced this patriotic work is, indeed, encouraging to all who have the soldier's welfare at heart, and we know that they will labor as long as the necessities of the soldier require it."

NOBLE WOMEN OF RICHMOND

[In A Rebel's Recollections, pages 66-69.]

In Richmond, when the hospitals were filled with wounded men brought in from the seven days' fighting with McClellan, and the surgeons found it impossible to dress half the wounds, a band was formed, consisting of nearly all the married women of the city, who took upon themselves the duty of going to the hospitals and dressing wounds from morning till night; and they persisted in their painful duty until every man was cared for, saving hundreds of lives, as the surgeons unanimously testified. When nitre was found to be growing scarce, and the supply of gunpowder was consequently about to give out, women all over the land dug up the earth in their smokehouses and tobacco barns, and with their own hands faithfully extracted the desired salt, for use in the government laboratories.

Many of them denied themselves not only delicacies, but substantial food also, when, by enduring semi-starvation, they could add to the stock of food at the command of the subsistence officers. I myself knew more than one houseful of women, who, from the moment that food began to grow scarce, refused to eat meat or drink coffee, living thenceforth only upon vegetables of a speedily perishable sort, in order that they might leave the more for the soldiers in the field. When a friend remonstrated with one of them, on the ground that her health, already frail, was breaking down utterly for want of proper diet, she replied, in a quiet, determined way, "I know that very well; but it is little that I can do, and I must do that little at any cost. My health and life are worth less than those of my brothers, and if they give theirs to the cause, why should not I do the same? I would starve to death cheerfully if I could feed one soldier more by doing so, but the things I eat can't be sent to camp. I think it a sin to eat anything that can be used for rations." And she meant what she said, too, as a little mound in the church-yard testifies.

Every Confederate remembers gratefully the reception given him when he went into any house where these women were. Whoever he might be, and whatever his plight, if he wore the gray, he was received, not as a beggar or tramp, not even as a stranger, but as a son of the house, for whom it held nothing too good, and whose comfort was the one care of all its inmates, even though their own must be sacrificed in securing it. When the hospitals were crowded, the people earnestly besought permission to take the men to their houses and to care for them there, and for many months almost every house within a radius of a hundred miles of Richmond held one or more wounded men as especially honored guests.

"God bless these Virginia women!" said a general officer from one of the cotton States, one day; "they're worth a regiment apiece." And he spoke the thought of the army, except that their blessing covered the whole country as well as Virginia.

FROM MATOACA GAY'S ARTICLES IN THE *PHILADELPHIA TIMES*

In a diary kept at the time by an official in the War Department I find this entry:

May 10, 1861.—The ladies are sewing everywhere, and are full of ardor. Love affairs are plentiful, but the ladies are postponing all engagements till their lovers have fought the Yankees. Their influence is very great. Day after day they go in crowds to the fair grounds, where the First South Carolina Volunteers are encamped, showering upon them smiles and every delicacy which the city can afford. They wine them and dine them, and they deserve it, for they are just from the taking of Sumter, and have won historic distinction. I was presented to several very distinguished looking young men, all of them privates, and was told by their captain that many of them were worth from a hundred thousand to half a million. These are the men the *Tribune* thought would all of them want to be captains; but that is only one of the hallucinations under which the North is now laboring.

THE WOMEN OF RICHMOND

[By Phoebe Y. Pember, in Hospital Life.]

But of what importance was the fact that I was homeless, houseless and moneyless, in Richmond, the heart of Virginia? Who ever wanted for aught that kind hearts, generous hands or noble hospitality could supply, that it was not here offered without even the shadow of a patronage that could have made it distasteful? What women were ever so refined in feeling and so unaffected in manner; so willing to share all that wealth gives, and so little infected with the pride of purse which bestows that power? It was difficult to hide one's needs from them; they found them out and ministered to them with their quiet simplicity and the innate nobility which gave to their generosity the coloring of a favor received, not conferred.

Would that I could do more than thank the dear friends who made my life for four years so happy and contented; who never made me feel by word or act that my self-imposed occupation was otherwise than one which would ennoble any woman. If ever any aid was given through my own exertions, or any labor rendered effective by me for the good of the South—if any sick soldier ever benefited by my happy face or pleasant smiles at his bedside, or death was ever soothed by gentle words of hope and tender care—such results were only owing to the cheering encouragement I received from them.

TWO GEORGIA HEROINES

[Mary L. Jewett, Corresponding Secretary Clement Evans Chapter, U. D. C.]

"To such women as these should a shaft of precious stone be erected."

'Twas thus an old soldier spoke of the wife of Judge Alexander Herrington, of Dougherty County, Georgia, many years ago, when the heroism of the Southern women was mentioned. She was president of the ladies' relief association during the war, and as such had thirty machines brought to her home and the neighbors gathered together and made leggings and clothing for "our boys," as they were called. Many and many days did she work with bleeding hands, caused by the constant use of the shears, for with her own hands she did the cutting for the others to stitch. This was a work that is far beyond the understanding of the present day, for she had never known a day's toil, being the wife of a wealthy planter and slave owner. Not only did she and Judge Herrington give money, cattle, cotton, and slaves to be used in the erecting of breastworks, but he being too old, and their only son being a mere child, they bravely sent two of their daughters to the field as army nurses, one of which served through the entire war. After the war, with slaves and money gone, her husband died, and it was then that she and her children suffered through the days of reconstruction, with never a murmur from her lips for the things she had given up and lost.

THE SEVEN DAYS' BATTLE

[Mrs. R. A. Pryor's Reminiscences.]

All the afternoon the dreadful guns shook the earth and thrilled our souls with horror. I shut myself in my darkened room. At twilight I had a note from Governor Letcher, telling me a fierce battle was raging, and inviting me to come to the governor's mansion. From the roof one might see the flash of musket and artillery.

No; I did not wish to see the infernal fires. I preferred to watch and wait alone in my room. And so the night wore on and I waited and watched. Before the dawn a hurried footstep brought a message from the battlefield to my door:

"The general, madame, is safe and well. Colonel Scott has been killed. The general has placed a guard around his body, and he will be sent here early to-morrow. The general bids me say he will not return. The fight will be renewed, and will continue until the enemy is driven away."

My resolution was taken. My children were safe with their grandmother. I would write. I would ask that every particle of my household linen, except a change, should be rolled into bandages, all my fine linen be sent to me for compresses, and all forwarded as soon as possible. I would enter the new hospital which had been improvised in Kent & Paine's warehouse, and would remain there as a nurse as long as the armies were fighting around Richmond.

But the courier was passing on his rounds with news to others. Presently Fanny Poindexter, in tears, knocked at my door.

"She is bearing it like a brave, Christian woman."

"She? Who? Tell me quick."

"Mrs. Scott. I had to tell her. She simply said, 'I shall see him once more.' The general wrote to her from the battlefield and told her how nobly her husband died, leading his men in the thick of the fight, and how he had helped to save the city."

Alas! that the city should have needed saving. What had Mrs. Scott and her children done? Why should they suffer? Who was to blame for it all?

Kent & Paine's warehouse was a large, airy building, which had, I understood, been offered by the proprietors for a hospital immediately after the battle of Seven Pines. McClellan's advance upon Richmond had heavily taxed the capacity of the hospitals already established.

When I reached the warehouse, early on the morning after the fight at Mechanicsville, I found cots on the lower floor already occupied, and other cots in process of preparation. An aisle between the rows of narrow beds stretched to the rear of the building. Broad stairs led to a story above, where other cots were being laid.

The volunteer matron was a beautiful woman, Mrs. Wilson. When I was presented to her as a candidate for admission, her serene eyes rested doubtfully upon me for a moment. She hesitated. Finally she said:

"The work is very exacting. There are so few of us that our nurses must do anything and everything—make beds, wait upon anybody, and often a half a dozen at a time."

"I will engage to do all that," I declared, and she permitted me to go to a desk at the farther end of the room and enter my name.

As I passed by the rows of occupied cots, I saw a nurse kneeling beside one of them, holding a pan for a surgeon. The red stump of an amputated arm was held over it. The next thing I knew I was myself lying on a cot, and a spray of cold water was falling over my face. I had fainted. Opening my eyes, I found the matron standing beside me.

"You see it is as I thought. You are unfit for this work. One of the nurses will conduct you home."

The nurse's assistance was declined, however. I had given trouble enough for one day, and had only interrupted those who were really worth something. A night's vigil had been poor preparation for hospital work. I resolved I would conquer my culpable weakness. It was all very well,—these heroics in which I indulged, these paroxysms of patriotism, this adoration of the defenders of my fireside. The defender in the field had naught to hope from me in case he should be wounded in my defence.

I took myself well in hand. Why had I fainted? I thought it was because ofthe sickening, dead odor in the hospital, mingled with that of acids and disinfectants. Of course, this would always be there—and worse, as wounded men filled the rooms. I provided myself with sal volatile and spirits of camphor,—we wore pockets in our gowns in those days,—and thus armed I presented myself again to Mrs. Wilson. She was as kind as she was refined and intelligent. "I will give you a place near the door," she said, "and you must run out into the air at the first hint of faintness. You will get over it, see if you don't."

Ambulances began to come in and unload at the door. I soon had occupation enough, and a few drops of camphor on my handkerchief tided me over the worst. The wounded men crowded in and sat patiently waiting their turn. One fine little fellow of fifteen unrolled a handkerchief from his wrist to show me his wound. "There's a bullet in there," he said proudly. "I am going to have it cut out, and then go right back to the fight. Isn't it lucky it's my left hand?"

As the day wore on I became more and more absorbed in my work. I had, too, the stimulus of a reproof from Miss Deborah Couch, a brisk, efficient, middle-aged lady, who asked no quarter and gave none. She was standing beside me a moment, with a bright tin pan filled with pure water, into which I foolishly dipped a finger to see if it were warm, to learn if I would be expected to provide warm water when I should be called upon to assist the surgeon.

"This water, madame, was prepared for a raw wound," said Miss Deborah, sternly. "I must now make the surgeon wait until I get more."

Miss Deborah, in advance of her time, was a germ theorist. My touch evidently was contaminating.

As she charged down the aisle, with a pan of water in her hand, everybody made way. She had known of my "fine-lady faintness," as she termed it, and I could see she despised me for it. She had volunteered, as all the nurses had, and she meant business. She had no patience with nonsense, and truly she was worth more than all the rest of us.

“Where can I get a little ice?” I one day ventured of Miss Deborah.

“Find it,” she rejoined, as she rapidly passed on; but find it I never did. Ice was an unknown luxury until brought to us later from private houses.

But I found myself thoroughly reinstated—with surgeons, matrons and Miss Deborah—when I appeared a few days later, accompanied by a man bearing a basket of clean, well-rolled bandages, with promise of more to come. The Petersburg women had gone to work with a will upon my table-cloths, sheets, and dimity counterpanes—and even the chintz furniture covers. My springlike green and white chintz bandages appeared on many a manly arm and leg. My fine linen underwear and napkins were cut, by the sewing circle at the Spotswood, according to the surgeons' directions, into two lengths two inches wide, then folded two inches, doubling back and forth in a smaller fold each time, until they formed pointed wedges or compresses.

Such was the sudden and overwhelming demand for such things that but for my own and similar donations of household linen the wounded men would have suffered. The war had come upon us suddenly. Many of our ports were already closed and we had no stores laid up for such an emergency.

The bloody battle of Gaines' Mill soon followed. Then Frazier's farm, within the week, and at once the hospital was filled to overflowing. Every night a courier brought me tidings of my husband. When I saw him at the door my heart would die within me. One morning John came in for certain supplies. After being reassured as to his master's safety, I asked, "Did he have a comfortable night, John?"

"He sholy did. Marse Roger sart'nly was comfortable las' night. He slep' on de field 'twixt two daid horses."

The women who worked in Kent & Paine's hospital never seemed to weary. After a while the wise matron assigned us hours, and we went on duty with the regularity of trained nurses. My hours were from 7 to 7 during the day, with the promise of night service should I be needed. Efficient, kindly colored women assisted us. Their motherly manner soothed the prostrate soldier, whom they always addressed as "son."

Many fine young fellows lost their lives for want of prompt attention. They never murmured. They would give way to those who seemed to be more seriously wounded than themselves, and the latter would recover, while from the slighter wounds gangrene would supervene from delay. Very few men ever walked away from that hospital. They died, or friends found quarters for them in Richmond. None complained. Unless a poor man grew delirious, he never groaned. There was an atmosphere of gentle kindness; a suppression of emotion for the sake of others.

Every morning the Richmond ladies brought for our patients such luxuries as could be procured in that scarce time. The city was in peril, and distant farmers feared to bring in their fruits and vegetables. One day a patient-looking, middle-aged man said to me, "What would I not give for a bowl of chicken broth like my mother used to give me when I was a sick boy?" I perceived one of the angelic matrons of Richmond at a distance, stooping over the cots, and found my way to her and said, "Dear Mrs. Maben, have you a chicken? And could you send some broth to No. 39?" She promised, and I returned with her promise to the poor, wounded fellow. He shook his head. "To-morrow will be too late," he said.

I had forgotten the circumstance next day, but at noon I happened to look toward cot No. 39, and there was Mrs. Maben herself. She had brought the chicken broth in a pretty china bowl, with napkin and silver spoon, and was feeding my doubting Thomas, to his great satisfaction.

It was at this hospital, I have reason to believe, that the little story originated, which was deemed good enough to be claimed by other hospitals, of the young girl who approached a sick man with a pan of water in her hand and a towel over her arm.

"Mayn't I wash your face?" said the girl, timidly.

"Well, lady, you may if you want to," said the man, wearily. "It has been washed fourteen times this morning. It can stand another time, I reckon."

I discovered that I had not succeeded, despite many efforts, in winning Miss Deborah. I learned that she was affronted because I had not shared my offerings of jelly and fruit with her, for her special patients. Whenever I ventured to ask a loan from her, of a pan or a glass of water, or the little things of which we never had enough, she would reply, "I must keep them for the nurses who understand reciprocity. Reciprocity is the rule some persons never seem to comprehend." When this was hammered into my slow perception, I rose to the occasion. I turned over the entire contents of a basket the landlord of the Spotswood had given me to Miss Deborah, and she made my path straight before me ever afterward.

At the end of a week the matron had promoted me. Instead of carving the fat bacon, to be served with corn bread, for the hospital dinner, or standing between two rough men to keep away the flies, or fetching water, or spreading sheets on cots, I was assigned to regular duty with one patient.

The first of these proved to be a young Colonel Coppens, of my husband's brigade. I could comfort him very little, for he was wounded past recovery. I spoke little French, and could only try to keep him, as far as possible, from annoyance. To my great relief, place was found for him in a private family. There he soon died—the gallant fellow I had admired on his horse a few months before.

Then I was placed beside the cot of Mr. (or Captain) Boyd, of Mecklenburg, and was admonished by the matron not to leave him alone. He was the most patient sufferer in the world—gentle, courteous, always considerate, never complaining.

"Are you in pain, Captain?"

"No, no," he would say gently.

One day when I returned from my "rest," I found the matron sitting beside him.

She motioned me to take her place, and then added, "No, no; I will not leave him."

The captain's eyes were closed, and he sighed wearily at intervals. Presently he whispered slowly: "There everlasting spring abides;" then sighed, and seemed to sleep for a moment.

The matron felt his pulse and raised a warning hand. The sick man's whisper went on: "Bright fields beyond the swelling flood, Stand dressed in living green;" and in a moment more the Christian soldier had crossed the river and lain down to rest under the trees.

Each of the battles of those seven days brought a harvest of wounded to our hospital. I used to veil myself closely as I walked to and from my hotel, that I might shut out the dreadful sights in the streets—the squads of prisoners, and worst of all, the open wagons in which the dead were piled. Once I did see one of these dreadful wagons. In it a stiff arm was raised, and shook as it was driven down the street, as though the dead owner appealed to Heaven for vengeance—a horrible sight, never to be forgotten.

After one of the bloody battles—I know not if it was Gaines' Mill or Frazier's Farm or Malvern Hill—A splendid young officer, Colonel Brokenborough, was taken to our hospital, shot almost to pieces. He was borne up the stairs and placed in a cot—his broken limbs in supports swinging from the ceiling. The wife of General Mahone and I were permitted to assist in nursing him. A young soldier from the camp was detailed to help us, and a clergyman was in constant attendance, coming at night that we might have rest. Our patient held a court in his corner of the hospital. Such a dear, gallant, cheery fellow, handsome, and with a grand air even as he lay prostrate. Nobody ever heard him complain. He would welcome us in the morning with the brightest smile. His aid said, "He watches the head of the stairs and calls up that look for your benefit."

"Oh," he said one day, "you can't guess what's going to happen. Some ladies have been here and left all these roses, and cologne, and such; and somebody has sent champagne. We are going to have a party."

Ah! but we knew he was very ill. We were bidden to watch him every minute and not be deceived by his own spirits. Mrs. Mahone spent her life hunting for ice. My constant care was to keep his canteen—to which he clung with affection—filled with fresh water from a spring not far away, and I learned to give it to him so well that I allowed no one to lift his head for his drink during my hours.

One day, when we were alone, I was fanning him, and thought he was asleep. He said gravely, "Mrs. Pryor, beyond that curtain they hung up yesterday, poor young Mitchell is lying. They don't know. But I heard when they brought him in. As I lie here I listen to his breathing. I haven't heard it now for some time. Would you mind seeing if he is all right?"

I passed behind the curtain. The young soldier was dead. His wide-open eyes seemed to meet mine in mute appeal. I had never seen or touched a dead man, but I laid my hands upon his eyelids and closed them. I was standing thus when his nurse, a young volunteer like myself, came to me.

"I couldn't do that," she said. "I went for the doctor. I'm so glad you could do it."

When I returned Colonel Brokenborough asked no questions and I knew that his keen senses had already instructed him.

To be cheerful and uncomplaining was the unwritten law of our hospital. No bad news was ever mentioned; no foreboding or anxiety. Mrs. Mahone was one day standing beside Colonel Brokenborough when a messenger from the front suddenly announced that General Mahone had received a flesh wound. Commanding herself instantly, she exclaimed merrily: "Flesh wound. Now you all know that is just impossible."

The general had no flesh. He was thin and attenuated as he was brave.

As Colonel Brokenborough grew weaker, I felt self-reproach that no one had offered to write letters for him. His friend the clergyman had said to me: "That poor boy is engaged to a lovely young girl. I wonder what is best? Would it grieve him to speak of her. You ladies have so much tact; you might bear it in mind. An opportunity might offer for you to discover how he feels about it."

The next time I was alone with him I ventured: "Now, Colonel, one mustn't forget absent friends, you know, even if fair ladies do bring perfumes and roses and what not. I have some ink and paper here. Shall I write a letter for you? Tell me what to say."

He turned his head and with a half-amused smile of perfect intelligence looked at me for a long time. Then an upward look of infinite tenderness; but the message was never sent—never needed from a true heart like this.

One night I was awakened from my sleep by a knock at my door, and a summons to "come to Colonel Brokenborough." When I reached his bedside I found the surgeon, the clergyman, and the colonel's aid. The patient was unconscious; the end was near. We sat in silence. Once, when he stirred, I slipped my hand under his head, and put his canteen once more to his lips. After a long time his breathing simply ceased, with no evidence of pain. We waited awhile, and then the young soldier who had been detailed to nurse him rose, crossed the room, and stooping over, kissed me on my forehead, and went out to his duty in the ranks.

Two weeks later I was in my room, resting after a hard day, when a haggard officer, covered with mud and dust, entered. It was my husband. "My men are all dead," he said, with anguish, and, falling across the bed, he gave vent to the passionate grief of his heart.

Thousands of Confederate soldiers were killed, thousands wounded. Richmond was saved!

DEATH OF MRS. SARAH K. ROWE, "THE SOLDIERS' FRIEND"

[From Southern Historical Papers.]

ORANGEBURG, S. C., *June 2, 1884.*

I feel warranted in informing you of the death of Mrs. Sarah K. Rowe, which occurred yesterday, the 1st of June, at her country home in this county. Mrs. Rowe was known for four and a half years, '61 to '65, as "the soldiers' friend." I detract nothing from great women all over the South, Cornelias of heroic type, when I state that Mrs. Rowe was pre-eminently the soldiers' friend. If this should meet the eye of Hood's Texans, of Polk's Tennesseeans, of Morgan's Kentuckians, or of Pickett's Virginians, any of whom passed on the South Carolina Railroad during the war, her face beaming with benevolence, her arms loaded with food, will be remembered as one of the sunny events of a dark time. From the first note of war Mrs. Rowe gave all she had and could collect by wonderful energy to the soldiers. She had her organized squads. The gay, strong soldier to Virginia was fed and cheered on; the mangled and sick were nursed and cared for. She had a mother's blessing for the brave; a mother's tears and sympathy for the dying and the dead. Mrs. Rowe emphatically lived and spent herself for the cause, and when it failed, like a noble woman she submitted, with the remark, "It is all right." The sight of a bandaged head or limb under her soft touch was an everyday picture. The echo of a thousand cheers as the troop trains passed her was recurring every day. She bandaged and waved God-speed as well. A few days ago Mrs. Rowe showed by request a part of her great legacy—the letters from the soldiers she had nursed to life again. Truly her reward was rich. She passed away, of paralysis, at a ripe old age. The soldiers and survivors buried her. The Young and "Old Guard" lowered her remains to mother earth. When Fame makes up its roll her precious name should stand out—the soldiers' friend.

Yours truly,

JOHN A. HAMILTON.

"YOU WAIT"

[Phoebe Y. Pember, in Hospital Life.]

Pleasant episodes often occurred to vary disappointments and lighten duties of hospital life.

"Kin you writ a letter?" drawled a whining voice from a bed in one of the wards, a cold day in '62.

The speaker was an up-country Georgian, one of the kind called "Goobers" by the soldiers generally—lean, yellow, attenuated, with wispy strands of hair hanging over his high, thin cheek-bones. He put out a hand to detain me and the nails were like claws.

"Why do you not let the nurse cut your nails?"

"Because I aren't got any spoon, and I use them instead."

"Will you let me have your hair cut then? You can't get well with all that dirty hair hanging about your eyes and ears."

"No, I can't git my hair cut, kase as how I promised my mammy that I would let it grow till the war be over. Oh, it's unlucky to cut it."

"Then I can't write any letter for you. Do what I wish you to do, and then I will oblige you."

This was plain talking. The hair was cut (I left the nails for another day), my portfolio brought, and sitting by the side of his bed I waited for further orders. They came with a formal introduction,—"for Mrs. Marthy Brown."

"My dear mammy:

"I hope this finds you well, as it leaves me well, and I hope that I shall git a furlough Christmas, and come and see you, and I hope you will keep well, and all the folks be well by that time, as I hopes to be well myself. This leaves me in good health, as I hope it will find you and—"

But here I paused as his mind seemed to be going round in a circle, and asked him a few questions about his home, his position during the last summer's campaign, how he got sick, and where his brigade was at that time. Thus furnished with some material to work upon, the letter proceeded rapidly. Four sides were conscientiously filled, for no soldier would think a letter worth sending home that showed any blank paper. Transcribing his name, the number of his ward and proper address, so that an answer might reach him— the composition was read to him. Gradually his pale face brightened, a sitting posture was assumed with difficulty (for, in spite of his determined effort to write a letter "to be well," he was far from convalescence). As I folded and directed it, contributed the expected five-cent stamp, and handed it to him, he gazed cautiously around to be sure there were no listeners.

"Did you writ all that?" he asked, whispering, but with great emphasis.

"Yes."

"Did I say all that?"

"I think you did."

A long pause of undoubted admiration—astonishment—ensued. What was working in that poor mind? Could it be that Psyche had stirred one of the delicate plumes of her wing and touched that dormant soul?

"Are you married?" The harsh voice dropped very low.

"I am not. At least, I am a widow."

He rose still higher in bed. He pushed away desperately the tangled hay on his brow. A faint color fluttered over the hollow cheek, and stretching out a long piece of bone with a talon attached, he gently touched my arm and with constrained voice whispered mysteriously:

"You wait!"

ANNANDALE—TWO HEROINES OF MISSISSIPPI

[By Anna B. A. Brown, in Memphis Commercial World.]

In these hurried days, when we spend the major portion of our lives trying to keep up with the electric currents that control the universe, it is good to be able to turn aside for a while in the byways of the South and feel the restfulness of old plantation life, whether it be a reality or an echo from the past. A day spent in touch with old Southern home life is a day full of restful peace and happy memories.

In Madison County, Mississippi, one finds many bits of ante-bellum life that the turbulent tide of commerce has not yet swept away—big plantations, historic old mansions, tumble-down slave quarters—that are the abiding proofs of the prosperity and hospitality of a people who lived and loved when knighthood was yet in flower, and whose children live yet to preserve the old traditions. Many of the old plantations are still tilled by the descendants of the original owners. Many have passed into stranger's hands. Some stand tenantless and lonely, with ghostly visitants slipping at midnight down the great stairways to tread a stately measure on the ball floor, a silent assemblage of long-ago belles and beaux returned from the cities of the dead or from the still trenches of Seven Pines, Chickamauga, or Shiloh.

One of these silent homes is Annandale, a bit of historic Mississippi architecture that stands near Canton, once the home of Southern chivalry and romance, now empty, save for the memories that cluster thickly within its walls. Annandale is the property, and was until recently the home of the Mississippi branch of the Johnstone family, and preserves to memory the name of the county in Scotland that cradled the ancestors who bore this illustrious name. It is still known as their home, though Vicksburg now claims the daughter of the house, and only in the summers are the doors opened again for that lavish hospitality for which the old place was noted. Two brothers of the Johnstone family came over from Scotland in 1734, having been sent by George III, on business of great import to the colonies. One had the appointment of governor to his majesty's colony of North Carolina, the other that of surveyor-general. The Johnstone family remained loyal to their king as long as native pride would permit, and then, true to the spirit that demanded the Magna Charta at Runnymede centuries before, they went to the American settlements in the fight for liberty. They were prominent in the Revolution, and after the war took part in the political work of building up the nation.

John T. Johnstone, a prominent member of this family, moved from North Carolina to Mississippi in 1836 and bought large tracts of land in Madison County. On the plantation near Annandale he built a comfortable home—a fine house for those days of pioneer effort. His neighbors were the families of Hardeman, Hinton, Ricks, Winters and Christmas, and there are still marvelous tales told in that locality of the lavish manner of living, the wonderful hospitality dispensed and the gay companies that assembled in the old home. A few years of this charmed life Mr. Johnstone called his, and then he was gathered to his illustrious fathers, and the burden of this great estate fell on the shoulders of his young widow. She stood the test of generalship, as other Southern women of her day have done, and the affairs of the plantation, the slave quarters and the household moved as smoothly as clock work and success smiled on her. The material side of her plantation's progress did not overshadow the religious side, and services for bond and free were held daily in a gothic church on the estate, the chapel of the cross which Mrs. Johnstone had erected in memory of her husband. The daughter of the house was carefully educated, and as she neared womanhood Mrs. Johnstone had a new home built, the present Annandale, and the same lavish hospitality was continued.

Then came the war. There was no husband, brother or son to send to the front, but the women, true to the patriotic sentiments of their house, gave of their best. The big mansion was turned into a factory for supplying Confederate needs. Mrs. Johnstone and her fair daughter, Helen, became the head of a busy body of working women, who gave of their time and talent for the South. All day was heard the whir of spinning-wheels, the slipping of the shuttles in the looms; all day busy fingers carded, wove, spun and sewed, that the soldiers might be made more comfortable. One company of soldiers was equipped throughout the war solely at Miss Johnstone's expense, while she and her mother furnished clothing to two hundred others. The setting of dainty stitches, the manufacture of rolled and whipped ruffles, were laid aside for the time. The rich carpets were torn from the floors and made into blankets; the rare bronzes and brasses were torn from their pedestals or their fastenings and sent to the foundries to be made into cannon; silk dresses were transformed into banners to lead the gray-clad men to victory, and dainty linen and cambric garments and rare household napery and linen were ruthlessly torn in strips to bandage the wounds of the men in the hospitals. The granaries, smokehouses, and wine cellars gave up their stores for the Confederacy, the wealth of these two loyal women being laid gladly on their country's altar. Yet, through all this troublous season, hospitality and merriment still reigned. The rebel lads adored the loyal women; the Union soldiers tried more than once to burn the house that sheltered such secessionists.

During the war the fair daughter of the house was married to Rev. George Carroll Harris, of Nashville, and for many years rector of Christ Church, and widely known throughout the South.

In 1880 Mrs. Johnstone died, and historic Annandale passed into her daughter's hands, and is still owned by her. A few years ago the son of Dr. and Mrs. Harris, George Harris, married Miss Cecile Nugent, of Jackson, Mississippi, and they live on his place in the Delta, and with the marriage of the daughter Helen to the son of the late Bishop Thompson the younger generation of Annandale closed another chapter of romances for the old home. But even though the windows are darkened and no material form passes daily over the threshold, the inner air is still palpitant with memories, and who knows what gay revels the ghostly companies of the past may not hold in the grand salon when midnight has come and the human world is wrapped in slumber?

A PLANTATION HEROINE

[In Southern Soldier Stories, pages 203-205.]

It was nearing the end. Every resource of the Southern States had been taxed to the point of exhaustion. The people had given up everything they had for "the cause." Under the law of a "tax in kind," they had surrendered all they could spare of food products of every character. Under an untamable impulse of patriotism they had surrendered much more than they could spare in order to feed the army.

It was at such a time that I went to my home county on a little military business. I stopped for dinner at a house, the lavish hospitality of which had been a byword in the old days. I found before me at dinner the remnants of a cold boiled ham, some mustard greens, which we Virginians called "salad," a pitcher of buttermilk, some corn pones and—nothing else. I carved the ham, and offered to serve it to the three women of the household. But they all declined. They made their dinner on salad, buttermilk, and corn bread, the latter eaten very sparingly, as I observed. The ham went only to myself and to the three convalescent wounded soldiers who were guests in the house. Wounded men were at that time guests in every house in Virginia.

I lay awake that night and thought over the circumstance. The next morning I took occasion to have a talk on the old familiar terms with the young woman of the family, with whom I had been on a basis of friendship in the old days that even permitted me to kiss her upon due and proper occasion.

"Why didn't you take some ham last night?" I asked urgently.

"Oh, I didn't want it," she replied.

"Now, you know you are fibbing," I said. "Tell me the truth, won't you?"

She blushed, and hesitated. Presently she broke down and answered frankly: "Honestly, I did want the ham. I have hungered for meat for months. But I mustn't eat it, and I won't. You see the army needs all the food there is, and more. We women can't fight, though I don't see at all why they shouldn't let us, and so we are trying to feed the fighting men—and there aren't any others. We've made up our minds not to eat anything that can be sent to the front as rations."

"You are starving yourselves," I exclaimed.

"Oh, no," she said. "And if we were, what would it matter? Haven't Lee's soldiers starved many a day? But we aren't starving. You see we had plenty of salad and buttermilk last night. And we even ate some of the corn bread. I must stop that, by the way, for corn meal is a good ration for the soldiers." A month or so later this frail but heroic young girl was laid away in the Grub Hill church-yard.

Don't talk to me about the "heroism" that braves a fire of hell under enthusiastic impulse. That young girl did a higher self-sacrifice than any soldier who fought on either side during the war ever dreamed of doing.

LUCY ANN COX

[In Southern Historical Papers, Volume 22, pages 54-55. From the Richmond *Star*, July 21, 1894.]

On the evening of October 15th an entertainment was given in Fredericksburg, Virginia, to raise funds to erect a monument to the memory of Mrs. Lucy Ann Cox, who, at the commencement of the war, surrendered all the comfort of her father's home, and followed the fortunes of her husband, who was a member of Company A, Thirteenth Virginia Regiment, until the flag of the Southern Confederacy was furled at Appomattox. No march was too long or weather too inclement to deter this patriotic woman from doing what she considered her duty. She was with her company and regiment on their two forays into Maryland, and her ministering hand carried comfort to many a wounded and worn soldier. While Company A was the object of her untiring solicitude, no Confederate ever asked assistance from Mrs. Cox but it was cheerfully rendered.

She marched as the infantry did, seldom taking advantage of offered rides in ambulances and wagon trains. When Mrs. Cox died, a few years ago, it was her latest expressed wish that she be buried with military honors, and, so far as it was possible, her wish was carried out. Her funeral took place on a bright autumn Sunday, and the entire town turned out to do honor to this noble woman.

The camps that have undertaken the erection of this monument do honor to themselves in thus commemorating the virtues of the heroine, Lucy Ann Cox.

"ONE OF THEM LEES"

[Phoebe Y. Pember, in Hospital Life.]

There was little conversation carried on, no necessity for introductions, and no names ever asked or given. This indifference to personality was a peculiarity strongly exhibited in hospitals; for after nursing a sick or wounded patient for months, he has often left without any curiosity as regarded my name, my whereabouts, or indeed anything connected with me. A case in point was related by a friend. When the daughter of our general had devoted much time and care to a sick man in one of the hospitals, he seemed to feel so little gratitude for the attention paid him that her companion to rouse him told him that Miss Lee was his nurse. "Lee, Lee?" he said. "There are some Lees down in Mississippi who keeps a tavern there. Is she one of them Lees?"

Almost of the same style, although a little worse, was the remark of one sick, poor fellow who had been wounded in the head and who, though sensible enough ordinarily, would feel the effect of the sun on his brain when exposed to its influence. After advising him to wear a wet paper doubled into the crown of his hat, more from a desire to show some interest in him than from any belief in its efficacy, I paused at the door long enough to hear him ask the ward-master, "who that was?"

"Why, that is the matron of the hospital; she gives you all the food you eat, and attends to things."

"Well," said he, "I always did think this government was a confounded sell, and now I am sure of it, when they put such a little fool to manage such a big hospital as this."

SOUTHERN WOMEN IN THE WAR BETWEEN THE STATES

[In Southern Historical Papers, Volume 32, pages 146-150. T. C. DeLeon, in New Orleans *Picayune*.]

The great German who wrote:

"Honor to woman! to her it is given

To garden the earth with roses of heaven!"

precisely described the Confederate conditions—a century in advance. True, constant, brave and enduring, the men were; but the women set even the bravest and most steadfast example. Nor was this confined to any one section of the country. The "girl with the calico dress" of the lowland farms; the "merry mountain maid" of the hill country, and the belles of society in the cities, all vied with each other in efforts to serve the men who had gone to the front to fight for home and for them. And there was no section of the South where this desire to do all they might and more was oftener in evidence than another. In every camp of the early days of the great struggle the incoming troops bore trophies of home love, and as the war progressed to need, then to dire want, the sacrifices of those women at home became almost a poem, and one most pathetic. Dress—misconceived as the feminine fetich—was forgotten in the effort to clothe the boys at the front; the family larder—ill-stocked at the best—was depleted to nothingness, to send to distant camps those delicacies—so equally freighted with tenderness and dyspepsia—which too often never reached their destination. And later, the carpets were taken from the floors, the curtains from the windows—alike in humble homes and in dwellings of the rich—to be cut in blankets for the uncomplaining fellows, sleeping on freezing mud.

So wide, so universal, was the rule of self-sacrifice, that no one reference to it can do justice to the zeal and devotion of "Our Girls." And the best proof of both was in the hospitals, where soon began to congregate the maimed and torn forms of those just sent forth to glory and victory. This was the trial that tested the grain and purity of our womanhood, and left it without alloy of fear or selfishness. And some of the women who wrought in home and hospital—even in trench and on the firing line—for the "boys," had never before handled aught rougher than embroidery, or seen aught more fearsome than its needle-prick. Yes, these untried women, young and old, stood fire like veteran regulars, indeed, even more bravely in moral view, for they missed the stimulus of the charge—the tonic in the thought of striking back.

During the entire war—and through the entire South—it was the hospital that illustrated the highest and best traits of the tried and stricken people. Doubtless, there was good work done by the women of the North, and much of it. Happily, for the sanity of the nation, American womanhood springs from one common stock. It is ever true to its own, as a whole—and, for aught I shall deny—individually. But behind that Chinese wall of wood and steel blockade, then nursing was not an episode. It was grave duty, grim labor; heartbreaking endurance—all self-imposed, and lasting for years, yet shirked and relinquished only for cause.

But the dainty little hands that tied the red bandages, or "held the artery" unflinching; the nimble feet that wearied not by fever cot, or operating table, the active months of war, grew nimbler still on bridle, or in the dances when "the boys" came home. This was sometimes on "flying furlough," or when an aid, or courier, with dispatches, was told to wait. Then "the one girl" was mounted on anything that could carry her; and the party would ride far to the front, in full view of the enemy, and often in point-blank range. Or, it was when frozen ruts made roads impassable for invader and defender; and the furlough was perhaps easier, and longer. Then came those now historic dances, the starvation parties, where rank told nothing, and where the only refreshment came in that intoxicant—a woman's voice and eyes.

Then came the "Dies Irae," when the Southern Rachel sat in the ashes of her desolation and her homespun was sackcloth. And even she rose supreme. By her desolate hearth, with her larder empty, and only her aching heart full, she still forced a smile for the home-coming "boy" through the repressed tears for the one left, somewhere in the fight.

In Richmond, Atlanta, Charleston and elsewhere was she bitter and unforgiving? If she drew her faded skirt—ever a black one, in that case— from the passing blue, was it "treason," or human nature? Thinkers who wore the blue have time and oft declared the latter. Was she "unreconstructed?" Her wounds were great and wondrous sore. She was true, then, to her faith. That she is to-day to the reunited land let the fathers of Spanish war heroes tell. She needs no monument; it is reared in the hearts of true men, North and South.

A MOTHER OF THE CONFEDERACY

[In Southern Historical Papers, Volume 22, pages 63-64. From the Memphis, Tenn., *Appeal-Avalanche*, June 30, 1894.]

Just upon the eve of preparations by ex-Confederates to celebrate the Fourth of July in a becoming manner and spirit, the sad news is announced of the death of the venerable Mrs. Law, known all over the South as one of the mothers of the Confederacy. She was also truly a mother in Israel, in the highest Christian sense. Her life had been closely connected with that of many leading actors in the late war, in which she herself bore an essential part. She passed away, June 28th, at Idlewild, one of the suburbs of Memphis, nearly 89 years of age.

She was born on the River Yadkin, in Wilson County, North Carolina, August 27, 1805, and at the time of her death was doubtless the oldest person in Shelby County. Her mother's maiden name was Charity King. Her father, Chapman Gordon, served in the Revolutionary War, under Generals Marion and Sumter. She came of a long-lived race of people. Her mother lived to be 93 years of age, and her brother, Rev. Hezekiah Herndon Gordon, who was the father of General John B. Gordon (now Senator from Georgia), lived to the age of 92 years.

Sallie Chapman Gordon was married to Dr. John S. Law, near Eatonton, Georgia, on the 28th day of June, 1825. A few years later she became a member of the Presbyterian Church, in Forsyth, Georgia, and her name was afterward transferred to the rolls of the Second Presbyterian Church in Memphis, of which church she remained a member as long as she lived.

She became an active worker in hospitals, and when nothing more could be done in Memphis she went through the lines and rendered substantial aid and comfort to the soldiers in the field. Her services, if fully recorded, would make a book. She was so recognized that upon one occasion General Joseph E. Johnston had 30,000 of his bronzed and tattered soldiers to pass in review in her honor at Dalton. Such a distinction was, perhaps, never accorded to any other woman in the South—not even Mrs. Jefferson Davis or the wives of great generals. Yet, so earnest and sincere in her work was she that she commanded the respect and reverence of men wherever she was known. After the war she strove to comfort the vanquished and encourage the down- hearted, and continued in her way to do much good work.

"THE GREAT EASTERN"

[In Christ in Camp, pages 94-98; J. William Jones, D. D.]

Here is another sketch of a soldier's friend who labored in some of our largest hospitals.

"She is a character," writes a soldier. "A Napoleon of her department, with the firmness and courage of Andrew, she possesses all the energy and independence of Stonewall Jackson. The officials hate her; the soldiers adore her. The former name her 'The Great Eastern,' and steer wide of her track, the latter go to her in all their wants and troubles, and know her by the name of 'Miss Sally.' She joined the army in one of the regiments from Alabama, about the time of the battle of Manassas, and never shrunk from the stern privations of the soldier's life from the moment of leaving camp to follow her wounded and sick Alabamians to the hospitals of Richmond. Her services are not confined, however, to the sick and wounded from Alabama. Every sick soldier has now a claim on her sympathy. Why, but yesterday, my system having succumbed to the prevailing malaria of the hospital, she came to my room, though a stranger, with my ward nurse, and in the kindest manner offered me her pillow of feathers, with case as tidy as the driven snow. The very sight of it was soothing to an aching brow, and I blessed her from heart and lips as well. I must not omit to tell why 'Miss Sally' is so disliked by many of the officials. Like all women of energy, she has eyes whose penetration few things escape, and a sagacity fearful or admirable, as the case may be, to all interested. If any abuse is pending, or in progress in the hospital, she is quickly on the track, and if not abated, off 'The Great Eastern' sails to headquarters. A few days ago one of the officials of the division sent a soldier to inform her that she must vacate her room instantly. 'Who sent you with that message to me?' she asked him, turning suddenly around. 'Dr.
——,' the soldier answered. 'Pish!' she replied, and swept on in ineffable contempt to the bedside, perhaps, of some sick soldier."

CORDIAL FOR THE BRAVE

[Eggleston's Recollections, pages 70-71.]

The ingenuity with which these good ladies discovered or manufactured onerous duties for themselves was surprising, and having discovered or imagined some new duty they straightway proceeded to do it at any cost.

An excellent Richmond dame was talking with a soldier friend, when he carelessly remarked that there was nothing which so greatly helped to keep up a contented and cheerful spirit among the men as the receipt of letters from their woman friends. Catching at the suggestion as a revelation of duty, she asked, "And cheerfulness makes better soldiers of the men, does it not?" Receiving yes for an answer, the frail little woman, already over-burdened with cares of an unusual sort, sat down and made out a list of all the men with whom she was acquainted even in the smallest possible way, and from that day until the end of the war she wrote one letter a week to each, a task which, as her acquaintance was large, taxed her time and strength very severely. Not content with this, she wrote on the subject in the newspapers, earnestly urging a like course upon her sisters, many of whom adopted the suggestion at once, much to the delight of the soldiers, who little dreamed that the kindly, cheerful, friendly letters which every mail brought into camp were a part of woman's self-appointed work for the success of the common cause. From the beginning to the end of the war it was the same.

HOSPITAL WORK AND WOMEN'S DELICACY

[Phoebe Y. Pember, in Hospital Life.]

There is one subject connected with hospitals on which a few words should be said—the distasteful one that a woman must lose a certain amount of delicacy and reticence in filling any office in them. How can this be? There is no unpleasant exposure under proper arrangements, and if even there be, the circumstances which surround a wounded man, far from friends and home, suffering in a holy cause and dependent upon a woman for help, care and sympathy, hallow and clear the atmosphere in which she labors. That woman must indeed be hard and gross who lets one material thought lessen her efficiency. In the midst of suffering and death, hoping with those almost beyond hope in this world; praying by the bedside of the lonely and heart-stricken; closing the eyes of boys hardly old enough to realize man's sorrow, much less suffer by man's fierce hate, a woman must soar beyond the conventional modesty considered correct under different circumstances.

If the ordeal does not chasten and purify her nature, if the contemplation of suffering and endurance does not make her wiser and better, and if the daily fire through which she passes does not draw from her nature the sweet fragrance of benevolence, charity, and love,—then, indeed, a hospital has been no fit place for her.

A WAYSIDE HOME AT MILLEN

[Electra Tyler Deloache, in Augusta *Chronicle*, October 29, 1905.]

Only a few of the present inhabitants of Millen know that it was once famous as the location of a Confederate Wayside Home, where, during the civil war, the soldiers were fed and cared for. The home was built by public subscription and proved a veritable boon to the soldiers, as many veterans now living can testify.

The location of the town has been changed slightly since the 60's, for in those days the car sheds were several hundred yards farther up the Macon track, and were situated where the railroad crossing is now. The hotel owned and run by Mr. Gray was first opposite the depot, and the location is still marked by mock-orange trees and shrubbery.

The Wayside Home was on the west side of the railroad crossing and was opposite the house built in the railroad Y by Major Wilkins and familiarly known here as the Berrien House. The old well still marks the spot. The home was weather-boarded with rough planks running straight up and down. It had four large rooms to the front, conveniently furnished with cots, etc., for the accommodation of any soldiers who were sick or wounded and unable to continue their journey. A nurse was always on hand to attend to the wants of the sick. Back of these rooms was a large dining hall and kitchen, where the weary and hungry boys in gray could minister to the wants of the inner man. And right royally they performed this pleasant duty, for the table was always bountifully supplied with good things, donated by the patriotic women of Burke county, who gladly emptied hearts and home upon the altar of country. This work was entirely under the auspices of the women of Burke. Mrs. Judge Jones, of Waynesboro, was the first president of the home. She was succeeded by Mrs. Ransom Lewis, who was second and last. She was quite an active factor in the work, and it was largely due to her efforts that the home attained the prominence that it did among similar institutions.

Miss Annie Bailey, daughter of Captain Bailey, of Savannah, was matron of the home. She was assisted in the work by committees of three ladies, who, each in turn, spent several days at the home. The regular servants were kept and extra help called in when needed.

This home was to the weary and hungry Confederate soldier as an oasis in the desert, for here he found rest and plenty beneath its shelter. And the social feature was not its least attraction, when a bevy of blooming girls from our bonny Southland would visit the home, and midst feast and jest spur the boys on to renewed vigor in the cause of the South. They felt amidst such inspirations it would be glorious to die but more glorious to live for such a land of charming women. One of our matrons with her sweet old face softened into a dreamy smile by happy reminiscences of those days of toil, care, and sorrow, where happy thoughts and pleasantries of the past crowded in and made little rifts of sunshine through the war clouds, remarked: "But with all the gloom and suffering, we girls used to have such fun with the soldiers at the home, and at such times we could even forget that our loved South was in the throes of the most terrible war in the history of any country!"

The home was operated for two years or more and often whole regiments of soldiers came to it, and all that could be accommodated were taken in and cared for.

It was destroyed by Sherman's army on their march to the sea. The car shed, depot, hotel and home all disappeared before the torch of the destroyer and only the memory, the well, and the trees remain to mark the historic spot where the heroic efforts of our Burke county women sustained the Wayside Home through long years of the struggle.

Mrs. Amos Whitehead and others who have "crossed the river" were prominently connected with this work; in fact, every one lent a helping hand, for it was truly a labor of love, and was our Southern women's tribute to patriotism and heroism.

A NOBLE GIRL

[From the *Floridian*, 1864.]

Upon the arrival of the troops at Madison sent to reinforce our army in East Florida, the ladies attended at the depot with provisions and refreshments for the defenders of their home and country. Among the brave war-worn soldiers who were rushing to the defence of our State there was, in one of the Georgia regiments, a soldier boy, whose bare feet were bleeding from the exposure and fatigue of the march. One of the young ladies present, moved by the impulse of her sex, took the shoes from her own feet, made the suffering hero put them on, and walked home herself barefooted. Wherever Southern soldiers have suffered and bled for their country's freedom, let this incident be told for a memorial of Lou Taylor, of Madison county.

THE GOOD SAMARITAN

[In Christ in Camp, pages 98-99; J. William Jones, D. D.]

At Richmond, Va., there was a little model hospital known as the "Samaritan," presided over by a lady who gave it her undivided attention, and greatly endeared herself to the soldiers who were fortunate enough to be sent there. "Through my son, a young soldier of eighteen," writes a father, "I have become acquainted with this lady superintendent, whose memory will live in many hearts when our present struggle shall have ended. But for her motherly care and skilful attention my son and many others must have died. One case of her attention deserves special notice. A young man, who had been previously with her, was taken sick in camp near Richmond. The surgeon being absent, he lay for two weeks in his tent without medical aid. She sent several requests to his captain to send him to her, but he would not in the absence of the surgeon. She then hired a wagon and went for him herself; the captain allowed her to take him away, and he was soon convalescent. She says she feels that not their bodies only but their souls are committed to her charge. Thus, as soon as they are comfortably fixed in a good, clean bed, she inquires of every one if he has chosen the good part; and through her instruction and prayers several have been converted. Her house can easily accommodate twenty, all in one room, which is made comfortable in winter with carpet and stove, and adorned with wreaths of evergreen and paper flowers, and in summer well ventilated, and the windows and yard filled with green-house plants. A library of religious books is in the room, and pictures are hung on the walls."

FEMALE RELATIVES VISIT THE HOSPITALS.

[Phoebe Y. Pember, in Hospital Life.]

There was no means of keeping the relations of patients from coming to them. There had been rules made to meet their invasion, but it was impossible to carry them out, as in the instance of a wife wanting to remain with her husband; and, besides, even the better class of people looked upon the comfort and care of a hospital as a farce. They resented the detention there of men who in many instances could lie in bed and point to their homes within sight, and argued that they would have better attention and food if allowed to go to their families. That *maladie du pays* called commonly nostalgia, the homesickness which rings the heart and impoverishes the blood, killed many a brave soldier, and the matron who day by day had to stand helpless and powerless by the bed of the sufferer, knowing that a week's furlough would make his heart sing with joy and save his wife from widowhood, learned the most bitter lesson of endurance that could be taught.

My hospital was now entirely composed of Virginians and Marylanders, and the nearness to the homes of the former entailed upon me an increase of care in the shape of wives, sisters, cousins, aunts, and whole families, including the historic baby at the breast. They came in troops, and, hard as it was to know how to dispose of them, it was harder to send them away. Sometimes they brought their provisions with them, but not often, and even when they did there was no place for them to cook their food. It must be remembered that everything was reduced to the lowest minimum, even fuel. They could not remain all day in the wards with men around them, and if even they were so willing, the restraint on wounded, restless patients who wanted to throw their limbs about with freedom during the hot days was unbearable.

Generally their only idea of kindness was giving the sick men what food they would take in any quantity and of every quality, and in the furtherance of their views they were pugnacious in the extreme. Whenever rules circumscribed their plans they abused the government, then the hospitals, and then myself. Many ludicrous incidents happened daily, and I have often laughed heartily at seeing the harassed ward-master heading away a pertinacious female who, failing to get past him at the door, would try the three others perseveringly. They seemed to think it a pious and patriotic duty not to be afraid or ashamed under any circumstances. One sultry day I found a whole family, accompanied by two young lady friends, seated around a sick man's bed. As I passed through six hours later, they held the same position.

"Had not you all better go home?" I said good-naturedly.

"We came to see my cousin," answered one very crossly. "He is wounded."

"But you have been with him all morning and that is a restraint upon the other men. Come again to-morrow."

A consultation was held, but when it ceased no movement was made, the older ones only lighting their pipes and smoking in silence.

"Will you come back to-morrow and go now?"

"No! You come into the wards when you please, and so will we."

"But it is my duty to do so. Besides, I always ask permission to enter, and never stay longer than fifteen minutes at a time."

Another unbroken silence, which was a trial to any patience left, and finding no movement made, I handed some clothing to the patient near.

"Here is a clean shirt and drawers for you, Mr. Wilson. Put them on as soon as I get out of the ward."

I had hardly reached my kitchen, when the whole procession, pipes and all, passed me solemnly and angrily; but, for many days, and even weeks, there was no ridding the place of this large family connection. Their sins were manifold. They overfed their relative who was recovering from an attack of typhoid fever, and even defiantly seized the food for the purpose from under my very nose. They marched on me *en-masse* at 10 o'clock at night, with a requisition from the boldest for sleeping quarters. The steward was summoned, and said "he didn't keep a hotel," so in a weak moment of pity for their desolate state, I imprudently housed them in my laundry. They entrenched themselves there for six days, making predatory incursions into my kitchen during my temporary absences, ignoring Miss G. completely. The object of their solicitude recovered and was sent to the field, and finding my writs of ejectment were treated with contemptuous silence, I sought an explanation. The same spokeswoman alluded to above met me half-way. She said a battle was imminent she had heard, and she had determined to remain, as her husband might be wounded. In the ensuing press of business she was forgotten, and strangely enough, her husband was brought in with a bullet in his neck the following week. The back is surely fitted to the burden, so I contented myself with retaking my laundry and letting her shift for herself, while a whole month slipped away. One morning my arrival was greeted with a general burst of merriment from everybody I met, white and black. Experience had made me sage, and my first question was a true shot, right in the center.

"Where is Mrs. Daniels?"

She had always been spokeswoman.

"In ward G. She has sent for you two or three times."

"What is the matter now?"

"You must go and see."

There was something going on either amusing or amiss. I entered ward G, and walked up to Daniel's bed. One might have heard a pin drop.

I had supposed, up to this time, that I had been called upon to bear and suffer every annoyance that humanity and the state of the country could inflict, but here was something most unexpectedly in addition; for lying composedly on her husband's cot (for he had relinquished it for the occasion) lay Mrs. Daniels and her baby (just two hours old).

The conversation that ensued is not worth repeating, being more of the nature of a soliloquy. The poor wretch had ventured into a bleak and comfortless portion of the world, and its inhuman mother had not provided a rag to cover it. No one could scold her at such a time, however ardently they might desire to do so. But what was to be done? I went in search of my chief surgeon, and our conversation although didactic was hardly satisfactory on the subject.

"Doctor, Mrs. Daniels has a baby. She is in ward G. What shall I do with her?"

"A baby! Ah, indeed! You must get it some clothes."

"What must I do with her?"

"Move her to an empty ward and give her some tea and toast."

This was offered, but Mrs. Daniels said she would wait until dinner time and have some bacon and greens.

The baby was a sore annoyance. The ladies of Richmond made up a wardrobe, each contributing some article, and at the end of the month, Mrs. D., the child, and a basket of clothing and provisions were sent to the cars with a return ticket to her home in western Virginia.

Sadie Curry And "Clara Fisher"

[I. L. U.]

In later years of the war a great many of the wounded soldiers were brought from east and west to Augusta, Ga. Immediately the people from the country on both sides of the Savannah River came in and took hundreds of the poor fellows to their homes and nursed them with every possible kindness. Ten miles up the river, on the Carolina side, was the happy little village of Curryton, named for Mr. Joel Curry and his father, the venerable Lewis Curry. Here, many a poor fellow from distant States was taken in most cordially and every home was a temporary hospital. Among those nursed at Mr. Curry's, whose house was always a home for the preacher, the poor man, and the soldier, was Major Crowder, who suffered long from a painful and fatal wound, and a stripling boy soldier from Kentucky, Elijah Ballard, whose hip wound made him a cripple for life.

Miss Sadie Curry nursed both, night and day, as she did others, when necessary, like a sister. Her zeal never flagged, and her strength never gave way. After young Ballard, who was totally without education, became strong enough, she taught him to read and write, and when the war ended he went home prepared to be a book-keeper. Others received like kindness.

But this noble girl had from the beginning of the war made it her daily business to look after the families of the poorer soldiers in the neighborhood. She mounted her horse daily and made her round of angel visits. If she found anybody sick she reported to the kind and patriotic Dr. Hugh Shaw. If any of the families lacked meal or other provisions, it was reported to her father, who would send meal from his mill or bacon from his smoke-house.

In appreciation of her heroic work, her father and her gallant brother-in-law, Major Robert Meriwether, who was in the Virginia army, now living in Brazil, bought a beautiful Tennessee riding horse and gave it to her. She named it "Clara Fisher" and many poor hearts in old Edgefield were made sad and many tears shed in the fall of 1864, when Sadie Curry and "Clara Fisher" moved to southwest Georgia.

Bless God, there were many Sadie Currys all over the South, wherever there was a call and opportunity. Miss Sadie married Dr. H. D. Hudson and later in life Rev. Dr. Rogers, of Augusta, where she died a few years ago.

MANIA FOR MARRIAGE

[In Diary of a Refugee, pages 329-330.]

There seems to be a perfect mania on the subject of matrimony. Some of the churches may be seen open and lighted almost every night for bridals, and wherever I turn, I hear of marriages in prospect.

"In peace Love tunes the shepherd's reed;

In war he mounts the warrior's steed,"

sings the "Last Minstrel" of the Scottish days of romance; and I do not think that our modern warriors are a whit behind them, either in love or war. My only wonder is, that they find time for love-making amid the storms of warfare. Just at this time, however, I suppose our valiant knights and ladies fair are taking advantage of the short respite, caused by alternate snows and sunshine of our variable climate having made the roads impassable to Grant's artillery and baggage-wagons.

A soldier in our hospital called to me as I passed his bed the other day, "I say, Mrs. ——, when do you think my wound will be well enough for me to go to the country?"

"Before very long, I hope."

"But what does the doctor say, for I am mighty anxious to go?"

I looked at his disabled limb and talked to him hopefully of his being able to enjoy country air in a short time.

"Well, try to get me up, for, you see, it ain't the country air I'm after, but I wants to get married, and the lady don't know that I am wounded, and maybe she'll think I don't want to come."

"Ah," said I, "but you must show her your scars, and if she is a girl worth having she will love you all the better for having bled for your country, and you must tell her that—

"'It is always the heart that is bravest in war

That is fondest and truest in love.'"

He looked perfectly delighted with the idea; and as I passed him again he called out, "Lady, please stop a minute and tell me the verse over again, for, you see, when I do get there, if she is affronted, I wants to give her the prettiest excuse I can, and I think that verse is beautiful."

GOVERNMENT CLERKSHIPS

[In Richmond During the War, pages 174-175.]

From the Treasury Department, the employment of female clerks extended to various offices in the War Department, the Post Office Department, and indeed every branch of business connected with the government. They were all found efficient and useful. By this means many young men could be sent into the ranks, and by testimony of the chiefs of bureaus, the work left for the women was better done; for they were more conscientious in their duties than the more self-satisfied, but not better qualified, male attaches of the government offices. The experiment of placing women in government clerkships proved eminently successful, and grew to be extremely popular under the Confederate government.

Many a young girl remembers with gratitude the kindly encouragement of our Adjutant-General Cooper, our chief of ordnance, Colonel Gorgas, or the first auditor of the Confederate treasury, Judge Bolling Baker, or Postmaster-General Reagan, and various other officials, of whom their necessities drove them to seek employment. The most high-born ladies of the land filled these places as well as the humble poor; but none could obtain employment under the government who could not furnish testimonials of intelligence and superior moral worth.

SCHOOLS IN WAR TIMES

[In Richmond During the War, pages 188-189.]

As the war went on a marked change was made in the educational interests of the South. For a certain number of pupils, the teachers of schools were exempt from military duty. To their credit be it recorded that few, comparatively, availed themselves of this exception, and the care of instructing the youth devolved, with other added responsibilities, upon the women of the country. Only the boys under conscript age were found in the schools; all older were made necessary in the field or in some department of government service, unless physical inability prevented them from falling under the requirements of the law. Many of our colleges for males suspended operation, and at the most important period in the course of their education our youths were instructed in the sterner lessons of military service.

HUMANITY IN THE HOSPITALS

[Richmond *Enquirer*, June 6, 1862.]

In our visits to the various hospitals, we cannot but remark, admire, and commend the kindly harmony and sweet-tempered familiarity which mark the intercourse of the ladies who have devoted themselves to the care of the sick and the wounded. There is a unity in the actions and solicitude of all which only a unity of motive could induce. The amiable and unpretending sister of mercy, the earnest bright-eyed Jewish girl and the womanly, gentle, and energetic Protestant, mingle their labors with a freedom and geniality which would teach the most prejudiced zealot a lesson that would never be forgotten. The necessity of charity, once demonstrated, teaches us that we are one kindred, after all, and whatever differences may exist in the peculiar tenets of the many, all hearts are alike open to the same impulses, and the couch of suffering at once commands their sympathy and reminds them of an identity of hope and a common fate.

MRS. DAVIS AND THE FEDERAL PRISONER

[Augusta, Ga., *Constitutionalist.*]

A clerical friend of ours in passing through one of our streets a few days since, to perform a ministerial duty—attending to the sick and wounded in the hospitals—encountered a stranger, who accosted him thus: "My friend, can you tell me if Mrs. Jeff Davis is in the city of Augusta?"

"No, sir," replied our friend. "She is not."

"Well, sir," replied the stranger, "you may be surprised at my asking such a question, and more particularly so when I inform you that I am a discharged United States soldier. But (and here he evinced great feeling), sir, that lady has performed acts of kindness to me which I can never forget. When serving in the valley of Virginia, battling for the Union, I received a severe and dangerous wound. At the same time I was taken prisoner and conveyed to Richmond, where I received such kindness and attention from Mrs. Davis that I can never forget her; and, now that I am discharged from the army and at work in this city, and understanding that the lady was here, I wish to call upon her, renew my expressions of gratitude to her, and offer to share with her, should she unfortunately need it, the last cent I have in the world."

Can it be truly charged on a nation that it was wantonly, criminally cruel, when a generous foe bears testimony to the mercy, kindness, and lowly service of the highest lady of the land?

SOCKS THAT NEVER WORE OUT

General Gordon tells of a simple-hearted country Confederate woman who gave a striking idea of the straits to which our people were reduced later in the war. She explained that her son's only pair of socks did not wear out, because, said she: "When the feet of the socks get full of holes, I just knit new feet to the tops, and when the tops wear out I just knit new tops to the feet."

BURIAL OF AUNT MATILDA

[Mrs. R. A. Pryor's Reminiscences.]

This precise type of a Virginia plantation will never appear again, I imagine. I wish I could describe a plantation wedding as I saw it that summer. But a funeral of one of the old servants was peculiarly interesting to me. "Aunt Matilda" had been much loved and, when she found herself dying, she had requested that the mistress and little children should attend her funeral.

"I ain' been much to church," she urged. "I couldn't leave my babies. I ain' had dat shoutin' an' hollerin' religion, but I gwine to heaven jes' de same"—a fact of which nobody who knew Aunt Matilda could have the smallest doubt.

We had a long, warm walk behind hundreds of negroes, following the rude coffin in slow procession through the woods, singing antiphonally as they went, one of those strange, weird hymns not to be caught by any Anglo-Saxon voice.

It was a beautiful and touching scene, and at the grave I longed for an artist (we had no kodaks then) to perpetuate the picture. The level rays of the sun were filtered through the green leaves of the forest, and fell gently on the dusky pathetic faces, and on the simple coffin surrounded by orphan children and relatives, very dignified and quiet in their grief.

The spiritual patriarch of the plantation presided. Old Uncle Abel said:

"I ain' gwine keep you all long. 'Tain' no use. We can't do nothin' for Sis' Tildy. All is done fer her, an' she done preach her own fune'al sermon. Her name was on dis church book here, but dat warn' nothin'; no doubt 'twas on de Lamb book, too.

"Now, whiles dey fillin' up her grave, I'd like you all to sing a hymn Sis' Tildy uster love, but you all know I bline in one eye, an' I dunno as any o' you all ken do it"—and the first thing I knew, the old man had passed his well- worn book to me, and there I stood at the foot of the grave, "lining out":

"'Asleep in Jesus, blessed sleep,

From which none ever wake to weep.'"

Words of immortal comfort to the great throng of negro mourners who caught it up line after line, on an air of their own, full of tears and tenderness,—a strange, weird tune no white person's voice could ever follow.

"ILLEGANT PAIR OF HANDS"

[Phoebe Y. Pember.]

A large number of the surgeons were absent, and the few left would not be able to attend to all the wounds at that late hour of the night. I proposed in reply that the convalescent men should be placed on the floor on blankets or bed-sacks filled with straw, and the wounded take their place, and, purposely construing his silence into consent, gave the necessary orders, eagerly offering my services to dress simple wounds, and extolling the strength of my nerves. He let me have my way (may his ways be of pleasantness and his paths of peace), and so, giving Miss G. orders to make an unlimited supply of coffee, tea, and stimulants, armed with lint, bandages, castile soap, and a basin of warm water, I made my first essay in the surgical line. I had been spectator often enough to be skilful. The first object that needed my care was an Irishman. He was seated upon a bed with his hands crossed, wounded in both arms by the same bullet. The blood was soon washed away, wet lint applied, and no bones being broken, the bandages easily arranged.

"I hope that I have not hurt you much," I said with some trepidation. "These are the first wounds that I have ever dressed."

"Sure, they be the most illegant pair of hands that ever touched me, and the lightest," he gallantly answered. "And I am all right now."

THE GUN-BOAT "RICHMOND"

[Scharf's Confederate Navy.]

The "Ladies' Defence Association" was then formed at Richmond, with Mrs. Maria G. Clopton, president; Mrs. General Henningsen, vice-president; Mrs.

R. H. Maury, treasurer, and Mrs. John Adams Smith, secretary. At its meeting, on April 9th, an address, prepared by Captain J. S. Maury, was read by Rev. Dr. Doggett. In this address it was eloquently stated that the first efforts of the association would be "directed to the building and putting afloat in the waters of the James River a steam man-of-war, clad in shot-proof armor; her panoply to be after the manner of that gallant ship, the noble *Virginia.*" Committees were appointed to solicit subscriptions, and so much encouragement was received that the managers of the association called upon President Davis for sanction of its purpose, which he gladly gave, and it was announced that the keel of the vessel would be laid in a few days; that Commander Farrand would be in charge of the work, and that he would be assisted by Ship-builder Graves.

Words can but inadequately represent the energy with which the women of Virginia undertook this work, or the sacrifices which they made to complete it. That their jewels and their household plate, heirlooms, in many instances, that had been handed down from generation to generation and were the embodiments of ancestral rank and tradition, were freely given up, is known. "Virginia," said they in their appeal, "when she sent her sons into this war, gave up her jewels to it. Let not her daughters hold back. Mothers, wives, sisters! what are your ornaments of silver and gold in decoration, when by dedicating them to a cause like this, you may in times like these strengthen the hand or nerve the arm, or give comfort to the heart that beats and strikes in your defence! Send them to us."

The organization, moreover, did not confine itself to urging upon the women of the State that this was particularly their contribution to the maintenance of the Confederacy. "Iron railings," the address continued, "old and new, scrap-iron about the house, broken ploughshares about the farm, and iron in any shape, though given in quantities ever so small, will be thankfully received if delivered at the Tredegar Works, where it may be put into the furnace, reduced, and wrought into shape or turned into shot and shell." A friendly invasion of the tobacco factories was made by a committee of ladies, consisting of Mrs. Brooke Gwathney, Mrs. B. Smith, and Mrs. George T. Brooker, and the owners cheerfully broke up much of their machinery that was available for the specified purpose. Mrs. R. H. Maury, treasurer of the association, took charge of the contributions in money, plate, and jewelry; the materials and tools were sent to Commodore Farrand, and an agent, S. D. Hicks, was appointed to receive the contributions of grain, country produce, etc., that were sent in by Virginia farmers to be converted into cash. By the end of April the construction had reached an advanced stage; President Davis and Secretary Mallory had congratulated the Ladies' Association upon the assured success of its self-allotted task, and by the sale of articles donated to a public bazaar or fair, almost a sufficient sum to complete the ship was secured.

The *Richmond* was completed in July, 1862, and although detailed descriptions are lacking all mention made of her is unanimous that she was an excellent ship of her type. Captain Parker says that "she was a fine vessel, built on the plan of the *Virginia*."

Note.—Mrs. General Henningsen received from New Orleans boxes containing articles to be sold for contribution to building the Richmond. Among the articles were two beautiful vases, which were bought by a gentleman of Richmond and are now in the possession of his family. The Richmond was destroyed on the evacuation of the Capital City.—J. L. U.

CAPTAIN SALLY TOMPKINS

[By J. L. Underwood.]

Southern women have cared little for public honors nor have they courted masculine titles. But a recent number of the Richmond *Times-Dispatch* recalls the pleasant bit of history that in the case of Miss Sallie Tompkins a remarkable honor was deservedly conferred upon a worthy Virginia girl by the Confederate authorities.

While yet a very young woman Miss Tompkins used her ample means to establish in Richmond a private hospital for Confederate soldiers. She not only provided for its support at her own expense, but devoted her time to the work of nursing the patients.

The wounded were brought into the city by the hundreds and there was hardly a private house without its quota of sick and wounded. Quite a number of private hospitals were established but, unlike Miss Tompkins's splendid institution, charges were made by some of them for services rendered. In course of time abuses grew with the system, and General Lee ordered that they all be closed—all except the hospital of Miss Tompkins. This was recognized as too helpful to the Confederate cause to be abolished.

In order to preserve it it had to be brought under government control, and to do this General Lee ordered a commission as captain in the Confederate army to be issued to Miss Sallie Tompkins. Though a government hospital from that time on, Captain Tompkins conducted it as before, paying its expenses out of her private purse.

The veterans are proud of her record, and a movement is now on foot among them to place Captain Tompkins in a position of independence as long as she lives.

THE ANGEL OF THE HOSPITAL

[From the Gray Jacket, pages 143-146.]

'Twas nightfall in the hospital. The day,
As though its eyes were dimmed with bloody rain
From the red clouds of war, had quenched its light,
And in its stead some pale, sepulchral lamps
Shed their dim lustre in the halls of pain,
And flitted mystic shadows o'er the walls.
No more the cry of "Charge! On, soldiers, on!"
Stirred the thick billows of the sulphurous air;
But the deep moan of human agony,
From the pale lips quivering as they strove in vain
To smother mortal pain, appalled the ear,
And made the life-blood curdle in the heart.
Nor flag, nor bayonet, nor plume, nor lance,
Nor burnished gun, nor clarion call, nor drum,
Displayed the pomp of battle; but instead
The tourniquet, the scalpel, and the draught,
The bandage, and the splint were strewn around —
Dumb symbols, telling more than tongues could speak
The awful shadows of the fiend of war.
Look! Look! What gentle form with cautious step
Passes from couch to couch as silently
As yon faint shadows flickering on the walls,
And, bending o'er the gasping sufferer's head,
Cools his flushed forehead with the icy bath,

From her own tender hand, or pours the cup
Whose cordial powers can quench the inward flame
That burns his heart to ashes, or with voice
As tender as a mother's to her babe,
Pours pious consolation in his ear.
She came to one long used in war's rude scenes —
A soldier from his youth, grown gray in arms,
Now pierced with mortal wounds. Untutored, rough,
Though brave and true, uncared for by the world.
His life had passed without a friendly word,
Which timely spoken to his willing ear,
Had wakened God-like hopes, and filled his heart
With the unfading bloom of sacred truth.
Beside his couch she stood, and read the page
Of heavenly wisdom and the law of love,
And bade him follow the triumphant chief
Who bears the unconquered banner of the cross.
The veteran heard with tears and grateful smile,
Like a long-frozen fount whose ice is touched
By the restless sun, and melts away,
And, fixing his last gaze on her and heaven,
Went to the Judge in penitential prayer.
She passed to one, in manhood's blooming prime,
Lately the glory of the martial field,
But now, sore-scathed by the fierce shock of arms,
Like a tall pine shattered by the lightning's stroke,

Prostrate he lay, and felt the pangs of death,
And saw its thickening damps obscure the light
Which make our world so beautiful. Yet those
He heeded not. His anxious thoughts had flown
O'er rivers and illimitable woods,
To his fair cottage in the Western wilds,
Where his young bride and prattling little ones—
Poor hapless little ones, chafed by the wolf of war—
Watched for the coming of the absent one
In utter desolation's bitterness.
O, agonizing thought! which smote his heart
With sharper anguish than the sabre's point.
The angel came with sympathetic voice,
And whispered in his ear: "Our God will be
A husband to the widow, and embrace
The orphan tenderly within his arms;
For human sorrow never cries in vain
To His compassionate ear." The dying man
Drank in her words with rapture; cheering hope
Shone like a rainbow in his tearful eyes,
And arched his cloud of sorrow, while he gave
The dearest earthly treasures of his heart,
In resignation to the care of God.
A fair man-boy of fifteen summers tossed
His wasted limbs upon a cheerless couch.
Ah! how unlike the downy bed prepared
By his fond mother's love, whose tireless hands
No comforts for her only offspring spared
From earliest childhood, when the sweet babe

slept,
Soft—nestling in her bosom all the night,
Like a half-blown lily sleeping on the heart
Of swelling summer wave, till that sad day
He left the untold treasure of her love
To seek the rude companionship of war.
The fiery fever struck his swelling brain
With raving madness, and the big veinsthrobbed
A death-knell on his temples, and his breath
Was hot and quick, as is the panting deer's,
Stretched by the Indian's arrow on the plain.
"Mother! Oh, mother!" oft his faltering tongue
Shrieked to the cold, bare wall, which echoed back
His wailing in the mocking of despair.
Oh! angel nurse, what sorrow wrung thy heart
For the young sufferer's grief! She knelt beside
The dying lad, and smoothed his tangled locks
Back from his aching brow, and wept and prayed
With all a woman's tenderness and love,
That the good Shepherd would receive this lamb,
Far wandering from the dear maternal fold,
And shelter him in His all-circling arms,
In the green valleys of Immortal rest.
And so the angel passed from scene to scene
Of human suffering, like that blessed One,
Himself the man of sorrows and of grief,
Who came to earth to teach the law oflove,
And pour sweet balm upon the mourner's heart,
And raise the fallen and restore the lost.

Bright vision of my dreams! thy light shall shine
Through all the darkness of this weary world—
Its selfishness, its coolness, and its sin,
Pure as the holy evening star of love,
The brightest planet in the host of heaven.

CHAPTER III
THEIR TRIALS

OLD MAIDS

[J. L. Underwood.]

This would be a dark world without old maids—God bless them! No one can measure their usefulness. Many a one of them has never married because she has never found a man good enough for her. The saddest mourners the world ever saw were some of our Southern girls whose hearts and hopes were buried in a soldier's grave in Virginia or the Far West. For four years the daughters of the South waited for their lovers, and alas! many waited in a life widowhood of unutterable sorrow. After the seven days' battles in front of Richmond a horseman rode up to the door of one of the houses on —— street in Richmond and cried out to an anxious mother: "Your son is safe, but Captain —— is killed." On the opposite side of the street a fair young girl was sitting. She was the betrothed of the ill-fated captain, and heard the crushing announcement. That's the way war made so many Southern girls widows without coming to the marriage altar.

"It matters little now, Lorena;

  The past is the eternal past.

Our heads will soon lie low, Lorena;

  Life's tide is ebbing out so fast

But, there's a future—oh, thank God—

  Of life this is so small a part;

'Tis dust to dust beneath the sod,

  But there—up there,—'tis heart to heart."

The writer is so partial to the old maids of the Confederacy that he is afraid of a charge of extravagance were he to say anything more. But the author of this book is not the only one to admire and love them. Hear what another old Confederate soldier says in the following letter in the Atlanta *Journal*:

SUGAR VALLEY, GA.

DEAR MISS THOMAS:

Will you permit an old Confederate soldier, who has nearly reached his three-score and ten, to occupy a seat while he says a few words?

The old maids of to-day were young girls in my youthful days. They were once young and happy and looked forward with bright hopes to the future, while the flowers opened as pretty, the birds sung as sweetly, and the sun shone as brightly as it does to the young girls of to-day. They had sweethearts; they loved and were loved in return; they had pleasant dreams of the coming future to be passed in their own happy homes surrounded by husband and children. But, alas! the dark war clouds lowered above the horizon and all their bright dreams of the future were overcast with gloom. They loved with a pure and unselfish devotion, but they loved their country best. The young men of the sixties were the first to respond to their country's call and marched away to the front, to undergo the hardships and dangers of a soldier's life.

Now, can you imagine the pangs that rent the maiden's breast as she bid farewell, maybe for the last time this side of eternity, to the one who was dearer than her own heart's blood, as she watched his manly form clothed in his uniform of gray disappear in the distance? She tried to be brave when she bade him go and fight the battles of his country. She remained at home and prayed to an all-wise and merciful God to spare him amidst the storm of iron and lead, but her heart seemed rent in twain and all of her bright hopes for the future seemed turned to ashes. The weary days and months passed in dread suspense.

Now and then a letter from the front revived her drooping spirits, as her soldier boy told of his many escapes amid the charging columns and roar of battle. After many months or maybe years she received the sad tidings that her gallant soldier was no more; his gallant spirit had flashed out with the guns, and his manly form, wrapped in a soldier's blanket, had been consigned to an unmarked grave far away from home and loved ones. The last rays of hope fled, and she resigned herself to her sad and lonely fate. They were true to their country in its sore distress, true to their heroes wearing the gray, and true to their God who doeth all things well. Could any one lead a more consecrated life? Now, let us, instead of deriding, cast the veil of charity over their desolate lives.

The once smooth cheek is furrowed with the wrinkles of time, the glossy braids have whitened with the snows of winter, the once graceful form is bending under the weight of years, while the bright eyes have grown dim watching, not for the soldier in gray, but for the summons that calls her to meet him on that bright and beautiful shore, there to be with loved ones who have gone before, and receive the reward of "Well done, thou good and faithful servant." Soon the last one of those patriotic women of the sixties will have passed over the river, and their like may never be seen again, but their love of home and country will be handed down to generations yet unknown.

With best wishes for the household,

W. H. ANDREWS.

A MOTHER'S LETTER

[From a dying soldier boy.]

The Alabama papers in 1863 published the following letter from Private John Moseley, a youth who gave up his life at Gettysburg:

BATTLEFIELD, GETTYSBURG, PA.,
July 4, 1863.

DEAR MOTHER:

I am here, prisoner of war and mortally wounded. I can live but a few hours more at furthest. I was shot fifty yards from the enemy's line. They have been exceedingly kind to me. I have no doubt as to the final result of this battle, and I hope I may live long enough to hear the shouts of victory before I die. I am very weak. Do not mourn my loss. I had hoped to have been spared, but a righteous God has ordered it otherwise, and I feel prepared to trust my case in His hands. Farewell to you all. Pray that God may receive my soul.

Your unfortunate son,

JOHN.

TOM AND HIS YOUNG MASTER

[In Richmond During the War, pages 178-179.]

A young soldier from Georgia brought with him to the war in Virginia a young man who had been brought up with him on his father's plantation. On leaving his home with his regiment, the mother of the young soldier said to his negro slave: "Now, Tom, I commit your master Jemmy into your keeping. Don't let him suffer for anything with which you can supply him. If he is sick, nurse him well, my boy; and if he dies, bring his body home to me; if wounded, take care of him; and oh! if he is killed in battle, don't let him be buried on the field, but secure his body for me, and bring him home to be buried!" The negro faithfully promised his mistress that all her wishes should be attended to, and came on to the seat of war charged with the grave responsibility placed upon him.

In one of the battles around Richmond the negro saw his young master when he entered the fight, and saw him when he fell, but no more of him. The battle became fierce, the dust and smoke so dense that the company to which he was attached, wholly enveloped in the cloud, was hidden from the sight of the negro, and it was not until the battle was over that Tom could seek for his young master. He found him in a heap of slain. Removing the mangled remains, torn frightfully by a piece of shell, he conveyed them to an empty house, where he laid them out in the most decent order he could, and securing the few valuables found on his person, he sought a conveyance to carry the body to Richmond. Ambulances were in too great requisition for those whose lives were not extinct to permit the body of a dead man to be conveyed in one of them. He pleaded most piteously for a place to bring in the body of his young master. It was useless, and he was repulsed; but finding some one to guard the dead, he hastened into the city and hired a cart and driver to go out with him to bring in the body to Richmond.

When he arrived again at the place where he had left it, he was urged to let it be buried on the field, and was told that he would not be allowed to take it from Richmond, and therefore it were better to be buried there. "I can't do it. I promised my mistress (his mother) to bring his body home to her if he got killed, and I'll go home with it or I'll die by it; I can't leave my master Jemmy here." The boy was allowed to have the body and brought it to Richmond, where he was furnished with a coffin, and the circumstances being made known, the faithful slave, in the care of a wounded officer who went South, was permitted to carry the remains of his master to his distant home in Georgia. The heart of the mother was comforted in the possession of the precious body of her child, and in giving it a burial in the church-yard near his own loved home.

Fee or reward for this noble act of fidelity would have been an insult to the better feelings of this poor slave; but when he delivered up the watch and other things taken from the person of his young master, the mistress returned him the watch, and said: "Take this watch, Tom, and keep it for the sake of my boy; 'tis but a poor reward for such services as you have rendered him and his mother." The poor woman, quite overcome, could only add: "God bless you, boy!"

"I KNEW YOU WOULD COME"

[In Southern Historical Papers, Volume 22, pages 58-59.]

Col. W. R. Aylett tells the following tender story:

Once during the war, when the lines of the enemy separated me from my home, I was an inmate of my brother's Richmond home while suffering from a wound. As soon as I could walk about a little, my first steps were directed to Seabrook's Hospital to see some of my dear comrades who were worse wounded than I. While sitting by the cot of a friend, who was soon to "pass over the river and rest under the shade of the trees," I witnessed a scene that I can hardly ever think of without quickened pulse and moist eye.

A beautiful boy, too young to fight and die, and a member of an Alabama regiment, was dying from a terrible wound a few feet off. His mother had been telegraphed for at his request. In the wild delirium of his dying moments he had been steadily calling for her, "Oh, mother, come; do come quickly!" Then, under the influence of opiates given to smooth his entrance into eternal rest, he dozed and slumbered. The thunders of the great guns along the lines of the immortal Lee roused him up. Just then his dying eyes rested upon one of the lovely matrons of Richmond advancing toward him. His reeling brain and distempered imagination mistook her for his mother. Raising himself up, with a wild, delirious cry of joy, which rang throughout the hospital, he cried: "Oh, mother! I knew you would come! I knew you would come! I can die easy now;" and she, humoring his illusion, let him fall upon her bosom, and he died happy in her arms, her tears flowing for him as if he had been her own son.

LETTERS FROM THE POOR AT HOME

[Phoebe Y. Pember.]

A thousand evidences of the loving care and energetic labor of the patient ones at home, telling an affecting story that knocked hard at the gates of the heart, were the portals ever so firmly closed; and with all these came letters written by poor, ignorant ones who often had no knowledge of how such communications should be addressed. These letters, making inquiries concerning patients from anxious relatives at home, directed oftener to my office than my home, came in numbers, and were queer mixtures of ignorance, bad grammar, worse spelling, and simple feeling. However absurd the style, the love that filled them chastened and purified them. Many are stored away, and though irresistibly ludicrous, are too sacred to print for public amusement. In them could be detected the prejudices of the different sections. One old lady in upper Georgia wrote a pathetic appeal for a furlough for her son. She called me "My dear sir," while still retaining my feminine address, and though expressing the strongest desire for her son's restoration to health, entreated in moving accents that if his life could not be spared, that he should not be buried in "Ole Virginny dirt"—rather a derogatory term to apply to the sacred soil that gave birth to the Presidents,—the soil of the Old Dominion.

Almost all of these letters told the same sad tale of destitution of food and clothing; even shoes of the roughest kind being either too expensive for the mass or unattainable by the expenditure of any sum, in many parts of the country. For the first two years of the war, privations were lightly dwelt upon and courageously borne, but when want and suffering pressed heavily, as times grew more stringent, there was a natural longing for the stronger heart and frame to bear part of the burden. Desertion is a crime that meets generally with as much contempt as cowardice, and yet how hard for the husband or father to remain inactive in winter quarters, knowing that his wife and little ones were literally starving at home—not even at home, for few homes were left.

LIFE IN RICHMOND DURING THE WAR

[Southern Historical Papers, Volume 19. From the *Cosmopolitan*, December, 1891; by Edward M. Alfriend.]

For many months after the beginning of the war between the States, Richmond was an extremely gay, bright, and happy city. Except that its streets were filled with handsomely attired officers and that troops constantly passed through it, there was nothing to indicate the horrors or sorrows of war, or the fearful deprivations that subsequently befell it. As the war progressed its miseries tightened their bloody grasp upon the city, happiness was nearly destroyed, and the hearts of the people were made to bleed. During the time of McClellan's investment of Richmond, and the seven days' fighting between Lee's army and his own, every cannon that was fired could be heard in every home in Richmond, and as every home had its son or sons at the front of Lee's army, it can be easily understood how great was the anguish of every mother's heart in the Confederate capital. These mothers had cheerfully given their sons to the Southern cause, illustrating, as they sent them to battle, the heroism of the Spartan mother, who, when she gave the shield to her son, told him to return with it or on it.

Happy Phases

And yet, during the entire war, Richmond had happy phases to its social life. Entertainments were given freely and very liberally the first year of the war, and at them wine and suppers were graciously furnished, but as the war progressed all this was of necessity given up, and we had instead what were called "starvation parties."

The young ladies of the city, accompanied by their male escorts (generally Confederate officers on leave) would assemble at a fashionable residence that before the war had been the abode of wealth, and have music and plenty of dancing, but not a morsel of food or a drop of drink was seen. And this form of entertainment became the popular and universal one in Richmond. Of course, no food or wine was served, simply because the host could not get it, or could not afford it. And at these starvation parties the young people of Richmond and the young army officers assembled and danced as brightly and as happily as though a supper worthy of Lucullus awaited them.

The ladies were simply dressed, many of them without jewelry, because the women of the South had given their jewelry to the Confederate cause. Often on the occasion of these starvation parties, some young Southern girl would appear in an old gown belonging to her mother or grandmother, or possibly a still more remote ancestor, and the effect of the antique garment was very peculiar; but no matter what was worn, no matter how peculiarly any one might be attired, no matter how bad the music, no matter how limited the host's or hostess's ability to entertain, everybody laughed, danced, and was happy, although the reports of the cannon often boomed in their ears, and all deprivations, all deficiencies, were looked on as a sacrifice to the Southern cause.

The Dress of a Grandmother

I remember going to a starvation party during the war with a Miss M., a sister of Annie Rive's mother. She wore a dress belonging to her great-grandmother or grandmother, and she looked regally handsome in it. She was a young lady of rare beauty, and as thoroughbred in every feature of her face or pose and line of her body as a reindeer, and with this old dress on she looked as though the portrait of some ancestor had stepped out of its frame.

Such spectacles were very common at our starvation parties. On one occasion I attended a starvation party at the residence of Mr. John Enders, an old and honored citizen of Richmond, and, of course, there was no supper. Among those present was Willie Allan, the second son of the gentleman, Mr. John Allan, who adopted Edgar Allan Poe, and gave him his middle name. About 1 o'clock in the morning he came to one other gentleman and myself, and asked us to go to his home just across the street, saying he thought he could give us some supper. Of course, we eagerly accepted his invitation and accompanied him to his house. He brought out a half dozen mutton chops and some bread, and we had what was to us a royal supper. I spent the night at the Allan home and slept in the same room with Willie Allan. The next morning there was a tap on the door, and I heard the mother's gentle voice calling: "Willie, Willie." He answered, "Yes, mother; what is it?" And she replied: "Did you eat the mutton chops last night?" He answered, "Yes," when she said, "Well, then, we haven't any breakfast."

Frightful Contrasts

The condition of the Allan household was that of all Richmond. Sometimes the contrasts that occurred in these social gayeties in Richmond were frightful, ghastly. A brilliant, handsome, happy, joyous young officer, full of hope and promise, would dance with a lovely girl and return to his command. Afew days would elapse, another "starvation" would occur, the officer would be missed, he would be asked for, and the reply come, "Killed in battle;" and frequently the same girls with whom he danced a few nights before would attend his funeral from one of the churches of Richmond. Can life have any more terrible antithesis than this?

A Georgia lady was once remonstrating with General Sherman against the conduct of some of his men, when she said: "General, this is barbarity," and General Sherman, who was famous for his pregnant epigrams, replied: "Madame, war is barbarity." And so it is.

On one occasion, when I was attending a starvation party in Richmond, the dancing was at its height and everybody was bright and happy, when the hostess, who was a widow, was suddenly called out of the room. A hush fell on everything, the dancing stopped, and every one became sad, all having a premonition in those troublous times that something fearful had happened. We were soon told that her son had been killed late that evening, in a skirmish in front of Richmond, a few miles from his home.

Wounded and sick men and officers were constantly brought into the homes of the people of Richmond to be taken care of, and every home had in it a sick or wounded Confederate soldier. From the association thus brought about many a love affair occurred and many a marriage resulted. I know of several wives and mothers in the South who lost their hearts and won their soldier husbands in this way, so this phase of life during the war near Richmond was prolific of romance.

General Lee Kissed the Girls

General Robert E. Lee would often leave the front, come into Richmond and attend these starvation parties, and on such occasions he was not only the cynosure of all eyes, but the young ladies all crowded around him, and he kissed every one of them. This was esteemed his privilege and he seemed to enjoy the exercise of it. On such occasions he was thoroughly urbane, but always the dignified, patrician soldier in his bearing.

Private theatricals were also a form of amusement during the war. I saw several of them. The finest I witnessed, however, was a performance of Sheridan's comedy, of Alabama, played by Mrs. Malaprop. Her rendition of the part was one of the best I ever saw, rivalling that of any professional. The audience was very brilliant, the President of the Confederacy, Mrs. Davis,

Judah P. Benjamin, and others of equal distinction being present.

Mrs. Davis is a woman of great intellectual powers and a social queen, and at these entertainments she was very charming. Mr. Davis was always simple, unpretentious, and thoroughly cordial in his manner. To those who saw him on these occasions it was impossible to associate his gentle, pleasing manner with the stern decision with which he was then directing his side of the greatest war of modern times. The world has greatly misunderstood Mr. Davis, and in no way more than in personal traits of his character. My brother, the late Frank H. Alfriend, was Mr. Davis's biographer, and through personal intercourse with Mr. Davis I knew him well. In all his social, domestic, and family relations, he was the gentlest, the noblest, the tenderest of men. As a father and husband he was almost peerless, for his domestic life was the highest conceivable.

Mr. Davis, at the executive mansion, held weekly receptions, to which the public were admitted. These continued until nearly the end of the war. The occasions were not especially marked, but Mr. and Mrs. Davis were always delightful hosts.

John Wise and His Big Clothes

The spectacle presented at the social gatherings, particularly the starvation parties, was picturesque in the extreme. The ladies often took down the damask and other curtains and made dresses of them. My friend, Hon. John S. Wise, formerly of Virginia, now of New York, tells the following story of himself: He was serving in front of Richmond and was invited to come into the city to attend a starvation party. Having no coat of his own fit to wear, he borrowed one from a brother officer nearly twice his height. The sleeves of his coat covered his hands entirely, the skirt came below his knees several inches, and the buttons in the back were down on his legs. So attired, Captain Wise went to the party. His first partner in the dance was a young lady of Richmond belonging to one of its best families. She was attired in the dress of her great-grandmother, and a part of this dress was a stomacher very suggestive in its proportions. Captain Wise relates with exquisite humor that in the midst of the dance he found himself in front of a mirror, and that the sight presented by himself and his partner was so ridiculous that he burst out laughing; and his partner turned and looked at him angrily, left his side and never spoke to him again.

Contrasts That Were Pretty

The varied and sometimes handsome uniforms of the Confederate officers commingling with each other and contrasting with the simple, pretty, sometimes antiquated dresses of the ladies, made pictures that were beautiful in their contrasts of color and of tone. An artist would have found these scenes infinite opportunity for his pencil or brush.

I am sure that this phase of social life in Richmond during the war is without parallel in the world's history. The army officers, of course, had only their uniforms, and the women wore whatever they could get to wear. In the last year of the war, particularly the last few months, the pinch of deprivation, especially as to food, became frightful. There were many families in Richmond that were in well-nigh a starving condition. I know of some that lived for days on pea soup and bread. Confederate money was almost valueless. Its purchasing power had so depreciated that it used to be said it took a basketful to go to market. Of course, the people had very few greenbacks, and very little gold or silver. The city was invested by two armies, Grant's and Lee's, and its railroad communications constantly destroyed by the Union cavalry. Supplies of food were very scarce and enormously costly; a barrel of flour cost several hundred dollars in Confederate money, and just before the fall of the Confederacy I paid $500 for a pair of heavy boots. The suffering of this period was dreadful, and when Richmond capitulated many of its people were in an almost starving condition. Indeed, there was little food outside, and the Southern troops were but little better off.

Loyalty of the Slaves

But in April, 1865, the Confederacy ceased to exist; it passed into history, and Richmond was occupied by the Northern army. Many of its people were without food and without money—I mean money of the United States. It was at this period that the colored people of Richmond, slaves up to the time the war ended, but now no longer bondsmen, showed their loyalty and love for their former masters and mistresses. They, of course, had access to the commissary of the United States, and many, very many, of these former negro slaves went to the United States commissary, obtained food seemingly for themselves, and took it in basketfuls to their former owners, who were without food or money. I do not recall any record in the world's history nobler than this—indeed, equal to it.

These are memories of a dead past, and thank God! we now live under the old flag and in a happy, reunited country, which the South loves with a patriotic devotion unsurpassed by the North itself.

THE WOMEN OF NEW ORLEANS

[J. L. Underwood.]

While the patriotic women of New Orleans saw very little of war's ravages, yet they endured three years of war's hardships. The Crescent City fell into the hands of the Federals in 1862, Commodore Farragut commanding the navy, and General B. F. Butler the land forces. The latter was made military governor. Farragut carried on war against combatants, and as an officer is to this day respected and honored by the Southern people. Butler carried on war on civilians and against defenceless women. The history of these women cannot be told without telling of their odious military tyrant.

President Davis in his proclamation said:

> The helpless women have been torn from their homes and subjected to solitary confinement, some in fortresses and prisons, and one, especially, on an island of barren sand under a tropical sun, have been fed with loathsome rations that had been condemned as unfit for soldiers, and have been exposed to the vilest insults.
>
> Egress from the city has been refused to those whose fortitude could withstand the test, even to lone and aged women and to helpless children; and after being ejected from their homes and robbed of their property, they have been left to starve in the streets or subsist on charity.

But this does not tell half the story. The civilized world stood aghast when General Butler issued his infamous "Order No. 28," which reads as follows:

> As the officers and soldiers of the United States have been subjected to insults from the women (calling themselves ladies) of New Orleans in return for the most scrupulous noninterference and courtesy on our part, it is ordered that hereafter when any female shall by word, gesture, or movement insult or show contempt for any officer or soldier of the United States, she shall be regarded and held liable to be treated as a woman of the town plying her avocation.
>
> By Command of Major General Butler.

Human language cannot describe the cowardice, the meanness, the brutality of such an order. All Europe denounced him, President Davis outlawed him, some of his own Northern newspapers would not at first believe that he had issued such an order.

From that time on the name of "Butler, the Beast," was fastened to him. In this day we pity women who are in danger of falling into the clutches of the black brute. These women of 1862 were under the heels of a white brute. Every American patriot will hang his head in shame for all time that President Lincoln kept Butler in high military office to the end of the war, and the government never did repudiate his infamous official outrage. Be it recorded to the everlasting honor of the Federal army that none of the soldiers of "The Beast" availed themselves of the license conferred by his order.

“INCORRIGIBLE LITTLE DEVIL”

[Eggleston’s Recollections, pages 65-66.]

In New Orleans, soon after the war, I saw in a drawing-room, one day, an elaborately framed letter, of which, the curtains being drawn, I could read only the signature, which to my astonishment was that of General Butler.

“What is that?” I asked of the young gentlewoman I was visiting.

“Oh, that’s my diploma, my certificate of good behavior from General Butler;” and taking it down from the wall, she permitted me to read it, telling me at the same time its history. It seems that the young lady had been very active in aiding captured Confederates to escape from New Orleans, and for this and other similar offenses she was arrested several times. A gentleman who knew General Butler personally had interested himself in behalf of her and some friends, and upon making an appeal for their discharge received this personal note from the commanding general, in which he declared his willingness to discharge all the others. “But that black-eyed Miss B.,” he wrote, “seems to me an incorrigible little devil, whom even prison fare won’t tame.” The young lady had framed the note, and she cherishes it yet, doubtless.

Later on Butler was given a command in the East and General Banks put in control at New Orleans. He was clean and soldierly, but more stern and overbearing in some respects than Butler. Dr. Stone, the most prominent citizen of New Orleans, said to the writer in 1863: “We could manage Butler better than we can Banks. We could scare Butler, but we can’t move Banks.” Our poor women, patient and prudent through it all, were out of the fire, but they were in the frying-pan.

THE BATTLE OF THE HANDKERCHIEFS

We are indebted to the Honorable W. H. Seymour for the following very interesting story:

There was a great stir and intense excitement one time during General Banks’s administration. A number of the “rebels” were to leave for the “Confederacy.” Their friends, amounting to some 20,000 persons, women and children principally, wended their way down to the levee to see them off and to take their last farewell. Such a quantity of women frightened the Federal officials: they were greatly exasperated at their waving of handkerchiefs, their loud calling to their friends, and their going on to vessels in the vicinity.

Orders were given to “stand back,” but no heed was given; the bayonets were pointed at the ladies, but they were not scared. A lady ran across to get a nearer view. An officer seized her by the arm, but she escaped, leaving a scarf in his possession. At last the military received orders to do its duty.

The affair was called the Pocket Handkerchief War and has been put in verse, as follows:

The Greatest Victory of the War—La Battaille des Mouchoirs.

[By Capt. James Dinkins, in New Orleans *Picayune*; Southern Historical Papers, Volume 31.]

[Fought Friday, February 20, 1863, at the head of Gravier Street.]

Of all the battles modern or old,

By poet sung or historian told;

Of all the routs that ever was seen

From the days of Saladin to Marshall Turenne,

Or all the victories later yet won,

From Waterloo's field to that of Bull Run;

All, all, must hide their fading light,

In the radiant glow of the handkerchief fight;

And a paean of joy must thrill the land,

When they hear of the deeds of Banks's band.

'Twas on a levee, where the tide of "Father
Mississippi" flows,

Our gallant lads, their country's pride,

Won this great victory o'er her foes,

Four hundred rebels were to leave

That morning for Secessia's shades,

When down there came (you'd scarce believe)

A troop of children, wives, and maids,

To wave their farewells, to bid God-speed,

To shed for them the parting tear,

To waft their kisses as the meed of praise to

soldiers' hearts most dear.
They came in hundreds; thousands lined
The streets, the roofs, the shipping, too;
Their ribbons dancing in the wind,
Their bright eyes flashing love's adieu.
'Twas then to danger we awoke,
But nobly faced the unarmed throng,
And beat them back with hearty stroke,
Till reinforcements came along.
We waited long; our aching sight
Was strained in eager, anxious gaze,
At last we saw the bayonets bright
Flash in the sunlight's welcome blaze.
The cannon's dull and heavy roll,
Fell greeting on our gladdened ear,
Then fired each eye, then glowed each soul,
For well we knew the strife was near.
"Charge!" rang the cry, and on we dashed
Upon our female foes,
As seas in stormy fury lashed,
Whene'er the tempest blows.
Like chaff their parasols went down,
As our gallants rushed;
And many a bonnet, robe, and gown
Was torn to shreds or crushed;
Though well we plied the bayonet,
Still some our efforts braved,
Defiant both of blow and threat,
Their handkerchiefs still waved.

Thick grew the fight, loud rolled the din,
When "charge!" rang out again
And then the cannon thundered in,
And scoured o'er the plain.
Down, 'neath the unpitying iron heels of horses children sank,
While through the crowd the cannon
Wheels mowed roads on either flank,
One startled shriek, one hollow groan,
One headlong rush, and then
"Huzza!" the field was all our own,
For we were Banks's men.
That night, released from all our toils,
Our dangers passed and gone,
We gladly gathered up the spoils
Our chivalry had won!
Five hundred 'kerchiefs we had snatched
From rebel ladies' hands,
Ten parasols, two shoes (not matched),
Some ribbons, belts, and bands,
And other things that I forgot;
But then you'll find them all
As trophies in that hallowed spot—
The cradle—Faneuil Hall!
And long on Massachusetts' shore
And on Green Mountain's side,
Or where Long Island's breakers roar,
And by the Hudson's tide,
In times to come, when lamps are lit,
And fires brightly blaze,

While round the knees of heroes sit
  The young of happier days,
Who listen to their storied deeds,
  To them sublimely grand,
Then glory shall award its meed
  Of praise to Banks's band,
And Fame proclaim that they alone
  (In Triumph's loudest note)
May wear henceforth, for valor shown,
  A woman's petticoat.

THE WOMEN OF NEW ORLEANS AND VICKSBURG PRISONERS

[By J. L. Underwood.]

General Pemberton's army at Vicksburg surrendered on the 4th of July, 1863. According to the liberal terms, the thirty thousand Confederates were paroled and allowed to march to their homes across the country. It was about a month before the sick and wounded could be removed. They were sent on Federal transports down the Mississippi River by the way of New Orleans and thence across the Gulf of Mexico by Fort Morgan to Mobile.

The first boatload consisted of the sick in the hospital, which was under the charge of Dr. Richard Whitfield, of Alabama. I went to Vicksburg as sergeant major of the Twentieth Alabama Regiment, but, at the request of the Thirtieth Alabama, had been commissioned captain and appointed chaplain of that command a few months before the surrender. On the very evening of the surrender I was taken very sick and for some days lay at the point of death. Under the kind nursing of friends in Vicksburg, and by the good medicines provided by the noble Chaplain Porter, of Illinois, of the Federal army, I began to rally in time to be moved to Dr. Whitfield's hospital and be put aboard the first boat for home. By the time we reached New Orleans I had nearly recovered my usual strength. At New Orleans we were transferred to a gulf steamer, which lay at the wharf for nearly two days. Soon after our arrival it looked as if the whole population of the Crescent City had crowded down to look at us and they stood there all day to comfort us with their smiles during our stay.

General Banks allowed Dr. Stone and five other physicians to come on our steamer and look after the sick, to furnish coffins for the dead and remove them for burial. No other citizens could pass the sentinels or a rope guard extending about thirty yards from the boat. A detail of Federal soldiers kept all our private Confederates on the boat. There were only three or four Confederate officers and we were allowed full liberty to go to the guard line and talk to the citizens. Very soon the people began to bring such supplies and refreshments as General Banks would allow, and they literally loaded the steamer with all sorts of good things, from hams and pickles down to fans, pipes, and tobacco. Every soldier had enough for his wants and as much as he could take home. Dr. Stone told me that General Banks would not allow his people to do half of what they were anxious to do. He said the people wanted to keep us a while and clothe us in new outfits.

I must just here put on record one of the most touching instances of soldierly generosity and kindness that ever occurred in war. Lieutenant Winslow, of Massachusetts, was in command of the Federal guard on our steamer, and Captain —— in charge of the guard on the wharf. These two gallant young Federal officers, although in full dress uniform, worked like beavers all day under a hot sun, in assisting me to get the refreshments and provisions from the hands of the ladies or servants at the guard line and take them to the boat, there to be handed to our men. The good women thought, of course, we had wounded men among us, but there was not one. An amazing quantity of lint and bandages was sent aboard. In the linen furnished for this purpose were whole garments of the finest fibre of female underwear, most of it all bright and new. Many a rusty Vicksburg soldier that night decked himself in a fine nightrobe with amazingly short sleeves, and many a soldier's wife accepted for her own use the dainty peace-offering when we reached home. None of these good people, men nor women, were allowed to cheer us. All that they could do was to give us sympathy by their presence and their smiles. I saw the police or the soldiers arrest man after man for some disloyal utterance.

The day we left the throng of beautiful women seemed to extend up and down the levee as far as the eye could reach. As the boat pushed off for Mobile our poor fellows crowded the deck and the excitement on shore grew intense. Neither side could cheer and the tension was painful. Finally the awfully trying stillness was broken by the waving of a little white handkerchief, in a fair woman's hand.

In a moment thousands of others were to be seen, silently telling us "Good-bye and God bless you." In a few moments we could see excitement in every face, and presently a little tender woman's voice screamed out "Hurrah! hurrah!" and then a thousand sweet throats took up the shout. That "Hurrah" from Southern women and those handkerchiefs waved under the point of hostile bayonets told with pathos of a world of patriotism in the breasts of those noble women. We old Confederates were overcome. One grim old North Carolinian, standing by my side, with Federal guards all around us, and the tears streaming down his sun-hardened cheeks, cried out at the top of his voice: "Men, they may kill me, but I tell you I am willing to die a hundred times for such women as them." We all felt so, and the living veterans feel that way yet.

"IT DON'T TROUBLE ME"

[Phoebe Y. Pember.]

There was but little sensibility exhibited by soldiers for the fate of their comrades in field or hospital. The results of war are here to-day and gone to-morrow. I stood still, spell-bound by that youthful death-bed, when my painful revery was broken upon by a drawling voice from a neighboring bed, which had been calling me such peculiar names and titles that I had been oblivious to whom they were addressed.

"Look here. I say, Aunty!—Mammy!—You!" Then in despair, "Missus Mauma! Kin you gim me sich a thing as a b'iled sweet pur-r-rta-a-a-tu-ur? I b'long to the Twenty-secun' Nor' Ka-a-a-li-i-na Regiment." I told the nurse to remove his bed from proximity to his dead neighbor, that in the low state of his health from fever the sight might affect his nerves, but he treated the suggestion with contempt.

"Don't make no sort of difference to me; they dies all around me in the field and it don't trouble me."

SAVAGE WAR IN THE VALLEY

[In the Rise and Fall of Confederate Government, Volume 2, pages 700-709.]

On June 19, 1864, Major-General Hunter began his retreat from before Lynchburg down the Shenandoah Valley. Lieutenant-General Early, who followed in pursuit, thus describes the destruction he witnessed along the route:

"Houses had been burned, and helpless women and children left without shelter. The country had been stripped of provisions, and many families left without a morsel to eat. Furniture and bedding had been cut to pieces, and old men and women and children robbed of all the clothing they had, except that on their backs. Ladies' trunks had been rifled, and their dresses torn to pieces in mere wantonness. Even the negro girls had lost their little finery. At Lexington he had burned the Military Institute with all its contents, including its library and scientific apparatus. Washington College had been plundered, and the statue of Washington stolen. The residence of ex-Governor Letcher at that place had been burned by orders, and but a few minutes given Mrs. Letcher and her family to leave the house. In the county a most excellent Christian gentleman, a Mr. Creigh, had been hung, because, on a former occasion, he had killed a straggling and marauding Federal soldier while in the act of insulting and outraging the ladies of his family."

MRS. ROBERT TURNER, WOODSTOCK, VA.

[J. L. Underwood.]

The patriotic husband was in Lee's army and had left his wife at home with two little girls and an infant in her arms. The home had fallen within the lines of the Federals and the officers had stationed a guard in the house for her protection. One night a marauding party of bummers, who were fleeing from a party of soldiers seeking to arrest them, came to her house and demanded that she should go and show them the road they wanted to take. The soldier guarding her said they were asking too much and refused to let her go. They shot him down so near her that his blood fell on her dress. She went with her little children in the dark night and showed them the road they asked for, and the poor woman hastened back to her home, only to hear the ruffians coming again. They overtook her in the yard and came with such rough threats that she thought they were going to kill her, and to save her oldest little girl, she tried to conceal her by throwing her into some thick shrubbery. Unfortunately the fall and the excitement inflicted an injury which followed the child all her life. The marauders followed the poor mother into the house and threatened to kill her. But as one of them held a pistol in her face the pursuing party rushed in and an officer knocked the pistol up and shot the ruffian, who proved to be the one who had killed the guard of the home.

Some one wrote to Mr. Turner of the situation of his family. General Lee saw the letter and sent Turner home to remove his little family to a place of safety. This he did, and promptly returned to his post in the army, where he served faithfully to the end of the war and then became a staunch citizen.

HIGH PRICE OF NEEDLES AND THREAD

[By Walter, a Soldier's Son; from Mrs. Fannie A. Beer's Memoirs, pages 293-295.]

My father was once a private soldier in the Confederate army, and he often tells me interesting stories of the war. One morning, just as he was going down town, mother sent me to ask him to change a dollar. He could not do it, but he said,

"Ask your mother how much change she wants?"

She only wanted a dime to buy a paper of needles and some silk to mend my jacket. So I went back and asked for ten cents. Instead of taking it out of his vest pocket, father opened his pocket-book and said,

"Did you say you wanted ten dollars or ten cents, my boy?"

"Why, father," said I, "who ever heard of paying ten dollars for needles and thread?"

"I have," said he. "I once heard of a paper of needles, and a skein of silk, worth more than ten dollars."

His eyes twinkled and looked so pleasant that I knew there was a story on hand, so I told mother and sis' Loo, who promised to find out all about it. After supper that night mother coaxed father to tell us the story.

We liked it so well that I got mother to write it down for the *Bivouac*.

After the battle of Chickamauga, one of "our mess" found a needle case which had belonged to some poor fellow, probably among the killed. He did not place much value upon the contents, although there was a paper of No. 8 needles, several buttons, and a skein or two of thread, cut at each end and neatly braided so that each thread could be smoothly drawn out. He put the whole thing in his breast-pocket, and thought no more about it. But one day while out foraging for himself and his mess, he found himself near a house where money could have procured a meal of fried chicken, corn-pone, and buttermilk, besides a small supply to carry back to camp. But Confederate soldiers' purses were generally as empty as their stomachs, and in this instance the lady of the house did not offer to give away her nice dinner. While the poor fellow was inhaling the enticing odor, and feeling desperately hungry, a girl rode up to the gate on horseback, and bawled out to another girl inside the house,

"Oh, Cindy, I rid over to see if you couldn't lend me a needle. I broke the last one I had to-day, and pap says thar ain't nary 'nother to be bought in the country hereabouts!"

Cindy declared she was in the same fix, and couldn't finish her new homespun dress for that reason.

The soldier just then had an idea. He retired to a little distance, pulled out his case, sticking two needles on the front of his jacket, then went back and offered one of them, with his best bow, to the girl on the horse. Right away the lady of the house offered to trade for the one remaining. The result was a plentiful dinner for himself; and in consideration of a thread or two of silk, a full haversack and canteen. After this our mess was well supplied, and our forager began to look sleek and fat. The secret of his success did not leak out till long afterward, when he astonished the boys by declaring he "had been 'living like a fighting-cock' on a paper of needles and two skeins of silk."

"And," added father, "if he had paid for all the meals he got in Confederate money, the amount would have been far more than ten dollars."

I know other boys and girls will think this a queer story, but I hope they will like it as well as mother and Loo and I did.

DESPAIR AT HOME—HEROISM AT THE FRONT

[Major Robert Stiles, in Four Years Under Marse Robert, pages 349-350.]

There is one feature of our Confederate struggle, to which I have already made two or three indirect allusions, as to which there has been such a strange popular misapprehension that I feel as if there rested upon the men who thoroughly understand the situation a solemn obligation to bring out strongly and clearly the sound and true view of the matter. I refer to an impression, quite common, that the desertions from the Confederate armies, especially in the latter part of the war, indicated a general lack of devotion to the cause on the part of the men in the ranks.

On the contrary, it is my deliberate conviction that Southern soldiers who remained faithful under the unspeakable pressure of letters and messages revealing suffering, starvation, and despair at home displayed more than human heroism. The men who felt this strain most were the husbands of young wives and fathers of young children, whom they had supported by their labor, manual or mental. As the lines of communication in the Confederacy were more and more broken and destroyed, and the ability, both of county and public authorities and of neighbors, to aid them became less and less, the situation of such families became more and more desperate, and their appeals more and more piteous to their only earthly helpers who were far away, filling their places in "the thin gray line." Meanwhile the enemy sent into our camps, often by our own pickets, circulars offering our men indefinite parole, with free transportation to their homes.

I am not condemning the Federal Government or military authorities for making these offers or putting out these circulars; but if there was ever such a thing as a conflict of duties, that conflict was presented to the private soldiers of the Confederate army who belonged to the class just mentioned, and who received, perhaps simultaneously, one of these home letters and one of these Federal circulars; and if ever the strain of such a conflict was great enough to unsettle a man's reason and to break a man's heart strings these men were subjected to that strain.

THE OLD DRAKE'S TERRITORY

[J. L. Underwood.]

When Sherman's army was making its celebrated "march to the sea," it cut a swath of fire and desolation from Atlanta to Savannah and on through the Carolinas. What food was not seized for the army was consumed by fire.

Mills and barns and hundreds of dwellings were consigned to the flames. Most of the people fled from the approach of the Federals and especially were the old men, who might be thought by negroes and bummers to have money concealed on their persons or premises, afraid to fall into their hands. Somewhere not far from Milledgeville, a well-to-do farmer lay hid in the woods where he saw the Federals enter his premises and carry off everything of any use or value. Not a strip of bedding, not an ear of corn, a hough of a cow nor the tail of a pig did they leave him. Before the Yankee brigade got entirely out of sight the old farmer came into his desolate home. One glance at the wreck and away he went in pursuit of the Federals. "Oh, General, General, stop your command," was the cry. On they marched without hearing him. On he rushed and cried as he ran, "Oh, General, oh, General, stop your command." Finally when he was nearly out of breath the cry was heard and the brigade halted.

"What's the matter, man?" said the soldiers, as he passed on by them, his face all flushed with excitement.

"Where's the General?"

"Yonder he is, sitting on that black horse."

Everybody stood still to hear the breathless message.

"Oh, General!"

"Well, what's the trouble, sir?"

"General, your men have been yonder to my house and literally ruined me. They have taken everything I have on God's earth; they have left me nothing but one old drake, and he says he is very lonesome, and he wishes you would come back and get him."

This was too much for the soldiers. Up went a shout of laughter and a yell all up and down the lines. The general was completely unhorsed by the desperate drollery of the old farmer, and rolled on the ground. Calling the man to him, he heard more of his story and finally had a list made of all the property which had been taken from him and had it all sent back to him, and the old rebel and the old drake felt better.

I saw much of that old drake's territory. It was the only drake or fowl of any kind I ever heard of being left by Sherman's bummers. I was with a cavalry company on Sherman's flanks or front all the way to Savannah. Miles and miles of smoke from burning houses, barns, and mills could be seen every day and the red line shone by night. He did not burn all the dwellings, but for months and years there stood the lone chimneys of hundreds of once happy homes. These chimneys were called "Sherman's sentinels." As he said, "War is hell." It is hell when conducted on the devil's plan instead of the principles of civilized warfare. For all time to come the march of Sherman and the burning of the Shenandoah Valley by Sheridan will cause the American patriot, North and South, to hang his head in shame.

The women and children in the burned district were, in many localities, reduced almost to starvation. There is a lady living now near Blakely, Ga., who, as a little girl fourteen years old, walked fifteen miles to bring a half bushel of meal for her mother's family. Some of the old men were murdered. The body of old Mr. Brewer, of Effingham county, father of Judge Harlan Brewer of Waycross, was never seen by his family after he was made prisoner. The charred remains of a man were found in a burned mill not far away. Sherman was the right man in the right place. He had lived in the South as a teacher and knew her people; and knew that in fair and honorable warfare the South never could be subdued. He knew, too, the devotion of Southern men to home and family, and he knew that the quickest way to thin the lines of Lee and Johnston was to fire the homes and beggar the families of the Confederate soldiers. As soon as I saw the lines of his fire I said confidentially to my captain, "Our men in Virginia can't stand this. Sherman has whipped us with fire. He drives the women and children out of Atlanta and then burns the country ahead of them. Our cause is lost." And it was.

"But the whole world was against us;

We fought our fight alone;

To the Conquerors Want and Famine,

We laid our standard down."

THE REFUGEE IN RICHMOND

[By A Lady of Virginia, in Diary of a Refugee, pages 252-254.]

Prices of provisions have risen enormously—bacon, $8 per pound, butter, $15, etc. Our old friends from the lower part of Essex, Mr. ——'s parishioners for many years, sent over a wagon filled most generously with all manner of necessary things for our larder. We have no right to complain, for Providence is certainly supplying our wants. The clerks' salaries, too, have been raised to $250 per month, which sounds very large; but when we remember that flour is $300 per barrel, it sinks into insignificance.

28th.—Our hearts ache for the poor. A few days ago, as E. was walking out, she met a wretchedly dressed woman, of miserable appearance, who said she was seeking the Young Men's Christian Association, where she hoped to get assistance and work to do. E. carried her to the door, but it was closed, and the poor woman's wants were pressing. She then brought her home, supplied her with food, and told her to return to see me the following afternoon. She came, and with an honest countenance and manner told me her history. Her name was Brown; her husband had been a workman in Fredericksburg; he joined the army, and was killed at the second battle of Manassas. Many of her acquaintances in Fredericksburg fled last winter during the bombardment; she became alarmed, and with her three little children fled, too. She had tried to get work in Richmond; sometimes she succeeded, but could not supply her wants. A kind woman had lent her a room and a part of a garden, but it was outside of the corporation; and although it saved house-rent, it debarred her from the relief of the associations formed for supplying the city poor with meal, wood, etc. She had evidently been in a situation little short of starvation. I asked her if she could get bread enough for her children by her work? She said she could sometimes, and when she could not, she "got turnip-tops from her piece of a garden, which were now putting up smartly, and she boiled them, with a little salt, and fed them on that."

"But do they satisfy their hunger?" said I.

"Well, it is something to go upon for awhile, but it does not stick by us like as bread does, and then we gets hungry again, and I am afraid to let the children eat them to go to sleep; and sometimes the woman in the next room will bring the children her leavings, but she is monstrous poor."

When I gave her meat for her children, taken from the bounty of our Essex friends, tears of gratitude ran down her cheeks; she said they "had not seen meat for so long." Poor thing, I promised her that her case should be known, and that she should not suffer so again. A soldier's widow shall not suffer from hunger in Richmond. It must not be, and will not be when her case is known.

DESOLATIONS OF WAR

[Diary of a Refugee, page 283-284.]

When the war is over, where shall we find our old churches, where her noble homesteads, scenes of domestic comfort and generous hospitality? Either laid low by the firebrand, or desecrated and desolated. In the march of the army, or in the rapid evolutions of raiding parties, woe betide the houses which are found deserted. In many cases the men of the family having gone to the war, the women and children dare not stay; then the lawless are allowed to plunder. They seem to take the greatest delight in breaking up the most elegant or the most humble furniture, as the case may be; cut the portraits from the frames, split pianos in pieces, ruin libraries in any way that suits their fancy; break doors from their hinges, and locks from the doors; cut the windows from the frames, and leave no pane of glass unbroken; carry off house-linen and carpets; the contents of the store-rooms and pantries, sugar, flour, vinegar, molasses, pickles, preserves, which cannot be eaten or carried off, are poured together in one general mass. The horses are of course taken from the stables; cattle and stock of all kinds driven off or shot in the woods and fields. Generally, indeed, I believe always, when the whole army is moving, inhabited houses are protected. To raiders such as Hunter and Co. is reserved the credit of committing such outrages in the presence of ladies—of taking their watches from their belts, their rings from their fingers, and their ear- rings from their ears; of searching their bureaus and wardrobes, and filling pockets and haversacks in their presence. Is it not, then, wonderful that soldiers whose families have suffered such things could be restrained when in a hostile country? It seems to me to show a marvellous degree of forbearance in the officers themselves and of discipline in the troops.

DEATH OF A SOLDIER

[Diary of a Refugee, pages 311-313.]

An officer from the far South was brought in mortally wounded. He had lost both legs in a fight below Petersburg. The poor fellow suffered excessively; could not be still a moment; and was evidently near his end. His brother, who was with him, exhibited the bitterest grief, watching and waiting on him with silent tenderness and flowing tears. Mr. —— was glad to find that he was not unprepared to die. He had been a professor of religion some years, and told him that he was suffering too much to think on that or any other subject, but he constantly tried to look to God for mercy. Mr. —— then recognized him, for the first time, as a patient who had been in the hospital last spring, and whose admirable character had then much impressed him. He was a gallant and brave officer, yet so kind and gentle to those under his control that his men were deeply attached to him, and the soldier who nursed him showed his love by his anxious care of his beloved captain. After saying to him a few words about Christ and his free salvation, offering up a fervent prayer in which he seemed to join, and watching the sad scene for a short time, Mr. —— left him for the night. The surgeons apprehended that he would die before morning, and so it turned out; at the chaplain's early call there was nothing in his room but the chilling signal of the empty "hospital bunk." He was buried that day, and we trust will be found among the redeemed in the day of the Lord.

This, it was thought, would be the last of this good man; but in the dead of night came hurriedly a single carriage to the gate of the hospital. A lone woman, tall, straight, and dressed in deep mourning, got out quickly, and moved rapidly up the steps into the large hall, where, meeting the guard, she asked anxiously, "Where's Captain T.?"

Taken by surprise, the man answered hesitatingly, "Captain T. is dead, madam, and was buried to-day."

This terrible announcement was as a thunderbolt at the very feet of the poor lady, who fell to the floor as one dead. Starting up, oh, how she made that immense building ring with her bitter lamentations. Worn down with apprehension and weary with traveling over a thousand miles by day and night, without stopping for a moment's rest, and wild with grief, she could hear no voice of sympathy—she regarded not the presence of one or many; she told the story of her married life as if she were alone—how her husband was the best man that ever lived; how everybody loved him; how kind he was to all; how devoted to herself; how he loved his children, took care of, and did everything for them; how, from her earliest years almost, she had loved him as herself; how tender he was of her, watching over her in sickness, never seeming to weary of it, never to be unwilling to make any sacrifice for her comfort and happiness; how that, when the telegraph brought the dreadful news that he was dangerously wounded, she never waited an instant nor stopped a moment by the way, day nor night, and now—"I drove as fast as the horses could come from the depot to this place, and he is dead and buried. I never shall see his face again. What shall I do? But where is he buried?"

They told her where.

"I must go there; he must be taken up; I must see him."

"But, madam, you can't see him; he has been buried some hours."

"But I must see him; I can't live without seeing him; I must hire some one to go and take him up; can't you get some one to take him up? I'll pay him well; just get some men to take him up. I must take him home; he must go home with me. The last thing I said to his children was that they must be good children, and I would bring their father home, and they are waiting for him now. He must go, I can't go without him; I can't meet his children without him;" and so, with her woman's heart, she could not be turned aside—nothing could alter her purpose.

The next day she had his body taken up and embalmed. She watched by it until everything was ready, and then carried him back to his own house and children, only to seek a grave for the dead father close by those he loved, among kindred and friends in the fair sunny land he died to defend.

MRS. HENRIETTA E. LEE'S LETTER TO GENERAL

HUNTER ON THE BURNING OF HER HOUSE

[In Southern Historical Papers, Volume 8, pages 215-216.]

The following burning protest against a cruel wrong deserves to be put on record, as a part of the history of General David Hunter's inglorious campaign in the Valley of Virginia, and we cheerfully comply with the request of a distinguished friend to publish it. The burning of this house and those of Col. A. R. Boteler and Andrew Hunter, esq., in the lower valley, and of Governor Letcher's and the Virginia Military Institute at Lexington give him a place in the annals of infamy only equaled by the contempt felt for his military achievements:

JEFFERSON COUNTY, *July 20, 1864.*

GENERAL HUNTER:

Yesterday your underling, Captain Martindale, of the First New York Cavalry, executed your infamous order and burned my house. You have had the satisfaction ere this of receiving from him the information that your orders were fulfilled to the letter; the dwelling and every out-building, seven in number, with their contents, being burned. I, therefore, a helpless woman whom you have cruelly wronged, address you, a Major-General of the United States army, and demand why this was done? What was my offence? My husband was absent, an exile. He had never been a politician or in any way engaged in the struggle now going on, his age preventing. This fact your chief of staff, David Strother, could have told you. The house was built by my father, a Revolutionary soldier, who served the whole seven years for your independence. There was I born; there the sacred dead repose. It was my house and my home, and there has your niece (Miss Griffith), who has tarried among us all this horrid war up to the present time, met with all kindness and hospitality at my hands. Was it for this that you turned me, my young daughter, and little son out upon the world without a shelter? Or was it because my husband is the grandson of the Revolutionary patriot and "rebel," Richard Henry Lee, and the near kinsman of the noblest of Christian warriors, the greatest of generals, Robert E. Lee? Heaven's blessing be upon his head forever. You and your Government have failed to conquer, subdue, or match him; and disappointment, rage, and malice find vent on the helpless and inoffensive.

Hyena-like, you have torn my heart to pieces! for all hallowed memories clustered around that homestead, and demon-like, you have done it without even the pretext of revenge, for I never saw or harmed you. Your office is not to lead, like a brave man and soldier, your men to fight in the ranks of war, but your work has been to separate yourself from all danger, and with your incendiary band steal unaware upon helpless women and children, to insult and destroy. Two fair homes did you yesterday ruthlessly lay in ashes, giving not a moment's warning to the startled inmates of your wicked purpose; turning mothers and children out of doors, you are execrated by your own men for the cruel work you give them to do.

In the case of Colonel A. R. Boteler, both father and mother were far away. Any heart but that of Captain Martindale (and yours) would have been touched by that little circle, comprising a widowed daughter just risen from her bed of illness, her three fatherless babies—the oldest not five years old—and her heroic sister. I repeat, any man would have been touched at that sight but Captain Martindale. One might as well hope to find mercy and feeling in the heart of a wolf bent on his prey of young lambs, as to search for such qualities in his bosom. You have chosen well your agent for such deeds, and doubtless will promote him.

A colonel of the Federal army has stated that you deprived forty of your officers of their commands because they refused to carry on your malignant mischief. All honor to their names for this, at least! They are men; they have human hearts and blush for such a commander!

I ask who that does not wish infamy and disgrace attached to him forever would serve under you? Your name will stand on history's page as the Hunter of weak women, and innocent children, the Hunter to destroy defenceless villages and refined and beautiful homes—to torture afresh the agonized hearts of widows; the Hunter of Africa's poor sons and daughters, to lure them on to ruin and death of soul and body; the Hunter with the relentless heart of a wild beast, the face of a fiend and the form of a man. Oh, Earth, behold the monster! Can I say, "God forgive you?" No prayer can be offered for you. Were it possible for human lips to raise your name heavenward, angels would thrust the foul thing back again, and demons claim their own. The curses of thousands, the scorns of the manly and upright, and the hatred of the true and honorable, will follow you and yours through all time, and brand your name infamy! infamy!

Again, I demand why you have burned my home? Answer as you must answer before the Searcher of all hearts, why have you added this cruel, wicked deed to your many crimes?

SHERMAN'S BUMMERS

[E. J. Hale, Jr.]

FAYETTEVILLE, N. C., *July 31st, 1865.*

MY DEAR GENERAL:

It would be impossible to give you an adequate idea of the destruction of property in this good old town. It may not be an average instance, but it is one, the force of whose truth we feel only too fully. My father's property, before the war, was easily convertible into about $85,000 to $100,000 in specie. He has not now a particle of property which will bring him a dollar of income. His office, with everything in it, was burned by Sherman's order. Slocum, who executed the order, with a number of other generals, sat on the veranda of a hotel opposite watching the progress of the flames, while they hobnobbed over wines stolen from our cellar. A fine brick building adjacent, also belonging to my father, was burned at the same time. The cotton factory, of which he was a large shareholder, was burned, while his bank, railroad, and other stocks are worse than worthless, for the bank stock, at least, may bring him in debt, as the stockholders are responsible. In fact, he has nothing left, besides the ruins of his town buildings and a few town lots which promise to be of little value hereafter, in this desolated town, and are of no value at present, save his residence, which (with brother's house) Sherman made a great parade of saving from a mob (composed of corps and division commanders, a nephew of Henry Ward Beecher, and so on down,) by sending to each house an officer of his staff, after my brother's had been pillaged and my father's to some extent. By some accidental good fortune, however, my mother secured a guard before the "bummers" had made much progress in the house, and to this circumstance we are indebted for our daily food, several months' supply of which my father had hid the night before he left, in the upper rooms of the house, and the greater part of which was saved.

You have, doubtless, heard of Sherman's "bummers." The Yankees would have you believe that they were only the straggling pillagers usually found with all armies. Several letters written by officers of Sherman's army, intercepted near this town, give this the lie. In some of these letters were descriptions of the whole burning process, and from them it appears that it was a regularly organized system, under the authority of General Sherman himself; that one-fifth of the proceeds fell to General Sherman, another fifth to the other general officers, another fifth to the line officers, and the remaining two-fifths to the enlisted men. There were pure silver bummers, plated-ware bummers, jewelry bummers, women's clothing bummers, provision bummers, and, in fine, a bummer or bummers for every kind of stealable thing. No bummer of one specialty interfering with the stealables of another. A pretty picture of a conquering army, indeed, but true.

REMINISCENCES OF THE WAR TIMES—A LETTER

[B. Winston, in Confederate Scrap-Book.]

SIGNAL HILL, *February 27th.*

MY DEAR ——:

Your very kind letter received. I delayed perhaps too long replying. I have hunted up a few little things. We are so unfortunate as to have nearly all our war relics burnt in an outhouse, so I have little left unless I took what I remember. We were left so bare of everything at that time. Our only pokers and tongs were pokers and ramrods; old canteens came into domestic service; we made our shoes of parts of old canvas tents, and blackened them with elderberry juice (the only ink we could command was elderberry juice); we plaited our hats of straw (I have a straw-splinter now, for which I gave $13; it did good service); the inside corn-shuck made dainty bonnets; sycamore balls, saturated with grease, made excellent tapers, though nothing superseded the time-honored lightwood knots.

The Confederate army was camped around us for months together. We often had brilliant assemblages of officers. On one occasion, when all went merry as a marriage-bell, and uniformed officers and lovely girls wound in and out in the dance, a sudden stillness fell—few words, sudden departures. The enemy were in full force, trying to effect a crossing at a strategic point. We were left at daybreak in the Federal camp, a sharp engagement around us—the beginning of the seven days' fight around Richmond. It was a bright, warm day in May. An unusual stillness brooded over everything. A few officers came and went, looking grave and important. In a short time, from a dense body of pines near us, curled the blue smoke, and volley after volley of musketry succeeded in sharp succession, the sharp, shrill scream of flying shells falling in the soft green of the growing wheat. Not long, and each opposing army emerged from ambush and stood in the battle's awful array. Our own forces (mostly North Carolinians) fell back into a railroad cut. The tide of battle swept past us, but the day was lost to us. At evening they brought our dead and wounded and made a hospital of our house. Then came the amputating surgeon to finish what the bullet had failed to do. Arms and legs lay in a promiscuous heap on our back piazza.

On another occasion I saw a sudden surprise in front of our house. A regiment of soldiers, under General Rosser's command, were camped around us. It was high, blazing noon. The soldiers, suspecting nothing, were in undress, lying down under every available shadow, when a sudden volley and shout made every man spring to his feet. The enemy were all around them, and panic was amongst our men; they were running, but as they rose a little knoll every man turned, formed, and fired. I saw some poor fellows fall.

AUNT MYRA AND THE HOE-CAKE

[In Our Women in the War, pages 419-420.]

Another instance was that of an old lady. Small and fragile-looking, with soft and gentle manners, it seemed as if a whiff of wind might have blown her away, and she was not one who was likely to tempt the torrent of a ruffian's wrath. But how often can we judge of appearances, for in that tiny body was a spirit as strong and fearless as the bravest in the land. The war had been a bitter reality to her. One son had been brought home shattered by a shell, and for long months she had seen him in the agony which no human tongue can describe; while another, in the freshness of his young manhood, had been numbered with the slain. She was a widow, and having the care of two orphan grandchildren upon her, was experiencing the same difficulty in obtaining food that we were. One morning she had made repeated efforts to get something cooked, but failed as often as she tried, for just as soon as it was ready to be eaten in walked a Federal soldier and marched off with it, expostulations or entreaties availing naught. Finally, after some difficulty, a little corn meal was found which was mixed with a hoe-cake and set in the oven to bake. Determined not to lose this, Aunt Myra, the lady in question, took her seat before the fire and vowed she would not leave the spot until the bread was safe in her own hands. Scarcely had she done so when, as usual, a soldier made his appearance, and, seeing the contents of the oven, took his seat on the opposite side and coolly waited its baking. I have since thought what a picture for a painter that would make—upon one side the old lady with the proud, high-born face of a true Southern gentlewoman, but, alas! stamped with the seal of care and sorrow; and upon the other, the man, strong in his assumed power, both intent upon that one point of interest, a baking hoe-cake. When it had reached the desired shade of browning, Aunt Myra leaned forward to take possession, but ere she could do so that other hand was before her and she saw it taken from her. Rising to her feet and drawing her small figure to its fullest height, the old lady's pent up feelings burst forth, and she gave expression to the indignation which "this last act caused to overflow."

"You thieving scoundrel!" she cried in her gathering wrath. "You would take the very last crust from the orphans' mouths and doom them to starvation before your very eyes."

Then, before the astonished man could recover himself, with a quick movement she had snatched the bread back again. Scarcely had she got possession, however, when a revulsion of feeling took place, and, breaking it in two, tossed them at him in the scorn which filled her soul as she said: "But if your heart is hard enough to take it, then you may have it."

She threw them with such force that one of the hot pieces struck him in the face, the other immediately following. Strange to say, he did not resent her treatment of him; but it was too much for Aunt Myra's excited feelings when he picked up the bread, and commenced munching upon it in the most unconcerned manner possible. Again snatching it from him, she flung it far out of the window, where it lay rolling in dirt, crying as she did so: "Indeed, you shan't eat it; if I can't have it, then you shan't."

"THE CORN WOMAN"

[Our Women in the War, page 276.]

"The corn woman" was a feature of the times. The men in the counties north of us were mostly farmers, owning small farms which they worked with the assistance of the family. Few owned slaves, and they planted garden crops chiefly. The men were now in the army, and good soldiers many of them made. During the last two years, for various reasons, many of the wives of these soldiers failed in making a crop, and were sent with papers from the probate judges to the counties south to get corn. No doubt these were really needy, and they were supplied abundantly, and then, thinking it an easy way to make a living, others not needing help came. They neglected to plant crops, as it was far more easy to beg all the corn they wanted than to work it. Women whose husbands were at home, who never had been in the army, young girls and old women came in droves—all railroad cars and steamboats were filled with "corn women."

They came twenty and thirty together, got off at the stations and landings for miles, visiting every plantation and never failing to get their sacks filled and sent to the depot or river for them. Some had bedticks; one came to me with a sack over two yards long and one yard wide that would have held ten bushels of corn, and she had several like it. They soon became perfect nuisances. When you objected to giving they abused you; they no longer brought papers; when we had no corn to spare we gave them money, which they said they would rather have. It would save the trouble of toting corn, and they could buy it at home for the money. I once gave them twenty-five dollars, all I had in the house at the time. "Well, this won't go to buy much corn, but as far as it do go we's obliged to you," were the thanks. I saw a party of them on a steamboat counting their money. They had hundreds of dollars and a quantity of corn. The boats and railroads took them free. I was afterward told by a railroad official that their husbands and fathers met them at the depot and either sold the corn or took it to the stills and made it into whiskey. They hated the army and all in it and despised the negro, who returned the compliment with interest. The very sight of a corn woman made them and the overseers angry. They regarded them as they did the army worm.

GENERAL ATKINS AT CHAPEL HILL

[In Last Ninety Days of the War, page 33.]

While the command of General Atkins remained in Chapel Hill—a period of nearly three weeks—the same work, with perhaps some mitigation, was going on in the country round us, and around the city of Raleigh, which had marked the progress of the Federal armies all through the South. Planters having large families of white and black were left without food, forage, cattle, or change of clothing. Being in camp so long, bedding became an object with the marauders; and many wealthy families were stripped of what the industry of years had accumulated in that line. Much of what was so wantonly taken was as wantonly destroyed and squandered among the prostitutes and negroes who haunted the camps. As to Raleigh, though within the corporate limits, no plundering of the houses was allowed; yet in the suburbs and the country the policy of permitting it to its widest extent was followed.

TWO SPECIMEN CASES OF DESERTION

[Heroes in the Furnace; Southern Historical Papers.]

We by no means excuse or palliate desertion to the enemy, which is universally recognized as one of the basest crimes known to military law; but most of the desertions from the Confederate army occurred during the latter part of the war, and many of them were brought about by the most heartrending letters from home, telling of suffering, and even starving families, and we cannot class these cases with those who deserted to join the enemy, or to get rid of the hardships and dangers of the army. Some most touching cases came under our observation, but we give only the following incidents as illustrating many other cases.

A distinguished major-general in the Western army has given us this incident. A humble man but very gallant soldier from one of the Gulf States, had enlisted on the assurance of a wealthy planter that he would see his young wife and child should not lack for support.

The brave fellow had served his country faithfully, until one day he received a letter from his wife, saying that the rich neighbor who had promised to keep her from want now utterly refused to give or to sell her anything to eat, unless she would submit to the basest proposals which he was persistently making her, and that unless he could come home she saw nothing but starvation before her and his child. The poor fellow at once applied for a furlough, and was refused. He then went to the gallant soldier who is my informant and stated the case in full, and told him that he must and would go home if he was shot for it the day he returned. The general told him while he could not give him a permit, he did not blame him for his determination.

The next day he was reported "absent without leave," and was hurrying to his home. He moved his wife and child to a place of safety and made provision for their support. Then returning to the neighborhood of his home, he caught the miscreant who had tried to pollute the hearthstone of one who was risking his life for him, dragged him into the woods, tied him to a tree, and administered to him a flogging that he did not soon forget. The brave fellow then hurried back to his regiment, joined his comrades just as they were going into battle, and behaved with such conspicuous gallantry as to make all forget that he had ever, even for a short time, been a "deserter."

The other incident which we shall give was related by General C. A. Battle, in a speech at Tuscumbia, Ala., and is as follows:

During the winter of 1862-3 it was my fortune to be president of one of the courts-martial of the Army of Northern Virginia. One bleak December morning, while the snow covered the ground and the winds howled around our camp, I left my bivouac fire to attend the session of the court. Winding for miles along uncertain paths, I at length arrived at the court-ground at Round Oak church. Day after day it had been our duty to try the gallant soldiers of that army charged with violations of military law; but never had I on any previous occasion been greeted by such anxious spectators as on that morning awaited the opening of the court. Case after case was disposed of, and at length the case of "The Confederate States vs. Edward Cooper" was called; charge, desertion. A low murmur rose spontaneously from the battle-scarred spectators as a young artilleryman rose from the prisoner's bench, and, in response to the question, "Guilty or not guilty?" answered, "Not guilty."

The judge advocate was proceeding to open the prosecution, when the court, observing that the prisoner was unattended by counsel, interposed and inquired of the accused, "Who is your counsel?"

He replied, "I have no counsel."

Supposing that it was his purpose to represent himself before the court, the judge-advocate was instructed to proceed. Every charge and specification against the prisoner was sustained.

The prisoner was then told to introduce his witnesses.

He replied, "I have no witnesses."

Astonished at the calmness with which he seemed to be submitting to what he regarded as inevitable fate, I said to him, "Have you no defence? Is it possible that you abandoned your comrades and deserted your colors in the presence of the enemy without any reason?"

He replied, "There was a reason, but it will not avail me before a military court."

I said, "Perhaps you are mistaken; you are charged with the highest crime known to military law, and it is your duty to make known the causes that influenced your actions."

For the first time his manly form trembled and his blue eyes swam in tears. Approaching the president of the court, he presented a letter, saying, as he did so, "There, colonel, is what did it." I opened the letter, and in a moment my eyes filled with tears.

It was passed from one to another of the court until all had seen it, and those stern warriors who had passed with Stonewall Jackson through a hundred battles wept like little children. Soon as I sufficiently recovered my self-possession, I read the letter as the prisoner's defence. It was in these words:

> My Dear Edward: I have always been proud of you, and since your connection with the Confederate army I have been prouder of you than ever before. I would not have you do anything wrong for the world; but before God, Edward, unless you come home we must die! Last night I was aroused by little Eddie's crying. I called and said, "What's the matter, Eddie?" and he said, "Oh, mamma, I'm so hungry!" And Lucy, Edward, your darling Lucy, she never complains, but she is growing thinner and thinner every day. And before God, Edward, unless you come home we must die.
>
> Your Mary.

Turning to the prisoner, I asked, "What did you do when you received this letter?"

He replied, "I made application for a furlough, and it was rejected; again I made application, and it was rejected; and that night, as I wandered backward and forward in the camp, thinking of my home, with the mild eyes of Lucy looking up to me, and the burning words of Mary sinking in my brain, I was no longer the Confederate soldier, but I was the father of Lucy and the husband of Mary, and I would have passed those lines if every gun in the battery had fired upon me. I went to my home. Mary ran out to meet me, her angel arms embraced me, and she whispered, 'O, Edward, I am so happy! I am so glad you got your furlough!' She must have felt me shudder, for she turned pale as death, and, catching her breath at every word, she said, 'Have you come without your furlough? O, Edward, Edward, go back! go back! Let me and my children go down together to the grave, but O, for heaven's sake, save the honor of our name! And here I am, gentlemen, not brought here by military power, but in obedience to the command of Mary, to abide the sentence of your court."

Every officer of that court-martial felt the force of the prisoner's words. Before them stood, in beatific vision, the eloquent pleader for the husband's and father's wrongs; but they had been trained by their great leader, Robert E. Lee, to tread the path of duty though the lightning's flash scorched the ground beneath their feet, and each in his turn pronounced the verdict: "Guilty." Fortunately for humanity, fortunately for the Confederacy, the proceedings of the court were reviewed by the commanding-general, and upon the record was written:

> Headquarters Army of Northern Virginia.
>
> The finding of the court is approved. The prisoner is pardoned, and will report to his company.

R. E. Lee, *General.*

During a subsequent battle, when shot and shell were falling "like torrents from the mountain cloud," my attention was directed to the fact that one of our batteries was being silenced by the concentrated fire of the enemy. When I reached the battery every gun but one had been dismantled, and by it stood a solitary soldier, with the blood streaming from his side. As he recognized me, he elevated his voice above the roar of battle, and said, "General, I have one shell left. Tell me, have I saved the honor of Mary and Lucy?" I raised my hat. Once more a Confederate shell went crashing through the ranks of the enemy, and the hero sank by his gun to rise no more.

SHERMAN IN SOUTH CAROLINA

[Cornelia B. Spencer, in Last Days of the War, pages 29-31.]

A letter dated Charleston, September 14, 1865, written by Rev. Dr. John Bachman, then pastor of the Lutheran Church in that city, presents many facts respecting the devastation and robberies by the enemy in South Carolina. So much as relates to the march of Sherman's army through parts of the State is here presented:

"When Sherman's army came sweeping through Carolina, leaving a broad track of desolation for hundreds of miles, whose steps were accompanied with fire, and sword, and blood, reminding us of the tender mercies of the Duke of Alva, I happened to be at Cash's Depot, 6 miles from Cheraw. The owner was a widow, Mrs. Ellerbe, 71 years of age. Her son, Colonel Cash, was absent. I witnessed the barbarities inflicted on the aged, the widow, and young and delicate females. Officers, high in command, were engaged tearing from the ladies their watches, their ear and wedding rings, the daguerreotypes of those they loved and cherished. A lady of delicacy and refinement, a personal friend, was compelled to strip before them, that they might find concealed watches and other valuables under her dress. A system of torture was practiced toward a weak, unarmed, and defenceless people which, as far as I know and believe, was universal throughout the whole course of that invading army. Before they arrived at a plantation, they inquired the names of the most faithful and trustworthy family servants; these were immediately seized, pistols were presented at their heads; with the most terrific curses, they were threatened to be shot if they did not assist them in finding buried treasures. If this did not succeed, they were tied up and cruelly beaten. Several poor creatures died under the infliction. The last resort was that of hanging, and the officers and men of the triumphant army of General Sherman were engaged in erecting gallows and hanging up these faithful and devoted servants. They were strung up until life was nearly extinct, when they were let down, suffered to rest awhile, then threatened and hung up again. It is not surprising that some should have been left hanging so long that they were taken down dead. Coolly and deliberately these hardened men proceeded on their way, as if they had perpetrated no crime, and as if the God of heaven would not pursue them with his vengeance. But it was not alone the poor blacks (to whom they professed to come as liberators) that were thus subjected to torture and death. Gentlemen of high character, pure and honorable and gray-headed, unconnected with the military, were dragged from their fields or beds, and subjected to this process of threats, beating, and hanging. Along the whole track of Sherman's army traces remain of the cruelty and inhumanity practiced on the aged and the defenceless. Some of those who were hung up died under the rope, while their cruel murderers have not only been left unreproached and unhung, but have been hailed as heroes andpatriots."

OLD NORTH STATE'S TRIALS

[Cornelia P. Spencer, in Last Ninety Days of the War, pages 95-97.]

By January, 1865, there was very little room for "belief" of any sort in the ultimate success of the Confederacy. All the necessaries of life were scarce, and were held at fabulous and still increasing prices. The great freshet of January 10th, which washed low grounds, carried off fences, bridges, mills, and tore up railroads all through the central part of the State, at once doubled the price of corn and flour. Two destructive fires in the same months, which consumed great quantities of government stores at Charlotte and at Salisbury, added materially to the general gloom and depression. The very elements seemed to have enlisted against us. And soon, with no great surplus of food from the wants of her home population, North Carolina found herself called upon to furnish supplies for two armies. Early in January an urgent and most pressing appeal was made for Lee's army; and the people, most of whom knew not where they would get bread for their children in three months' time, responded nobly, as they had always done to any call for "the soldiers." Few were the hearts in any part of the land that did not thrill at the thought that those who were fighting for us were in want of food. From a humble cabin on the hill-side, where the old brown spinning-wheel and the rude loom were the only breastworks against starvation, up through all grades of life, there were none who did not feel a deep and tender, almost heartbreaking solicitude for our noble soldiers. For them the last barrel of flour was divided, the last luxury in homes that had once abounded cheerfully surrendered. Every available resource was taxed, every expedient of domestic economy was put into practice—as, indeed, had been done all along; but our people went to work even yet with fresh zeal. I speak now of central North Carolina, where many families of the highest respectability and refinement lived for months on corn-bread, sorghum, and peas; where meat was seldom seen on the table, tea and coffee never, where dried apples and peaches were a luxury; where children went barefoot through winter, and ladies made their own shoes, and wove their own homespuns; where the carpets were cut up into blankets, and window-curtains and sheets were torn up for hospital uses; where the soldiers' socks were knit day and night, while for home service clothes were twice turned, and patches were patched again; and all this continually, and with an energy and a cheerfulness that may well be called heroic.

There were localities in the State where a few rich planters boasted of having "never felt the war;" there were ladies whose wardrobes encouraged the blockade-runners, and whose tables were still heaped with all the luxuries they had ever known. There were such doubtless in every State in the

Confederacy. I speak not now of these, but of the great body of our citizens—the middle class as to fortune, generally the highest as to cultivation and intelligence—these were the people who denied themselves and their little ones, that they might be able to send relief to the gallant men who lay in the trenches before Petersburg, and were even then living on crackers and parched corn.

The fall of Fort Fisher and the occupation of Wilmington, the failure of the peace commission, and the unchecked advance of Sherman's army northward from Savannah, were the all-absorbing topics of discussion with our people during the first months of the year 1865. The tide of war was rolling in upon us. Hitherto our privations, heavily as they had borne upon domestic comfort, had been light in comparison with those of the people in the States actually invaded by the Federal armies; but now we were to be qualified to judge, by our own experience, how far their trials and losses had exceeded ours. What the fate of our pleasant towns and villages and of our isolated farm-houses would be we could easily read by the light of the blazing roof-trees that lit up the path of the advancing army. General Sherman's principles were well known, for they had been carefully laid down by him in his letter to the Mayor of Atlanta, September, 1864, and had been thoroughly put in practice by him in his further progress since. To shorten the war by increasing its severity: this was his plan—simple, and no doubt to a certain extent effective.

SHERMAN IN NORTH CAROLINA

[Cornelia P. Spencer, in Last Ninety Days of the War, pages 214-215.]

General Sherman's reputation had preceded him, and the horror and dismay with which his approach was anticipated in the country were fully warranted. The town itself was in a measure defended, so to speak, by General Schofield's preoccupation; but in the vicinity and for twenty miles around the country was most thoroughly plundered and stripped of food, forage, and private property of every description. One of the first of General Sherman's own acts, after his arrival, was of peculiar hardship. One of the oldest and most venerable citizens of the place, with a family of sixteen or eighteen children and grandchildren, most of them females, was ordered, on a notice of a few hours, to vacate his house, which of course was done. The gentleman was nearly 80 years old, and in very feeble health. The outhouses, fences, grounds, etc., were destroyed, and the property greatly damaged during its occupation by the general. Not a farm-house in the country but was visited and wantonly robbed. Many were burned, and very many, together with outhouses, were pulled down and hauled into camps for use. Generally not a live animal, not a morsel of food of any description was left, and in many instances not a bed or sheet or change of clothing for man, woman, or child. It was most heartrending to see daily crowds of country people, from three score and ten years down to the unconscious infant carried in its mother's arms, coming into the town to beg food and shelter, to ask alms from those who had despoiled them. Many of these families lived for days on parched corn, on peas boiled in water without salt, or scraps picked up about the camps. The number of carriages, buggies, and wagons brought in is almost incredible. They kept for their own use what they wished, and burned or broke up the rest. General Logan and staff took possession of seven rooms in the house of John C. Slocumb, esq., the gentleman of whose statements I avail myself. Every assurance of protection was given to the family by the quartermaster; but many indignities were offered to the inmates, while the house was effectually stripped as any other of silver plate, watches, wearing apparel, and money. Trunks and bureaus were broken open and the contents abstracted. Not a plank or rail or post or paling was left anywhere upon the grounds, while fruit trees, vines, and shrubbery were wantonly destroyed. These officers remained nearly three weeks, occupying the family beds, and when they left the bed-clothes also departed.

It is very evident that General Sherman entered North Carolina with the confident expectation of receiving a welcome from its Union-loving citizens. In Major Nichol's "Story of the Great March," he remarks, on crossing the line which divides South from North Carolina:

> The conduct of the soldiers is perceptibly changed. I have seen no evidence of plundering; the men keep their ranks closely; and more remarkable yet, not a single column of the fire or smoke, which a few days ago marked the positions of the heads of columns, can be seen upon the horizon. Our men seem to understand that they are entering a State which has suffered for its Union sentiment, and whose inhabitants would gladly embrace the old flag again if they can have the opportunity, which we mean to give them.

But the town meeting and war resolutions of the people of Fayetteville, the fight in her streets, and Governor Vance's proclamation, soon undeceived them, and their amiable dispositions were speedily corrected and abandoned.

MRS. VANCE'S TRUNK—GENERAL PALMER'S GALLANTRY

[Cornelia B. Spenser, in Southern Historical Papers.]

On the road from Statesville a part of the command was dispatched in the direction of Lincolnton, under General Palmer. Of this officer the same general account is given as of General Stoneman, that he exhibited a courtesy and forbearance which reflected honor on his uniform, and have given him a just claim to the respect and gratitude of our western people. The following pleasant story is a sample of his way of carrying on war with ladies: Mrs. Vance, the wife of the governor, had taken refuge, from Raleigh, in Statesville with her children. On the approach of General Stoneman's army, she sent off to Lincolnton, for safety, a large trunk filled with valuable clothing, silver, etc., and among other things two thousand dollars in gold, which had been entrusted to her care by one of the banks. This trunk was captured on the road by Palmer's men, who of course rejoiced exceedingly over this finding of spoil, more especially as belonging to the rebel General Vance. Its contents were speedily appropriated and scattered. But the circumstances coming to General Palmer's knowledge, within an hour's time he had every article and every cent collected and replaced in the trunk, which he then immediately sent back under guard to Mrs. Vance with his compliments. General Palmer was aiming for Charlotte when he was met by couriers announcing news of the armistice.

THE EVENTFUL THIRD OF APRIL

[Correspondent of New York *Herald*, Southern Historical Papers.]

It was known about this time to the people of Richmond that the negro troops in the Union army had requested General Grant to give them the honor of being the first to enter the fallen capital. The fact gave rise to a fear that they would unite with the worst class of resident negroes and burn and sack the city. When, therefore, the black smoke and lurid flames arose on that eventful 3d of April, caused by the Confederates themselves, the terror-stricken inhabitants at first thought their fears were to be realized, but were soon relieved when they saw the manful fight made by many of the negroes and Union troops to suppress the flames. At no time did they fear their own servants; indeed, I was afterwards assured that the many negroes who filled the streets and welcomed the Union troops would have resisted any attack upon the households of their old masters.

The behavior of many of the old family servants was very marked in the care and great solicitude shown by them for their masters during this trying period. As an amusing instance of this, I will tell you this incident:

An old lady had a very bright, good-looking maid servant, to whom some of the Union officers had shown considerable attention by taking her out driving. The girl came in one morning and asked her old mistress if she would not take a drive with her in the hack which stood at the door, with her sable escort in waiting. Doubtless this was done not in a spirit of irony, but really in feeling for her old mistress.

In another family, on the day the troops entered the city, when all the males had fled, leaving several young ladies with their mother alone, “Old Mammy,” the faithful nurse, was posted at the front door with the baby in her arms, while the trembling females locked themselves in an upper room. When the hurrahing, wild Union troops passed along, many straggled into the house and asked where the white ladies were.

“Old Mammy” replied: “Dis is de only white lady; all de rest ar’ culled ladies,” and she laughed and tossed up the baby, which seemed to please the soldiers, who chucked the baby and passed on.

Spartan Richmond Ladies

The ladies of Richmond who bore such an active part on that terrible 3d of April, many of whom with blackened faces mounted the tops of their roofs, and with their faithful servants swept off the flying firebrands as they were wafted over the city, or bore in their arms the sick to places of safety, or sent words of comfort to their husbands and their sons who were battling against the flames—these were the true women of the South, who had never given up the hope of final victory until Lee laid down his sword at Appomattox. They were calm even in defeat; and though strong men lost their reason and shed tears in maniacal grief over the destruction of their beautiful city, yet her noble women still stood unflinching, facing all dangers with heroism that has never been equalled since the days of Sparta.

Sauntering along the street, making a few purchases preparatory to leaving the doomed city, I was suddenly accosted by a friend, who with trembling voice and terrified countenance exclaimed:

“Sir, I have just heard that the Petersburg and Weldon railroad will be cut by the Yankees in a few days. My daughter, who is in North Carolina, will be made a prisoner. I will give all I have to get her home.”

I saw the intense anguish of the father, and learning that he could not get a pass to go through Petersburg, I said, “Mr. T——, if you will pay my expenses, I will have your daughter here in two days.”

He overwhelmed me with thanks, crammed my pockets full of Confederate notes, filled my haversack with rations for several days, and I left next morning for Petersburg. The train not being allowed to enter the city, we had to make a mile or more in a conveyance of some kind at an exorbitant price. Learning that the Weldon train ran only at night for fear of the Yankee batteries, which were alarmingly near, I had time to inspect the city. I found here a marked contrast to Richmond. As I passed along its streets, viewing the marks of shot and shell on every side, hearing now and then the heavy, sullen boom of the enemy's guns, seeing on every hand the presence of war, I noticed its business men had, nevertheless, a calm, determined look. Its streets were filled with women and children, who seemed to know no fear, though at any moment a shrieking shell might dash among them, but each eye would turn in loving confidence to the Confederate flag which floated over the headquarters of General Lee, feeling that they were secure as long as he was there.

That night, when all was quiet and darkness reigned, with not a light to be seen, our train quietly slipped out of the city, like a blockade-runner passing the batteries. The passengers viewed in silence the flashing of the guns as they were trying to locate the train. It was a moment of intense excitement, but on we crept, until at last the captain came along with a lantern and said, "All right!" and we breathed more freely; but from the proximity of the batteries, I surmised that it would not be "all right" many days hence.

Hastening on my journey, I found the young lady, and telling her she must face the Yankee batteries if she would see her home, I found her even enthusiastic at the idea, and we hastily left, though under protest of her friends.

Returning by the same route—which, indeed, was the only one now left—we approached to within five miles of Petersburg and waited for darkness. The lights were again extinguished, the passengers warned to tuck their heads low, which in many cases was done by lying flat on the floor, and then we began the ordeal, moving very slowly, sometimes halting, at every moment fearing a shell from the belching batteries, which had heard the creaking of the train and were "feeling" for our position. The glare and the boom of the guns, the dead silence broken only by a sob from some terrified heart, all filled up a few moments of time never to be forgotten.

But we entered the city safely just as the moon was rising, and the next morning I handed my friend his daughter. A few days after the batteries closed the gap on the Weldon road, cutting off Petersburg and Richmond from the South, and compelling General Lee to prepare for retreat.

THE FEDERALS ENTER RICHMOND

[Phoebe Y. Pember.]

Before the day was over the public buildings were occupied by the enemy, and the minds of the citizens relieved from all fear of molestation. The hospitals were attended to, the ladies being still allowed to nurse and care for their own wounded; but rations could not be drawn yet, the obstructions in the

James River preventing the transports from coming up to the city. In a few days they arrived, and food was issued to those in need. It had been a matter of pride among the Southerners to boast that they had never seen a greenback, so the entrance of the Federal army had thus found them entirely unprepared with gold and silver currency. People who had boxes of Confederate money and were wealthy the day previously looked around in vain for wherewithal to buy a loaf of bread. Strange exchanges were made on the street of tea and coffee, flour, and bacon. Those who were fortunate in having a stock of household necessaries were generous in the extreme to their less wealthy neighbors, but the destitution was terrible. The sanitary commission shops were opened, and commissioners appointed by the Federals to visit among the people and distribute orders to draw rations, but to effect this, after receiving tickets, required so many appeals to different officials, that decent people gave up the effort. Besides, the musty cornmeal and strong codfish were not appreciated by fastidious stomachs; few gently nurtured could relish such unfamiliar food.

But there was no assimilation between the invaders and invaded. In the daily newspapers a notice had appeared that the military bands would play in the beautiful capitol grounds every afternoon, but when the appointed hour arrived, except the Federal officers, musicians and soldiers, not a white face was to be seen. The negroes crowded every bench and path. The next week another notice was issued that the colored population would not be admitted; and then the absence of everything and anything feminine was appalling. The entertainers went alone to their own entertainment. The third week still another notice appeared: "Colored nurses were to be admitted with their white charges," and lo, each fortunate white baby received the cherished care of a dozen finely dressed black ladies, the only drawback being that in two or three days the music ceased altogether, the entertainers feeling at last the ingratitude of the subjugated people.

Despite their courtesy of manner—for, however despotic the acts, the Federal authorities maintained a respectful manner—the newcomers made no advance toward fraternity. They spoke openly and warmly of their sympathy with the sufferings of the South, but committed and advocated acts that the hearers could not recognize as "military necessities." Bravely-dressed Federal officers met their former old classmates from colleges and military institutions and inquired after the relatives to whose houses they had ever been welcome in days of yore, expressing a desire to "call and see them;" while the vacant chairs, rendered vacant by Federal bullets, stood by the hearth of the widow and bereaved mother. They could not be made to understand that their presence was painful. There were but few men in the city at this time; but the women of the South still fought their battles for them: fought it resentfully, calmly, but silently. Clad in their mourning garments, overcome, but hardly subdued, they sat within their desolate homes, or if compelled to leave that shelter went on their errands to church or hospital with veiled faces and swift steps. By no sign or act did the possessors of their fair city know that they were even conscious of their presence. If they looked in their faces they saw them not; they might have supposed themselves a phantom army. There was no stepping aside with affectation to avoid the contact of dress; no feigned humility in giving the inside of the walk; they simply totally ignored their presence.

SOMEBODY'S DARLING

[In Richmond During the War, pages 152-154.]

Our best and brightest young men were passing away. Many of them, the most of them, were utter strangers to us; but the wounded soldier ever found a warm place in our hearts, and they were strangers no more. A Southern lady has written some beautiful lines, suggested by the death of a youthful soldier in one of our hospitals. So deeply touching is the sentiment, and such the exquisite pathos of the poetry, that we shall insert them in our memorial to those sad times. When all sentiment was well nigh crushed out, which courts the visit of the nurse, these lines sent a thrill of ecstasy to our hearts, and comfort and sweetness to the bereaved in many far-off homes of the South. Of "Somebody's Darling," she writes:

Into a ward of the whitewashed halls
  Where the dead and dying lay;
Wounded by bayonets, shells, and balls,
  Somebody's darling was borne one day.
Somebody's darling so young and so brave,
  Wearing yet on his sweet, pale face,
Soon to be laid in the dust of the grave,
  The lingering light of his boyhood's grace.
Matted and damp are the curls of gold,
  Kissing the snow of that fair youngbrow;
Pale are the lips of delicate mould,
  Somebody's darling is dyingnow!
Back from his beautiful blue-veined brow,

Brush the wandering waves of gold;
Cross his hands on his bosom now—
Somebody's darling is still and cold.
Kiss him once, for somebody's sake,
Murmur a prayer, soft and low.
One bright curl from its fair mates take,
They were somebody's pride, you know.
Somebody's hand hath rested there,
Was it a mother's, soft and white;
Or have the lips of a sister fair
Been baptized in their waves of light?
God knows best! He has somebody's love,
Somebody's heart enshrined him there;
Somebody wafted his name above,
Night and morn, on the wings of prayer.
Somebody wept when he marched away,
Looking so handsome, brave and grand!
Somebody's kiss on his forehead lay,
Somebody clung to his parting hand.
Somebody's waiting, and watching for him,
Yearning to hold him again to her heart,
And there he lies—with his blue eyes dim,
And his smiling, child-like lips apart!
Tenderly bury the fair young dead,
Pausing to drop o'er his grave a tear;
Carve on the wooden slab at his head,
"'Somebody's darling' is lying here!"

CHAPTER IV
THEIR PLUCK

FEMALE RECRUITING OFFICERS

[J. L. Underwood.]

The young women and girls brightly and cordially cheered every Confederate volunteer. Nothing was too good for him, and smiles of sisterly esteem and love met him at every turn. There was a sort of intoxication in the welcome and applause that everywhere greeted the young volunteer. To many it was full pay for the sacrifice. Many an expectant bride sadly but resolutely postponed marriage, and sent her affianced lover to the army.

"Wouldst thou have me love thee, dearest,

With a woman's proudest heart,

Which shall ever hold thee nearest,

Shrined in its inmost part?

"Listen then! My country's calling

On her sons to meet the foe!

Leave these groves of rose and myrtle;

Like young Koerner, scorn the turtle

When the eagle screams above."

But there were many young men who did not want to hear Koerner's war eagle scream. They wanted a battle, but they wanted to "smell it afar off." They believed in the righteousness of the war more strongly than anybody. Yes, many of them were the first to don the blue cockade of the "minute men;" that is, the militia organized with the avowed object of fighting on a moment's warning. They were ever so ready to be soldiers at home for a "minute," but held back when it came to volunteering for six months, a year, or three years. Then the young women would turn loose their little tongues, and their jeers and sarcasm would drive the skulker clear out of their society, and eventually in self-defense he would have to "jine the cavalry," or infantry one, to get away from the darts of woman's tongue. A hornet could not sting like that little tongue.

One of these girls was a lone sister, with many brothers, in a very wealthy family, which we will call the DeLanceys, in one of the richest counties of Alabama. A cavalry company had been organized and drilled for the war, but not a DeLancey's name was on the roll. The company was to leave the home camp for the front. The whole county gathered to cheer them and bid them good-bye. Presents and honors were showered upon the young patriots. The sister mentioned above owned a very fine favorite horse, named "Starlight," which she presented to the company in a touching little speech, which brought tears to many eyes, and which wound up with the following apostrophe, "Farewell, Starlight! I may never see you again; but, thank God, you are the bravest of the DeLanceys."

All through the war cowards were between two fires, that of the Federals at the front and that of the women in the rear.

MRS. SUSAN ROY CARTER

[Thomas Nelson Page.]

Old Mathews and Gloucester, Virginia, as they are affectionately termed by those who knew them in the old times, were filled with colonial families and were the home of a peculiarly refined and aristocratic society. Miss Roy was the daughter of William H. Roy, esq., of "Green Plains," Mathews county, and of Anne Seddon, a sister of Hon. James A. Seddon, Secretary of War of the Confederate States. She was a noted beauty and belle, even in a society that was known throughout Virginia for its charming and beautiful women. Her loveliness, radiant girlhood, and early womanhood is still talked of among the survivors of that time. Old men, who have seen the whole order of society in which they spent their youths pass from the scene, still refresh themselves with the memory of her brilliant beauty and of her gracious charms. She was the centre and idol of that circle.

In 1855, on November 7th, she gave her hand and heart to Dr. Thomas H. Carter, esq., of Shirley, and from that time to the day of her death their life was one of the ideal unions which justify the saying that "marriages are made in heaven." "It has always been a honeymoon with us," he used to say. The young couple almost immediately settled at "Pampatike," on the Pamunkey, an old colonial estate. Here Mrs. Carter lived for thirty-four years, occupied in the duties of mistress of a great plantation, dispensing that gracious hospitality which made it noted even in Old Virginia; shedding the light of a beautiful life on all about her, and exemplifying in herself the character to which the South points with pride and affection as a refutation of every adverse criticism.

Such a plantation was a world in itself, and the life upon it was such as to entail on the master and mistress labors and responsibilities such as are not often produced under any other conditions. In addition to the demands of hospitality, which were exacting and constant, the conduct of such a large establishment, with the care of over one hundred and fifty servants, whose eyes were ever turned to their mistress, called forth the exercise of the highest powers from those who felt themselves answerable to the Great Master of All for the full performance of their duty. No one ever performed this duty with more divine devotion than did this young mistress. She was at once the friend and the servant of every soul on the place. Mrs. Carter was a fine illustration of the rare quality of the character formed by such conditions. In sickness and in health she watched over, looked after, and cared for all within her province.

It is the boast of the South, and one founded on truth, that when during the war the men were withdrawn from the plantations to do their duty on the field, the women rose to the full measure of every demand, filling often, under new conditions that would have tried the utmost powers of the men themselves, a place to which only men had been supposed equal.

When, on the outbreak of war, her husband was among the first who took the field as a captain of artillery, Mrs. Carter took charge of the plantation and during all the stress of that trying period she conducted it with an ability that would have done honor to a man of the greatest experience. The Pampatike plantation, lying not far from West Point, the scene of so many operations during the war, was within the "debatable land" that lay between the lines and was alternately swept by both armies. The position was peculiarly delicate, and often called for the exercise of rare tact and courage on the part of the mistress. It was known to the enemy that her husband was a gallant and rising officer and a near relative of General Lee, and the plantation was a marked one.

On one occasion a small party of mounted Federal troops on a foraging expedition visited the place and were engaged in looting, when a party of Confederate cavalry suddenly appeared on the scene, and a brisk little skirmish took place in the garden and yard. The Federals were caught by surprise, and getting the worst of it, broke and retreated across the lawn, with the enemy close to their heels in hot chase. A Union trooper was shot from his horse and fell just in front of the house, but rising, tried to run on. Mrs. Carter, seeing his danger, rushed out, calling to him to come to her and she would protect him. Turning, he staggered to her, but though she sheltered him, his wound was mortal, and he died at her feet. The surprise and defeat of this party having been reported at West Point, a stronger force was sent up to wreak vengeance on the place. But on learning of Mrs. Carter's act in rushing out amid the flying bullets to save this man at the risk of her life, the officer in command posted a guard, and orders were given that the place should be henceforth respected.

The hospital service on the Confederate side during the war, as wretched as it was, without medicines or surgical appliances, would have been far more dreadful but for the devotion with which the Southern women consecrated themselves to it. Every woman was a nurse if she were within reach of wounds and sickness. Every house was a hospital if it was needed; and to their honor be it said that the principle enunciated by Dr. Dunant, and finally established in the creation of the Red Cross Society, found its exemplification here some time before the Geneva Congress. To them a wounded man of whatever side was sacred, and to his service they consecrated themselves. Unhappily, devotion, even as divine as theirs, could not make up for all.

At the battle of Seven Pines—"Fair Oaks"—Captain Carter's battery rendered such efficient service that the commanding general declared he would rather have commanded that battery that day than to have been President of the Confederate States. But the fame of the battery was won at the expense of about sixty per cent of its officers and men killed and wounded. The Carter plantation was within sound of the guns, and Mrs. Carter immediately constituted herself the nurse of the wounded men of her husband's battery. And from this time she was regarded by them as their guardian angel—an affection that was extended to her by all of the men of her husband's command, as he rose from rank to rank, until he became a colonel and acting chief of artillery in the last Valley campaign.

When the war closed nothing remained except the lands and a few buildings, but the energy of the master and mistress began from the first to build up the plantation again. The servants were free; the working force was broken up and scattered, yet large numbers of them, including all who were old and infirm, remained on the place and had to be cared for and fed. To this master and mistress alike applied all their abilities, with the result that defeat was turned into success and the place became known as one of the estates that had survived the destruction of war.

Having a family of young children, the best tutors were secured, and owing largely to the knowledge of the good influence to which the boys would be subjected under Mrs. Carter's roof, many applied to send their boys to them, and "Pampatike School" soon became known far beyond the limits of Virginia. Among those who have testified to the influence upon them of their life at Pampatike are men now nearing the top of every profession in many States.

It was at this period that the writer came to know her. And he can never forget the impression made on him by her—an impression that time and fuller knowledge of her only served to deepen. Of commanding and gracious presence, with a face of rare beauty and loveliness, and manners, whose charm can never be described, she might have been noble Brunhilda, softened and made sweet by the chastening influence of Christianity and unselfish love. No one that ever saw her could forget her. It was, indeed, the beautifying influences of a simple piety and devoted love that guided her life, which stamped their impress on that noble face. In every relation of life she was perfect. And the influence of such a life can never cease. Many besides her children rise up and call her blessed.

In closing this incomplete sketch of one whose life illustrated all that was best in life, and admits of justice in no sketch whatsoever, the writer feels that he cannot do better than to use the words of him who knew and loved her best:

> Every day an anthem of love and praise swells up from all over the land to do her honor. Old boys of Pampatike schooling, new boys of the University, girls and old people, recall her delight to make them happy and to give them pleasure. It was her greatest happiness to make others happy; for she was absolutely the most unselfish and generous being on earth. Her generosity was not always of abundance, for abundance was not always hers; but a generosity out of everything that she had.
>
> Her beautiful life has passed away, and is now only a memory, but a memory fraught and fragrant with all that is sweetest and loveliest and purest and best in noblest womanhood. Who that ever saw her can forget her noble and beautiful face, resplendent with all that was exalted and high-souled, gracious, and kindest to others—the Master's index to the heart within!

J. L. M. CURRY'S WOMEN CONSTITUENTS

[J. L. Underwood.]

Hon. J. L. M. Curry had ever since the war with Mexico been the idol of his district in Alabama, which kept him steadily in the United States Congress and sent him to the Confederate House of Representatives. Toward the latter part of the war in the Congressional campaign Mr. Curry found an opponent in Mayor Cruickshank, of Talladega. The latter skilfully played upon the hardships and hopelessness of the war and in some of the upper mountain counties considerable opposition to Mr. Curry was developed. At a gathering of the mountaineers, largely composed of women, Mr. Curry was appealing with his usual favor to his people to continue their efforts to secure the independence of the Confederacy and not to listen to any suggestion of submission to the Northern States. About the time his eloquence reached its highest point, up rose an old woman and hurled at him what struck him like a thunderbolt:

"I think it time for you to hush all your war talk. You go yonder to Richmond and sit up there in Congress and have a good time while our poor boys are being all killed; and if you are going to do anything it's time for you to stop this war."

In a moment up sprang another mountain woman. "Go on, Mr. Curry," said she. "Go on, you are right. We can never consent to give up our Southern cause. Don't listen to what this other woman says. I have sent five sons to the army. Three of them have fallen on the battlefield. The other two are at their post in the Virginia army and they will all stand by Lee to the last. This woman here hasn't but two sons and they had to be conscripted. One of them has deserted and it takes all of Lewis's Cavalry to keep the other one in ranks. Go on, Mr. Curry. We are with you." And Curry went on, more edified by this last woman's speech, said he afterward, than any speech he ever heard in his life.

NORA MCCARTHY

[In The Gray Jacket, pages 26-29.]

Norah McCarthy won by her courage the name of the "Jennie Deans" of the West. She lived in the interior of Missouri—a little, pretty, black-eyed girl, with a soul as huge as a mountain, and a form as frail as a fairy's, and the courage and pluck of a buccaneer into the bargain. Her father was an old man—a secessionist. She had but a single brother, just growing from boyhood to youthhood, but sickly and lame. The family had lived in Kansas during the troubles of '57, when Norah was a mere girl of fourteen or thereabouts. But even then her beauty, wit and devil-may-care spirit were known far and wide; and many were the stories told along the border of her sayings and doings. Among other charges laid at her door it is said that she broke all the hearts of the young bloods far and wide, and tradition goes even so far as to assert that, like Bob Acres, she killed a man once a week, keeping a private church-yard for the purpose of decently burying her dead. Be this as it may, she was then, and is now, a dashing, fine-looking, lively girl, and a prettier heroine than will be found in a novel, as will be seen if the good-natured reader has a mind to follow us to the close of this sketch.

Not long after the Federals came into her neighborhood, and after they had forced her father to take the oath, which he did partly because he was a very old man, unable to take the field, and hoped thereby to save the security of his household, and partly because he could not help himself; not long after these two important events in the history of our heroine, a body of men marched up one evening, while she was on a visit to a neighbor's, and arrested her sickly, weak brother, bearing him off to Leavenworth City, where he was lodged in the military guard-house.

It was nearly night before Norah reached home. When she did so, and discovered the outrage which had been perpetrated, and the grief of her old father, her rage knew no bounds. Although the mists were falling and the night was closing in, dark and dreary, she ordered her horse to be resaddled, put on a thick surtout, belted a sash round her waist, and sticking a pair of ivory-handled pistols in her bosom, started off after the soldiers. The post was many miles distant. But that she did not regard. Over hill, through marsh, under cover of the darkness, she galloped on to the headquarters of the enemy. At last the call of a sentry brought her to stand, with a hoarse "Who goes there?"

"No matter," she replied. "I wish to see Colonel Prince, your commanding officer, and instantly, too."

Somewhat awed by the presence of a young female on horseback at that late hour, and perhaps struck by her imperious tone of command, the Yankee guard, without hesitation, conducted her to the fortifications, and thence to the quarters of the colonel commanding, with whom she was left alone.

"Well, madam," said the Federal officer, with bland politeness, "to what do I owe the honor of this visit?"

"Is this Colonel Prince?" replied the brave girl, quietly.

"It is, and you are—"

"No matter. I have come here to inquire whether you have a lad by the name of McCarthy a prisoner?"

"There is such a prisoner."

"May I ask why he is a prisoner?"

"Certainly! For being suspected of treasonable connection with the enemy."

"Treasonable connection with the enemy! Why the boy is sick and lame. He is, besides, my brother; and I have come to ask his immediate release."

The officer opened his eyes; was sorry he could not comply with the request of so winning a supplicant; and must "really beg her to desist and leave the fortress."

"I demand his release," cried she, in reply.

"That you cannot have. The boy is a rebel and a traitor, and unless you retire, madam, I shall be forced to arrest you on a similar suspicion."

"Suspicion! I am a rebel and a traitor, too, if you wish; young McCarthy is my brother, and I don't leave this tent until he goes with me. Order his instant release or,"—here she drew one of the aforesaid ivory handles out of her bosom and levelled the muzzle of it directly at him—"I will put an ounce of lead in your brain before you can call a single sentry to your relief."

A picture that!

There stood the heroic girl; eyes flashing fire, cheek glowing with earnest will, lips firmly set with resolution, and hand outstretched with a loaded pistol ready to send the contents through the now thoroughly frightened, startled, aghast soldier, who cowered, like blank paper before flames, under her burning stare.

"Quick!" she repeated, "order his release, or you die."

It was too much. Prince could not stand it. He bade her lower her infernal weapon, for God's sake, and the boy should be forthwith liberated.

"Give the order first," she replied, unmoved.

And the order was given; the lad was brought out; and drawing his arm in hers, the gallant sister marched out of the place, with one hand grasping one of his, and the other holding her trusty ivory handle. She mounted her horse, bade him get up behind, and rode off, reaching home without accident before midnight.

Now that is a fact stranger than fiction, which shows what sort of metal is in our women of the much abused and traduced nineteenth century.

WOMEN IN THE BATTLE OF GAINESVILLE, FLA.

[From Dickinson and His Men, pages 99-100.]

As Captain Dickinson and our brave defenders charged the enemy through the streets, many of the ladies could be seen, whose inspiring tones and grateful plaudits cheered these noble heroes on to deeds of greater daring. While charging the enemy, near the residence of Judge Dawkins, Mrs. Dawkins and her lovely sister, Miss Lydia Taylor, passed from their garden into the street, and in the excitement of the moment, actuated by the heroic spirit that ever animated our noble women, united their voices in repeating the captain's word of command. "Charge, charge!" was heard with the musical rhythm of a benediction from their grateful hearts.

The enemy, halting, made a stand a few yards below the entrance to their residence, firing up the street almost a hailstorm of Minie balls from their Spencer rifles. Apparently indifferent to their danger, these heroic ladies stood unmoved, cheering on our gallant soldiers, among whom were many near and dear to them. Captain Dickinson earnestly entreated them to return to the house, as they were in imminent danger of being killed.

Many ladies brought buckets of water for the heated, famished soldiers who had no time to give even to this needed refreshment. Through all the desperate fight not a citizen was hurt. The sweet incense of prayer arose from hundreds of agonized hearts to the mercy-seat, in behalf of husbands, sons, fathers, and brothers who were in the battle.

"SHE WOULD SEND TEN MORE"

[Judge John H. Reagan's address in 1897.]

To illustrate the character and devotion of the women of the Confederacy, I will repeat a statement made to me during the war by Governor Letcher, of Virginia. He had visited his home in the Shenandoah Valley, and on his return to the State capitol called at the house of an old friend who had a large family. He found no one but the good old mother at home, and inquired about the balance of the family. She told him that her husband, her husband's father and her ten sons were all in the army. And on his suggestion that she must feel lonesome, having had a large family with her and now to be left alone, her answer was that it was very hard, but if she had ten more sons they should all go to the army. Can ancient or modern history show a nobler or more unselfish and patriotic devotion to any cause?

WOMEN AT VICKSBURG

[J. L. Underwood.]

On first thought it would be expected that women would be greatly excited when under fire and amid other scenes of actual war. But almost invariably they exhibited during our war a calm fearlessness that was amazing. My girl wife and her war companion, Mrs. Lieutenant Lockett, of Marion, Ala., a daughter of Alabama's noble war governor, A. B. Moore, spent several months of the spring of 1863 at Vicksburg and its vicinity, to be near their husbands. They were boarding in the city the night when Porter's fleet ran down the river by the batteries. The cannonading was terrific. I was with my regiment, the Thirtieth Alabama, some few miles away. Next morning, as soon as regimental duties would allow, I hastened to the city. To my astonishment I found that neither "the girls" nor the ladies of the city had been at all alarmed. They seemed to look upon it as a sort of enjoyable episode.

In May we were at Warrenton, 10 miles below the city, where the two ladies were quartered with old Mr. Withington and his good wife, in one of the most independent and comfortable plantation homes in the land. When our brigade, under command of the brave but ill-fated Gen. Ed. Tracy, was ordered to Grand Gulf, I was left under orders to take the ladies to Vicksburg and send them home out of danger. But before we could get away from Mr. Withington's news came that a battle was raging at Bayou Pierre. I told the ladies that I could not stay away from my command while it was engaged in battle and that they would just have to do the best they could where they were. Their cheeks never blanched; nor was a protest uttered. After the battle I hurried back and got them to Vicksburg, hoping to have them beyond Jackson before Grant's flanking army could reach it. The idea of having them shut up in Vicksburg during a siege was a horror to me. What was my chagrin when, on reaching the railroad station, I was informed by the officials that not another train would be allowed to go out. There were numbers of officers' wives and other women all round the depot, eager to go. They bore their bitter disappointment even cheerfully. Their courage and cheerfulness soon took another happy turn when under orders I passed around to whisper to them, "Be ready to jump quickly and quietly on a train which has been provided to carry off soldiers' wives in a few minutes."

Away they went and reached their homes safely, though we at Vicksburg never learned this until after the surrender. The siege lasted forty-seven days. Day and night, not only the entrenchments but the entire city was exposed to artillery and rifle fire day and night. Many a man was killed far away from the front lines. Many a private house was torn by shells from Grant's rifle cannon or Porter's mortar fleet. While the shot and shell did not fall incessantly at any one point there was no place they did not reach. I knew several poor fellows to receive fresh wounds while lying on their cots in the hospitals.

Porter did not spare the city hospital, although carrying the yellow flag. In it I had an old college friend, Capt. Ben Craig, of Alabama, sick with fever, whose wife and venerable father had remained to nurse him. Just before one of my visits a thirteen-inch shell came down through the roof, leaving an ugly hole in the floor within six inches of poor Craig's bed. His brave little wife, (formerly Miss Eliza Tucker, of Milledgeville, Ga.) never flinched.

A great many families of the city had dug caves in the soft clay of the Vicksburg hills and could hide in them in perfect safety. Many did not avail themselves of this refuge, but bravely remained in their houses and took chances. Even the cave dwellers had to come out to cook their food. Nobly did these good women render whatever attention they could to our sick and wounded. They were as brave and as calm as the soldiers.

"MOTHER, TELL HIM NOT TO COME"

[Major Robert Stiles, in Four Years Under Marse Robert, pages 322-326.]

I sat in the porch, where were also sitting an old couple, evidently the joint head of the establishment, and a young woman dressed in black, apparently their daughter, and, as I soon learned, a soldier's widow. My coat was badly torn, and the young woman kindly offering to mend it I thanked her and, taking it off, handed it to her. While we were chatting, and groups of men sitting on the steps and lying about the yard, the door of the house opened and another young woman appeared. She was almost beautiful, was plainly but neatly dressed, and had her hat on. She had evidently been weeping and her face was deadly pale. Turning to the old woman, as she came out, she said, cutting her words off short, "Mother, tell him if he passes here he is no husband of mine," and turned again to leave the porch. I rose, and placing myself directly in front of her, extended my arm to prevent her escape. She drew back with surprise and indignation. The men were alert on the instant, and battle was joined.

"What do you mean, sir?" she cried.

"I mean, madam," I replied, "that you are sending your husband word to desert, and that I cannot permit you to do this in the presence of my men."

"Indeed! and who asked your permission, sir? And pray, sir, is he your husband or mine?"

"He is your husband, madam, but these are my soldiers. They and I belong to the same army with your husband, and I cannot suffer you, or any one, unchallenged, to send such a demoralizing message in their hearing."

"Army! do you call this mob of retreating cowards an army? Soldiers! if you are soldiers, why don't you stand and fight the savage wolves that are coming upon us defenceless women and children?"

"We don't stand and fight, madam, because we are soldiers, and have to obey orders, but if the enemy should appear on that hill this moment I think you would find that these men are soldiers, and willing to die in defense of women and children."

"Quite a fine speech, sir, but rather cheap to utter, since you very well know the Yankees are not here, and won't be, till you've had time to get your precious carcasses out of the way. Besides, sir, this thing is over, and has been for some time. The government has now actually run off, bag and baggage,— the Lord knows where,—and there is no longer any government or any country for my husband to owe allegiance to. He does owe allegiance to me and to his starving children, and if he doesn't observe this allegiance now, when I need him, he need not attempt it hereafter when he wantsme."

The woman was quick as a flash and cold as steel. She was getting the better of me. She saw it, and, worst of all, the men saw and felt it, too, and had gathered thick and pressed up close all round the porch. There must have been a hundred or more of them, all eagerly listening, and evidently strongly to the woman's side. This would never do. I tried every avenue of approach to that woman's heart. It was congealed by suffering, or else it was encased in adamant. She had parried every thrust, repelled every advance, and was now standing defiant, with her arms folded across her breast, rather courting further attack. I was desperate, and with the nonchalance of pure desperation —no stroke of genius—I asked the soldier-question:

"What command does your husband belong to?"

She started a little, and there was a trace of color in her face as she replied, with a slight tone of pride in her voice: "He belongs to the Stonewall Brigade, sir."

I felt, rather than thought it—but, had I really found her heart? We would see.

"When did he join it?"

A little deeper flush, a little stronger emphasis of pride.

"He joined in the spring of '61, sir."

Yes, I was sure of it now. Her eyes had gazed straight into mine; her head inclined and her eyelids drooped a little now, and there was something in her face that was not pain and was not fight. So I let myself out a little, and turning to the men, said:

"Men, if her husband joined the Stonewall Brigade in '61, and has been in the army ever since, I reckon he's a good soldier."

I turned to look at her. It was all over. Her wifehood had conquered. She had not been addressed this time, yet she answered instantly, with head raised high, face blushing, eyes flashing: "General Lee hasn't a better in his army!" As she uttered these words she put her hand in her bosom, and drawing out a folded paper, extended it toward me, saying: "If you doubt it, look at that."

Before her hand reached mine she drew it back, seeming to have changed her mind, but I caught her wrist, and without much resistance possessed myself of the paper. It had been much thumbed and was much worn. It was hardly legible, but I made it out. Again I turned to the men.

"Take off your hats, boys, I want you to hear this with uncovered heads"— and then I read an endorsement on an application for furlough, in which General Lee himself had signed a recommendation of this woman's husband for a furlough of special length on account of extraordinary gallantry in battle.

During the reading of this paper the woman was transfigured, glorified. No Madonna of old master was ever more sweetly radiant with all that appeals to what is best and holiest in man. Her bosom rose and fell with deep, quiet sighs; her eyes rained gentle, happy tears.

The men felt it all—all. They were all gazing upon her, but the dross was clean, purified out of them. There was not, upon any one of their faces, an expression that would have brought a blush to the cheek of the purest womanhood on earth. I turned once more to the soldier's wife.

"This little paper is your most precious treasure, isn't it?"

"It is."

"And the love of him whose manly courage and devotion won this tribute is the best blessing God ever gave you, isn't it?"

"It is."

"And yet, for the brief ecstasy of one kiss, you would disgrace this hero-husband of yours, stain all his noble reputation, and turn this priceless paper to bitterness; for the rear-guard would hunt him from his own cottage, in half an hour, a deserter and a coward."

Not a sound could be heard save her hurried breathing. The rest of us held our breath. Suddenly, with a gasp of recovered consciousness, she snatched the paper from my hand, put it back hurriedly in her bosom, and turning once more to her mother, said: "Mother, tell him not to come."

I stepped aside at once. She left the porch, glided down the path to the gate, crossed the road, surmounted the fence with easy grace, climbed the hill, and as she disappeared in the weedy pathway I caught up my hat and said:

"Now, men, give her three cheers."

Such cheers. Oh, God, shall I ever again hear a cheer which bears a man's whole soul in it? For the first time I felt reasonably sure of my battalion. It would follow anywhere.

BRAVE WOMAN IN DECATUR, GA.

[Miss Mary A. H. Gay, in Life in Dixie, pages 127-132.]

Garrad's Cavalry selected our lot, consisting of several acres, for headquarters, and soon what appeared to us to be an immense army train of wagons commenced rolling into it. In less than two hours our barn was demolished and converted into tents, which were occupied by privates and noncommissioned officers, and to the balusters of our portico and other portions of the house were tied a number of large ropes, which, the other ends being secured to the trees and shrubbery, answered as a railing to which at short intervals apart a number of smaller ropes were tied, and to these were attached horses and mules, which were eating corn and oats out of troughs improvised for the occasion out of bureau, washstand, and wardrobe drawers. Men in groups were playing cards on tables of every size and shape, and whisky and profanity held high carnival. Thus surrounded, we could but be apprehensive of danger; and, to assure ourselves of as much safety as possible, we barricaded the doors and windows, and arranged to sit up all night; that is, my mother and myself.

As we sat on a lounge, every chair having been taken to the camps, we heard the sound of footsteps entering the piazza, and in a moment, loud rapping, which meant business. Going to the window nearest the door, I removed the fastenings, raised the sash, and opened the blinds. Perceiving by the light of a brilliant moon that at least a half dozen men in uniforms were on the piazza, I asked: "Who is there?"

"Gentlemen," was the laconic reply.

"If so, you will not persist in your effort to come into the house. There is only a widow and one of her daughters, and two faithful servants in it," said I.

"We have orders from headquarters to interview Miss Gay. Is she the daughter of whom you speak?"

"She is, and I am she."

"Well, Miss Gay, we demand seeing you, without intervening barriers. Our orders are imperative," said he who seemed to be the spokesman of the delegation.

"Then wait a moment," I amiably responded. Going to my mother, I repeated in substance the above colloquy, and asked her if she would go with me out of one of the back doors and around the house into the front yard. Although greatly agitated and trembling, she readily assented, and we noiselessly went out. In a few moments we announced our presence, and our visitors descended the steps and joined us. And these men, occupying a belligerent attitude toward ourselves and all that was dear to us, stood face to face with us and in silence we contemplated each other. When the silence was broken, the aforesaid officer introduced himself as Major Campbell, a member of General Schofield's staff. He also introduced the accompanying officers each by name and title. This ceremony over, Major Campbell said:

"Miss Gay, our mission is a painful one, and yet we will carry it out unless you satisfactorily explain acts reported to us."

"What is the nature of those acts?"

"We have been told that it is your proudest boast that you are a rebel, and that you are ever on duty to aid and abet in every possible way the wouldbe destroyers of the United States government. If this be so, we can not permit you to remain within our lines. Until Atlanta surrenders, Decatur will be our headquarters, and every consideration of interest to our cause requires that no one inimical to it should remain within our boundaries established by conquest."

In reply to these charges, I said:

"Gentlemen, I have not been misrepresented, so far as the charges you mentioned are concerned. If I were a man, I should be in the foremost ranks of those who are fighting for rights guaranteed by the Constitution of the United States. The Southern people have never broken that compact, nor infringed upon it in any way. They have never organized mobs to assassinate any portion of people sharing the privileges granted by that compact. They have constructed no underground railroads to bring into our midst incendiaries and destroyers of the peace, and to carry off stolen property. They have never sought to array the subordinate element of the North in deadly hostility to the controlling element. No class of the women of the South have ever sought positions at the North which secured entrance into good households, and then betrayed the confidence reposed by corrupting the servants and alienating the relations between the master and the servant. No class of women in the South have ever mounted the rostrum and proclaimed falsehoods against the women of the North—falsehoods which must have crimsoned with shame the very cheeks of Beelzebub. No class of the men of the South have ever tramped over the North with humbugs, extorting money either through sympathy or credulity, and engaged at the same time in the nefarious work of exciting the subordinate class to insurrection, arson, rapine, and murder. If the South is in rebellion, a well-organized mob at the North has brought it about. Long years of patient endurance accomplished nothing. The party founded on falsehood and hate strengthened and grew to enormous proportions. And, by the way, mark the cunning of that party. Finding that the Abolition party made slow progress and had to work in the dark, it changed its name and took in new issues, and by a systematic course of lying in its institutions of learning, from the lowly school-house to Yale College, and from its pulpits and rostrums, it inculcated lessons of hate toward the Southern people, whom it would hurl into the crater of Vesuvius if endowed with the power. What was left us to do but to try to relieve that portion of the country which had permitted this sentiment of hate to predominate of all connection with us, and of all responsibility for the sins of which it proclaimed us guilty? This effort the South has made, and I have aided and abetted in every possible manner, and will continue to do so as long as there is an armed man in the Southern ranks. If this is sufficient cause to expel me from my home, I await your orders. I have no favors to ask."

Imagine my astonishment, admiration, and gratitude when that group of Federal officers with unanimity said:

"I glory in your spunk, and am proud of you as my countrywoman; and so far from banishing you from your home, we will vote for your retention within our lines."

GIVING WARNING TO MOSBY

[From original manuscript, now in the Confederate Museum.]

My Dear Friend: * * * Soon after the Yankees went into winter quarters in Warrenton, I was requested by a soldier friend to avail myself of every opportunity to obtain and transmit information that might be of service to our scouts and guerrillas, and this of course I was most willing to do. Our house was at that time within the lines in the day time, and beyond them at night. I walked up to Warrenton one bright but very cold morning, (the 22d of December) and as soon as I arrived was informed by a lady friend, who was also on the lookout, that she had just seen a negro, who looked like a newcomer, escorted by several officers to the provost marshal's office. I immediately concluded that he was bearer of some tidings, most probably from "Mosby's Confederacy," and that I must know what it might be, but how could I accomplish it? A sentinel was placed always before the office. I had my purse with me. I fell into conversation with him. I offered him so much to let me pass into the basement of the house on pretense of wishing to transact some business with the negroes who occupied it. He accepted it, and I went— not into the room which the negroes occupied, but into the one adjoining it—a place very damp and dark, where I could hear, but not be seen, and suiting my purpose admirably, as it was immediately under the office. I listened; heard the negro questioned and heard him answer that he could and would guide a force to Mosby's headquarters, to the houses where he knew many of his men boarded, to the place where the command had stored a quantity of corn. About the corn they seemed to care little, but oh! to catch Mosby,—they waxed warm at the thought—they talked long and loudly (all for my convenience, no doubt) and the result of the consultation was a plan to go "riding on a raid" with the "reliable contraband" acting as guide—to go that very night if certain reinforcements arrived in time, or should they fail to do so, the next night. I had heard enough. I came out of my cell, walked through town to a picket post, with the remaining contents of my purse bribed the faithful soldier of the Union to let me pass, then walked two miles to a neighbor's where I thought I could get a horse, which was most gladly furnished me when my errand was made known. By this time it was late in the afternoon; it had been turning colder all day, and was now intensely cold with a blustering wind, the sky covered with moving masses of black clouds. My friends wrapped me up as best they could. I mounted and rode three miles to a neighbor's house, where I took a little boy up behind me for escort. My object now was to ride in what seemed the right direction until I met some Southern soldier to whom I could impart the information I gathered, and commission him to convey it to those whom it most nearly concerned. I rode on for miles—the country becoming entirely new to me—the cold increasing —the darkness deepening—the wind rising higher and higher. Mosby's men were always hanging about the outposts of the enemy. Why was it that I could not meet one of them? Did they think the night too terrible to be out? Oh! how I ached with cold, and when I thoughtlessly said as much, my gallant little escort, who was not less so, I am sure, begged that he might be allowed to take off his overcoat and put it around me. Suddenly, just before me, I saw a large fire—the temptation was too great—I forgot that its light might reveal me to those whom the darkness hid, drew the reins—old Kitty Grey stood still, and I stretched out my hands toward the genial warmth. I then discovered that I was near the "View Tree" to reach which, though only four miles from Warrenton, I had traveled eight or ten. The fire, thought I to myself, was built by some Southern scouts, but they left it as I came on lest it should endanger them. The thought aroused me. I started on, but had scarcely done so when the moon came out, and almost immediately Walter called my attention to a body of men on my right, in the form of a V, each with his carbine levelled, and moving slowly toward me: I expected them to fire any moment, but I neither quickened nor slackened my pace. The moon went under a cloud and I passed into the sheltering darkness, wondering much why they did not fire. My curiosity on that point was afterwards satisfied. On I rode. It was not long before I saw a single horseman with his raised weapon just in front of me.

"Halt," he said.

Boldness alone I believed could save me. The cold wind made my voice hoarse; stern purpose made it strong. I tell you I was astonished at the manliness of its tone, as lifting my arm I said, "Surrender or I'll blow your brains out."

I only knew that a moment afterwards I heard his horse's retreating hoofs clattering on the stony road. Now surely, thought I, I am safe; surely the last picket is passed, and my spirits rose. Soon after this, deceived by the darkness and my ignorance of the mountain ways, I lost my direction and took a wrong road; but believing myself right and at last out of danger, I moved on as fast as I could over the rough, frozen ground, when on reaching the top of the hill, what was my amazement and horror on finding that instead of proceeding I was retracing my steps, though by a different route. I saw distinctly, perhaps three miles off, the lights of the town of Warrenton. And this was all that I had accomplished after riding at least twelve miles. What should I do? Was I to fail altogether of my mission? To keep going toward Warrenton would inevitably lead me to the Yankees. If I turned and lost my way entirely, what would become of me on such a night? Just then there came into my mind those sweet quaint lines which I did not know that I could repeat:

"God shall charge his angel legions
  Watch and ward o'er thee to keep,
Tho' thou walk thro' hostile regions,
  Tho' in desert wilds thou sleep."

They were to me then an inspiration—a harbinger of safety and success. It would have been still further inspiration, could I have seen how just at the time, dear old Mrs. ——, who had helped to wrap me up when I started, and had encouraged me by her sympathy and interest, was watching for my return, keeping up a big fire—warming some of her own clothes for me; and when at last she laid down, it was with her lamp still burning, a pillow arranged for me close by her kind heart, and with a prayer for me on her lips, that she slept. God bless her!

Turning my back to the lights once more, I rode on. I had only gone a few hundred yards when I saw just before me a horse and his dismounted rider. The man stepped out, laid his hand on my bridle and said: "Stop, lady, you can go no further; but where are you going?"

I answered in the very tone of candor: "I was trying to go to the neighborhood of Salem to see a sick friend. It was later than I thought when I set off. My poor old borrowed horse traveled very slowly; night overtook me suddenly and I determined to make my way back to my home near Warrenton, but have lost my way."

He then said: "It is my painful duty to take you to the reserves, where you will be detained all night and taken to headquarters in the morning."

I replied: "You can shoot me on the spot, but I will not spend this night unprotected among your soldiers. I cannot consent that you should perform your duty."

"Nor am I willing to perform it!" he exclaimed.

After a few moments' hesitation, which seemed to me a century, he pointed out to me a light at some distance and said, "Go to that house; no one will be so cruel as to turn you away on such a night."

I turned into what I thought the right path, but presently he called out to me in a tone of earnest entreaty: "Not that way, for God's sake; that leads to the reserves."

He then came to me, and leading my horse into the right path said: "Good-by, I shall be three hours on picket to think of a freezing lady."

Keeping the light in my eye, I soon reached the house, which was not far off, and although the inmates evidently looked upon me with suspicion, they agreed to let me stay all night and let me feed my horse. I gave them an assumed name, asked to go to bed immediately, had a hot brick put to my feet and plenty of cover; but I was too thoroughly cold to be warmed easily, so I lay and shivered and wept the live-long night.

Next morning six Yankees, just off post, rode up to the house. At first I feared the kind picket had proved as treacherous as the rest, had informed on me, and that they had come to arrest me. I hurried down to meet them and was not a little relieved to find that they only wanted to buy milk and eggs. There was a captain among them.

"We had an alarm last night," said he to me.

"Ah! how was it?"

"Why, the rebels wanted to attack our soldiers and they thought to fool us by sending one man on ahead as if he were alone, thinking we would all fire on him and not be ready for the rest when they came up; but we were too sharp for them, did not fire at all and the rascals were afraid to try it."

Ah! what mistakes we sometimes make! I learned from them by a little judicious questioning that no raiding party had passed up during the night, and hoped that I might still be in time.

After they left I found that the mistress of the house was a true Southern woman. I told her my real name and my errand; she went with me to a house in the mountains, where were some of Mosby's men. We also met several on the way. I entreated them to give due notice and then joyfully turned my face homewards. Gentle, faithful, old Kitty Grey stood me in good stead upon more than one occasion, but the Yankees have since stolen her, too. I soon returned her to her owners and had nothing to do but get through the lines to our house. This I accomplished without difficulty, and when I got in sight of the camp, just about sundown, I saw every preparation making for a raid—the raid which was to catch Mosby and his men. I had the satisfaction to learn in a few days that it met with very poor success. Not a few soldiers have since told me that the warning saved them from capture. Several were in bed when they received it. One had not left his boarding-house twenty minutes when it was surrounded by the enemy. They preferred one night in the mountains of Virginia to a winter in a Yankee dungeon. Am I not more than repaid by their thanks?

A few days after this, during Christmas, some friends in the neighborhood came through the lines to spend the day and night with us. To show you how difficult it was to overcome a Yankee sentinel's stern sense of duty, I must tell you that one of the young ladies of the party bribed the incumbent of the post on this occasion to let them all pass for the small consideration of two ginger-cakes and one turn-over pie.

Between 11 and 12 that night, as we girls were undressing and chatting around the fire, we heard a gentle tapping on the window below, and immediately mother came up and whispering as softly and mysteriously as if she feared the walls, which they so closely watched, or the winds, that whistled so keenly around the corners of the house, and also their ears might repeat her words to the pickets, informed me that Colonel Mosby and a few of his men were in the yard and wished to see me. I put on the first dress I came to and crept down noiselessly, lest I should arouse our spy of a guard. The colonel wanted to know the exact position of the pickets and videttes. I told him as well as I could, and in order to give him a more correct idea, I offered to go with any of them whom he might select to a certain hill, where I could point out their positions more definitely. Capt. Wm. R. Smith begged leave to go with me. He led his horse and we walked along, talking in a low tone. There was a full moon, but she wore a veil of fleecy clouds.

When we had gone about two hundred yards, very unexpectedly there rode out from behind a tree a Yankee picket.

"Halt," he cried.

It was but the work of an instant for Captain Smith to spring on his horse, and with an effort of his strong arm, "Light to the croup the fair lady he swung." The next instant a bullet seemed to graze our ears; in quick succession six bullets came, but they soon fell far behind us. We heard the whole line take up the alarm. As we flew along, Captain Smith said, very calmly, "A little romance for you." We soon reached our reserve and after some further conversation, bade one another goodnight—they going forth to meet other adventures and I to my friends, who having heard the firing, were awaiting my return somewhat anxiously. When I took off the dress I had worn, I discovered a very jagged rent, evidently made by the spur of a cavalier. Brave, brave Captain Smith! soon he gave his young life to our cause.

"AIN'T YOU ASHAMED OF YOU'UNS?"

[Phoebe Y. Pember.]

Directly in front of me sat an old Georgia up-country woman, placidly regarding the box cars full of men on the parallel rails, waiting, like ourselves, to start. She knitted and gazed, and at last inquired "who was them ar' soldiers, and whar' was they a-going to?" The information that they were Yankee prisoners startled her considerably. The knitting ceased abruptly (all the old women in the Southern States knitted socks for the soldiers while traveling), and the cracker bonnet of dark brown homespun was thrown back violently, for her whole nervous system seemed to have received a galvanic shock. Then she caught her breath with a long gasp, lifted on high her thin, trembling hand, accompanied by the trembling voice, and made a speech:

"Ain't you ashamed of you'uns," she piped. "A-coming down here a-spiling our country, and a-robbing our hen-roosts? What did we ever do to you'uns that you should come a-killing our brothers and sons? Ain't you ashamed of you'uns? What for do you want us to live with you'uns, you poor white trash? I ain't got a single nigger that would be so mean as to force himself where he warn't wanted, and what do we-uns want with you? Ain't you—" but there came a roar of laughter from both cars, and, shaking with excitement, the old lady pulled down her spectacles, which in the excitement she had pushed up on her forehead, and tried in vain to resume her labors with uncertain fingers.

FALSE TEETH

[In Richmond During the War, pages 165-166.]

In connection with the battle of the Cross Keys, we are just here reminded of an amusing stratagem of a rebel lady to conceal her age and charms from the enemy, who held possession of her house. She says: "Mr. K., you know, was compelled to evacuate his premises when the Federals took possession, and succeeding in making good their escape, left me here, with my three children, to encounter the consequences of their intrusion upon my premises. Not wishing to appear quite as youthful as I really am, and desiring to destroy, if possible, any remains of my former beauty, I took from my mouth a set of false teeth, (which I was compelled to have put in before I was 20 years old,) tied a handkerchief around my head, donned my most sloven apparel, and in every way made myself as hideous as possible. The disguise was perfect. I was sullen, morose, sententious. You could not have believed I could so long have kept up a manner so disagreeable; but it had the desired effect. The Yankees called me 'old woman.' They took little thought I was not 30 years of age. They took my house for a hospital for their sick and wounded, and allowed me only the use of a single room, and required of me many acts of assistance in nursing their men, which under any circumstances my own heart-promptings would have made a pleasure to me. But I did not feel disposed to be compelled to prepare food for those who had driven from me my husband, and afterwards robbed me of all my food and bed-furniture, with the exception of what they allowed me to have in my room. But they were not insulting in their language to the 'old woman,' and I endured all the inconveniences and unhappiness of my situation with as much fortitude as I could bring into operation, feeling that my dear husband, at least, was safe from harm. After they left," she continued, "I was forced to go into the woods, near by, and with my two little boys pick up fagots to cook the scanty food left to me." This is the story of one of the most luxuriously reared women of Virginia, and is scarcely the faintest shadow of what many endured under similar circumstances.

EMMA SANSOM

[Gen. T. Jordan and J. P. Pryor, in Campaigns of General Forrest, pages 267-270.]

The Federal column under Colonel Streight was again overtaken by 10 A. M., on the 2d; and the Confederate general selected fifty of the best mounted men, with whom his escort charged swiftly upon its rear in the face of a hot fire. For ten miles now, to Black Creek, an affluent of the Coosa, a sharp, running conflict occurred. The Federals, however, effected the passage of the stream without hindrance, by a bridge, which, being old and very dry, was in flames and impassable as the Confederates approached; besides which it was commanded by Streight's artillery, planted on the opposite bank. Black Creek is deep and rapid, and its passage in the immediate presence of the Federal force was an impossibility before which even Forrest was forced to pause and ponder. But while reflecting upon the predicament, he was approached by a group of women, one of whom, a tall, comely girl of about 18 years of age, stepped forward and inquired, "Whose command?"

The answer was, "The advance of General Forrest's cavalry."

She then requested that General Forrest should be pointed out, which being done, advancing, she addressed him nearly in these words:

"You are General Forrest, I am told. I know of an old ford to which I could guide you, if I had a horse. The Yankees have taken all of ours."

Her mother, stepping up, exclaimed:

"No, Emma; people would talk about you."

"I am not afraid to trust myself with as brave a man as General Forrest, and don't care for people's talk," was the prompt rejoinder of this Southern girl, her face illuminated with emotion.

The general then remarked, as he rode beside a log nearby: "Well, Miss ——, jump up behind me."

Quickly or without an instant of hesitation, she sprang from the log behind the redoubtable cavalry leader, and sat ready to guide him—under as noble an inspiration of unalloyed, courageous patriotism as that which has rendered the Maid of Zaragossa famous for all time. Calling for a courier to follow, guided by Miss Sansom, Forrest rode rapidly, leaping over fallen timber, to a point about half a mile above the bridge, where, at the foot of a ravine, she said there was a practicable ford. There, dismounting, they walked to the river- bank, opposite to which, on the other side, were found posted a Federal detachment, who opened upon both immediately with some forty small arms, the balls of which whistled close by, and tore up the ground in their front as they approached. Inquiring naively what caused the noise, and being answered that it was the sound of bullets, the intrepid girl stepped in front of her companion, saying, "General, stand behind me; they will not dare shoot me." Gently putting her aside, Forrest observed he could not possibly suffer her to do so, or to make a breastwork of herself, and gave her his arm so as to screen her as much as possible. By this time they had reached the ravine. Placing her behind the shelter afforded by the roots of a fallen tree, he asked Miss Sansom to remain there until he could reconnoitre the ford, and proceeded at once to descend the ravine on his hands and knees. After having gone some fifty yards in this manner, looking back, to his surprise and regret, she was immediately at his back; and in reply to his remark that he had told her to remain under shelter, replied: "Yes, General, but I was fearful that you might be wounded; and it is my purpose to be near you."

The ford-mouth reached and examined, they then returned as they came, through the ravine, to the crown of the bank, under fire, when she took his arm as before—an open mark for the Federal sharpshooters, whose fire for some instants was even heavier than at first; and several of their balls actually passed through her skirts, exciting the observation, "They have only wounded my crinoline." At the same time, withdrawing her arm, the dauntless girl, turning round, faced the enemy, and waved her sun-bonnet defiantly and repeatedly in the air. We are pleased to be able to record that, at this, the hostile fire was stopped; the Federals took off their own caps, and, waving them, gave three hearty cheers of approbation. Remounting, Forrest and Miss Sansom returned to the command, who received her with unfeigned enthusiasm.

The artillery was sent forward, and with a few shells, well thrown, quickly drove away the Federal guard at the ford, which Major McLemore was directed to seize with his regiment. The stream was boggy, with high, declivitous banks on both sides, and it was necessary to take the ammunition from the caissons by hand, and to force the animals down the steep slopes, and to take the ford, but, nevertheless, the passage was successfully effected in less than two hours. Meantime, the Confederate general delivered his fair, daring young guide back safely into the hands of her mother, took a knightly farewell, inspired by the romantic coloring of the occurrence, and dashed after his command to resume the chase, as soon as the passage of the creek was effected.

PRESIDENT ROOSEVELT'S MOTHER AND GRANDMOTHER

[By J. L. Underwood.]

The story has often been told of Mrs. Roosevelt, formerly Miss Bulloch, of Georgia, and mother of President Roosevelt, that early in the war between the States, when a regiment of Federal soldiers was marching past her residence in New York, she displayed a Confederate flag at her window and refused to take it down when ordered to do so.

In October, 1905, a similar story was told by the Philadelphia correspondent of the Richmond *Times-Dispatch* that Mrs. Bulloch, the grandmother of the President, at some period of the war did the same thing in that city. The author of this volume was about to insert both incidents when a moment's reflection caused him to hesitate. He remembered that both the ladies mentioned were typical Southern women, of one of the best and most knightly families. The stories lack *vraisemblance*. Whatever may have been their sympathies during the war between the States, such a needless display as that indicated in the stories does not sound like the Bullochs of Georgia. Southern women were not given to showing their patriotism by waving flags. It is rather too cheap. Southern women of the best type, while members of Northern families or guests of Northern friends, during the war, would not volunteer to flaunt before the public a family division of political sentiment under such sad circumstances. In addition to this, the author has too much regard for the sanctity of home, be it ever so humble or so highly exalted, to enter its portals for a striking story without knocking for admission. Under the circumstances he felt it due to consult our magnanimous President himself as to the authenticity of either or both incidents. President Roosevelt kindly forwarded the following reply:

"THE WHITE HOUSE,
WASHINGTON, D. C., *Nov. 20, 1905.*

Personal.

Dear Sir: It is always a pleasure to hear from an old Confederate soldier, and I thank you for your letter and for the kind way in which you speak of me; but that incident about my mother never took place. This is the first time I ever heard the story about my grandmother and I am sure it is equally without basis. My grandmother was very infirm during the war and I do not believe she ever lived at Philadelphia. She was with us in New York.

Sincerely yours, Theodore Roosevelt.

Rev. J. L. Underwood, *Kellam's Hospital, Richmond, Va.*"

Elsewhere in this volume it is shown that John G. Whittier's famous story of [217] Barbara Freitchie and the Federal flag is a myth, pure and simple. This letter of the President consigns the two stories above mentioned to a similar fate. The Southern people will thank him for it. They desire nothing but simple truth about their honored President and his family.

THE LITTLE GIRL AT CHANCELLORSVILLE

General Fitz Hugh Lee loved to tell of the little girl in the house where Stonewall Jackson breathed his last, who said to her mother that she "wished that God would let her die instead of the general, for then only her mother would cry; but if Jackson died all the people of the country would cry."

SAVED HER HAMS

In Mississippi a farmer's wife heard that a regiment of Federal cavalry was coming. She had a smoke-house full of fine hams and shoulder meat. Immediately she went to work, and when the soldiers came they found the meat lying all about the yard with a knife hole stuck deep into each piece. The Yankees rushed in and began to pick it up.

"What's the matter with this meat, madam? How came these holes in it?"

"Now, look here," said she, "you know the Confederate cavalry has just been here, and if you all get poisoned by that meat you must not blame me."

They left the meat.

HEROISM OF A WIDOW [218]

[Mrs. Allie McPeek, in Southern Historical Papers, Volume 23, page 328; from the Atlanta (Ga.) *Constitution*, November 9, 1905.]

It was on the first and second days of September, 1864, General Hardee of the Southern forces was sent to Jonesboro from Atlanta with 22,000 men to head off a formidable flank movement of the enemy, which had for its purpose to cut off Southern communication and thereby compel the evacuation of the city of Atlanta. The flank movement consisted of 40,000 men, and was commanded chiefly by Major-General John M. Schofield, together with General Sedgwick, who was also a corps commander, and consisted of the best fighters of the Federal army.

As the two armies confronted each other two miles to the north andnorthwest of Jonesboro, it so happened that the little house and farm of a poor old widow was just between the two lines of battle when the conflict opened, and, having nowhere to go, she was necessarily caught between the fire of the two commanding lines of battle, which was at comparatively close range and doing fierce and deadly work. The house and home of this old lady was soon converted into a Federal hospital, and with the varying fortunes she was alternately within the lines of each contending army, when not between them on disputed ground.

During the whole of this eventful day this good and brave woman, exposed as she was to the incessant showers of shot and shell from both sides, moved fearlessly about among the wounded and dying of both sides alike, and without making the slightest distinction. Finally night closed the scene with General Schofield's army corps in possession of the ground, and when the morning dawned it found this grand old lady still at her post of duty, knowing, too, as she did, the fortunes, or rather misfortunes, of war had stripped her of the last vestige of property she had except her little tract of land which had been laid waste. Now it was that General John M. Schofield, having known her suffering and destitute condition, sent her, under escort and arms, a large wagon-load of provisions and supplies, and caused his adjutant-general to write her a long and touching letter of thanks, and wound up the letter with a special request that she keep it until the war was over and present it to the United States government, and they would repay all her losses.

She kept the letter, and soon after the Southern Claims Commission was established she brought it to the writer, who presented her claim in due form, and she was awarded about $600—all she claimed, but not being all she lost. The letter is now on file with other proofs of the exact truth of this statement with the files of the Southern Claims Commission at Washington. Her name was Allie McPeek, and she died several years ago.

WINCHESTER WOMEN

[Fremantle's Three Months in Southern Lines.]

Winchester used to be a most agreeable town, and its society extremely pleasant. Many of its houses are now destroyed or converted into hospitals, the outlook miserable and dilapidated. Its female inhabitants (for the able- bodied males are all absent in the army) are familiar with the bloody realities of war. As many as 5,000 wounded have been accommodated here at one time. All the ladies are accustomed to the bursting of shells and the sight of fighting, and all are turned into hospital nurses or cooks.

SPARTA IN MISSISSIPPI

[Gen. J. B. Gordon.]

The heroines of Sparta who gave their hair for bow-strings have been immortalized by the muse of history; but what tongue can speak or pen indite a tribute worthy of the Mississippi woman who with her own hands applied the torch to more than half a million dollars' worth of cotton, reducing herself to poverty rather than have that cotton employed against her people. The day will come, and I believe it is rapidly approaching, when in all will be seen evidences of appreciation of these inspiring incidents; when all lips will unite in expressing gratitude to God that they belong to such a race of men and women.

"WOMAN'S DEVOTION"—A WINCHESTER HEROINE

[Gen. D. H. Maury, in Southern Historical Papers.]

The history of Winchester is replete with romantic and glorious memories of the late war. One of the most interesting of these has been perpetuated by the glowing pencil of Oregon Wilson, himself a native of this valley, and the fine picture he has made of the incident portrayed by him has drawn tears from many who loved their Southern country and the devoted women who elated and sanctified by their heroic sacrifices the cause which, borne down for a time, now rises again to honor all who sustained it.

That truth, which is stranger than fiction, is stronger, too. The simple historic facts which gave Wilson the theme of his great picture gains nothing from the romantic glamour his beautiful art has thrown about the actors in the story.

In 1864, General Ramseur, commanding a Confederate force near Winchester, was suddenly attacked by a Federal force under General Averell, and after a sharp encounter was forced back through the town. The battlefield was near the residence of Mr. Rutherford, about two miles distant, and the wounded were gathered in his house and yard. The Confederate surgeons left in charge of these wounded men appealed to the women of Winchester (the men had all gone off to the war) to come out and aid in dressing the wounds and nursing the wounded. As was always the way of these Winchester women, they promptly responded to this appeal, and on the —— day of July more than twenty ladies went out to Mr. Rutherford's to minister to their suffering countrymen. There were more than sixty severely wounded men who had been collected from the battlefield and were lying in the house and garden of Mr. Rutherford. The weather was warm, and those out of doors were as comfortable and as quiet as those within. Amongst them was a beardless boy named Randolph Ridgely; he was severely hurt; his thigh was broken by a bullet, and his sufferings were very great; his nervous system was shocked and unstrung, and he could find no rest. The kind surgeon in charge of him had many others to care for; he felt that quiet sleep was all important for his young patient, and he placed him under charge of a young girl who had accompanied these ladies from Winchester; told her his life depended on his having quiet sleep that night; showed her how best to support his head, and promised to return and see after his condition as soon and as often as his duties to the other wounded would permit.

All through that anxious night the brave girl sat, sustaining the head of the wounded youth and carefully guarding him against everything that could disturb his rest or break the slumber into which he gently sank, and which was to save his life. She only knew and felt that a brave Confederate life depended on her care. She had never seen him before, nor has she ever seen him since. And when at dawn the surgeon came to her, he found her still watching and faithful, just as he had left her at dark—as only a true woman, as we love to believe our Virginia women, can be. The soldier had slept soundly. He awoke only once during the night, when tired nature forced his nurse to change her posture; and when after the morning came she was relieved of her charge, and she fell ill of the exhaustion and exposure of that night. Her consolation during the weary weeks she lay suffering was that she had saved a brave soldier for her country.

In the succeeding year, Captain Hancock, of the Louisiana Infantry, was brought to Winchester, wounded and a prisoner. He lay many weeks in the hospital, and when nearly recovered of his wounds, was notified that he would be sent to Fort Delaware. As the time drew near for his consignment to this hopeless prison, he confided to Miss Lenie Russell, the same young girl who had saved young Ridgely's life, that he was engaged to be married to a lady of lower Virginia, and was resolved to attempt to make his escape. She cordially entered into his plans, and aided in their successful accomplishment. The citizens of Winchester were permitted sometimes to send articles of food and comfort to the sick and wounded Confederates, and Miss Russell availed herself of this to procure the escape of the gallant captain. She caused him to don the badge of a hospital attendant, take a market basket on his arm and accompany her to a house, whence he might, with least danger of detection and arrest, effect his return to his own lines. Captain Hancock made good use of his opportunity and safely rejoined his comrades; survived the war; married his sweetheart, and to this day omits no occasion for showing his respect and gratitude for the generous woman to whose courage and address he owes his freedom and his happiness.

SPOKEN LIKE CORNELIA

[From The Gray Jacket, page 529.]

A young lady of Louisiana, whose father's plantation had been brought within the enemy's lines in their operations against Vicksburg, was frequently constrained by the necessities of her situation to hold conversation with the Federal officers. On one of these occasions, a Yankee official inquired how she managed to preserve her equanimity and cheerfulness and so many trials and privations, and such severe reverses of fortune. "Our army," said he, "has deprived your father of two hundred negroes, and literally desolated two magnificent plantations."

She said to the officer—a leader of that army, which had, for months, hovered around Vicksburg, powerless to take it with all their vast appliances of war, and mortified by their repeated failures: "I am not insensible to the comforts and elegances which fortune can secure, and of which your barbarian hordes have deprived me; but a true Southern woman will not weep over them, while her country remains. If you wish to crush me, take Vicksburg."

A SPECIMEN MOTHER

[Mrs. Fannie A. Beers' Memories, pages 208-209.]

At the commencement of the war there lived in Sharon, Miss., Mr. and Mrs. O'Leary, surrounded by a family of five stalwart sons. Mrs. Catherine O'Leary was a fond and loving mother, but also an unfaltering patriot, and her heart was fired with love for the cause of Southern liberty. Therefore when her brave sons, one after another, went forth to battle for the right, she bade them God-speed. "Be true to your God and your country," said this noble woman, "and never disgrace your mother by flinching from duty."

Her youngest and, perhaps, dearest, was at that time only 14. For a while she felt that his place was by her side; but in 1863, when he was barely 17, she no longer tried to restrain him. Her trembling hands, having arrayed the last beloved boy for the sacrifice, rested in blessings on his head ere he went forth. Repressing the agony which swelled her heart, she calmly bade him, also, "Do your duty. If you must die, let it be with your face to the foe." And so went forth James A. O'Leary, at the tender age of 17, full of ardor and hope. He was at once assigned to courier duty under General Loring. On the 28th of July, 1864, at the battle of Atlanta, he was shot through the hip, the bullet remaining in the wound, causing intense suffering, until 1870, when it was extracted, and the wound healed for the first time. Notwithstanding this wound, he insisted upon returning to his command, which, in the mean time, had joined Wood's regiment of cavalry. This was in 1865, and, so wounded, he served three months, surrendering with General Wirt Adams at

Gainesville. A short but very glorious record. Mrs. O'Leary still lives in Sharon. The old fire is unquenched.

MRS. ROONEY

[Mrs. Fannie A. Beers' Memories, pages 217-220.]

There is one bright, shining record of a patriotic and tireless woman which remains undimmed when placed beside that of the most devoted Confederate women. I refer to Mrs. Rose Rooney, of Company K, Fifteenth Louisiana Regiment, who left New Orleans in June, 1861, and never deserted the "b'ys" for a day until the surrender.

She was no hanger-on about camp, but in everything but actual fighting was as useful as any of the boys she loved with all her big, warm, Irish heart, and served with the undaunted bravery which led her to risk the dangers of every battlefield where the regiment was engaged, unheeding havoc made by the solid shot, so that she might give timely succor to the wounded or comfort the dying. When in camp she looked after the comfort of the regiment, both sick and well, and many a one escaped being sent to the hospital because Rose attended to him so well. She managed to keep on hand a stock of real coffee, paying at times $35 per pound for it. The surrender almost broke her heart. Her defiant ways caused her to be taken prisoner. I will give in her own words an account of what followed:

"Sure, the Yankees took me prisoner along with the rest. The next day, when they were changing the camps to fix up for the wounded, I asked them what they would do with me. They tould me to 'go to the devil.' I tould them, 'I've been long in his company; I'd choose something better.' I then asked them where any Confederates lived. They tould me about three miles through the woods. On my way I met some Yankees. They asked me, 'What have you in that bag?' I said, 'Some rags of my own.' I had a lot of rags on the top, but six new dresses at the bottom; and sure, I got off with them all. Then they asked me if I had any money. I said no; but in my stocking I had two hundred dollars in Confederate money. One of the Yankees, a poor devil of a private soldier, handed me three twenty-five cents of Yankee money. I said to him, 'Sure, you must be an Irishman.' 'Yes,' said he. I then went on till I got to the house. Mrs. Crump and her sister were in the yard, and about twenty negro women—no men. I had not a bite for two days, nor any water, so I began to cry from weakness. Mrs. Crump said, 'Don't cry; you are among friends.' She then gave me plenty to eat,—hot hoecakes and buttermilk. I stayed there fifteen days, superintending the cooking for the sick and wounded men. One half of the house was full of Confederates and the other of Yankees. They then brought us to Burkesville, where all the Yankees were gathered together. There was an ould doctor there, and he began to curse me, and to talk about all we had done to their prisoners. I tould him, 'And what have you to say to what you done to our poor fellows?' He tould me to shut up, and sure I did. They asked me fifty questions after, and I never opened me mouth. The next day was the day when all the Confederate flags came to Petersburg. I had some papers in my pocket that would have done harrum to some people, so I chewed them all up and ate them; but I wouldn't take the oath, and I never did take it. The flags were brought in on dirt-carts and as they passed the Federal camps them Yankees would unfurl them and shake them about to show them. My journey from Burkesville to Petersburg was from 11 in the morning till 11 at night, and I sitting on my bundle all the way. The Yankee soldiers in the car were cursing me, and calling me a damn rebel, and more ugly talk. I said, 'Mabbe some of you has got a mother or wife; if so, you'll show some respect for me.' Then they were quiet. I had to walk three miles to Captain Buckner's headquarters. The family were in the house near the battle-ground, but the door was shut, and I didn't know who was inside, and I couldn't see any light. I sat down on the porch, and thought I would have to stay there all night. After a while I saw a light coming from under the door, and so I knocked; when the door was opened and they saw who it was, they were all delighted to see me because they were afraid I was dead. I wanted to go to Richmond, but would not go on a Yankee transportation. When the brigade came down, I cried me heart out because I was not let go on with them. I stayed three months with Mrs. Cloyd, and then Major Rawle sent me forty dollars and fifty more if I needed it, and that brought me home to New Orleans."

Mrs. Rooney is still cared for and cherished by the veterans of Louisiana. At the Soldiers' Home she holds the position of matron, and her little room is a shrine never neglected by visitors to "Camp Nichols."

WARNING BY A BRAVE GIRL

[Our Women in the War, pages 63-64.]

I know of a girl who rode through the storm of a winter's night, many miles, to give information to our soldiers when Sherman was on his way to Atlanta. The country far and wide was filled with soldiers, and skirmishing was of constant occurrence. By her efforts many lives were saved, and as she returned homeward the shot and shell were falling thick and fast around her. Later, a desperate encounter took place in her father's yard between contending armies, and her courage was wonderful in assisting the wounded and baffling inquiries from the Yankee officers, who made headquarters in her home. She still managed to give important information, and defied detection.

This girl is of an ancient family, and soldier blood is in her veins. Her grandfather was a general in the United States army before her mother was grown.

A PLUCKY GIRL WITH A PISTOL

[Our Women in the War, pages 37-39.]

Charleston was under an iron heel, the heel of despair. Every house had its shutters closed and darkened; all the rooms overlooking the streets were abandoned; the women endeavored to give a deserted and dreary aspect to every mansion, and lived as retiringly as possible in the back portions of their dwellings, hoping that the Northern soldiery in the city would suppose such houses to be deserted and therefore would not search them.

But this did not save Mr. Cunningham's house. By a strange coincidence it was again a company of black Michigan troops, with a negro in command, that burst open the locked gate, tore up the flower garden, and finally streamed up the back piazza steps, armed with muskets and glittering bayonets that shone in the noonday sun, their faces blacker than ink, their eyes red with drink and malice. The three girls saw them from the dining- room and shivered, but not one moment was lost. Cecil pushed the other two into the room, saying, "Stay here, I will go close this door and meet them," and advancing quickly she reached the entrance to the piazza just as the captain set his foot on the last step, and would have entered, but that her slight person filled up the narrow space.

"What do you want here?" she asked. "Why do you and your troops rush into my house?"

"We want quarters here, and quarters we will have. Move aside and let us in."

"I shall not; we don't take boarders, and I have not invited you as guests. Go away at once, or I will report you to the general in command."

"D——n you, move aside, or I will throw you down."

"Keep your hands off if you are wise," said Cecil, instantly placing one ofher own in her pocket, and never removing her steady eyes from hisface.

"By God! I believe you have got a pistol; let's search her person for arms."

"I have a pistol and shall shoot the first person that touches me, even if you all strike and kill me afterwards. Leave this yard, and do it at once. By 3 o'clock I will give you an answer if you come here for quarters then; now go!"

"You little rebel devil! We will be back, and we will stay next time, be sure;

and will take that same pistol from you, too."

With an extra volley of fearful curses they departed and the girls rushed to Cecil, who, after the excitement was over and nerve no longer needed, turned white and faint. Then they all sat down and cried, feeling like desolate orphans.

MOSBY'S MEN AND TWO NOBLE GIRLS

[In Wearing of the Gray, pages 545-547.]

The force at Morgan's Lane was too great to meet front to front, and the ground so unfavorable for receiving their assault, that Mountjoy gave the order for his men to save themselves, and they abandoned the prisoners and horses, put spurs to their animals, and retreated at full gallop past the mill, across a little stream, and up the long hill upon which was situated the mansion above referred to. Behind them the one hundred Federal cavalrymen came on at full gallop, calling upon them to halt, and firing volleys into them as they retreated.

We beg now to introduce upon the scene the female *dramatis personae* of the incident—two young ladies who had hastened out to the fence as soon as the firing began, and now witnessed the whole. As they reached the fence, the fifteen men of Captain Mountjoy appeared, mounting the steep road like lightning, closely pursued by the Federal cavalry, whose dense masses completely filled the narrow road. The scene at the moment was sufficient to try the nerves of the young ladies. The clash of hoofs, the crack of carbines, the loud cries of "halt! halt!! halt!!!"—this tramping, shouting, banging, to say nothing of the quick hiss of bullets filling the air, rendered the "place and time" more stirring than agreeable to one consulting the dictates of a prudent regard to his or her safety.

Nevertheless, the young ladies did not stir. They had half mounted the board fence, and in this elevated position were exposed to a close and dangerous fire; more than one bullet burying itself in the wood close to their persons. But they did not move—and this for a reason more creditable than mere curiosity to witness the engagement, which may, however, have counted for something. This attracted them, but they were engaged in "doing good," too. It was of the last importance that the men should know where they could cross the river.

"Where is the nearest ford?" they shouted.

"In the woods there," was the reply of one of the young ladies, pointing with her hand, and not moving.

"How can we reach it?"

"Through the gate," and waving her hand, the speaker directed the rest, amid a storm of bullets burying themselves in the fence close beside her.

The men went at full gallop towards the ford. Last of all came Mountjoy—but Mountjoy, furious, foaming almost at the mouth, on fire with indignation, and uttering oaths so frightful that they terrified the young ladies much more than the balls or the Federal cavalry darting up the hill.

The partisan had scarcely disappeared in the woods, when the enemy rushed up, and demanded which way the Confederates had taken.

"I will not tell you," was the reply of the youngest girl. The trooper drew a pistol, and cocking it, levelled it at her head.

"Which way?" he thundered.

The young lady shrunk from the muzzle, and said: "How do I know?"

"Move on!" resounded from the lips of the officer in command, and the column rushed by, nearly trampling upon the ladies, who ran into the house.

Here a new incident greeted them, and one sufficiently tragic. Before the door, sitting on his horse, was a trooper, clad in blue—and at sight of him the ladies shrunk back. A second glance showed them that he was bleeding to death from a mortal wound. The bullet had entered his side, traversed the body, issued from the opposite side, inflicting a wound which rendered death almost certain.

"Take me from my horse!" murmured the wounded man, stretching out his arms and tottering.

The young girls ran to him.

"Who are you—one of the Yankees?" they exclaimed.

"Oh, no!" was the faint reply. "I am one of Mountjoy's men. Tell him, when you see him, that I said, 'Captain, this is the first time I have gone out with you, and the last!'"

As they assisted him from the saddle, he murmured: "My name is William Armistead Braxton. I have a wife and three little children living in Hanover—you must let them know—"

The poor fellow fainted; and the young ladies were compelled to carry him in their arms into the house, where he was laid upon a couch, writhing in agony.

They had then time to look at him, and saw before them a young man of gallant countenance, elegant figure—in every outline of his person betraying the gentleman born and bred. They afterwards discovered that he had just joined Mosby, and that, as he had stated, this was his first scout. Poor fellow! it was also his last.

A SPARTAN DAME AND HER YOUNG

[From The Gray Jacket, page 488.]

"We were once," says General D. H. Hill, "witness to a remarkable piece of coolness in Virginia. A six-gun battery was shelling the woods furiously near which stood a humble hut. As we rode by, the shells were fortunately too high to strike the dwelling, but this might occur any moment by lowering the angle or shortening the fire. The husband was away, probably far off in the army, but the good housewife was busy at the wash-tub, regardless of all the roar and crash of shells and falling timber. Our surprise at her coolness was lost in greater amazement at observing three children, the oldest not more than 10, on top of a fence, watching with great interest the flight of the shells. Our curiosity was so much excited by the extraordinary spectacle that we could not refrain from stopping and asking the children if they were not afraid. 'Oh, no,' replied they, 'the Yankees ain't shooting at us, they are shooting at the soldiers.'"

SINGING UNDER FIRE

[A Rebel's Recollections, pages 72-73.]

They [the women of Petersburg] carried their efforts to cheer and help the troops into every act of their lives. When they could, they visited camp. Along the lines of march they came out with water or coffee or tea—the best they had, whatever it might be; with flowers, or garlands of green when their flowers were gone. A bevy of girls stood under a sharp fire from the enemy's lines at Petersburg one day, while they sang Bayard Taylor's "Song of the Camp," responding to an encore with the stanza:

"Ah! soldiers, to your honored rest,

  Your truth and valor bearing;

The bravest are the tenderest,

  The loving are the daring!"

Indeed, the coolness of women under fire was always a matter of surprise to me. A young girl, not more than 16 years of age, acted as guide to a scouting party during the early years of the war, and when we urged her to go back after the enemy had opened a vigorous fire upon us, she declined, on the plea that she believed we were "going to charge those fellows," and she "wanted to see the fun." At Petersburg women did their shopping and went about their duties under a most uncomfortable bombardment, without evincing the slightest fear or showing any nervousness whatever.

A WOMAN'S LAST WORD

[Eggleston, in Southern Soldier Stories, pages 225-227.]

The city of Richmond was in flames. We were beginning that last terrible retreat which ended the war. Fire had been set to the arsenal as a military possession, which must on no account fall into the enemy's hands. As the flames spread, because of a turn of the wind, other buildings caught. The whole business part of the city was on fire. To make things worse, some idiot had ordered that all the liquor in the city should be poured into the gutters. The rivers of alcohol had been ignited from the burning buildings. It was a time and scene of unutterable terror.

As we marched up the fire-lined street, with the flames scorching the very hair off our horses, George Goodsmith—the best cannoneer that ever wielded a rammer—came up to the headquarters squad, and said: "Captain, my wife's in Richmond. We've been married less than a year. She is soon to become a mother. I beg permission to bid her good-bye. I'll join the battery later."

The permission was granted readily, and George Goodsmith put spurs to his horse. He had just been made a sergeant, and was therefore mounted. It was in the gray of the morning that he hurriedly met his wife. With caresses of the tenderest kind, he bade her farewell. Realizing for a moment the utter hopelessness of our making another stand on the Roanoke, or any other line, he said in the bitterness of his soul: "Why shouldn't I stay here and take care of you?"

The woman straightened herself and replied: "I would rather be the widow of a brave man than the wife of a coward."

That was their parting, for the time was very short. Mayo's bridge across the James River was already in flames when Goodsmith perilously galloped across it.

Three or four days later—for I never could keep tab on time at that period of the war—we went into the battle at Farmville. Goodsmith was in his place in command of the piece. Just before fire opened he beckoned to me, and I rode up to hear what he had to say.

"I'm going to be killed, I think," he said. "If I am, I want my wife to know that she is the widow of a—brave man. I want her to know that I did my duty to the last. And—and if you live long enough and this thing don't kill Mary—I want you to tell the little one about his father."

Goodsmith's premonition of his death was one of many that were fulfilled during the war. A moment later a fearful struggle began. At the first fire George Goodsmith's wife became the "widow of a brave man." His body was heavy with lead.

His son, then unborn, is now a successful broker in a great city. There is nothing particularly knightly or heroic about him, for this is not a knightly or heroic age. But he takes very tender care of his mother—that "widow of a brave man."

TWO MISSISSIPPI GIRLS HOLD YANKEES AT PISTOL POINT

[In Richmond Enquirer, July 22, 1862, page 3.]

A Memphis correspondent of the *Appeal*, in referring to the bad treatment of citizens by the Federal soldiers, related the following:

The most unmanly and brutal act that I know of is their treatment of two Misses Coe. Levin Coe, their brother, was at home, discharged from the army. They surrounded the house before the family knew they were on the place. Fortunately young Coe had gone fishing, and two of his sisters escaped to the garden and ran to warn him not to come home. The Yankees saw the way they went, and followed them, but the sisters outran them and gave their brother the information of their coming. They came up with the ladies at a house in the vicinity of the creek, and attempted to arrest them, but they were both armed and dared the six big, strapping Yankees to lay their hands on them. One would say to another, "She's got a pistol; take it away from her." And she, a weak woman, stood at bay and told them to touch her at their peril. And the craven wretches dared not do it. At last, to get them from the neighborhood of their brother, they agreed to go to headquarters with them. It was then noon, and these girls had run two miles, and then these scoundrels marched them off on foot four miles to town. At every step they tried to get their pistols from them, threatening them with instant death if they did not give them up. Three times they placed their pistols at the girls' hearts with them cocked and their fingers on the trigger, telling them they would kill them. Each time the girls replied, "Shoot; I can shoot as quick as you can." And they never did give them up until their brother-in-law came up with them and told them to do so, and he gave himself up in their place. Levin Coe escaped.

"WAR WOMEN" OF PETERSBURG

[Southern Soldier Stories, pages 72-73.]

During all those weary months the good women of Petersburg went about their household affairs with fifteen-inch shells dropping occasionally into their boudoirs or uncomfortably near to their kitchen ranges. Yet they paid no attention to any danger that threatened themselves. Their deeds of mercy will never be adequately recorded until the angels report. But this much I want to say of them—they were "war women" of the most daring and devoted type. When there was need of their ministrations on the line, they were sure to be promptly there; and once, as I have recorded elsewhere in print, a bevy of them came out to the lines only to encourage us, and, under a fearful fire, sang Bayard Taylor's "Song of the Camp," giving as an encore the lines:

"Ah! soldiers, to your honored rest,
  Your truth and valor bearing;
The bravest are the tenderest,
  The loving are the daring."

With inspiration such as these women gave us, it was no wonder that, as I heard General Sherman say soon after the war: "It took us four years, with all our enormous superiority in resources, to overcome the stubborn resistance of those men."

JOHN ALLEN'S COW

While General Milroy was in possession of Winchester he was extremely harsh and vindictive towards the people. A great many of them were reduced to the borders of starvation. Miss Allen, a 15-year-old Southern girl, was a member of a family almost absolutely dependent on a good cow's milk for sustenance. In a short time the cow's food was exhausted and the prospect looked dark indeed. There was a good pasturage just outside the town, beyond the guard lines of the Federal troops. The brave girl volunteered to lead the cow out and attend her while grazing. A permit to pass the lines from General Milroy was necessary. She went to the general and laid her case before him and asked for a permit. He flatly refused her request and rudely insulted the poor girl.

"I can't do anything for you rebels and I will not let you pass. The rebellion has got to be crushed," said he.

"Well," answered the girl, "if you think you can crush the rebellion by starving John Allen's old cow, just crush away."

THE FAMILY THAT HAD NO LUCK

[Eggleston, in Southern Soldier Stories, pages 23-24.]

At the battle of Fredericksburg, as we tumbled into the sunken road, an old man came in bearing an Enfield rifle and wearing an old pot hat of the date of 1857 or thereabouts. With a gentle courtesy that was unusual in war, he apologized to the two men between whom he placed himself, saying: "I hope I don't crowd you, but I must find a place somewhere from which I can shoot."

At that moment one of the great assaults occurred. The old man used his gun like an expert. He wasted no bullet. He took aim every time and fired only when he knew his aim to be effective. Yet he fired rapidly.

Tom Booker, who stood next to him, said as the advancing column was swept away: "You must have shot birds on the wing in your time."

The old man answered: "I did up to twenty years ago; but then I sort o' lost my sight, you know, and my interest in shootin'."

"Well, you've got 'em both back again," called out Billy Goodwin, from down the line.

"Yes," said the old man. "You see I had to. It's this way: I had six boys and six gells. When the war broke out I thought the six boys could do my family's share o' the fightin'. Well, they did their best, but they didn't have no luck. One of 'em was killed at Manassas, two others in a cavalry raid, and the other three fell in different actions—'long the road, as you might say. We ain't seemed to a had no luck. But it's just come to this, that if the family is to be represented, the old man must git up his shootin' agin, or else one o' the gells would have to take a hand. So here I am."

Just then the third advance was made. A tremendous column of heroic fellows was hurled upon us, only to be swept away as its predecessors had been. Two or three minutes did the work, but at the end of that time the old man fell backward, and Tom Booker caught him in his arms.

"You're shot," he said.

"Yes. The family don't seem to have no luck. If one of my gells comes to you, you'll give her a fair chance to shoot straight, won't you, boys?"

BRAVE WOMEN AT RESACA, GA.

[By J. L. Underwood.]

In a letter to Mrs. E. J. Simmons, of Calhoun, Ga., dated June 7, 1896, Rev. Jno. C. Portis, of Union, Miss., formerly of the Eighteenth Mississippi Regiment, and now a Congregational Methodist minister, writes:

"My good right arm lies about a mile south of Resaca, Ga., just north of a church at the root of a large oak or chestnut tree. It was put in a board box and buried by a comrade. Hence you see I feel an interest in the wild hills of Resaca. I was a private in Company B, Eighth Mississippi Volunteer Inf., and was wounded in right shoulder and throat about dark in a charge on the enemy's works, May 14, 1864, on the side of a hill just west of the village on the north side of the river. I was carried back to the bluff below the bridge, where about three or four hundred poor fellows were lying torn, bleeding, and some dying. After a time I crossed the bridge, and, faint and sick, I was trying to make my way to Cheatham's Division Hospital, which was in the church. A man came into the road with an ox wagon loaded in part with beds which appeared to be very white. Some one called him Motes and asked him about his family (Motes's family), and he said they had gone on to Calhoun. Mr. Motes insisted that I should ride, and said his wife would not care if all her beds were dyed with rebel blood. He carried me to the old church. I would like to know what became of Mr. Motes; I could not see his face. The night was dark. Sunday morning, May 15, about eight o'clock, my right arm was amputated at the shoulder joint. Thirty-two years have passed since then, and strange it may seem that a boy soldier, that few thought could live, is writing this reminiscence of those two days of carnage. Never shall I forget the morning of that fateful 14th of May, when at early dawn the signal guns told us in tones of thunder that both armies were ready for the work of death. Bright rose the sun, tipping mountain peak with blooming rays of silver and bathing valley and woodland in a flood of golden light, a scene never to be witnessed again by hundreds of the boys who wore the blue and the gray. In the streets of Resaca that day I saw enacted a deed of heroism which challenged the admiration of all who witnessed it. A wagon occupied by several ladies was passing along north of the river and just west of the railroad, when a Yankee battery opened fire on it and, until it had passed over the bridge, poured a storm of shells around it. A young woman stood erect in the wagon waving her hat, which was dressed with red or had a red ribbon or plume on it, seemingly to defy the cowards who would make war on defenceless women. I felt then, as I do to-day, for that woman a man could freely die. Many a rebel boy felt as I did that day. I was taken from the church to a bush-arbor on the west side of the railroad, where I expected to die. A middle-aged woman dressed in black came with nourishment and (God forever bless her) fed me, and during that awful day ministered to the wants of the wounded and dying. If I remember correctly she came often to me with food and drink. Who she was I may never know, but she was a noble woman."

The fearlessness of the Southern women under cannon and rifle fire mentioned in the above incident was exhibited time and again during the war. The women seemed to have their souls and bodies keyed up for any and all emergencies. There may be something of an explanation in the fact that they belonged to a race of marksmen and expected bullets and cannon balls to hit what they were aimed to hit, and as they didn't think anybody was trying to kill them, they apprehended no danger.

A WOMAN'S HAIR

[Southern Soldier Stories, pages 82-84.]

About 10 o'clock in the morning the sharpshooters began. Our captain instantly divided us into two squads, and without military formalities said: "Now, boys, ride to the right and left and corner 'em."

That was the only command we received, but we obeyed it with a will. The two sharpshooting citizens who were there that morning escaped on good horses, but we captured the pickets.

Among them was a woman—a Juno in appearance, with a wealth of raven black hair twisted carelessly into a loose knot under the jockey cap she wore. She was mounted on a superb chestnut mare, and she knew how to ride. She might easily have escaped, and at one time seemed to do so, but at the critical moment she seemed to lose her head and so fell into our hands.

When we brought her to Charlie Irving she was all smiles and graciousness, and Charlie was all blushes.

"You'd hang me to a tree, if I were a man, I suppose," she said. "And serve me right, too. As I'm only a woman, you'd better send me to General Stuart, instead."

This seemed so obviously the right way out of it Charlie ordered Ham Seay and me to escort her to Stuart's headquarters, which were under a tree some miles in the rear.

When we got there Stuart seemed to recognize the young woman. Or perhaps it was only his habitual and constitutional gallantry that made him come forward with every manifestation of welcome, and himself help her off her horse, taking her by the waist for that purpose.

Ham Seay and I, being mere privates, were ordered to another tree. But we could not help seeing that cordial relations were quickly established between our commander and this young woman. We saw her presently take down her magnificent black hair and remove from it some papers. They were not "curl papers," or that sort of stuffing which women call "rats." Stuart was a very gallant man, and he received the papers with much fervor. He spread them out carefully on the ground, and seemed to be reading what was written or drawn upon them. Then he talked long and earnestly with the young woman and seemed to be coming to some definite sort of understanding with her. Then she dined with him on some fried salt pork and some hopelessly indigestible fried paste. Then he mounted her on her mare again and summoned Ham

Seay and me.

"Escort this young lady back to Captain Irving," he said. "Tell him to send her to the Federal lines under flag of truce, with the message that she was inadvertently captured in a picket charge, and that as General Stuart does not make war on women and children, he begs to return her to her home and friends."

We did all this.

The next day, Stuart with a strong force advanced to Mason's and Munson's mills. From there we could clearly see a certain house in Washington. It had many windows, and each had a dark Holland shade. When we stood guard we were ordered to observe minutely and report accurately the slidings up and down of those Holland shades. We never knew what three shades up, two half up, and five down might signify. But we had to report it, nevertheless, and Stuart seemed from that time to have an almost preternatural advance perception of the enemy's movements. That young woman certainly had a superb shock of hair.

A BREACH OF ETIQUETTE

[Eggleston, in Southern Soldier Stories, pages 121-123.]

Finally we went near to Martinsburg, and came upon a farm-house. The farm gave no appearance of being a large one, or one more than ordinarily prosperous, yet we saw through the open door a dozen or fifteen "farm hands" eating dinner, all of them in their shirt-sleeves. Stuart rode up, with a few of us at his back, to make inquiries, and we dismounted. Just then a slip of a girl, —not over 14, I should say—accompanied by a thickset young bull-dog, with an abnormal development of teeth, ran up to meet us.

She distinctly and unmistakably "sicked" that dog upon us. But as the beast assailed us, the young girl ran after him and restrained his ardor by throwing her arms around his neck. As she did so, she kept repeating in a low but very insistent tone to us: "Make 'em put their coats on! Make 'em put their coats on! Make 'em put their coats on!"

Stuart was a peculiarly ready person. He said not one word to the young girl as she led her dog away, but with a word or two he directed a dozen or so of us to follow him with cocked carbines into the dining-room. There he said to the "farm hands:" "Don't you know that a gentleman never dines without his coat? Aren't you ashamed of yourselves? And ladies present, too! Get up and put on your coats, every man jack of you, or I'll riddle you with bullets in five seconds."

They sprang first of all into the hallway, where they had left their arms; but either the bull-dog or the 14-year-old girl had taken care of that. The arms were gone. Then seeing the carbines levelled, they made a hasty search of the hiding-places in which they had bestowed their coats. A minute later they appeared as fully uniformed but helplessly unarmed Pennsylvania volunteers.

They were prisoners of war at once, without even an opportunity to finish that good dinner. As we left the house the young girl came up to Stuart and said: "Don't say anything about it, but the dog wouldn't have bit you. He knows which side we're on in this war."

As we rode away this young girl—she of the bull-dog—cried out: "To think the wretches made us give 'em dinner; and in their shirt-sleeves, too."

LOLA SANCHEZ'S RIDE

[Women in The War.]

During the war for Southern independence there lived just opposite Palatka, on the east bank of the St. Johns River, Florida, a Cuban gentleman, Mauritia Sanchez by name, who early in life had left the West Indies to seek a home in the State of Florida. Many years had passed since then and Mr. Sanchez was at the time of the following incident an old man, infirm and in wretched health. The family consisted of an invalid wife, one son, who was in the service of the Confederacy, and three daughters, Panchita, Lola, and Eugenia.

Suspicion had long fastened upon Mr. Sanchez as a spy for the Confederates, and at the time of this incident, the old man had been torn from his home and family and was a prisoner in the old Spanish Fort San Marcos (now Fort Marion), at St. Augustine. The girls occupied the old home with their mother and were entirely unprotected. Many times at night their house was surrounded by white and negro soldiers expecting to surprise them and find Confederates about the place, for the Yankees knew some one was giving information, but thought it was Mr. Sanchez. The Southern soldiers were higher up the St. Johns, on the west side. It was usual for the Yankee officers to visit frequently at the Sanchez home, and the girls, for policy, (and information) were cordial in their reception of them, and thereby gained some protection from the thieving soldiery.

One warm summer's night three Yankee officers came to the Sanchez home to spend the evening. After a short time the three sisters left the officers and went to the dining room to prepare supper. The soldiers, thinking themselves safe, entered into the discussion of a plan to surprise the Confederates on Sunday morning by sending the gunboats up the river, and also by planning that a foraging party should go out from St. Augustine.

On hearing this Lola Sanchez stopped her work and listened. After hearing of the road the foraging party would take and gaining all necessary information, she told Panchita to entertain them until she returned. Stealing softly from the house, she sped to the horse lot, and throwing a saddle on her horse rode for life to the ferry, a mile distant; there the ferryman took her horse, and gave her a boat. She rowed herself across the St. Johns, met one Confederate picket, who knew her and gave her his horse. Out into the night through the woods she rode like the wind to Camp Davis, a mile and a half away. Reaching the camp, she asked for Captain Dickinson, (afterwards General Dickinson) and told him the Yankees were coming up the river Sunday morning and that the troop from St. Augustine would go out foraging in a southerly direction. Then leaving the camp, Lola Sanchez rode for her life indeed. She knew she must not be missed from home. Giving the picket his horse, she recrossed the ferry, then mounting her waiting animal she struck out for home. Dismounting some distance from the house, she turned her horse loose, and reached home in time for supper and pleasantly entertained her guests until a late hour.

That night Captain Dickinson marched his men to intercept the Yankees. He crossed from the west to the east side and surprised them on Sunday. A severe fight ensued. The Yankee General Chatfield was killed and Colonel Nobles wounded and captured. On that same Sunday morning the Yankee gunboats went up the St. Johns to surprise the Confederates. They were very much surprised in turn. The Confederates were ready for them, disabled a gunboat and captured a transport; also many prisoners were taken by the Confederates.

The foraging party lost all their wagons, and everything they had stolen, and again many prisoners were taken, and Captain Dickinson sent for the three sisters to be at the ferry (the one Lola Sanchez crossed) to see the prisoners and wagons that had been taken.

Time and again this daughter of the Confederacy aided and abetted the Southern cause. Some time after a pontoon was captured, and renamed "The Three Sisters" in compliment to these brave young women. The pontoon was coming from Picolata to Orange Mills. Mr. Sanchez still languished in Fort San Marco, however, and Panchita grieved continuously over her father's unjust incarceration. The old man was truly innocent, his daughters were the informers, but he did not know this. Panchita determined to obtain his release if possible. After some time spent in applying, she got a pass to go through the Yankee lines, and boarding one of their transports, this young woman went alone to St. Augustine, and gained her father's freedom, taking him with her back to the old homestead.

There is the "Emily Geiger Ride," and "Lill Servosse's Ride," but none more daring than that of Lola Sanchez, the young Floridian of the Southern Confederacy. The U. D. C. should look to it that one chapter at least should be Lola Sanchez Chapter.

Lola Sanchez married Emanuel Lopez, a Confederate soldier of the St. Augustine Blues; Eugenia married Albert Rogers, another soldier of the St. Augustine Blues; Panchita is the widow of the late John R. Miot, of Columbia, S. C. Lola Sanchez died about seven years ago. May the memory of this Southern woman never fade.

These facts were recently related to me by Mrs. Eugenia Rogers, of St. Augustine.

ELIZABETH W. MULLINGS.

THE REBEL SOCK
A TRUE EPISODE IN SEWARD'S RAIDS ON THE OLD LADIES OF MARYLAND

BY TENELLA.

[The Gray Jacket, pages 510-513.]

In all the pride and pomp of war
  The Lincolnite was dressed;
High beat his patriotic heart
  Beneath his armoured vest.
His maiden sword hung by his side,
  His pistols both were right,
  His coat was buttoned tight.
His shining spurs were on his heels;
A firm resolve sat on his brow,
  For he to danger went.
By Seward's self that day he was
  On secret service sent.
"Mount and away!" he sternly cried
  Unto the gallant band.
Who all equipped from head to heel

Awaited his command.
"But halt, my boys—before we go
These solemn words I'll say,
Lincoln expects that every man
His duty'll do to-day!"
"We will! we will!" the soldiers cried,
"The President shall see
That we will only run away
From Jackson or from Lee!"
And now they're off, just four score men,
A picked and chosen troop.
And like a hawk upon a dove
On Maryland they swoop.
From right to left, from house to house,
The little army rides.
In every lady's wardrobe look
To see that there she hides;
They peep in closets, trunks, and drawers,
Examine every box;
Not rebel soldiers now they seek,
But rebel soldiers' socks!
But all in vain—too keen for them
Were those dear ladies there,
And not a sock or flannel shirt
Was taken anywhere.
The day wore on to afternoon,
That warm and drowsy hour,
When Nature's self doth seem to feel
A touch of Morpheus' power.

A farm-house door stood open wide,
  The men were all away,
The ladies sleeping in their rooms,
  The children at their play;
The house dog lay upon the steps,
  But never raised his head,
Though cracking on the gravel walk
  He heard a stranger's tread.
Old grandma, in her rocking chair,
  Sat knitting in the hall,
When suddenly upon her work
  A shadow seemed to fall.
She raised her eyes and there she saw
  Our Fed'ral hero stand.
His little cap was on his head;
  His sword was in his hand;
While circling round and round the house
  His gallant soldiers ride
To guard the open kitchen door
  And chicken coop beside.
Slowly the dear old lady rose
  And tottering forward came,
And peering dimly through her "specks,"
  Said, "Honey, what's your name?"
Then as she raised her withered hand
  To pat his sturdy arm—
"There's no one here but grandmamma,
  And she won't do you harm;
Come, take a seat and don't be scared;

Put up your sword, my child,
I would not hurt you for the world,"
She gently said and smiled.
"Madam, my duty must be done,
And I am firm as rock!"
Then pointing to her work he said,
"Is that a rebel sock!"
"Yes, honey, I am getting old,
And for hard work ain't fit,
But for Confederate soldiers still
I, thank the Lord, can knit."
"Madam, your work is contraband,
And Congress confiscates
This rebel sock, which I now seize,
To the United States."
"Yes, honey, don't be scared, for I
Will give it up to you."
Then slowly from the half knit sock
The dame her needles drew,
Broke off her thread, wound up herball
And stuck her needles in.
"Here, take it, child, and I to-night
Another will begin!"
The soldier next his loyal heart
The dear-bought trophy laid,
And that was all that Seward got
By this "old woman's raid."

CHAPTER V
THEIR CAUSE

INTRODUCTORY NOTE TO "THEIR CAUSE"

In no sense does the author offer the suggestions in this section as an apology for the course of Southern women or men in the war between the States. They are presented simply as a part of history, showing the political principles which guided and moved the South in the momentous struggle. They explain the lofty zeal and heroic fortitude of the Confederate women. They cannot be attributed to partisanship or sectional bias on the part of the author, for sufficient quotations are herewith presented from well-known Northern, English, and Continental public men to show that if there is an extreme Southern view it is held by other people as well as by our own.

Right or wrong, each Southern man in the field and each woman at home, toiled in that war with a *mens sibi conscia recti*. It was a movement of the people. In the ranks of the army were found hundreds of college graduates and men carrying muskets whose property was valued at a hundred thousand dollars, and at home the rich and the poor women toiled with equal zeal for the cause so dear to their hearts.

"WHEN THIS CRUEL WAR IS OVER"

Mrs. W. W. Gordon, of Savannah, the wife of the brave ex-Confederate officer who was commissioned brigadier general by President McKinley, and served with distinguished gallantry in the Spanish War, had kindred in the Federal army, which under Sherman captured Savannah. As the troops were entering the city she stood with her children watching them as they marched under the windows of her Southern home. Just then the splendid brass band at the head of one of the divisions began to play the old familiar air, "When this cruel war is over." Just as soon as the notes struck the ear of her little daughter this enthusiastic young Confederate exclaimed, "Mamma, just listen to the Yankees. They are playing, 'When this cruel war is over,' and they are just doing it themselves."

NORTHERN MEN LEADERS OF DISUNION

In 1860 it was plain to the world that the people of the North were determined to spurn the compact of union with the Southern States and to deny to those

States all right to control their own affairs. Here are the sentiments of the Northern leaders:

"There is a higher law than the Constitution which regulates our authority over the domain. Slavery must be abolished, and we must do it."—*Wm. H. Seward.*

"The time is fast approaching when the cry will become too overpowering to resist. Rather than tolerate national slavery as it now exists, let the Union be dissolved at once, and then the sin of slavery will rest where it belongs."—*New York Tribune.*

"The Union is a lie. The American Union is an imposture—a covenant with death and an agreement with hell. We are for its overthrow! Up with the flag of disunion, that we may have a free and glorious republic of our own."—*Wm. Lloyd Garrison.*

"I look forward to the day when there shall be a servile insurrection in the South; when the black man, armed with British bayonets, and led on by British officers, shall assert his freedom and wage a war of extermination against his master. And, though we may not mock at their calamity nor laugh when their fear cometh, yet we will hail it as the dawn of a political millennium."—*Joshua Giddings.*

"In the alternative being presented of the continuance of slavery or a dissolution of the Union, we are for a dissolution, and we care not how quick it comes."—*Rufus P. Spaulding.*

"The fugitive-slave act is filled with horror; we are bound to disobey this act."—*Charles Sumner.*

"The *Advertiser* has no hesitation in saying that it does not hold to the faithful observance of the fugitive-slave law of 1850."—*Portland Advertiser.*

"I have no doubt but the free and slave States ought to be separated. * * * The Union is not worth supporting in connection with the South."—*Horace Greeley.*

"The times demand and we must have an anti-slavery Constitution, an anti-slavery Bible, and an anti-slavery God."—*Anson P. Burlingame.*

"There is merit in the Republican party. It is this: It is the first sectional party ever organized in this country. * * * It is not national; it is sectional. It is the North arrayed against the South. * * * The first crack in the iceberg is visible; you will yet hear it go with a crack through the center."—*Wendell Phillips.*

"The cure prescribed for slavery by Redpath is the only infallible remedy, and men must foment insurrection among the slaves in order to cure the evils. It can never be done by concessions and compromises. It is a great evil, and must be extinguished by still greater ones. It is positive and imperious in its approaches, and must be overcome with equally positive forces. You must commit an assault to arrest a burglar, and slavery is not arrested without a violation of law and the cry of fire."—*Independent Democrat*, leading Republican paper in New Hampshire.

THE UNION VS. A UNION

[J. L. Underwood.]

Early in the war a son of the Emerald Isle, but not himself green, was taken prisoner not far from Manassas Junction. In a word, Pat was taking a quiet nap in the shade; and was aroused from his slumber by a Confederate scouting party. He wore no special uniform of either army, but looked more like a spy than an alligator and on this was arrested.

"Who are you?" "What is your name?" and "Where are you from?" were the first questions put to him by the armed party.

Pat rubbed his eyes, scratched his head, and answered: "Be me faith, gintlemen, them is ugly questions to answer, anyhow; and before I answer any of them, I be after axing yo, by yer lave, the same thing."

"Well," said the leader, "we are out of Scott's army and belong to Washington."

"All right," said Pat. "I knowed ye was a gintleman, for I am that same. Long life to General Scott."

"Ah ha!" replied the scout. "Now you rascal, you are our prisoner," and seized him by the shoulder.

"How is that," inquired Pat, "are we not friends?"

"No," was the answer; "we belong to General Beauregard's army."

"Then ye tould me a lie, me boys, and thinking it might be so, I told you another. An' now tell me the truth, an' I'll tell you the truth too."

"Well, we belong to the State of South Carolina."

"So do I," promptly responded Pat, "and to all the other States uv the country, too, and there I am thinking, I hate the whole uv ye. Do ye think I would come all the way from Ireland to belong to one State when I have a right to belong to the whole of 'em?"

This logic was rather a stumper; but they took him up, as before said, and carried him for further examination.

This Irishman's unionism is a fair sample of what sometimes passes in this country as broad patriotism. "We don't believe in so much State and State's right. We want a nation and we want it spelt with a big N." This is the merest twaddle. From the very nature of the formation of our government there can be no organized Nation. Alexander Hamilton wrote, "The State governments are essentially necessary to the form and spirit of the general system. * * * They can never lose their powers till the whole of America are robbed of their liberties." It is a Union of States and can be made nothing else. Bancroft, the great historian, says: "But for Staterights the Union would perish from the paralysis of its limbs. The States, as they gave life to the Union, are necessary to the continuance of that life."

Madison wrote as follows: "The assent and ratification of the people, not as individuals composing the entire nation, but as composing the distinct and independent States to which they belong, are the sources of the Constitution. It is therefore not a National but a Federal compact."

The Irishman could only belong to the "whole of 'em" by belonging to one of them. No man can love all the other States without loving his own State. A Swiss loves Schwyz or Unterwalden or some other canton before he loves the Confederation of Cantons. The loyal Scotchmen love Scotland before they love the British Empire. The Union man loves the Union through his immediate part of Union. Daniel Webster loved the Union, but his speeches show how he loved Massachusetts first. Calhoun loved the Union, but he loved it as a Federal Union with his beloved Carolina. Many of the best people of the North loved their several States and in loyalty to them took sides against the South.

The Southern people, Whigs and Democrats, were devoted to the Union of the fathers as long as it was a reality. But as soon as they realized that it had become only a confederation of the Northern majority States, with the protecting features of the old Constitution directly discarded, the love for their own States led them heart and soul into the Confederate cause. Our Irishman might be satisfied with A Union, but nothing but THE Union of the fathers could satisfy Southern men. They loved the definite Union of 1789; they fought the indefinite Union of 1861. The former was a union on a Constitution without a flag; the latter was a mere sentimental union under a flag without a Constitution. The Constitution had been thrown away.

The writer's father, a plain old farmer-merchant of Alabama, was a fair specimen of the staunchest Southern Union man. A Whig all his life, he almost adored Henry Clay and idolized the Union. The great old Union paper, the *National Intelligencer*, of Washington City, was his political Bible, and he made it follow his son all through school and college. Like all other Whigs, he believed in the right of secession, but did not think the time had come for such a step. He opposed with all his might the secession of Alabama. But when it was an accomplished fact, he wrote sadly to his son, who was then a student in a foreign land:

> Alabama has seceded. She has the right to do so, but I didn't want her to exercise it. I belong to my State, and I secede with her. And I know the other States have no right to coerce her. My son, your old father is like a Tennessee hog, he can be tolled, but he can't be driven.

Savoyard tells us truly that no State embraced secession with more reluctance than North Carolina, and yet no State supported the Southern cause with more heroism or fortitude. When the news flashed over the wires that President Lincoln had issued a call for volunteers to coerce the sovereign Southern States, Zebulon B. Vance was addressing an immense audience, pleading for the Union and opposing the Confederacy. His hand was raised aloft in appealing gesture when the fatal tidings came, and in relating the incident to a New England audience a quarter of a century later, he said:

> When my hand came down from that impassioned gesticulation it fell slowly and sadly by the side of a secessionist. I immediately, with altered voice and manner, called upon the assembled multitude to volunteer, not to fight against but for South Carolina. If war must come, I preferred to be with my own people. If we had to shed blood I preferred to shed Northern rather than Southern blood.

North Carolina took her favorite son at his word, turned secessionist with him, and volunteered for the conflict.

Robert E. Lee felt in Virginia just like Zeb Vance felt in North Carolina. The women of the South were the women of Lee and Vance and Alex. Stephens and Judah P. Benjamin, Charles J. Jenkins and Ben Hill. They loved the Union, but when it was gone, they, with their States, opposed what, to them, was only a Union of invading, coercing States.

"We were not the first to break the peace

  That blessed our happy land;

We loved the quiet calm and ease,

  Too well to raise a hand,

Till fierce oppression stronger grew,

  And bitter were your sneers.

Then to our land we must be true,

  Or show a coward's fears!

We loved our banner while it waved

An emblem of our Union.
The fiercest dangers we had braved
To guard that sweet communion.
But when it proved that ‘stripes’ alone
Were for our Sunny South,
And all the ‘stars’ in triumph shone
Above the chilly North,
Then, not till then, our voices rose
In one tumultuous wave:
‘We will the tyranny oppose,
Or find a bloody grave.’”

It was Southern devotion to the Union which led so many men of Kentucky and Tennessee into the Federal army. It was the same traditional love for the Union of the fathers that held back Virginia and the other border States from secession too long. It led them to make the mistake of the crisis. The writer, like nearly all the Southern men of his ultra Unionism, at the time thought South Carolina made the mistake of too much haste in her secession. He does not think so now. He has not thought so since calmly and thoroughly studying the history of those times.

The new party in the North was in a triumphant majority and was determined to deprive the minority States of the South of their share in the government. Delay on the part of Southern border States did no good. It did harm. It misled the Northern people as to the true feeling in Virginia and the other border States. Had they all seceded on the same day with South Carolina there would have been no war.

Now that the Northern people, through the broad, patriotic administrations of Cleveland, McKinley and Roosevelt, have restored the Union, and Florida is again a coequal State with New York, and Texans once more fellow-citizens with Pennsylvanians, what section shows more loyalty to the Union and the common country than the South?

Our patriot mothers and grandmothers of 1860 loved the Union. Those who yet survive, and their children, love the Union in 1905. No State is under the ban now. The captured battle flags of Confederate States have been restored to the States by a Republican Congress. The Federal government volunteers to take care of Confederate soldiers’ graves. President, and Congress and Army and Navy follow General Wheeler’s coffin to an honored grave. A

Republican President publicly avows his attachment to Confederate veterans and shows his faith by his appointments. Thank God, our Union to-day is again *the* Union of equal States.

THE NORTHERN STATES SECEDE FROM THE UNION

[By J. L. Underwood.]

The denial of the equal rights of the Southern States in the public territorial domain, and the nullification by the Northern States of the acts of Congress and the decisions of the Supreme Court on territorial questions, and the formation and triumph of a party pledged to hostility to the South, were not the only considerations that convinced the Southern States that their only honorable course lay in secession. The compact of the written Constitution was the only Union that had existed. A breach or repudiation of that compact was a breach of the Union. It was secession without its name.

In 1850, after a violent sectional agitation, which shook the country, over the admission of California as a free State, a compromise measure, proposed by Mr. Clay and advocated by Webster and Calhoun, was adopted by Congress. It was known as the "omnibus bill." It provided, among other things, that California should be a free State; that the slave trade should be abolished in the District of Columbia, and that slaves escaping from their owners, from one State into another, could be arrested anywhere and returned to their owners. Article four, section two of the Federal Constitution makes this provision in the plainest of terms. It was similar to the New England Fugitive Slave law of 1643 enacted by Massachusetts, Connecticut, Plymouth and New Haven. Mr. Webster in his great speech in Faneuil Hall in Boston, in defense of his vote for the "omnibus bill," read the words of the Constitution and showed that the fugitive slave section of the omnibus bill was almost a literal reiteration of the constitutional provision.

The majority of the Northern States repudiated this feature of the act of Congress and declared that it should not be enforced. Here was the boldest nullification, the most direct breaking up of the old Union. Here was the arch rebellion of the century. The question was not what should be done with the fugitive slaves, but whether the Northern States would do what, in the Constitution, they had agreed to do. The South waited for the Northern States to revoke such a flagrant disregard of their rights under the Constitution and such a bold repudiation of the original terms of Union. Patriotic little Rhode Island did rescind her action in the matter, but she was alone. Most of the other States had become desperate in their hostility to the South and, when the South, seeing all hope of justice, all vestige of the old Union, all prospect of peace, hopelessly gone, resorted to quiet, peaceable withdrawal from these domineering States, the resolution was formed and carried out by the party in power, to subjugate the Southern States to the will of the majority States, and keep them in what was called the Union against their will.

The South in seceding made no threat, and contemplated no attempt to invade a Northern State in pursuit of slaves, but simply sought to sever all connection with the States and people who were so determined to ignore her rights, and who nullified their own plighted terms of union. She did not secede in the interest of slavery nor for the purpose of war. The Southern States seceded to take care of the fragments of a broken Union. Slavery, it is true, was the occasion of the rupture. Peaceable secession on the one hand and coercion on the other was the issue of the war. Emancipation was adopted as a war measure two years later by the Northern administration and finally consummated in 1865 as a punitive measure to further crush the conquered South. Such was the public opinion at the time of the fall of Fort Sumter that not a regiment could have been raised at the North to invade Virginia if it had been distinctly called out for the purpose of setting the negroes free. Fanatics by the thousands made a demigod of the murderous John Brown, but it was not fanatics who were in control at Washington. It was the politicians, not working from humanitarian sentiment, true or false, but impelled by a determination to cripple the South and break up her controlling influence in national politics,—a preeminence which had existed from the first days of the government. The politicians shrewdly employed the anti-slavery excitement to gain power for themselves and especially to aggravate the South into secession, and then, smothering every whisper of war for the freedom of the negroes, they raised the rallying cry of "Save the Union" and marshalled the Northern hosts for subjugation. President Davis justly said to a self- constituted umpire visiting him in Richmond, "We are not fighting for slavery; we are fighting for independence. The war will go on unless you acknowledge our right to self-government."

FRENZIED FINANCE AND THE WAR OF 1861

[By J. L. Underwood.]

Was the war between the States in 1861 a war in behalf of slavery on the one side and freedom on the other? Not at all. After all the noisy and fanatical agitation on the subject, only a small minority of the Northern people had expressed any desire to have the negroes of the South emancipated at that time, and no State nor people of the South had said that slavery should be perpetual. All the parties which in 1860 cast any electoral votes distinctly disavowed any intention to interfere with slavery where it existed. This was the declaration even of the Republican party which was triumphant and was now in power. Mr. Lincoln, the President-elect, repeatedly declared that slavery was not to be disturbed in the States, although he said the country could not remain "half slave and half free." Here, then, the North and the South were thoroughly agreed that slavery within the States should continue undisturbed. As to emancipation, both sections of the country and all parties except the ultra-Abolitionists were pro-slavery. The Abolitionists admitted that under the Federal Constitution there could be no power in the national government to free the slaves. They cursed and burned the Constitution as "a compact with the devil and a league with hell," and defiantly repudiated all laws which carried out its provisions. Under the plea of what they called "higher law," they defied law. They were really anarchists. The Free Soil party, which had assumed the name of Republican for party purposes, secretly encouraged the Abolitionists in their mad crusade and welcomed their votes, but persistently disavowed their aims. All rational men knew that the time had not come to turn loose millions of half-civilized Africans in this country; while many, North and South, deplored the existence of slavery and would not advocate it in the abstract, yet they believed that emancipation was not best for the negro and would be accompanied by tremendous peril to the white people. The truth is that the Abolitionists of the North kept up such a blatant and fanatical agitation against the South that it was out of the question, in the excitement of the times, for conservative men, North or South, to think or speak of such an alternative as the immediate freedom of the negroes.

The Republican party, now the dominant party, and its leader, Mr. Lincoln, stood against the immediate freedom of the slaves. But this party had come into power on two ground principles which made its triumph a direct attack on the rights and interests of the Southern States in the Territories.

It gloried in its free-soil doctrine, which was a declaration that the Southern States should no longer enjoy their share in the Territories of the government. It never mounted the steed of abolitionism until 1862 when the emancipation of the slaves was adopted as a war measure, and was so declared by Mr. Lincoln himself. In defiance of the decisions of the Supreme Court, the triumphant party held that Congress should not allow the Southern people the right to take their slave property, although distinctly recognized as property by the Constitution, into the Territories. The Northern legislatures deliberately defied the Supreme Court and its people denounced it and reiterated their free soil demand. Of course this was a direct insult to the South and a public outlawry of the South that no self-respecting people ought to submit to. The Territories were common property to all the States. The South held that while they were Territories the Southern people had as much right to enter and enjoy them as the people of the North, but the South was always willing that the people of the Territory, in organizing a State government, should decide for themselves as a State whether it should be admitted as a slave or free State. The new party declared that under no circumstances should another slave State be admitted. The territorial demands of the new party had been endorsed by the formal acts of a majority of Northern States in their legislatures. The catchword of the new party was "no more extension of slavery." The South had never brought a slave into the country, and never did propose to add another slave to it, but its rights in the common property of the Union it could not surrender to the dictation of the more numerous and populous Northern States.

Then what? Declare war? No. Simply fall back on the right of original sovereignty, on their several Constitutional rights, as the people of New England, when they were in the minority, had threatened to do, and withdraw from the Union with States who declared so distinctly a purpose not to abide by the terms of Union. Then came secession, the only peaceable remedy. In it the South made no claim on territorial or other property. In fact, it was a voluntary surrender of everything not on its own soil to the remaining States. It was old Abraham's alternative to Lot. "Let there be no strife, I pray thee, between me and thee, and between my herdsmen and thy herdsmen, for we be brethren. Is not the whole land before thee? Separate thyself, I pray thee, from me; If thou wilt take the left hand, then I will go to the right; or if thou depart to the right hand, then I will go to the left." Then why should there be war? Indeed, why?

So natural and just was the step of secession that the more enlightened and conscientious Abolitionists conceded the right of South Carolina to withdraw from the Union. Horace Greeley, the powerful editor of the great Abolition organ, the New York *Tribune*, boldly protested against any interference with her departure. Wendell Phillips, the great lawyer and Abolition orator of Boston, said in a public speech: "Deck her brow with flowers, pave her way with gold, and let her go." But Greeley and Phillips were not the politicians nor the party in control of the country. We have shown how the Free Soil aim of the triumphant party led the Northern States to adopt such a course as really to drive the Southern States into secession. What was the main spring of the Free Soil crusade? This brings us to tell in one word what brought on the war. What was the ground issue which held the Northern States so desperately on their crusade against the South? It was the "tariff." New England ideas dominated the thought of the North and Northwest, and it was always a ruling New England idea to get all money possible from the government. New England never lost sight of business, and especially her own business interests. It was only by Virginia's surrender of her vast territories that New England could be brought into the Union and it took subsidies, appropriations for internal improvement, and fishing and tariff bounties to keep her in it.

Very soon she set up a persistent demand for high duties on imports to assist in building up her increasing manufactures. The moderate protective tariffs of the twenties, the tariff of Henry Clay, did not satisfy her. Her cry up to the final passage of the trust-breeding Dingley tariff bill of our day has been that of the horse leech, "Give! give!" The Southern States were agricultural and the prevailing doctrine as to tariff duties was a "tariff for revenue only." The old Southern Whigs, like Clay, only favored a moderate protective tariff as a compromise sop to New England in behalf of her infant industries. But New England was not satisfied with the tariff of the twenties. A little taste of incidental protection had only increased her greed. In the thirties she demanded more. The tariff of 1832 was enacted and proved such a heavy tax on the consumers for the benefit of the manufacturers that South Carolina took the bold stand of nullification against it. By the combined efforts of Clay and Calhoun a compromise was effected and the tariff modified and the country saved. In 1846 the moderate Walker tariff, the "free-trade tariff," was adopted and under it the people of all classes and all sections enjoyed more general prosperity up to 1861 than the country has ever before or since seen.

But New England "frenzied finance" was at work. The taste for public pap had grown by what it fed on. The "almighty dollar" idea in politics was sweeping the North. The *auri sacra fames* had formed a league with a fanatical sectional party. The seed sowing was over; the harvest of financial politics had come. New England must have a higher tariff and votes from agricultural States meant more anti-tariff votes and the tariff advocates decreed that there should be no slave States carved out of the Territories. To secure this the Southern people with their property must be excluded from the occupancy of the Territorial soil. Frenzied finance triumphed, and in the election of Mr. Lincoln the North declared the national territory forbidden ground to the South. Free soil exclusion from their property was openly flaunted in the face of the slave States.

What could the Southern States do under such an insulting ultimatum from the triumphant North? What did they do? Why, they simply fell back on their original right of State sovereignty and, as the North had already broken the Union, peaceably seceded from it.

Then why not, as Greeley and Phillips and thousands of Northern patriots urged, why not let these States go? Frenzied Finance replied in the words of Mr. Lincoln, "If we let the South go, where will we get our revenues?" There it is. They were needed to furnish their cotton and their trade to support the North. It was the frenzied Pharoah of finance that refused to let tribute- paying, brick-making Israel go. Hence the war of subjugation.

It is a grotesque and sad bit of history that while patriots like Crittenden, of Kentucky, Bayard, of Delaware, Black, of Pennsylvania and Seymour, of New York, were anxiously trying to avert war and save the old Union, while the whole world was watching with bated breath the storm gathering around Fort Sumter, the party of frenzied finance, now in control of Congress, defiantly discarded all propositions of peace compromise and concentrated all its mighty energies on the passage of its darling Morrill Tariff Bill. The Morrill tariff bill was enacted April 2, 1861. Fort Sumter fell April 14, 1861. There is the record of cold-blood-money worship. It was not Nero "fiddling while Rome was burning" but it was the legislators of the great American Republic fiddling on a scheme for the financial gain of private business while the glorious Union that we loved and our fathers loved was falling to pieces! The laborer's groans, the widow's sobs, the roar of cannon and the crash of States could not drown the mad New England cry for private subsidy from the public treasury.

THE RIGHT OF SECESSION

[In Southern Historical Papers, Volume 31, pages 87-88.]

It may not be amiss, however, to call attention to the fact that the North already admits that the people of the South were honest in their contentions, and that they at least thought they were right. Furthermore, it is even conceded that the South was not without great support for its contentions from legal, moral and historical points of view. For instance, Professor Goldwin, of Canada, an Englishman, a distinguished historian, resident of and sympathizing with the North during the civil war, recently said:

> Few who have looked into the history can doubt that the Union originally was, and was generally taken by the parties to it to be, a compact; dissoluble, perhaps most of them would have said, at pleasure, dissoluble certainly on breach of the articles of Union.

To the same effect, but in even stronger terms, are the words of Mr. Henry

Cabot Lodge, now a Senator from Massachusetts, who said in one of his historic works:

> When the Constitution was adopted by the votes of States at Philadelphia, and accepted by the votes of States in popular conventions, it is safe to say that there was not a man in the country from Washington and Hamilton on the one side to George Clinton and George Mason on the other, who regarded the new system as anything but an experiment entered upon by the States and from which each and every State had the right peaceably to withdraw, a right which was very likely to be exercised.

As far back as 1887, General Thomas C. Ewing, of Ohio, said in a speech in New York:

> The North craves a living and lasting peace with the South; it also asks no humiliating conditions; it recognizes the fact that the proximate cause of the war was the constitutional question of the right of secession—a question which, until it was settled by the war, had neither a right side nor a wrong side to it. Our forefathers in framing the Constitution purposely left the question unsettled; to have settled it distinctly in the Constitution would have been to prevent the formation of the Union of the thirteen States. They, therefore, committed that question to the future, and the war came on and settled it forever. And, right here, let me say that the South has accepted that settlement in good faith, and will forever abide by it as loyally as the North, although we will never admit that our people were wrong in making the contest.

This question was calmly and logically discussed by Mr. Charles Francis Adams in a late speech delivered in Charleston, S. C., when he said:

> When the Federal Constitution was framed and adopted, "an indestructible union of imperishable States," what was the law of treason, to what or to whom in case of final issue did the average citizen own allegiance? Was it to the Union or to his State? As a practical question, seeing things as they were then—sweeping aside all incontrovertible legal arguments and metaphysical disquisitions—I do not think the answer admits of doubt. If put in 1788, or indeed at any time anterior to 1825, the immediate reply of nine men out of ten in the Northern States, and ninety-nine out of a hundred in the Southern States, would have been that, as between the Union and the State, ultimate allegiance was due to the State.

THE CAUSE NOT LOST

[From Memorial Day, pages 30-31.]

A few weeks ago Dr. E. Benjamin Andrews, president of Brown University, a leading institution of learning in a New England State, in a lecture delivered in the city of New Orleans upon the life and character of the General of the Confederate armies, uttered this language:

> People are prone to allude to all Lee fought for as the "Lost Cause." Yet, like Oliver Cromwell, Lee has accomplished what he fought for, and more than could have been accomplished had he been victorious. At the close of the war we find the Supreme Court of the United States deciding the status of individual States, and the result is found to be that while the Union is declared to be indestructible, each State is regarded as an indestructible unit of that nation. Who would dare to wipe out to-day a State's individuality? And do we not find to-day, instead of centralized power in Congress adjudicating things pertaining to the States, the States themselves settling these matters?
>
> Inasmuch as the war brought out these utterances with regard to the States of the Union upon

matters then in question, who can say that Lee fought in vain?

SLAVERY AS THE SOUTH SAW IT

[Vice-President Alexander H. Stephens, in War Between the States, page 539.]

The matter of slavery, so called, which was the proximate cause of these irregular movements on both sides, and which ended in the general collision of war, was of infinitely less importance to the seceding States than the recognition of the great principles of constitutional liberty. There was with us no such thing as slavery in the true and proper sense of that word. No people ever lived more devoted to the principles of liberty, secured by free democratic institutions, than were the people of the South. None had ever given stronger proofs of this than they had done. What was called slavery amongst us was but a legal subordination of the African to the Caucasian race. This relation was so regulated by law as to promote, according to the intent and design of the system, the best interests of both races, the black as well as the white, the inferior as well as the superior. Both had rights secured and both had duties imposed. It was a system of reciprocal service and mutual bonds. But even the two thousand million dollars invested in the relations thus established between private capital and the labor of this class of population under system, was but the dust in the balance compared with the vital attributes of the rights of independence and sovereignty on the part of the several States.

VINDICATION OF SOUTHERN CAUSE

[In Southern Historical Papers, pages 332-336.]

Mr. Percy Greg, the justly famous English historian, says: "If the Colonies were entitled to judge their own cause, much more were the Southern States. Their rights—not implied, assumed, or traditional, like those of the Colonies, but expressly defined and solemnly guaranteed by law—had been flagrantly violated; the compact which alone bound them, had beyond question been systematically broken for more than forty years by the States which appealed to it."

After showing the perfect regularity and legality of the secession movement, he then says: "It was in defence of this that the people of the South sprang to arms 'to defend their homes and families, their property and their rights, the honor and independence of their States to the last, against five fold numbers and resources a hundred fold greater than theirs.'"

He says of the cause of the North: "The cause seems to me as bad as it well could be—the determination of a mere numerical majority to enforce a bond, which they themselves had flagrantly violated, to impose their own mere arbitrary will, their idea of national greatness, upon a distinct, independent, determined, and almost unanimous people."

And then he says as Lord Russell did: "The North fought for empire which was not and never had been hers; the South for an independence she had won by the sword, and had enjoyed in law and fact ever since the recognition of the thirteen sovereign and independent States, if not since the foundation of Virginia. Slavery was but the occasion of the rupture, in no sense the object of the war."

Let me add a statement which will be confirmed by every veteran before me —no man ever saw a Virginia soldier who was fighting for slavery.

This letter then speaks of the conduct of the Northern people as "unjust, aggressive, contemptuous of law and right," and as presenting a striking contrast to the "boundless devotion, uncalculating sacrifice, magnificent heroism, and unrivalled endurance of the Southern people."

But I must pass on to what a distinguished Northern writer has to say of the people of the South, and their cause, twenty-one years after the close of the war. The writer is Benjamin J. Williams, Esq., of Lowell, Mass., and the occasion which brought forth this paper (addressed to the Lowell *Sun*) was the demonstration to President Davis when he went to assist in the dedication of a Confederate monument at Montgomery, Ala. He says of Mr. Davis:

"Everywhere he receives from the people the most overwhelming manifestations of heartfelt affection, devotion, and reverence, exceeding even any of which he was the recipient in the time of its power; such manifestations as no existing ruler in the world can obtain from his people, and such as probably were never given before to a public man, old, out of office, with no favors to dispense, and disfranchised. Such homage is significant; it is startling. It is given, as Mr. Davis himself has recognized, not to him alone, but to the cause whose chief representative he is, and it is useless to attempt to deny, disguise, or evade the conclusion that there must be something great and noble and true in him and in the cause to evoke this homage."

Mr. Davis, in his speech on the occasion referred to, alluded to the fact that the monument then being erected was to commemorate the deeds of those "who gave their lives a free-will offering in defence of the rights of their sires, won in the war of the Revolution, the State sovereignty, freedom and independence which were left to us as an inheritance to their posterity forever."

Mr. Williams says of this definition: "These masterful words, 'the rights of their sires, won in the war of the Revolution, the State sovereignty, freedom and independence which were left to us an inheritance to their posterity forever,' are the whole case, and they are not only a statement but a complete justification of the Confederate cause to all who are acquainted with the origin and character of the American Union."

He then proceeds to tell how the Constitution was adopted and the government formed by the individual States, each acting for itself, separately and independently of the others, and then says:

"It appears, then, from this view of the origin and character of the American Union, that when the Southern States, deeming the constitutional compact broken, and their own safety and happiness in imminent danger in the Union, withdrew therefrom and organized their new Confederacy, they but asserted, in the language of Mr. Davis, the rights of their sires, won in the war of the Revolution, the State sovereignty, freedom, and independence, which were left to us as an inheritance to their posterity forever,' and it was in defence of this high and sacred cause that the Confederate soldiers sacrificed their lives. There was no need of war. The action of the Southern States was legal and constitutional, and history will attest that it was reluctantly taken in the extremity."

He now goes on to show how Mr. Lincoln precipitated the war, and describes the unequal struggle in which the South was engaged in these words: "After a glorious four years' struggle against such odds as have been depicted, during which independence was often almost secured, where successive levies of armies, amounting in all to nearly three millions of men, had been hurled against her, the South, shut off from all the world, wasted, rent, and desolate, bruised and bleeding, was at last overpowered by main strength; out-fought, never; for from first to last, she everywhere out-fought the foe. The Confederacy fell, but she fell not until she had achieved immortal fame. Few great established nations in all time have ever exhibited capacity and direction in government equal to hers, sustained as she was by the iron will and fixed persistence of the extraordinary man who was her chief; and few have ever won such a series of brilliant victories as that which illuminates forever the annals of her splendid armies, while the fortitude and patience of her people, and particularly of her noble women, under almost incredible trials and sufferings, have never been surpassed in the history of the world."

And then he adds: "Such exalted character and achievement are not all in vain. Though the Confederacy fell, as an actual physical power, she lives, illustrated by them, eternally in her just cause—the cause of constitutional liberty."

NORTHERN VIEW OF SECESSION

[Charles L. C. Minor's Real Lincoln.]

W. H. Russell, the famous correspondent of the *London Times*, in his diary (page 13) quotes Bancroft, the historian, afterwards Minister to England, for the opinion, in 1860, that the United States had no authority to coerce the people of the South; and Russell reports the same opinion prevailing in March, 1861, in New York and in Washington.

The life of Charles Francis Adams, Lincoln's Minister to England, says that up to the very day of the firing on the flag the attitude of the Northern States, even in case of hostilities, was open to grave question, while that of the border States did not admit of a doubt; that Mr. Seward, the member of the President's Cabinet, repudiated not only the right but the wish even to use armed force in subjugating the Southern States.

Morse's Lincoln (Volume I, page 131) makes the following remarkable statement: "Greeley and Seward and Wendell Phillips, representative men, were little better than secessionists. The statement sounds ridiculous, yet the proof against each one comes from his own mouth. The *Tribune* had retracted none of these disunion sentiments of which examples have been given."

Even so late as April 10, 1861, Seward wrote officially to Charles Francis Adams, Minister to England:

"Only an imperial and despotic government could subjugate thoroughly disaffected and insurrectionary members of the State."

On April 9th, the rumor of a fight at Sumter being spread abroad, Wendell Phillips said:

"Here are a series of States girding the gulf who think that their peculiar institutions require that they should have a separate government; they have a right to decide the question without appealing to you and to me. * * * Standing with the principles of '76 behind us, who can deny them that right?"

Woodrow Wilson's Division and Reunion says (page 214) that President Buchanan agreed with the Attorney General (Hon. Jere Black, of Pennsylvania) that there was no constitutional means for coercing a State (as his last message shows beyond a doubt) and adds that such for the time seemed to be the general opinion of the country.

MAJOR J. SCHEIBERT (OF THE PRUSSIAN ARMY) ON

CONFEDERATE HISTORY

[In Southern Historical Papers, Volume 18, pages 425-428.]

Tariff

Besides the differences of race and religion, nature itself, through the varied geographical position of the States, had created relations of varied character that not only must conflict ensue, but the least law affecting the whole Union often aroused diametrically and sharply opposed interests; the consequences of which were to embitter sectional opinions to an intolerable degree.

When the North demanded tariff protection for their industries as against European competition, the Southern States insisted upon free trade, so as not to be compelled to buy costly products of the North. The New England States strove for concentration of power in the national government; the Southerners believed that the independence of the individual States must be maintained, and when the Southerners demanded protection for their labor, which was performed by imported negroes, the North answered with evasion of the laws, while, in direct opposition to these laws, it denied to the master the right to his escaped negroes. From any point of view, there existed, and exist to-day, interests almost irreconcilably opposed, which make it difficult for the most earnest student of American affairs to find a clew in such a tangled labyrinth. The difficulty in the present undertaking is to make good the fact that the so-called Confederates, who have been by almost all the German writers represented as "Rebels," stood firm upon a ground of right oflaw.

If the central government at Washington was the sovereign power, then the (Southern) States were in the wrong, and their citizens were simply rebels. If, on the other hand, the individual States were separate and sovereign political bodies, then their secession, independent of consideration of expediency or selfishness, was a politically justifiable withdrawal from a previous limited alliance; and in this case it was the duty of citizens of the States to go with their States. As a proper consequence of these different views, the Federals considered as a traitor every citizen who opposed the central government, however his individual State may have determined; while the Confederates, after the declaration of war on the part of the Union, looked on the Federalists indeed as enemies, but considered as traitors only those citizens who, in opposition to the vote of their States, yet adhered to the Union. * * * * Instead of inquiring into emotion and sympathies, the question is an historical one as to the origin of the Union; that is, to seek in the founding of the United States in what relation,—at that time, the States stood to the central government, the mode of their covenant, and how the relation of the several States to the common union was developed. The colonies, therefore, united not because the citizens in general were oppressed by the British Government, but because one colony felt, whether rightly or not, that it was oppressed and insulted as an independent political body. In the first movement of independence was exhibited clearly the consciousness that the colonies felt themselves separate political bodies. Even at that time the assembly of delegates designated itself "as a congress of twelve independent political bodies," and in the Union each of the colonies issued its separate declaration. When the delegates of the thirteen colonies met in their first Congress the first permanent Union was founded; which was ratified by each colony as a separate body, as one by one they entered the Union.

Slavery

With the question as to the origin of the war, the enemies of the South have mingled another—the slavery question—which strictly does not belong to it. This slavery question was inscribed on the banners of the war when it was seen that thereby could be enlisted on the side of the North the sympathies of the old world, and of a great part of their own inhabitants, especially of the German immigrants. This question could never legally be the cause of the war, for the Constitution expressly says that the question of slavery should be regulated by the State legislatures. * * * * At the time of the founding of the Union, eleven of the thirteen States were slave-holding, and it is a remarkable fact that it then occurred to no writer nor humanitarian in America or Europe even to think that this ownership (of slaves) was a wrong or a crime. It is enough to say that the institution was accepted not only as a matter of course, but that it was also especially protected, the farming interest being granted an increased suffrage in proportion to the number of negroes on their plantations.
* * * * * Even in the last days, before the outbreak of war, when the press and demagogues raised the slavery question in order to inflame the masses, the statesman (of the North) carefully avoided such a blunder, since the slavery question was not the ground of the war, and could not be proclaimed as such.

CHAPTER VI
MATER REDIVIVA

INTRODUCTORY NOTE

[By J. L. Underwood.]

For twenty years after the close of the war most of the Southern States, through the bayonet-enforced amendments to the Constitution and the carpet- bag negro governments established under them, were kept under military rule. The men met the awful responsibility and their hideous trials with an amazing courage and sought to counteract, in every possible way, the work of Congress at Washington and the work of the Union Leagues and other secret societies among the negroes at home, and to build up the South in spite of the demoralization of labor. The Ku Klux Klan, a secret vigilance committee, did much good in terrifying the carpet-bag deposits and breaking up the secret armed midnight meetings of the negroes. Rowdy imitators of the Ku Klux afterwards in many instances did much harm.

But the women kept on at work. They have never faltered, and never shown any weariness. Thousands left penniless who were once wealthy, took up whatever work came to hand. The writer knew the daughter-in-law of a wealthy Congressman and the daughter of a governor of two States to plow her own garden with a mule. He saw all over the country the members of the oldest and wealthiest families of the Atlantic coast teaching school, even far in the west. Not a murmur escaped their lips. They cheered each other as they strengthened the nerves of the men.

But they kept up their work for the Confederate soldiers, and keep it up to this day. Soldiers' graves were everywhere looked after. Memorial associations were organized all over the South. The two great societies of Richmond, the Hollywood and the Oakwood, each looking after thousands of graves, the names of whose occupants are unknown, are doing the most sublime work the world ever saw. The Southern women soon extended their efforts to building Confederate monuments all over the South, providing soldiers' homes in the various States and securing what pensions the Southern States could afford. As long as they live they work for the cause they loved; when they die their spirit lives on in their worthy daughters.

THE EMPTY SLEEVE

[By Dr. G. W. Bagby.]

[In Living Writers of the South, pages 28-29.]

Tom, old fellow, I grieve to see
  That sleeve hanging loose at your side.
The arm you lost was worth to me
  Every Yankee that ever died.
But you don't mind it at all.
  You swear you've a beautiful stump,
And laugh at the damnable ball.
  Tom, I knew you were always a trump!
A good right arm, a nervy hand,
  A wrist as strong as a sapling oak,
Buried deep in the Malvern sand—
  To laugh at that is a sorry joke.
Never again your iron grip
  Shall I feel in my shrinking palm.
Tom, Tom, I see your trembling lip.
  How on earth can I be calm?
Well! the arm is gone, it is true;
  But the one nearest the heart
Is left, and that's as good as two.
  Tom, old fellow, what makes you start?
Why, man, she thinks that empty sleeve
  A badge of honor; so do I
And all of us,—I do believe
  The fellow is going to cry.
"She deserves a perfect man," you say.
  You, "not worth her in your prime."
Tom, the arm that has turned to clay

Your whole body has made sublime;
For you have placed in the Malvern earth
The proof and the pledge of a noble life,
And the rest, henceforward of higher worth,
Will be dearer than all to your wife.
I see the people in the street
Look at your sleeve with kindling eyes;
And know you, Tom, there's nought so sweet,
As homage shown in mute surmise.
Bravely your arm in battle strove,
Freely for freedom's sake you gave it;
It has perished, but a nation's love
In proud remembrance will save it.
As I look through the coming years,
I see a one-armed married man;
A little woman, with smiles and tears,
Is helping as hard as she can
To put on his coat, and pin his sleeve,
Tie his cravat, and cut his food,
And I say, as these fancies I weave,
"That is Tom, and the woman he wooed."
The years roll on, and then I see
A wedding picture, bright and fair;
I look closer, and it's plain to me
That is Tom, with the silver hair.
He gives away the lovely bride,
And the guests linger, loth to leave
The house of him in whom they pride,—
Brave Tom, old Tom, with the empty sleeve.

THE OLD HOOPSKIRT

[J. L. Underwood.]

The only ante-bellum property which Sherman and Thad Stevens left the Confederate woman was her old hoopskirt. They could neither confiscate nor burn, nor set this free. Like slavery, it was so closely connected with her life that it cannot be ignored in her history.

The Southern woman always kept well up with the latest fashions in dress. In the fifties the modistes of Paris, whose word, however absurd, was law to the women of the civilized world, sent out the famous hoopskirt. It was not an article of dress, but a mere contrivance for sustaining and exhibiting the clothes that were worn over it. It was made of a succession of small but strong steel wires bent into circles and fastened to each other by cross bars of tape. The lower hoop was usually from four to eight feet in diameter, according to taste, and the top one but little larger than the woman's waist, from which the whole net-work was hung. It held whatever clothes were put over it in the shape of a church bell or a horizontal section of a balloon.

Like all new fashions, some carried this one to grotesque extremes. One of the bon-ton set of Columbia, S. C., in 1858 was the remarkably beautiful and charming Mrs. ——, the wife of one of the professors in South Carolina College. It is a fact that, on average sidewalks in that beautiful city, wherever she was met by gentlemen they had to step into the street and give the whole pavement to her tremendous skirt. Most of our Southern beauties were more merciful.

When the hoopskirt first came, it looked as if Paris had sent out the greatest of all the absurdities. The men laughed, the boys jeered, and the newspapers poured out invectives against the monster. The country preachers anathematized it and urged its excommunication from the church. But the hoopskirt came to stay. *Veni, vidi, vici.* It whipped the fight, and when the war between the States came on it was in control of the Southern female wardrobe. It enlisted for "three years or the war." It clung to our mothers like Ruth to Naomi. "Entreat me not to leave thee, or to return from following after thee; for whither thou goest, I will go, and where thou lodgest I will lodge." It proved a godsend on account of the Federal blockade of the ports. Articles of clothing soon became scarce, and when the silks had all gone into flags and the gingham into shirts for the soldiers, with a dainty homespun skirt stretched over the hoopskirt, our mothers looked like they were dressed whether they were or not.

It was a good umbrella as far as it went and it was a special convenience to the refugee women who had to camp in the woods. At night a short pole was set in the ground with a short horizontal cross piece tacked across its top. Over this was stretched the hoopskirt and over it a sheet, and, behold a beautiful, cozy Sibley tent for two or three children to sleep under. It was our mother's faithful friend and companion to the end of the war. Like the old soldier's sword it came out very much battered and worn by long service. Like the old soldier himself, it had been wounded and broken and mended and spliced until it was hardly its former self. In their fatigue outfit our mothers laid aside the hoopskirt and tucked up what was left. But on dress parade, in meeting, company, and attending church it was her constant friend and companion. The South embalms in its memories the deeds of its men and the toil of its women. Father's old sword and John's gray jacket are sacred heirlooms. So are the old spinning wheel and hand loom,

"And e'en the old hoopskirt which hung on the
wall,

The old hoopskirt

The steel-ribbed shirt,

The old hoopskirt which hung on the wall."

One thing in the management of the hoopskirt the men never could understand. How in the world could all those steel wires be bundled and controlled when a woman rode horseback or had to be packed in a buggy or carriage?

It was always a like wonder how the women could dance so nimbly and gracefully with long trains and never get tripped or tangled in them. Our women managed the trains and the hoopskirts just as tactfully and thoroughly and gracefully as they did their hard-headed husbands and silly sweethearts. How they did it nobody can tell, but they did it.

About the very last days of the war one of these old hoopskirts played a conspicuous part in a tragedy in the suburbs of Camilla, then a very small village, the county seat of Mitchell County, Ga. A farmer by the name of Taylor lived near the Hoggard Swamp. He had a friend living in the town by the name of O'Brien. Both of them often visited a very thrifty widow by the name of Woolley. On her disappearance Taylor had put out the report that she had moved back to South Carolina, but the truth was he had murdered her for her money and buried her body under some peach trees near the swamp. No suspicion was aroused until Taylor returned from a trip to Albany without O'Brien, who had gone off with him, and a report came down from Albany that O'Brien's dead body had been found near there in the woods. Then suspicion put in its work. Murder was in the air, but nowhere else as yet.

People held their breath. Some women late one afternoon happened to pass the peach trees mentioned and noticed the suspicious looking fresh soil under them. As soon as they reached home they reported the circumstance and a party was soon made up to go that night and make an examination. The women guided them to the spot. They were afraid to make a bright fire and they used only a dim light by burning corn cobs. Their blood ran cold when in a very few moments they were satisfied that they were digging into the poor woman's grave. Suddenly on the quick removal of a shovel or two more of dirt, up flew a woman's dress and white underclothing pretty high in the air. Then there was a stampede for life. Terror seized the men's very bones. After a while they mustered courage enough to return and find that the woman was dead and her hoopskirt had been weighted down by the soil and as soon as this was sufficiently removed, it flew up with all its fearful elasticity. There was life in it even in the grave. Taylor was tried, convicted, andhung.

THE POLITICAL CRIMES OF THE NINETEENTH CENTURY

[By J. L. Underwood.]

The first of the great crimes of the last century was the great rebellion of the Northern States against the Federal constitutional Union, "the best government the world ever saw." Nine of these States in solemn legislative action, in the fifties, utterly repudiated their contract in the Federal Constitution. They nullified the acts of Congress and repudiated and defied the decisions of the Supreme Court.

This rebellion at the North broke up "the glorious Union of our fathers," and drove the South, like poor Hagar, into the wilderness to look out for herself, without a charge from any quarter that a Southern State had committed one single act in violation of Federal law or in hostility to the Constitution. Then came the second great crime, the crime so vigorously denounced at the time by William Lloyd Garrison, the most consistent and the most heroic of the Northern Abolitionists, Horace Greeley and Wendell Phillips, the crime of coercion of the weaker by the stronger States, the military invasion of the South under the prostituted flag of the Union, and the final subjugation of her people by fire and sword. *O tempora! O mores!*

The acts of congress for years after the Southern army had honorably laid down its arms and gone home to plow and plant the fields make the blackest pages in the history of modern times. The writer dreads to put in print his estimate of such a political monster as Thad Stevens, the misanthropic genius of reconstruction, the Robespierre of America. Robespierre's guillotine cut off the heads of its victims. Thad Stevens's guillotine cut off all hopes from Southern hearts. He avowed it his purpose to exterminate the Southern white people, to confiscate their property into the hands of the negroes, and with these negroes to keep the country forever under the dominion of his party. According to him and his followers to this day this party of (so-called) high moral ideas must be kept in power no matter what crimes are committed in securing the ascendency. This is political Jesuitism run mad.

The saddest, strangest part of the history is that it was twenty years before the Northern people came to their reason and put a check on this ruinous fratricidal policy. If the writer shall go to his grave with a holy horror of the bald malignity, the reckless folly, the cowardly spite, the sweeping curse of the reconstruction measures of Thad. Stevens and his Congress, he will find himself in good company. He once heard the great and good Dr. John A. Broadus, of the Southern Baptist Theological Seminary, say, "I can easily forgive and forget the war. It was war, and all the wrongs done in it diedaway with the cannon's roar. But I find it so hard to forgive the excuseless wrongs done to the Southern people since the war."

Dr. Broadus was a Southern man, but Rev. Dr. H. M. Field, the fair-minded and patriotic author of "Bright Skies and Dark Shadows," is not a Southern man. Hear what he says in his book:

> In South Carolina and the Gulf States negro government had a clean sweep, and if we are to believe the records of the times, it was a period of corruption such as had never been known in the history of the country. The blacks having nothing to lose, were ready to vote to impose any tax, or to issue any bonds of town, country or State provided they had a share in the booty; and this negro government manipulated by the carpet baggers, ran riot over the South. It was chaos come again. The former masters were governed by their servants, while the latter were governed by a set of adventurers and plunderers. The history of these days is one which we cannot recall without indignation and shame. After a time the moral sense of the North was so shocked by their performances that a Republican administration had to withdraw its proconsuls, when things resumed their former condition and the management of affairs came back into the old hands.

These national crimes which so woefully afflicted the people of the South after peace was made were:

1. The refusal to carry out Mr. Lincoln's cherished plan of reconstruction by immediate readmission of seceding States after an orderly and legal abolition of slavery.

2. The sudden emancipation of millions of African slaves. Gradual emancipation would have been so much better for their interests and for the welfare of the country.

3. The conferring of civil rights so early upon the freedmen. If they had not been made citizens they could have been colonized in due time and provided

for, as the Indians have been, with land and homes.

4. Enfranchisement of these grossly ignorant Africans.

5. Disfranchisement of the best people of the South.

6. Arming the blacks and disarming the white people.

7. The un-American crime of uniting church and state and the employment of a religious society to carry out directly the schemes of a political faction. Jesus Christ never authorized any such work. He never gave the least authorization of any church machinery through which such a union could be effected. God wants the good lives of men, and not compact and imposing church organizations. They can be so easily perverted to unholy purposes and made so effective in destroying human liberty and crushing human rights. The union of church and state was the curse of the middle ages and the blight of modern Europe.

It was an ominous day for America and a woeful day for the South, when, upon the enfranchisement of the negroes, the politicians in power and the fanatical Northern Methodist Episcopal Church organized and transplanted in the South the African Methodist Episcopal Church and employed it directly in manipulating the votes of the ignorant negroes. The great iron wheel controlling the whole machine was put into the hands of a political boss committee in Washington. Just within this was the wheel turned by an absolute bishop in each State. The most malignant of all the Southern negro politicians, Bishop H. M. Turner, had the control of the Georgia wheel and turns it to this day. Then came the smaller wheels, turned by the presiding elder in each Congressional district, enclosing the little wheels in the hands of the preachers and circuit riders and stewards. The ignorant negroes were wound tightly by the ropes into a solid mass, and voted like slaves by the officers of the new imported Northern church and the strikers of the Union League. It was enough to make a patriot despair of the country and a Christian to despair of religion to witness these scenes. It made the white people of the South get together in self-defence. It inevitably set race against race in politics. This slimy trail of this union of church and state has done sad work for the South and dangerous work for the whole country. The church iron wheel organized a solid mass of ignorant negro voters on one side of the Southern ballot box. This necessitated a "solid South" of white voters on the other side.

8. Demoralizing the negroes for generations by making them believe themselves to be special wards of the nation and holding out to them the delusive promise of "forty acres and a mule" as a pension for slavery and a reward for party loyalty.

9. Taking away by act of Congress, without a dollar of compensation, the slave property of orphans, widows and Union men, the property recognized by the Constitution of the government.

10. By force of bayonets keeping in the Southern high places of power the carpet-bag adventurer from the North and the irresponsible, unprincipled scalawag who had for the sake of office turned his back upon his native South.

11. Unlawful confiscation of Southern lands, much of it belonging to orphans and widows.

12. Enormous and unjust tax on cotton, at that time the only marketable product of the Southern farms.

These were the woes which the "Reconstruction" measures of the Federal Congress made for our Southern people, a burden mountain-high, Ossa on Pelion, Pelion upon Ossa. But grimly, patiently, bravely did our men bear up under it. Political crimes always hurt the women more than the men. Our women stood by and cheered and comforted and helped as only such women can help through all the toil, the gloom and wrongs of those dark days. God bless their memories!

BRAVE TO THE LAST

[Eggleston's Recollections, pages 73-76.]

But if the cheerfulness of the women during the war was remarkable, what shall we say of the way in which they met its final failure and the poverty that came with it? The end of the war completed the ruin which its progress had wrought. Women who had always lived in luxury, and whose labors and sufferings during the war were lightened by the consciousness that in suffering and laboring they were doing their part toward the accomplishment of the end upon which all hearts were set, were now compelled to face not temporary but permanent poverty, and to endure, without a motive or a sustaining purpose, still sorer privations than they had known in the past. The country was exhausted, and nobody could foresee any future but one of abject wretchedness. Everybody was poor except the speculators who had fattened upon the necessities of the women and children, and so poverty was essential to anything like good repute. The return of the soldiers made some sort of social festivity necessary, and "starvation parties" were given, at which it was understood that the givers were wholly unable to set out refreshments of any kind. In the matter of dress, too, the general poverty was recognized, and every one went clad in whatever he or she happened to have. The want of means became a jest, and nobody mourned over it; while all were laboring to repair their wasted fortunes as they best could. And all this was due solely to the unconquerable cheerfulness of the Southern women. The men came home moody, worn out, discouraged, and but for the influence of woman's cheerfulness the Southern States might have fallen into a lethargy from which they could not have recovered for generations. Such prosperity as they have since achieved is largely due to the courage and spirit of their noble women.

SALLIE DURHAM

[From Life In Dixie, pages 304-308, by Mary A. H. Gay.]

Dr. Durham came to Decatur, Ga., in 1859. Well do I remember the children —two handsome sons, John and William—two pretty brown-eyed girls, Sarah and Catherine.

The Durham residence, which was on Sycamore Street, then stood just eastward of where Colonel G. W. Scott now lives. The rear of the house faced the site where the depot had been before it was burned by the Federals, the distance being about 350 yards. Hearing an incoming train, Sallie went to the dining-room window to look at the cars, as she had learned in some way that they contained Federal troops. While standing at the window, resting against the sash, she was struck by a bullet fired from the train. It was afterwards learned that the cars were filled with negro troops on their way to Savannah, who were firing off their guns in a random, reckless manner. The ball entered the left breast of this dear young girl, ranging obliquely downward, coming out just below the waist, and lodging in the door of a safe, or cupboard, which stood on the opposite side of the room. This old safe, with the mark of the ball, is still in the village. The wounded girl fell, striking her head against the dining table, but arose, and, walking up a long hall, she threw open the door of her father's room, calling to him in a voice of distress.

Springing from the bed, he said: "What is it, my child?"

"Oh, father," she exclaimed, "the Yankees have killed me!"

Every physician in the village and city and her father's three brothers were summoned, but nothing could be done except to alleviate her sufferings. She could only lie on her right side, with her left arm in a sling suspended from the ceiling. Every attention was given by relatives and friends. Her grandmother Durham came and brought with her the old family nurse. Sallie's schoolmates and friends were untiring in their attentions.

During the week that her life slowly ebbed away, there was another who ever lingered near her, a sleepless and tireless watcher, a young man of a well known family, to whom this sweet young girl was engaged to be married. Sallie was shot on Friday at 7.30 A. M., and died the following Friday at 3.30 A. M. General Stephenson was in command of the Federal post at Atlanta. He was notified of this tragedy, and sent an officer to investigate. This officer refused to take anybody's word that Sallie had been shot by a United States soldier from the train; but, dressed in full uniform, with spur and sabre rattling upon the bare floor, he advanced to the bed where the dying girl lay, and threw back the covering "to see if she had really been shot." This intrusion almost threw her into a spasm. This officer and the other at Atlanta promised to do all in their power to bring the guilty party to justice, but nothing ever came of the promise, so far as we know.

As a singular coincidence, as well as an illustration of the lovely character of Sallie, I will relate a brief incident given by the gifted pen already quoted: "One of the most vivid pictures in my memory is that of Sallie Durham emptying her pail of blackberries into the hands of Federal prisoners on a train that had just stopped for a moment at Decatur, in 1863. We had been gathering berries at Moss's Hill, and stopped on our way home for the train to pass."

THE NEGRO AND THE MIRACLE

[In Grady's New South, pages 97-118.]

What of the negro? This of him. I want no better friend than the black boy who was raised by my side, and who is now trudging patiently, with downcast eyes and shambling figure, through his lowly way in life. I want no sweeter music than the crooning of my old "mammy," now dead and gone to rest, as I heard it when she held me in her loving arms and bending her old black face above me stole the cares from my brain, and led me smiling into sleep. I want no truer soul than that which moved the trusty slave, who for four years, while my father fought with the armies that barred his freedom, slept every night at my mother's chamber door, holding her and her children as safe as if her husband stood guard, and ready to lay down his humble life for her household. History has no parallel to the faith kept by the negro in the South during the war. Of five hundred negroes to a single white man, and yet through these dusky throngs the women and children walked in safety, and the unprotected homes rested in peace. Unmarshalled, the black battalions moved patiently to the fields in the morning to feed the armies their idleness would have starved, and at night gathered anxiously at the big house to "hear the news from marster," though conscious that his victory made their chains enduring. Everywhere humble and kindly; the body-guard of the helpless; the observant friend; the silent sentry in his lowly cabin; the shrewd counsellor; and when the dead came home, a mourner at the open grave. A thousand torches would have disbanded every Southern army, but not one was lighted. When the master, going to a war in which slavery was involved, said to his slave, "I leave my home and loved ones in your charge," the tenderness between man and master stood disclosed. And when the slave held that charge sacred through storm and temptation he gave new meaning to faith and loyalty. I rejoice that when freedom came to him after years of waiting, it was all the sweeter, because the black hands from which the shackles fell were stainless of a single crime against the helpless ones confided to his care.

This friendliness, the most important factor of the problem, the saving factor now as always, the North has never, and it appears will never, take account of. It explains that otherwise inexplicable thing—the fidelity and loyalty of the negro during the war to the women and children left in his care. Had "Uncle Tom's Cabin" portrayed the habit rather than the exception of slavery, the return of the Confederate armies could not have stayed the horrors of arson and murder their departure would have invited. Instead of that, witness the miracle of the slave in loyalty closing the fetters about his own limbs, maintaining the families of those who fought against his freedom, and at night on the far-off battlefield searching among the carnage for his young master, that he might lift the dying head to his humble breast and with rough hands wipe the blood away and bend his tender ear to catch the last words for the old ones at home, wrestling meanwhile in agony and love, that in vicarious sacrifice he would have laid down his life in his master's stead. This friendliness, thank God, survived the lapse of years, the interruption of factions and the violence of campaigns in which the bayonet fortified and the drum-beat inspired. Though unsuspected in slavery, it explains the miracle of 1864; though not yet confessed, it must explain the miracle of1888.

GEORGIA REFUGEES

[Mrs. W. H. Felton, in Georgia Land and People, pages 404-405.]

From the time that Oglethorpe planted his colony upon Yamacraw Bluff, Georgia has never passed through such an ordeal as the present. Nine-tenths of her sons were practically disfranchised because they had served the Southern Confederacy, and all the conditions of life were new; their servants were no longer subject to their control, and most of their property was scattered to the four winds of heaven. It tested the blood that had come down to them from Cavalier and Huguenot, from Scotch and Irish ancestry. The private life of many Georgians for the first few years after the war beggars description; but the women rose to the occasion.

The surrender found a gentle, shrinking Georgia woman on the Florida line, nearly four hundred miles from her luxurious home, from which she had fled in haste as Sherman "marched to the sea." The husband was with General Lee in Virginia. The last tidings came from Petersburg—before Appomattox—and his fate was uncertain. Hiring a dusky driver, with his old army mule and wagon, she loaded the latter with the remnant of goods and chattels that were left to her, and, placing her four children on top, this brave woman trudged the entire distance on foot, cheering, guiding, and protecting the driver and her little ones in the tedious journey. Under an August sun through sand and dust she plodded along, footsore and anxious, until she reached the dismantled home and restored her little stock of earthly goods under their former shelter. When her soldier husband had walked from Virginia to Georgia, he found, besides his noble wife and precious children, the nucleus of a new start in life, glorified by woman's courage and fidelity under a most trying ordeal. For a twelve-month the exigencies of their situation deprived her of a decent pair of shoes; still she toiled in the kitchen, the garden, and, perhaps, the open fields, without a repining word or complaining murmur. The same material is found in a steel rail as in the watch spring, and the only difference between the soldier and his wife was physical strength.

This was no exceptional case. The hardships of Georgia women were extreme and long-continued.

THE NEGROES AND NEW FREEDOM

[In Last Ninety Days of the War, pages 186-187.]

The negroes, however, behaved much better, on the whole, than Northern letter-writers represent them to have done. Indeed, I do not know a race more studiously misrepresented than they have been and are at this present time. They behaved well during the war; if they had not, it could not have lasted eighteen months. They showed a fidelity and a steadiness which speaks not only well for themselves but well for their training and the system under which they lived. And when their liberators arrived, there was no indecent excitement on receiving the gift of liberty, nor displays of impertinence to their masters. In one or two instances they gave "missus" to understand that they desired present payment for their services in gold and silver, but, in general, the tide of domestic life flowed on externally as smoothly as ever. In fact, though of course few at the North will believe me, I am sure that they felt for their masters, and secretly sympathized with their ruin. They knew that they were absolutely penniless and conquered; and though they were glad to be free, yet they did not turn round, as New England letter-writers have represented, to exult over their owners, nor exhibit the least trace of New England malignity. So the bread was baked in those latter days, the clothes were washed and ironed, and the baby was nursed as zealously as ever, though both parties understood at once that the service was voluntary. The Federal soldiers sat a good deal in the kitchens; but the division being chiefly composed of Northwestern men, who had little love for the negro, (indeed I heard some d——n him as the cause of the war, and say that they would much rather put a bullet through an Abolitionist than through a Confederate soldier,) there was probably very little incendiary talk and instructions going on. In all of which, compared with other localities we were much favored.

THE CONFEDERATE MUSEUM IN THE CAPITAL OF THE CONFEDERACY

This house, built for a gentleman's private residence, was thus occupied until 1862, when Mr. Lewis Crenshaw, the owner, sold it to the city of Richmond for the use of the Confederate government. The city, having furnished it, offered it to Mr. Davis, but he refused to accept the gift. The Confederate government then rented it for the "Executive Mansion" of the Confederate States. President Davis lived here with his family, using the house both in a private and official capacity. The present "Mississippi" room was his study, where he often held important conferences with his great leaders. In this house, amid the cares of state, joy and sorrow visited him; "Winnie," the cherished daughter, was born here, and here "little Joe" died from the effects of a fall from the back porch. It remained Mr. Davis's home until the evacuation of the city of Richmond. He left with the government officials on the night of April 2, 1865. On the morning of April 3, 1865, General Godfrey Witzel, in command of the Federal troops, upon entering the city, made this house his headquarters. It was thus occupied by the United States Government during the five years Virginia was under military rule, and called "District No. 1."

In the present "Georgia" room, a day or two after the evacuation, Mr. Lincoln was received. He was in the city only a few hours. When at last the military was removed and the house vacated, the city at once took possession, using it as a public school for more than twenty years. In order to make it more comfortable for school purposes, a few unimportant alterations were made. It was the first public school in the city. War had left its impress on the building, and the constant tread of little feet did almost as much damage. It was with great distress that our people (particularly the women), saw the "White House of the Confederacy" put to such uses, and rapidly falling into decay. To save it from destruction, a mass-meeting was called to take steps for its restoration. A society was formed, called the "Confederate Memorial Literary Society," whose aim was the preservation of the mansion. Their first act was to petition the city to place it in their hands, to be used as a memorial to President Davis and a museum of those never-to-be-forgotten days, '61-'65. It was amazing to see the wide-spread enthusiasm aroused by the plan. With as little delay as possible the city, acting through alderman and council, made the deed of conveyance, which was ratified by the then Mayor of Richmond, the Hon. J. Taylor Ellyson.

The dilapidation of the entire property was extreme, but to its restoration and preservation the society had pledged itself. They had no money—the city had already given its part—what could be done? To raise the needed funds it was decided to hold a "memorial bazaar" in Richmond for the joint benefit of the museum and the monument to the private soldier and sailor.

All through the South the plan of the museum and the bazaar was heartily endorsed; so that donations of every kind poured in. Each State of the Confederacy was represented by a booth, with the name, shield, and flag of her State. The whole sum realized was $31,400. Half of this was given to complete the monument to the private soldiers and sailors now standing on Libby Hill, and the other half went to the museum.

The partition walls were already of brick, and the whole house had been strongly and well built, but the entire building was now made fireproof, and every other possible precaution taken for its safety. In every particular the old house in its entirety was preserved, the wood work (replaced by iron) being used for souvenirs. The repairs were so extensive that the building was not ready for occupancy until late in 1895.

On February 22, 1896, the dedication service was held, and the museum formally thrown open to the public.

But the house was entirely empty. Rapidly the memorials were gathered from each loyal State and placed in their several rooms. From start to finish the whole work has been free-will offering to the beloved cause.

The treasury had been nearly exhausted by the restoration of the building. The current expenses were met only by the strictest economy, and largely carried on by faith. In the past nine years much has been accomplished. The institution is free from debt; and the museum is now widely known. But much lies ahead in the ideal the patriotic women have set before them and the work grows larger, more important and far reaching as it is approached. Such is the interest felt in the museum that during the past year they have had 7,459 visitors, of whom 3,717 were from the North. It is by these door-fees that the expenses are met.

It would be quite impossible to enumerate all the articles of interest to be found here. The memorials gathered are not only interesting in themselves, but invaluable for the truth and lessons which they teach. Historians in search of information can here obtain original data in regard to the "War between the States." The United States Government has already made use of these records for its new Navy Register. Each confederate State is hereby represented by a room, set apart in special honor of her sons and their deeds. A regent in that State has it in charge, and is responsible for its contents and appearance. A vice-regent (as far as possible a native of that State, but residing in Richmond) gives her personal supervision to the room and its needs. The labor is incessant, and would be impossible, but for the fact that it is impelled by a sense of sacred love and duty.

Of the women of the Confederacy, of our brave and uncomplaining soldiers, of their great leaders, as well as of our illustrious chief, it well may be said:

"Would you see their monument?

Look around."

The Mary DeRenne Collection

The late Dr. Everard DeRenne bequeathed to the Georgia room "The Mary DeRenne (of Georgia) collection." Mrs. Mary DeRenne, of Savannah, Ga., was his mother, an enthusiastic Georgian, and patriotic Confederate. Soon after the close of the war between the States, finding that an officer of the Northern army was making a collection of Southern relics, she felt that there were few in the South who had the means to do the same, but that it ought to be done. She determined at once to begin, and while life lasted she spared neither effort nor expense in gathering relics, books, papers, and all that added to their value. Mrs. DeRenne soon found that persons were glad to put together what made history, when isolated relics or papers told so little. The result tells an absorbing story.

Miss C. N. Usina, of Savannah, Georgia, presented in 1903 a liberal addition to this library.

FEDERAL DECORATION DAY—ADOPTION FROM OUR MEMORIAL

[Taken from Confederate Dead in Hollywood Cemetery, page 7.]

MRS. JOHN A. LOGAN WITNESSED OBSERVANCE IN RICHMOND AND MADE THE SUGGESTION.

The New York *Herald* contains the following contribution from Mrs. John A. Logan, in which she says that the "Decoration Day" in the North was an adoption from the South's "Memorial Day."

To the editor of the Herald:

In the spring of 1868, General Logan and I were invited to visit the battle-grounds of the South with a party of friends. As certain important matters kept him from joining the party, however, I went alone, and the trip proved a most interesting and impressive one. The South had been desolated by the war. Everywhere signs of privation and devastation were constantly presenting themselves to us. The graves of the soldiers, however, seemed as far as possible the objects of the greatest care and attention.

One graveyard that struck me as being especially pathetic was in Richmond. The graves were new, and just before our visit there had been a "Memorial Day" observance, and upon each grave had been placed a small Confederate flag and wreaths of beautiful flowers. The scene seemed most impressive to me, and when I returned to Washington I spoke of it to the General and said I wished there could be concerted action of this kind all over the North for the decoration of the graves of our own soldiers. The General thought it a capital idea, and with enthusiasm set out to secure its adoption.

At that time he was commander-in-chief of the Grand Army. The next day he sent for Adjutant-General Chipman, and they conferred as to the best means of beginning a general observance. On the 5th day of May in that year the historic order was put out. General Logan often spoke of the issuing of this order as the proudest act of his life.

It was marvelous how popular the idea became. The papers all over the land copied the order, and the observance was a general one. The memorial ceremonies that took place at Arlington that year were perfectly inspiring to all the old soldiers. Generals Grant, Sherman, and Sheridan and many of those who have since passed away attended the first solemn observance of that day.

Mrs. John A. Logan.

THE DAUGHTERS AND THE UNITED DAUGHTERS OF THE CONFEDERACY

The following valuable bit of history is taken from the Macon (Ga.) *Telegraph's* account of the meeting of the United Daughters of the Confederacy in Macon, October, 1905.

"In the presentation to Mrs. L. H. Raines of a gold pin, a testimonial from the United Daughters of Georgia, a very pretty climax to the morning's session was reached. The speech with which Miss Mildred Rutherford presented the pin in behalf of the Daughters will be memorable to every one present, for it was touched with emotion and instruction as a bit of history. Miss Rutherford explained that when the war between the States ended, the Ladies' Aid Societies resolved themselves into associations whose work it was to care for the graves of the fallen heroes and to collect the bodies from far-off fields.

"There was a woman in Nashville, who had ever been foremost in

Confederate work—a Mrs. M. C. Goodlet, who in 1892 was president of the auxiliary to the Cheatham Bivouac. She had just aided in building the soldiers' home near Nashville and felt that there was a work not included in the work of the auxiliaries as then constituted. So she resolved to form an organization to be called the 'Daughters of the Confederacy.' The purpose of this organization was to be the care of aged veterans and the wives and children of veterans, the building of monuments, the collection and preservation of records.

"Mrs. L. H. Raines was one of the first to write for information to Mrs. Goodlet, and on reply she took the matter before the Savannah auxiliary. This auxiliary, while not willing to lose its individuality in the new organization, quickly formed within its own ranks a chapter of the Daughters of the Confederacy. So the charter chapter of Georgia came into existence."

Miss Rutherford then related how the chapters grew in number until it occurred to Mrs. Raines that strength would come through union. She wrote to Mrs. Goodlet suggesting a "United Daughters of the Confederacy," and Mrs. Goodlet agreed with the idea, so that a constitution and by-laws were formulated and a convention of the various chapters called at Nashville in 1894, "Mother" Goodlet presiding. The convention of the United Daughters at San Francisco formally recognized Mrs. Goodlet as founder of the Daughters of the Confederacy and Mrs. Raines as founder of the United Daughters.

A DAUGHTER'S PLEA

The following is an extract from the Macon (Ga.) *Telegraph's* report of the proceedings of the United Daughters of the Confederacy in Macon on the 26th of October, 1905:

Mrs. Plaine had not then learned that Virginia opened last year a large and comfortable home for Confederate women on Grace street in the city of Richmond. It is a noble monument to our mothers and grandmothers and a needed asylum for some of the very lonely. Mrs. Plaine among other things said:

"We have corrected many falsehoods disseminated throughout the South in Northern histories and readers, substituting impartial and truthful Southern books; and we have children's chapters as auxiliaries to the United Daughters of the Confederacy that they may learn even more of the imperishable grandeur of the men and women of the old South. But, my dear friends, have we not failed in one paramount duty? Should we not in all these years have made some organized effort for the succor and support of the aged women of the Confederacy whose noble deeds we have been busily recording? Texas is the only State which has made any decided move in this direction. The United Daughters of the Confederacy of that State have purchased a lot in Austin and have several thousand dollars towards building a home to be known as 'Heroines' Home.' They propose to have for these precious old ladies pleasant and comfortable housing, good food cheerfully served, efficient attendants, nurses and physicians, books, and all the little pastimes with which cherished mothers should be provided to keep them satisfied and happy as the depressing shadows grow longer.

"When we of Atlanta were working so hard to have the State accept and maintain the soldiers' home which had been built by public subscription eight years before and was fast going to decay, the only opposition we had was from those who thought there were too few soldiers left to need such a home. But what has been the result of opening it to them? Why, hundreds of old, infirm and needy veterans have found there a comfortable place in which to pass the remnant of their lives, and we feel more than repaid for our small share in opening it for their use.

"Now, in the effort to establish a home for the aged women of the Confederacy, the same objection will be raised of 'so few to occupy it.'

"Where are the women who represented the six hundred thousand valiant soldiers who constituted the grandest army the world has yet known?

"Where are those who with unflinching courage sent forth husbands, sons, fathers, brothers and lovers to swell that immortal host which marched and suffered beneath the 'Stars and Bars?' Where the little girls who carded and spun and knitted to help their mothers clothe the naked soldiers? Where the young girls who stood by the wayside to feed the hungry and quench the thirst of the men on their long and weary marches? Where the women who with tireless energy ministered night and day to the sick and wounded and spoke words of hope to the dying? Where those who stood at the threshold of desolate homes to welcome with smiles and loving caresses their uncrowned heroes, and who by their courage and patient endurance, amidst want and poverty, saved from despair and even suicide the men by whose heroic efforts a new and greater South has arisen from the ashes of the old?

"Hundreds of these women, my dear friends, some of them once queens in the old Southern society of which we still boast, and who would even now grace the court of the proudest monarch on earth, are still with us, but many of them in poverty and obscurity, suffering in silence rather than acknowledge their changed condition.

"I know personally of four cultured, refined women, born and bred in luxury, who gave some of the best years of their lives to help the Southern cause, and who for the love of it still work with their feeble hands to make the money with which to pay their dues as members of the United Daughters of the Confederacy.

"I know of another, reared by aristocratic, wealthy parents in this city, who drove with her patriotic mother almost daily to take in their private carriage the sick and wounded from the trains to the hospitals, and who on one occasion retired behind one of the brick pillars of your depot and tore off her undergarments to furnish bandages for bleeding arteries. She is now quite advanced in years, nearly all her relatives dead, and she is in very straitened circumstances. But she is proud and brave still, and makes no moan.

"A few years ago it was announced in an Atlanta paper that a lady from Sharpsburg, Md., was visiting a friend in Atlanta. A gentleman in Griffin, after seeing the notice, took the next train to Atlanta and called to see the lady without giving his name. As she entered the parlor he stared at her for a moment and then grasped both her hands in his and tears sprang to his eyes as he said with great emotion, 'Yes, yes, this is Miss Julia, only grown older—the same sweet face that looked so compassionately into mine, and the same person who with her beautiful sister Alice and her mother, worthy to have been the mother of Napoleon, nursed me into life as you did so many poor fellows after that awful battle. I have come to take you home with me. My wife and children love you and all your family; your names are honored household words with us.' Everything in the fine old mansion of that family was literally soaked in the blood of Southern soldiers. To these two young girls, Julia and Alice, scores of Southern families owe the recovery of the bodies of their dead upon the memorable and bloody field of Antietam or Sharpsburg. Most of the people around there were Northern sympathizers, and took pleasure in desecrating Confederate graves, and these young ladies, with the assistance of a gentleman, who posed as a Yankee, made, secretly, diagrams of the burial places of our dead, marking distances from trees, fences and other objects, and sometimes burying pieces of iron or other indestructible articles near by, that they might be able, if need be, to recover the bodies, and thus many were restored to their friends. So much was this family hated by the Yankee element in the surrounding country it became unsafe for them to keep a light in the house after night, for fear of being fired into. I have myself seen since the war the bullets which lodged in the inside walls of the rooms. Just at the close of the war these brave girls, in order to send the body of a noble Confederate captain to his wife, then living in Macon, drove with it in a wagon seventeen miles at night, crossing the broad Potomac in a ferryboat, their only companion a boy of twelve, and delivered the casket to the express agent at Leesburg, Va. Both of these Southern heroines are still living. Poverty long since overtook them; the dear old home has passed into strange hands, and they are left almost alone—one a widow, the other never married.

"Think you that such as these are not deserving the help of those of us who have been more fortunate? In the language of Mrs. Vincent, of Texas, a native Georgian, 'because they have stifled their cries, and in silent self-reliance labored all these years for subsistence, are we Daughters to close our ears to their appeals, now that the patient hands and the feeble footsteps hesitate in the oncoming darkness?'

"The time will come—is already here—when marble shafts will arise to commemorate the deeds of the Spartan women of the South, but a better and more enduring monument would be a home for such of them as are still alive and in need, and for the benefit of the female descendants of the men and women of the Confederacy who may yet become old and homeless, and are eligible to the United Daughters of the Confederacy.

"Memorial Hall in course of erection by the Daughters of the American Revolution, commemorative of the deeds of our Revolutionary ancestry, is a worthy and patriotic enterprise, but a home for the aged heroines of the Confederacy would serve not alone as a memorial of our dead heroes and heroines, but what is still better, it would be a blessing to worthy, suffering humanity."

HOME FOR CONFEDERATE WOMEN

[J. L. Underwood.]

These women of the South not only work for the men, but when the men undertake to work for them, they take up the work and do it for themselves. In March, 1897, the Ladies' Auxiliary of the George E. Pickett Camp, Confederate Veterans, began a movement to establish a home for the wives, sisters, and daughters of dead and disabled Confederate soldiers. Of this Auxiliary Society Mrs. R. N. Northern was president, Miss Alice V. Loehr, secretary. A call was made to the people of the State and a Confederate festival, in charge of a committee of which Mrs. Mary A. Burgess was chairman, was held in the Regimental Armory in Richmond from the 19th to 29th of May for the purpose of raising funds. The movement was most heartily endorsed by the veterans, by Governor C. T. O'Ferrall, and the people generally, and was continued to complete success. A very desirable building was secured on Grace street and the home dedicated and opened in 1904 and is now occupied by a number of grateful inmates. In all the historic memorials about noble old Richmond there is no monument more touching than this practical offering to the women of the Confederacy. A similar home has already been provided in Texas and the R. A. Smith Camp of Veterans at Macon, Ga., which recently laid the corner-stone of a monument to the Confederate Women, has already begun a movement for the establishment of a home in that city and the United Daughters of the Confederacy are at work for its accomplishment.

JEFFERSON DAVIS MONUMENT

[J. L. Underwood.]

The project to erect an appropriate monument to the great Chieftain of the Confederacy was undertaken by the veterans years ago. They raised about $20,000. The Daughters of the Confederacy, just as they always do, then took hold of the matter and they have increased the fund to $70,000. The Georgia United Daughters of the Confederacy, who have built a Winnie Davis dormitory at the Georgia Normal School, have been very active in the work for the Davis Monument at Richmond, and Georgia has the credit of leading all the States in the amount contributed. The city of Richmond has donated a very eligible lot at the crossing of Franklin and Cedar streets, near the splendid R. E. Lee monument. It is fitting that the monuments to the leading civil and military heroes of the great cause shall be so near each other. Very near to these will be monuments each to Gen. J. E. B. Stuart, and to Gen. Fitz Hugh Lee. These monuments will all stand in the Lee district, the new and coming choice residence section of the glorious city.

It is expected that the splendid monument to Mr. Davis will be unveiled at the Confederate reunion in 1907. Work has already begun and the foundations are being laid. Dirt was formally broken on the 7th of November, 1905, by Mrs. Thomas McCullough, of Staunton, president of the Davis Monument Association. Hon. J. Taylor Ellyson, lieutenant-governor elect, a noble veteran, and others, also took part in the historic ceremonies. The picks and shovels will be preserved in the Confederate Museum. The monument will be unique in its design and will worthily tell future generations of the great man and the great cause. The writer confesses to a great pleasure, while preparing this volume, of almost daily visits to see the foundation work of this monument going on. He spent five years of his life in Mississippi in the old days, and he knows Mr. Davis before our war to have been a gentleman, a patriot, and a Christian, and the kindest of masters to his slaves. He was a Chevalier Bayard, a knight *sans peur et sans reproche*, and yet, under the responsibility laid on him by the Confederate States, he became the mark for all the abuse and slander that could be heaped on the Confederate cause by the fanatics among our foes. His grave in Hollywood Cemetery and the

Confederate Memorial Museum building, which was Mr. Davis's home during the sad war, have been precious though mournful Meccas to the author during many months of hospital suffering in Richmond, and, by courtesy of the Ladies' Memorial Literary Society, a large part of the actual work on this memorial volume was done in the very rooms occupied by our great leader. May God bless our noble women for the monument which promises to be worthy of its mission.

RECIPROCAL SLAVERY

[J. L. Underwood.]

Humanity and kindness were the rule which marked the treatment of the slaves in the South. For this the Southern people have claimed no credit. A man deserves no credit for taking care of a $50 cow. Much more will his very self interest treat well a $250 horse. How much more to his interest to feed, house, clothe and nurse a $1,500 negro. As in all things human, there were evils connected even with Southern slavery, and Southern patriots rejoice that it is all gone. But history will only render simple justice to the men and women of the South when it records that any real cruel treatment of the negro was very rare.

The writer's life has nearly all been spent in the negro belts of Alabama, Mississippi, Georgia and South Carolina, and he knew of but three cases where slave owners were charged with habitual cruel treatment of the slaves. One of these, in the Alabama canebrake, gave his slaves the best of medical attention, but they were evidently not supplied with the clothing they ought to have. The other two, one man and one woman, had the reputation of giving way to a cruel temper when chastising their slaves. All of them stood branded with public odium.

The truth is that in Southern slavery there was a sort of mutuality. The owner belonged to the negro as truly as the negro belonged to the white man. In many respects the master rendered service to the slave. The State laws, to say nothing of humanity and religion, made it so, but you say "it was a very pleasant sort of slavery for the master." Yes, and a very pleasant sort of slavery for the negro. They were the jolliest set of working people the world ever saw. The chains of the negro were not the only shackles removed by the great revolution. When the time came the slave owners felt that a great burden had been rolled from their own shoulders.

As far as the writer knows, the universal feeling of the slave owners was expressed in the language of a good old couple who had worked hard and finally become the owners of a hundred slaves. Said the old man, "I didn't enslave the negroes, and I didn't set them free, and I am glad the whole of the great responsibility has been lifted from my shoulders." His wife, sitting by, said, "I feel like a new woman. I am now set free from a great burden."

The truth is, while negro slavery was the most convenient property ever owned in America, it made heavy and constant exactions of care, attention, and worry on the part of the owner. The ignorant, childish Africans needed a master more than any master needed them. There lived near the author's home in Sumter county, Ala., a Mr. Jere Brown. He was of a fine family and a graduate of South Carolina College. He was a splendid type of the intelligent, polished, Christian gentleman of the old school. He owned at least a thousand negro slaves and kept them all near him. While he had overseers and foremen to direct the farm labor, he devoted all his time to attendance upon his slaves. He was their physician and their nurse and very rarely ever left the boundaries of his own land. His slaves all loved him, and it was long said of him that he wore himself out looking after the negroes. They belonged to him and he to them. This identity of interest, the closeness of relationship, the mutual, kind feeling between owners and slaves was never realized by the fanatics and party politicians of the North until since the emancipation. The eyes of the world have been opened to the fact that nearly all of the substantial help for the negro's school, his church and for himself and his family when in distress, has been rendered by the old slave owners and their children. This practical help has been rendered all over the South.

Alas! this mutual interest is growing weaker very fast. The slave owners and their children, the true friends to the negro, will soon be all dead. How much sympathy the negro is to get from the next generation is for the negro himself to say. He has used his ballot in such a way as to cut himself off from his neighbors, employers and life-long friends; and to bring down the contempt of the world. For years he used it as a bludgeon to beat the life out of what had been sovereign States and free people. Later on he has made it a toy to be sold for a drink of whiskey or thrown into the gutter. The whole American people know this negro ballot to be a travesty on liberty. His natural civil rights are secure in the North and in the South. But his own folly has raised the question of the continuance of the privilege of voting. Anglo Saxons will continue to rule America. They are not a people who will long put up with child's play and stupidity in politics. They mean business. And if the negro expects to use the ballot, he must catch the step of a freeman. He must vote for the interest of his State and his section and through a prosperous united State, work for the well being of the whole Union. In this Christian land he has met with unbounded sympathy in his helplessness. That sympathy is being at times sorely tried. It is waning, sadly waning. If he expects the privilege of an American, he must act like an American. It saddens the

Confederate veterans of 1861 to see how far white and black have drifted apart within the last twenty years. The "friendliness" of which Henry Grady wrote in 1888 will not, it is feared, last to 1908. God grant they may get closer together in all that makes for the good of both races.

BARBARA FRIETCHIE

[J. L. Underwood.]

Here is a part of the story of the Maryland woman and the Federal flag in the famous poem of John G. Whittier:

"Bravest of all in Fredericktown

She took up the flag the men hauled down;

In her attic window the staff she set

To show that one heart was loyal yet.

Up the street came the rebel tread,

Stonewall Jackson riding ahead:

Under his slouch hat left and right

He glanced; the old flag met his sight.

'Halt!' the dust-brown ranks stood fast,

'Fire!' Out blazed the rifle blast,

It shivered the window pane and sash,

It rent the banner with seam and gash.

Quick as it fell from the broken staff,

Dame Barbara snatched the silken scarf."

This is poetry, but it is not history. It is not truth. It does not sound like it. Nobody but men like Whittier, blinded by New England prejudice and steeped in ignorance of Southern people, would for a moment have thought Stonewall Jackson capable of giving an order to fire on a woman. None of the story sounds at all like "Stonewall Jackson's way." To their credit the later editions of Whittier's poems cast a grave doubt on the truth of the story, and now Mr. John McLean, an old next-door neighbor to the genuine Barbara Frietchie, has given to Mr. Smith Clayton, of the Atlanta *Journal*, the true story showing Whittier's tale to be nothing but a myth. Mr. Clayton says:

"Coming up to Washington from Richmond the other day I brushed up an acquaintance with a very pleasant, intelligent and, by the way, handsome gentleman, Mr. John McLean, a conductor on the Richmond, Fredericksburg and Washington Railroad. In the course of conversation he mentioned Frederick, Md. I laughed and said:

"Did you ever meet Barbara Frietchie?"

"Why, my dear sir," he replied, "she lived just across the street from my father's home."

"You don't say so?"

"It's a fact; and let me tell you, that poem is a 'fake,' pure and simple. I was a child during the war, but I'll give you the truth about Barbara Frietchie as I got it from the lips of my father and mother."

And then he told me this interesting story:

"Ever been to Frederick?"

"No."

"Well, just where the turnpike enters the town my father and mother lived in the old homestead. Directly across the way lived Mr. Frietchie. He was a tailor, and a good, clever man and honest citizen. His house had two stories. On the ground, or street floor, was his shop. The family lived up stairs. There was a balcony to the upper story of the house facing the street. It was from that balcony that the flag was waved, but Barbara Frietchie had no more to do with it than you. General Stonewall Jackson, returning from Monocacy, passed through Frederick at the head of his army. He entered the town by the turnpike and marched between the house of Mr. Frietchie and the home of my parents. There was a United States flag in the tailor's house. His eldest daughter, Mary Quantrell, thinking that the Union army was coming, mistaking Jackson's men for the Federals, seized this flag, ran out upon the balcony and waved it. Observing her, General Stonewall Jackson, who was riding at the head of his troops, took off his hat, and ordered his men to uncover their heads. They did so, and General Jackson said that he gave the order to uncover because he wanted his men to show proper appreciation of a woman who had the loyalty and patriotism to stand up for her side. Those are the facts. My parents were there. They told me. I tell you. There was no sticking any flag staff in any window. No order by General Jackson to 'Halt' and 'Fire;' no seizing of the flag and waving it after it had been shot from the staff; no begging General Jackson to shoot anybody's grey head but to 'spare the flag of his country'—all of this is described in the poem—but none of it happened. Very funny about Barbara Frietchie being four score and ten."

"Who was Barbara Frietchie?"

"Why she was the young daughter of Mr. Frietchie—the young sister of Mary Quantrell, who waved the flag—that's all."

Mr. McLean told me that he had three brothers in the Federal army. His brother was doorkeeper of the Maryland assembly, and his uncle a member during the stormy sessions held at Frederick, when that body hotly discussed, for many days, the question as to whether Maryland should secede.

SOCIAL EQUALITY BETWEEN THE RACES

[J. L. Underwood.]

When the men of the writer's generation see or read of the growing sensitiveness in all parts of the country, at the North and South, as to negro social equality, there rush up memories from the days of slavery that make the present jealousy to some extent ridiculous. As to religious equality, the slaves joined the churches of their own choice. In the cities there were some churches composed entirely of negro slaves and nearly all had white preachers. The country has had few if any preachers more eloquent and accomplished than Dr. Giradeau, who in late years was professor in the Presbyterian Theological Seminary at Columbia, S. C. He spent all of his ministry up to the breaking out of the war as pastor of one of these negro churches in Charleston.

In the country towns and villages seats were provided for the negroes to attend the 11 o'clock and night services of the whites. They shared in the ordinances and communed from the same plate and cup in perfect Christian equality with the whites. In the afternoon the house was turned over to their exclusive use and the white pastor was required to preach to them and worthy preachers from among themselves were always encouraged. It always appeared to the writer, all through his boyhood days, that the white preachers preached better sermons to the negroes than they did to the whites. The negro was thus blessed with the most thorough and efficient evangelist work ever done for the benighted. The negroes trained under it have been the salt of the earth to their race in their churches since the war. In those days in the South the white evangelist Phillip rode in the wagon with the Ethiopian and taught him, and both were blessed. When the lamented good old deacon Alex. Smith, of Thomasville, Ga., was ordained a deacon, one of the ordaining elders was his negro slave. At Bainbridge, Ga., Rev. Jesse Davis officiated as a member of the Presbytery ordaining to the ministry his slave, Ben. Munson. What a calamity that this close brotherly association in religious matters should have been so rudely broken in many directions by the politics of the wild reconstruction which was forced on the South.

At home some features of the life amounted to more than social equality. There was "mammy," for instance, the good old negro nurse, housekeeper, hospital matron, superintending cook, boss of the whole family, and what not. She was father's friend to counsel and cheer him, and she was mother's staff and companion. To us children she was just everything. Those strong old arms supported us in babyhood and dandled us and fondled us in childhood.

Her old bosom was a city of refuge from even the pursuing father and mother. How quietly peach-tree switches dropped from parental hands when Mammy begged for us. Mammy's cabin was the white children's paradise. Well does the writer remember that when his mother had to take a trip for her health away from home, he and a sister a little older than himself were left in the home of a neighboring kindred to be cared for. Kinsfolk did very well till night approached, then our poor little hearts sighed for home and we ran away to Mammy Cynthia and remained in her cabin and slept in her arms in her nice clean bed until mother's return. The most cruel work done by the reconstruction politics was to enforce the orders of the carpet-baggers and scalawags in compelling these "mammies" to forsake their old "missus" and old homes. Many of them never could be tempted or forced to leave the old home.

Then there was "Daddy Jacob," the nabob of the farm. Like "mammy" he was given just enough work to keep up appearances and keep him in practice. But it was usually special work, like presiding at the gin or hauling with the two-ox wagon. Many a meal has the little white boy eaten from old daddy's dinner bucket or from the blue-edged plates in his cabin.

Then there was "Mandy," the young girl given by the parents to her young white mistress near her age. Mandy caught Miss Mary's manners, fell heir to her dresses and bonnets, waited on the table, joined the children in their sports, and felt that she was about as good as anybody. And she was, until the devil came along with the bayonets and brought the monster curse to the negro, the "Yankee school marm." These women were deluded, blind guides of the blind Africans. Reconstruction work has left the negro women, especially the young ones, the most giddy, most idle and aimless and the least virtuous of any set of women in any civilized country. The white Yankee school teachers sent down South by the thousands, forty years ago, sowed the seed of false notions of life and duty and opportunity, and the country is now afflicted with the harvest.

"Jere" was the negro boy companion of young "Mars Henry." He and Mars Henry played marbles together, fished or swam the millpond, searched the woods for chinquapins or hickory nuts. They rode on the same lever at the old gin and leaped into the lint room together to pack back the loose cotton, and then mounted the mules and rode them to the barn. But the 'possum hunt was the glory of Henry and Jere's united life. After supper, in which Henry had swapped biscuit from the table for Jere's pork and roasted potatoes or sweet ash cake, they would put a few potatoes in their pockets, gather an axe, whistle up old "Tige," the dog, and were soon away in the woods. When the game was captured, and a failure was a rare thing, with the nocturnal

Nimrods, a small short hickory pole was split and the tail of the 'possum inserted in the crack and soon each boy had a 'possum pole on his shoulder. But a boy gets sleepy quickly. Worn out with their ramble they would rake up a pile of leaves on the south side of a big log, kindle a fire near their feet and put the potatoes to roasting. "Tige" knew what it all meant and he enjoyed the camping too. He would lie next to the 'possums so that he could keep an eye on them. (The writer's Tige had but one eye.) A 'possum is the meekest of all animals, when you get his tail in a vice and a dog in three feet of him. Jere would lie next to Tige, close enough to get some of his warmth, and Mars Henry would lie close to Jere. With their feet to the fire they got a few hours of the sweetest sleep the world ever gave. It was Mars Henry's active, rollicking, rough and tumble open-air life with Jere that gave such vigor, in camp and on the march, to the Confederate soldier.

The only man who has understood the negro, knew his wishes and his failings, knew how to be kind to him when a slave, and a safe counsellor now that he is free, is the man who, when a boy, played with Jere and slept by his side in the midnight campfire. It is mammy's people, and daddy Jacob's and Mandy's and Jere's people, that understand the negro and have always been his best friends. Had the country abided by Grant and Sherman and Lincoln and Johnson as to the status of the restored Union and left the rights of the emancipated slaves in the hands of their old owners and their interests to be regulated by the Mars Henrys of the South how much better it would have been for the poor negro and infinitely better for the white people. Southern people know best how far the negro may go and where it is best for him to stop. Now when the fearful problems which have been brought about by vindictive politics, personal demoralization and fanatical race prejudices, for which the people of the South are not responsible, the whole country is beginning to realize that if these problems are to be solved in the negro's favor he himself is to do the solving. "Mars Henry" and "Jere" would once have died for each other. But "Mars Henry" can't help "Jere" much now. Reconstruction politics led "Jere" too far away from "Mars Henry" and kept him too long. In a very few years there will be no "Mars Henry," no "Jere." "Mars Henry's" children know how to take care of themselves. May God teach poor "Jere's" children to work out their own good.

DREAM OF RACE SUPERIORITY

[J. L. Underwood.]

In a previous article the author has given an account of what was nearer social equality between the white and black races than will ever again be seen in the South or anywhere else. But the deluded negro has been led to look for something higher than social equality. The most awfully destructive work done by the Northern attempt to reconstruct Southern society has been seen in the complete demoralization of the generation of the negroes succeeding the playmates of the young Southerners of 1861-1865. They were thrown directly under Northern teachers profoundly ignorant of the negro race, their condition, and their danger; but teachers supremely bent on injury, as far as possible, to the white people of the South. From them and the literature which they circulated, and his own folly, the young negroes became imbued with the idea, not of social equality with the white people, but of social superiority to them. They themselves were heralded in the highest places as the "wards of the nation;" the white people were branded as its enemies; they were the lions and the heroes of the revolution, the white people were its victims. They were the acknowledged pets of the triumphant Northern people, while the whites were their doomed enemies. They were to have offices, endowments, and bounties from the government. This government gave them a Freedmen's Bank and a Freedmen's Bureau and they saw no bank nor bureau for white people. They saw the white people to whom nothing was promised with no prospect but that of poverty and degradation. The North gave them colleges and the South taxed itself to give them schools. They were lauded in Congress, on the hustings, in the Northern pulpits, and in the party newspapers, as the innocent Uncle Tom-like, angelic people who were to redeem the South and glorify America, while the white people, only living by Northern sufferance, were branded as traitors and rebels and enemies of the government. To insure the triumph of the negro and the degradation of Southern whites Congress kept the ominous Force Bills before the public. Who can wonder that the heads of these poor ignorant people were turned and their moral natures poisoned?

Then, with all this, came the awful lawlessness under which this young generation grew up. There was no longer "old massa and old missus" to see that they were controlled. Their parents gave way to delusive dreams and devoted their energies to "going to town" by day "going to meetin'" by night. Home life in the family was, and is to this day, almost a thing unknown. There was no parental control whatever. When undertaken much of it was so childish or so brutal as to do more harm than good. Some of these boys went to school enough to learn to read a little and sign their names, and right there the most of them graduated. A large portion cannot read now. They seldom went to church, except just enough to be baptized and to join in a special revival shout of

"We are all going to heaven,

Hallelujah!"

At other times when they did go they stood out on the church grounds and smoked cigarettes. The negro preachers, in nine cases out of ten, knew nothing and could teach nothing. The aim of most of them seemed to be to have a happy Sunday religion and enjoy the honor of religious office and prominence. What a passion this has been with the free negro. Then the inevitable collection of the preacher, and all would scatter without a thought of a religion to make good their lives through the remaining six days of the week. Mrs. Stowe's Topsy said she did not know anything about herself except, "I specs I growed." Those young reconstruction negroes just "growed." They "growed" without law at their so-called homes; they "growed" ignorant of, or defiant of the laws of the State, and they "growed" without any aim except self-indulgence in ease and pleasure.

Then there before their eyes rose the Paradise tree of the forbidden fruit—the white women beyond their reach. There was in every State the law against intermarriage of the white and black races which stood and will stand in Median and Persian unchangeableness. Then came, wherever these young negroes were scattered, at the North as well as the South, the mighty resolve of passion, pride, and revenge—"these white women are ours, we are better than they are, they shall not be monopolized by white men."

The record is awful and the blackest page of American history. This is the saddest chapter the author has ever written. He has been all his long life known and recognized by the negroes as one of their best friends. There is nothing but sorrow in his heart over the wide-spread demoralization of the negro race. He and all other true Southern men rejoice over the great progress of the few. He deplores the enslavement and degradation of the many by whiskey, idleness, and lust. The strong, young African tiger has been found lurking, not in American jungles, but in American homes, highways, barns and fields. His arch crime woman cannot hear named. And to mention it to Southern men is to make their blood boil in their veins and their brains to reel.

The heroism of Southern women cannot be told without this dark page. The trials of the war were nothing compared to the ordeal through which Southern women have just passed. In the wreck of the South brought on by Northern ballots and bayonets, the culminating damage is the demoralization of the generation of negroes now recently grown. In the face of the worse than Gorgan horrors our women have borne themselves with a courage, a patience, and fortitude that are sublime. But let friends of the negro and friends of our women hope. Thank God, the crime is on the decrease. White men somehow will protect such women as God has given our sunny land. The tiger is on the retreat, and thousands of the negro race are awakening to the fact that there must speedily be another emancipation, a redemption of their sons and daughters from their new slavery. The negro has had race emancipation; he needs family emancipation and personal emancipation from the chains of sense and appetite. Good negroes are working and praying for it. The negroes must break their own chains this time. But let patriotic and Christian white men help them everywhere.

ROOSEVELT AT LEE'S MONUMENT

"Come Closer, Comrades!"

[J. L. Underwood.]

When the victorious Federal army marched home, at the close of the war between the States, the famous Brooklyn preacher, Henry Ward Beecher, said that in twenty-five years any man in America would be ashamed to admit that he was ever a Confederate soldier. And yet in twenty-five years half of the Cabinet at Washington was composed of Confederate soldiers. In little more than twenty-five years the country sees William McKinley, the Republican President of the United States, himself a veteran of the Federal army, down among the Confederate veterans in Georgia, wearing the Confederate badge, and otherwise fraternizing as a soldier with those who wore the gray, and in his official capacity calling upon Congress to care for the graves of the dead Confederate soldiers just as the Government provides for the dead who wore the blue. And the whole country, North and South, applauded the noble McKinley.

Here is President Roosevelt, forty years after the war, making the same recommendations and Congress actually restoring the captured battle flags to the several Southern States. It is a pity Beecher didn't live to be inRichmond, Va., on the 18th of October, 1905, and see President Roosevelt by special appointment meet the Confederate Veterans at the foot of the monument of General Robert E. Lee. When he began his talk he said, "Come closer, comrades." The President of the United States calling those old "rebels" of Beecher his comrades and all the way on his long Southern tour, having at his own request a voluntary escort at every point composed of the veterans from both armies!

Shade of Beecher! Come back to Washington and see President and Cabinet and Congress and Army and Navy gather in tears around the coffin and do the grand honors at the grave of the Confederate General Wheeler!

The truth is the true comrades from both sides have been coming "closer" to each other ever since the bloodshed at Gettysburg and Vicksburg, whenever the politicians would let them. The old "vets" understand each other whether other people do or not. We are "comrades" indeed. Now, comrades of the North, let an old "Confederate vet" who has gloried in the privilege of frequently grasping your hands for forty years, say a parting word to you. Your country is our country. Your heroes are our heroes. We claim the honor of having such patriotic countrymen as Lincoln, such heroes as Thomas, Meade and Hancock, and McClellan and Grant, and McPherson and Farragut. If there were such men as Butler and Milroy and Hunter, they were our countrymen, too, and if they did things worthy of condemnation, let Southerners condemn them with a feeling of sorrow over the failings of erring countrymen—just as Northern men should look truthfully at the lives of Southern leaders and condemn, when it is just, but condemn in sorrow our erring countrymen.

But, comrades, "come closer." Read the humble tribute of this book to the memory of Southern women of 1861-1865. They were your countrywomen. Their virtues are the glory of all America. We have tried to help you and the world to know them better. We have all come forth from the ashes now. We are rejoicing in a prosperous South and a prosperous North. Our women nobly did their part in the war and nobly have they helped to rebuild the South, not only for our children, but for your sons and your daughters. Our sunny South belongs to the whole country. Our noble women and their children love their whole country. They have shown themselves true to principle and true to duty. "Come closer, comrades," and study these Southern women. If you find anything wrong in their spirit or conduct, hold it up to just retribution. If they have set a glorious example of courage, of sacrifice and of patriotism, help your children and our children to "come closer" in following their example.

www.ingramcontent.com/pod-product-compliance
Lightning Source LLC
Chambersburg PA
CBHW060805310726
48980CB00002B/244

* 9 7 8 3 7 3 2 6 2 1 2 2 4 *